THE MEASURE OF ELLA

THE MEASURE OF ELLA

by

Toni Bird Jones

www.penmorepress.com

The Measure of Ella by Toni Bird Jones

ISBN-13: 978-1-950586-15-8(Paperback)
ISBN: -978-1-950586-16-5 (E-book)

BISAC Subject Headings:
FIC002000 FICTION / Action & Adventure
FIC022080FICTION / Mystery & Detective /
International Mystery & 　 Crime
FIC047000FICTION / Sea Stories

The Book Cover Whisperer:
ProfessionalBookCoverDesign.com

Address all correspondence to:

Penmore Press LLC
920 N Javelina Pl
Tucson AZ 85748

For Ralph

Acknowledgements

This book draws loosely on people I met and experiences I had while messing about with boats in Florida, the Bahamas and the Lesser Antilles. I'd like to thank the captains and fellow crew, from whom I learned so much about the sea, for welcoming me into the sailing community.

To my brilliant husband, Ralph Jones, without whom I could not have written this novel, I am deeply grateful for your unwavering support and insightful editing of the numerous drafts for all my stories, bringing my work into a sharper focus.

To Nina Schuyler, thanks for years of guidance in story development. When I asked Nina to review my short story, she told me it wasn't a short story but a novel—then apologized, knowing how much work it would entail.

Many thanks to my talented editors, Anne Dubuisson, who helped wrestle the POV problem to the ground, and to the skilled editor Chris Wozney. To Michael James at Penmore Press, I am deeply grateful for your appreciation of *The Measure Of Ella* and for taking a chance on my debut novel. To Ron Walz at OceanGrafix, thank you for authorizing the use of the Caribbean chart.

Special thanks to my sister, Bonnie Liebhold, and my brother, Scott Bird, who have supported me in so many ways through the years and provided reliable feedback on my work. To my dear friend

Jennifer Barry, your tireless support and readings of numerous drafts have gone far beyond any friendship I've known. My heartfelt thanks to Amy and Michael Chapman for their encouragement and the care they took reading multiple drafts. Thank you to my niece, Genevieve, for reading a work-in-progress; to Michael McCulloch, who encouraged me to take the first step in owning my passion for writing; and to Ron Spinka, whose guidance has kept me on track.

And to my oldest friends, Sandy and Andy Peterson, still out there floating on the far Pacific Ocean, thank you for rescuing me. Thanks also to Kim M. Hollins, for teaching me to sail and, best of all, for sharing extraordinary tales of your adventures.

REVIEWS

"A page-turning thriller set in the murky underworld of the Caribbean. The sailing life is beautifully rendered. A must for all who wish to enter an exciting new environment for an adventure."
– Michael Chapman, cinematographer: *Taxi Driver, Raging Bull*

"Toni Jones is a true storyteller, weaving a tension-filled tale of Ella, a savvy sailor who risks crewing on a drug run to fund her dream. Set in the islands of the Caribbean and South Florida, it's a high-stakes adventure of crime, love and deception that puts her moral code to the test against a cast of dangerous characters."
—Nina Schuyler, author: *The Translator, The Painting*

In *The Measure of Ella*, Jones has deftly created a true original, a sailing heroine with agency. With storytelling prowess and an expert's eye for the perils of life on the water and off, she keeps us turning the pages as we urge Ella on.
—Anne Dubuisson, Writing and Publishing Consultant

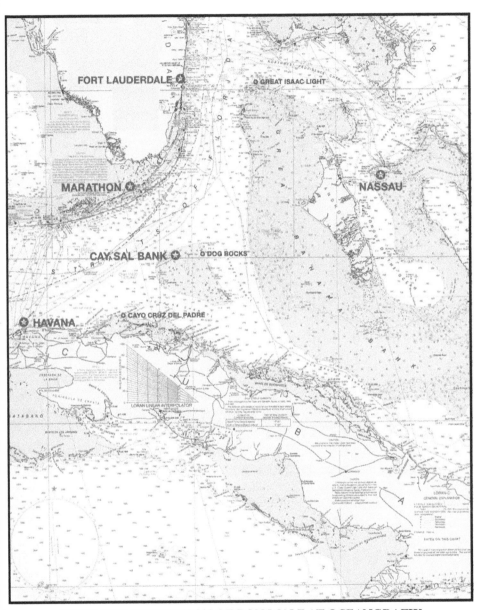

WITH THE PERMISSION OF RON WALZ AT OCEANGRAFIX
CHART OF THE STRAITS OF FLORIDA

"NO MAN IS RICH ENOUGH TO BUY BACK HIS PAST."

– OSCAR WILDE

CHAPTER 1

The worst kind of trouble, Ella Morgan thought, is the kind you didn't see coming. On a moonless night in the Straits of Florida due west of the Great Bahama Bank, she smelled rain in the freshening wind. She couldn't see a squall line, but stars to the west had begun to disappear, darkening the night and deepening her unease. When lightning branched across the sky, illuminating a tower of boiling clouds, it confirmed her sense that the night could get ugly.

The wind built and the waves began to crest, their tops streaming away in veins. The straining canvas lifted *Grace's* ninety-eight tons of wood and iron in a slow, heavy rise, and the hundred-foot pilot schooner plowed through the mounting seas like a great whale. Her sails hardened and her rigging groaned under the strain. Breakers slammed broad on her port bow, spewing plumes of spray across her deck.

Braced against the forward mast, Ella crouched and counted the seconds between each strike and the rumble of thunder that followed, trying to gauge the velocity and direction of the squall. Another flash, this one closer, brought her to her feet. She looked back. In the dim light thrown from the cabin, she made out the lone shape of the captain at the helm. She darted aft, moving in rhythm with the rise and fall of the boat, dodging sheets of stinging spray that whipped across the deck. Down below, the contents of the ship shifted and something crashed.

Ella ducked her head into the companionway. "Need help, Carlos?" she shouted to the first mate.

"I've got it—wine broke lose."

"The owner's?"

"No, our cheap stuff."

She pulled her watch cap further down. "Looks like this squall's got some teeth," she yelled to the captain.

Captain Rich Wells pressed into the wheel with one hand gripping a spoke and the other shoved deep into his pocket. "Carlos," he called out, squatting to see into the cabin, "what's the radar show?"

"It's moving easterly."

Rich turned back to Ella. "Take the helm. Keep her heading at a hundred-twenty-two degrees—as best you can."

Ella grabbed the wheel, shifting from leeward to windward and back again, trying to catch sight of the storm in the flashes of lightning. "Think it'll pass in front of us?"

"Possibly." Rich tugged the bill of his cap around back. "Kill the cabin lights, Carlos. I want to see what the lightning can show us."

The lights blinked out, plunging them into darkness. Phosphorescent flashes of breaking crests tumbled out of the black toward the boat. Lightning struck again, and Ella looked high off the water to see the ragged peaks of the squall line.

Carlos stuck his head out of the companionway, gripping the hatch rails to keep his balance. "It's building in the northeast— moving east near the six-mile mark."

"Looks closer than six miles," said Ella.

"It's coming right at us!" Rich shouted over the wind that now began to howl through the rigging. "Carlos, wake up Davis, we're shortening sail. God damn, we're in for a fight." He rubbed his hands together, smiling. "Make ready to reef the main!"

"Davis is up," said Carlos. "You want Jake too?"

"No." Rich ducked a sheet of spray. "Ella, flip on the spreader lights." Rich turned back to Carlos. "Alright, get the kid on deck. Just keep him out of the way. His father wanted him toughened up; this should do the trick."

Ella flipped on the lights just as Davis was coming up the companionway, zipping his foul weather jacket, heavy with sleep. His raven curls, caught by the wind, beat about a craggy face made handsome by dark eyes that flickered with a touch of wild. He threw Ella a smile.

"Welcome to the party," hollered Ella.

"You want me to take the helm?" Davis motioned to the wheel.

"No way!" Ella shouted through the wind. "Let you have all the fun?"

Over the year they'd been together, Ella's admiration for Davis had grown, and she'd opened her heart to him, a man unlike most, who lived life by the fistful. He was twenty years older than she was, an ex-Guardsman, ex-Merchant Marine and gale-tested captain with years of experience on the water delivering boats; a man who had crafted his life in the way that suited him, she thought, a trait she had respected in her father.

A distant bolt of lightning ripped open the night sky, affording her a glimpse of the storm's magnitude, its towering thunderhead dumping a wall of water into the building seas. With anxious excitement she steadied against the gunwale and gripped the wheel like a fighter going into battle, bending her knees in rhythm with the boat as it lumbered over the swells.

"She's sailing smartly," Davis yelled to Rich. "Let's wait to shorten sail."

Rich held onto the backstay, taking the measure of the sails in the flash of lighted sky. "And risk shredding them?"

"We can sail at the storm's edge. Still keep close to our course. We don't need to reef."

"Not tonight, Sinbad," said Rich. "Ella!" he shouted, pointing into the wind. "Prepare to head her up. We're shortening sail."

"Roger that." Ella smiled, her long braid buffeting against her back. She lifted her face to take a read on the wind that was kicking up the seas into four-foot whitecaps and shearing off their tops.

Rich held his eyes half-shut against the driving rain and turned to Carlos. "We're reefing deep!" He shot a look at Davis, and then took account of his crew. "Where the hell's the kid?"

"Here." Jake emerged from below. Wincing at the abrupt slap of wind, he tucked his head in and put his back to it. "I was asleep. What time is it?"

"No time for comfort," Rich shouted. "It's going to get nasty out here, so pay attention!"

"Going to?" Jake gripped the safety of the companionway and huddled against a blast of sea spray.

Ella cringed at the sight of the well-mannered boy, tall and thin as parchment. A strong gust could blow him away. He didn't belong here, on this stormy night sea.

"Get in position." Rich turned to take in the kid, then reached in the locker for a tether line, clipped one end to Jake's life vest and the other to the lifeline.

"What the hell, you're putting me on a leash? I'll trip over it."

"Then watch yourself!" Rich muttered.

Carlos held a tight grip on the mast. "Do you want to leave the jib up?"

"There's no time to hank on a storm jib. Reef the main deep, second reefing line. We'll drop the jib," said Rich. "It's a squall. It'll be over in an hour."

Ella watched Rich and Carlos work together, admiring their competence. She had sailed with enough captains and crews whose bungling ways led to dicey consequences. They're a good team, she thought, remembering Rich saying that Carlos had been his preferred first mate for the past five years, and Rich thought of him as a brother.

"Head up!" Rich looked back at Jake. "Kid, snap that tether onto the lifeline. You take it off one more time, I'll throw you overboard myself." He shot his arm up at the mainsail. "Grab hold of the sail and pull it down inside the lazy jacks. Tie off at the second reef." Rich turned to Carlos. "Keep an eye on him."

Davis had been right; they caught the edge of the squall line. But still, the wind was a stiff thirty knots with gusts to forty, screaming through the rigging, pounding against the sails and battering them with sheets of pelting rain. The sails snapped and strained and the great hull heeled with the driving wind hitting her on the beam.

Ella pulled the wheel hand over hand, bringing *Grace's* nose into the wind. The hood of her foul weather jacket billowed and flapped against her face, blinding her. She shoved it back and held the lumbering hull pointing up into the wind, every muscle from her clenched jaw down to her white-knuckled hands straining against the force of the waves.

Carlos eased the halyard and the men yanked the massive sail down to the second reefing point. The wind caught the sail, snapping the thick canvas out of their hands and sending it flailing in great billowing folds. Without a sail to steady her, *Grace* moaned and heaved as she mounted the waves, throwing the men off balance. They leaned into the boom, using their bodies to flatten the sail, and tied off the reefs. When the job was done they headed to the bow.

Jake stood clinging to the boom, watching the men bring down the jib.

"Jake!" Ella hollered, signaling the boy. "Come back to the cockpit."

Heedless of wind or wave, Jake let go of the boom. Ella watched with dread as he stretched to reach the stay, then the boat took a sudden jolt and the boy tumbled off the cabin top.

"Jake!"

In an instant, the sea opened beneath them and the ship plunged into what seemed an endless drop as Ella sensed a terrifying mass rising in the darkness.

"Incoming! Port bow!" she screamed. "Davis, grab Jake!" But her words were lost to the wind.

Illuminated by the spreader lights, the towering rogue wave reared up like a fist coiling back for a punch and smashed into the hull, a massive wall of green water exploding over the deck and crew. Ella pressed her body into the wheel, wrapping her arms around its spokes, and tried to hold their course with all her strength as seawater flooded the deck and swept over her head.

For a long moment, she was underwater and terror shot through her like a bullet. Were they going down? All she could feel was a tangle of ropes sweeping past. She fought her instinct to let go of the wheel, free herself from the boat and struggle to surface for air. If she did, she'd be swept away. Panic overtook her, driven by the involuntary urge to breathe. Choking on the saltwater, she lost her grip and was swept aft with the current until her body hit hard against the backstay and she grabbed on. After what seemed an eternity, the ship threw off the sea and shuddered to the surface, and Ella gulped the precious air. Then the spreader lights flickered for a moment and went out. She could hear Rich calling out for the crew to sound off, Carlos's reply and then Davis's.

"Ella!" Rich called out, racing back toward the cockpit. "*Ella!*"

She fought her way back to the wheel and sputtered, "Here! I'm here."

"You okay?"

She swept the strands of wet hair from her eyes. Her shoulders shook uncontrollably. "I'm good." The wind pressed her wet clothes to her frame, making her look as small as a drenched cat.

Rich stood for a moment holding onto the shroud, looking at her. "Hang in there. One of us will relieve you when all's secured," he hollered over the wind. "Besides, it's the safest spot on deck."

"Not so sure about that." Ella stood. "Where's Jake?"

"Jake?" Rich spun around. "Jake. Jake!"

She grabbed the high-powered searchlight from the cockpit and thrust it at Rich.

"Carlos, Davis, where's Jake?" Rich made his way forward across the heaving deck, shining the light along the rail, looking for Jake's safety tether.

"Starboard!" yelled Carlos.

"Was he tethered?" Rich ran the light along the topsides.

"Don't know."

"He's here!" Rich found the boy hanging over the side. "Jake, hold fast, we'll get you." *Grace* dropped into a trough and a wave plowed the boy under.

"Ella," Davis called out, "man overboard. Tethered. Leeward side."

"Holy hell," Ella screamed. "Carlos, we're doing a short tack. Now!"

Carlos ran to the cockpit and manned the winches.

"He's underwater," Davis hollered.

"Oh God." Ella screamed "Tacking!" and brought the bow through the wind, lifting the leeward side out of the water and Jake along with it. Carlos worked at a racer's speed pulling in the sheets.

"Is he conscious?" Ella asked.

"Not sure." Rich shone the light onto the boy, and then his tether: it was tangled among the lines and had somehow wrapped around a stanchion. "How in the hell?"

"Get me up!" Jake cried, gasping as he came up for air and banged hard against the rolling hull. "Stop it!" His hands, fiercely gripping the tether, were visible with every break in the waves, and then he was lost again—underwater.

"Hang on, Jake. We'll get you," Rich bellowed. "Ella, once we grab him, heave-to."

"She knows." Davis grabbed hold of the lifeline and swung his legs over the side. "We've practiced this."

"Davis, hold the light."

Rich lay flat against the rail, hooking his foot on a stanchion and stretching for the boy. "We've got you." He grabbed Jake's life vest, but the tether was taut and tangled and he couldn't pull the boy up.

And then the storm let loose a downpour. Rain rattled on the deck so hard that it sounded like hail and the rigging banged against the mast, adding to the cacophony of the hardening wind and sea.

"Rich!" Jake cried, catching his breath. "Get me up!"

"Shit!" Rich grimaced at the pelting rain. "Can't get him in."

Davis tore at the wet lines, trying to free them from the tangled mess, but the tether was still caught up around the stanchion. "Easiest to unclip him and pull him in."

"You're right," said Rich. "It's getting hung up somewhere. I can't see."

"Jake!" Davis leaned over the rail and shouted to the boy. "We need you to unclip the tether so we can pull you in."

"No way! I can't."

"We'll have hold of you," Rich shouted. "Fastest way to get onboard."

"No!" Jake shot a look over his shoulder into the black void of night.

"Christ," muttered Rich. "We'll have to cut the tether."

Rich turned to the helm. Ella had somewhat stabilized the boat by heaving to and tying off the wheel while Carlos trimmed the sails to balance the ride.

"Carlos!" Rich signaled him over.

"Keep a good hold on him, Rich," said Davis. "I'll lower over and wrap my legs around him. Carlos, cut the tether."

8

Davis seized the lifeline with one hand and Jake's tether with the other. *Grace* rode up a wave, lifting Jake free from the water, and Davis quickly lowered himself over the side, snagging the boy with his legs to keep him from being swept under.

"Got him." Rich grabbed Jake's life vest with one hand and a handful of jeans with the other. "Cut the line, Carlos."

"No!" Jake screamed as Carlos severed the tether.

"We got you," said Rich.

The three men pulled the boy under the lifelines, heaving him onboard. When he hit the deck, he scrambled to the cockpit on his hands and knees and cowered against the coaming, looking too afraid to stand up, as though the wind might blow him off deck again and into the sea, in the middle of nowhere, in the middle of the black night. He sat in the shelter of the cockpit trembling, clutching the cabin's handrail.

"Jake, get below and stay there," said Rich.

"No problem," said Jake.

"And take off those wet clothes, or you'll get pneumonia." Rich watched him go down the companionway. "Hopeless," he muttered under his breath.

"Okay, men," Rich twisted around to smile at Ella. "Let's get her back on course."

*****

Grace had sailed out of Port Everglades en route to Nassau, Bahamas, for a night crossing of the powerful Gulf Stream. Now, on the axis where the river of seawater flowed north with a steady force, the crew aboard *Grace* sailed along a major shipping lane where merchant ships and sailors took advantage of the prevailing winds, like migrating birds on a flyway, to all points of the Caribbean and beyond.

Ella brought up a sandwich and thermos of strong coffee and set it next to Rich at the helm. He had taken Jake's watch. Even though the squall had passed, it had left a confused sea and the kid was permanently relieved for anything but fair weather sailing. Davis and Carlos had coiled the tangled lines and checked the boat for damages, then they too went below to rest, leaving only Ella and Rich on deck.

"Want me to take the wheel while you change into dry clothes?"

"I'll wait," said Rich. "I want to be sure this squall is finished with us. Can you sit for a minute?"

"Sure. What's up?"

"You kept a cool head tonight."

"Not much choice, was there?"

"Good answer," he said, studying her. "Look, there's something coming up that needs a special crew. What I'm about to ask can't go any further, not to a soul—not even Davis. Will that be a problem?"

"He doesn't need to hear about everything I do." Ella kept her back to the wind, hugging herself against the cold, and sat down. "Besides, lately we're seldom in port at the same time. So, what's up?"

"Another passage. I need a capable crew I can trust, people like you. It'd be a commitment of about a week, the pay is phenomenal, but it involves some risk."

"What kind of risk?" Ella suspected what was coming—in this part of the world, secrecy and boats often meant drugs.

Rich looked hard at her before he spoke. "Sailing a load of weed into Florida."

Not Rich, too, she thought, checking over her shoulder to see if they were alone.

"Premium marijuana, no cocaine."

"That's unexpected, I never had the slightest ..." Ella sat back, realizing she sounded disapproving. She had been asked before by people she wouldn't have trusted to organize a picnic. She remembered how upset Davis had been when she'd told him, and his warning against taking such risk: smuggling marijuana across a

U.S. border was a Federal offense that carried a heavy jail sentence, even though it had been legalized in some states.

"I mean, you're the last person I would have suspected."

"That's good. I just run an occasional trip to help fund my research work."

"Your entomology studies?" It was easy to forget that Rich was a scientist; he seemed a man most suited for the sea, not bending over a microscope to study insects.

"Funding is drying up," said Rich.

"Aren't you worried about the risk? If you got caught, you'd be sent to prison."

"Sure." Rich wolfed down half of his sandwich, followed by a swig of hot coffee. "But with careful planning and known resources —it's an acceptable risk, price of being committed to what you love. Good coffee, Ella."

"Thanks."

Rich stood to get a clear read on the compass, then sat back down behind the wheel. "We could use a strong woman and you're a damn good sailor—a natural, with good judgment. A lot of people would have panicked when Jake fell overboard."

"At least he was on a tether," Ella said, remembering her father bragging to his shipmates that she was a natural. "Why do you want a woman onboard?"

"Deflect suspicion. Sailing into port we'll look like a couple coming in from a day sail."

Ella looked away, out at the sea, feeling more disappointed in Rich than complimented by his trust. An invitation into a secret world with the lure of fast money: it was against all she had been taught by her father, who regarded people in the drug trade as criminals unwilling to perform an honest day's work for what they wanted.

"You know I'm planning on opening a restaurant? I put a deposit on a place in the Keys."

"I've heard that."

"Captain Morgan's Table, named for my dad. He's the one who taught me to sail." Ella leaned against the coaming and pulled her knees to her chest. "I'd never do a run, Rich. Curious though— how much does it pay?"

"Still being worked out, but around twenty, twenty-five thousand."

"A pile of money for one week's work," said Ella.

"That's right."

Enough money to buy the latest kitchen appliances instead of used ones as she had planned, Ella thought—but not enough to risk going to prison. And not enough to make a mockery of the sacrifices her father had made to send her to the culinary academy.

"I'm flattered you asked, Rich, that you trust me enough. But, I have to say no."

"I thought that would be your answer."

Ella looked up at the night sky that was now clearing, allowing a few stars to shine through, and wondered if crewing for him would now be over.

"Will we still work together?"

"Sure, of course."

"Good." Ella nodded, giving Rich a smile. "I'd love for you to see my restaurant: a beautiful old Florida house shaded by a grove of pine and Jacaranda trees, right on the water."

"Sounds nice," Rich's voice tapered off.

"It's a little rundown, but the frame is solid and the wood floors are in okay shape. And the kitchen..." Ella shook her head. "My God, it's huge, with plenty of room for commercial appliances and two walls of windows that open out. I can hardly wait to prepare my recipes in a real kitchen."

"When does this happen?"

"It'll take some work to bring it up to code. I'll have to gut the dining and living room, except for the fireplace, which is made out of coral and so massive you can practically walk into it. I still can't believe I found it. It even has a solid pier where I can dock my boat and for customers that come by water."

"Sounds like you're on a good course."

"I am." Ella straightened her back. "I know exactly what it'll look like: old Florida intrigue, seaside dining in the romantic tropics. It's really going to be something."

"Big plans take a lot of money. Couldn't use a little more?" Rich asked.

"I'll have enough," she said. "You remember my father passed away last year?"

"I remember. That's why you came down here," said Rich.

"Partly. Everything back home reminded me of him; he was all the family I had left. And partly because I've always wanted to live in the tropics." Ella rubbed her arms, trying to keep warm in the pressing wind. "I have a buyer for his tugboat. I'm hoping to have a signed sale agreement waiting when I return to Lauderdale."

"Depending on the shape it's in, that should bring you a nice chunk of change," said Rich.

"It's contingent on a survey, of course, but he took good care of things. That was like him. Always on the up and up."

"Sounds like someone I would have liked to know."

"Yeah," said Ella. "He would have liked you, too."

"I think the squall's through with us." Rich stood up, pulling the wet sweatshirt away from his chest. "Take the wheel while I go change."

At the helm, Ella shone a light on the sails and eased the mainsheet for a smoother ride. The boat was working too hard and everyone onboard was exhausted from the boy's rescue, the storm, and the late hour. She watched the eastern sky brighten a little, the sun still well below the horizon.

In the morning they would reach the Berry Islands where Davis would step off *Grace* and pick up a yacht waiting for delivery to

Venezuela. She wanted to go along, but Davis had said it was out of his hands; a crew had been assigned. Now it could be a month before she saw him again.

Rich came on deck in a hooded sweatshirt and pants, carrying a mug of coffee. "There's a fresh pot," he said, raising his mug to Ella.

"I'm getting some sleep." Ella looked below and saw Davis enter her cabin. Maybe not, she thought. She wanted him tonight, even if it was only to say good-bye.

"Tell Davis we should be reaching the Berry Islands in about three hours," said Rich.

"You need something more to eat? More coffee?"

"No, I'm good. Carlos will relieve me soon."

Ella lowered her voice. "Please be careful."

"Always. If you change your mind... I can't do anything until I get back to the States."

"Thanks. And don't worry, I can keep a secret."

"I know," he smiled. "Good night, Ella."

She patted his shoulder as she stepped past him. She walked below, unwinding her braid as she went, shaking her hair loose before opening her cabin door.

CHAPTER 2

First light came slowly, turning sky and sea into a palette of pale, metallic pinks and blues, blending together along the milky horizon. The sea was still running high, but the wind had calmed to a moderate breeze. The early morning sun began to heat up the water and the air took on the intoxicating sultry scent of the tropics.

Ella stood at the galley stove and leaned back against its strap for support. Her sailing and culinary skills had earned her a place among the crew on this passage, and she had thought herself lucky: of all the boats she had crewed on over the past year, none could compare to the majestic beauty of *Grace*.

Through the porthole, she watched the changing colors of the sky as she turned over the frying bacon, pulling strips out of the pan one by one to drain on paper towels. Her thoughts were on her restaurant. The words 'liquor license' rushed her mind and she began to worry over its additional start-up costs. She couldn't successfully run a restaurant in the Florida Keys without serving alcohol—no one would come. But worry over the problems she faced was pointless until her dad's tug was sold and the money was in her hand. She was musing over which was riskier: opening a restaurant or running drugs, when Jake's shouts from the helm roused her from thoughts.

"Ella, I see Great Isaac's light. Hey, Ella!" Jake had spotted a flash of light in the distance and was shouting with the enthusiasm of a once-hopeless survivor.

"Yeah?" Ella popped her head up from below, drying her hands on a dishtowel. "How many seconds between flashes?"

"I don't know." Jake stood at the helm wrapped in a blanket, trying to focus the binoculars on the light. "It's the only lighthouse out here."

"Never take anything for granted. Not on the water. Have you kept our course?"

"Yeah."

"If you haven't, it could be the North Bimini light."

"Where's Rich?"

"He's asleep. When he gets up I'll tell him you spotted the light. Good work." Ella watched the flashing light for a moment.

"Fifteen seconds. That *is* Great Isaac." She ducked back into the galley to make coffee.

"Tell me what?" Rich lumbered up, grabbed a strip of bacon and headed on deck. He was disheveled and drowsy from the little sleep he'd had. His hair was taking on new forms of wild, his mustache bent toward his nose and his wrinkled clothes hung askew on his solid frame. But even in this condition, there was no mistaking his strength.

"Jake spotted the Great Isaac light," she called after him.

Ella heard Davis stride back from the bow to the helm. She saw him grab the binoculars out of Jake's hands and focus them on the lighthouse. He took over the wheel from Jake and trimmed the mainsails, then the jib, bringing *Grace* on a tighter course. The boat heeled, picking up a little speed.

Rich bent over the compass to get a read on Davis's course and then went below to check the charts.

"Everything okay?" said Ella.

"Yeah. It's a good course," said Rich.

"Rich," Jake stuck his head into the cabin. "Thanks for last night, for getting me back on deck."

"No problem. You know without that tether, we never would have found you."

Jake hesitated. "Rich?"

"Yeah?"

"There's no need to tell my dad I fell overboard."

"Not in my interest to tell Falco that I nearly lost his son at sea," said Rich. "Between you and me, kid."

To Ella, Jake seemed too young for his years. She could see why his father wanted to toughen him up. But one passage couldn't make him a man, though the guidance of a loving father might.

"Thanks." Jake shook his head. "Not my kind of sailing. Frigging sails were going ballistic! The wind," He fanned his hand. "I like adventures I can control."

"That's an oxymoron," Ella said, handing Jake mugs of coffee to distribute. She joined the others on deck. Davis made room, lifting his arm for her to tuck in alongside him at the helm. Cushions, bedding and clothing lay drying in the cockpit; the old deck had a few leaks, and no one had had a dry night's sleep.

"Seas are calming down." Ella held the warm coffee to her chest and curled closer to Davis, facing the morning sun.

"You do this for a living?" Jake was too young to conceal the note of disapproval in his voice.

"It's steady work while I'm in school; some boat owners won't sail open waters." Ella smiled at Davis. "Besides, it's fun."

"Fun?" said Jake, glancing at Davis.

"Danger is seductive." Carlos said, coming up from below.

"Ask your dad," Davis muttered, "he knows."

Jake's face darkened at the mention of his dad, and he stood up on the seat, facing the sunrise, looking for the lighthouse.

"Kid needs a break," Ella whispered to Davis.

17

"A slow trip through hell really isn't my thing." Jake shot a worried glance to the aft deck where Rich had stretched out and lay with his eyes closed.

Ella followed his glance and smiled at Rich. Through half-closed eyes, he caught her smile and returned it. She enjoyed the familial closeness on these passages that came with being together day and night, a temporary family where she belonged, making it possible for her to feel whole again after the loss of her own.

Stretched out on the teak cockpit seat, resting in Davis's arms, Ella turned to her own thoughts of weekends spent sailing with her father offshore Rhode Island when she was Jake's age.

She hadn't really gotten to know her father until she was eight. Ross Morgan was a tugboat captain who was seldom home before her bedtime. All that changed when, in the middle of a cold night during Christmas break, she'd woken to the deep, pained howl of her father's cries. She'd run into the hall to see him lying on the floor alongside her mother, holding her in his arms, rocking and calling out her name, begging her to come back. She had had a massive heart attack. The center of Ella's life was gone.

Shortly after her mother died, her father bought a neglected Herreshoff 27 sloop and named it *Gina Marie* after his wife. He put everything he had into it—money, time, but mostly his grief. It was as if he were trying to bring Gina back to life. And for Ella, comfort came in the form of the inclusive sailing community and life on the water, where everything had a reason and a purpose.

By the time she turned twelve, her father had taught her how to study the wind patterns and clouds for advance warnings of storms, and how to recognize the smell of rain before it fell. Under his guidance, she'd grown to understand sail shape and trim until it became intuitive. It had been a beginning for them, and over time he and Ella had become friends, two survivors sharing the same lifeboat.

"When's breakfast?" said Jake.

"I think I just heard my cue." Ella smiled, uncurling from under Davis's arm. "I'm making a frittata."

"Ahh, Ella, that's why we all love you," Rich said from the aft deck. "No gooey oatmeal when you're onboard."

Davis handed off the wheel to Carlos and followed Ella below.

"Can I help?" He tugged on her braid, pulling her head back, and kissed her.

"That's not a handle," she laughed, jerking her braid free. "Who is Jake's father? He seems afraid of him."

"He should be. Falco's a fucking drug baron. Don't know why the kid is even down here. He lives with his mother in New York."

"Is Falco *Grace's* owner?"

"No." Davis bent around Ella to steal a morsel of the frittata's crust.

"Hey, it's not ready." Ella slapped at his hand. "Then, why is Jake onboard—is Rich a friend of his father?"

"Falco doesn't have friends."

"Poor kid. So why did Rich agree to take him on this trip?"

"Probably owes Falco a favor. Delivery captains can't be choosey about who we work for—we'd go broke."

"What kind of a favor?"

"Don't know." Davis tugged at Ella's braid again.

"Would you quit doing that?"

"Come here, you. I'm going to miss you."

"Then take me with you. It'd be so cool sailing into Caracas."

"I told you, I've already got my crew."

Davis hugged her tightly, lifted her off the cabin sole and buried his face in her neck, kissing her and making her laugh.

Ella pushed away, finding her footing. "I wish you had asked me first."

"You've got your dad's tug to sell," said Davis.

"It's in Rhode Island. I can sell it from anywhere. Your crew probably can't sail as well as me and you'll be eating canned beans for weeks."

"Hey, Ella." Jake stuck his head below. "When do we get breakfast?'

"I'm on it." She watched Davis bound up the stairs two at a time. "I thought you wanted to help!"

*****

A frigate bird glided down across the bow, turned on the wind and flew away—a sign that land was near. They sailed out of the deep, black-blue waters of the Gulf Stream and into the turquoise waters of paradise—the Bahama Banks. Rounding Great Isaac Lighthouse, they continued into the Northwest Providence Channel and dropped anchor at Great Harbour Cay, Berry Islands, to ferry Davis ashore.

Ella stood leaning into Davis, her hand, resting on his shoulder, slid lightly down to the small of his back, committing to memory the feel of his toned muscles as she watched Rich and Carlos launch the dinghy.

"Well, I'm off." Davis handed Carlos his duffle and shot Jake a glance, giving the kid a nod. Then he gripped Rich's hand, giving it a hard shake. "Thanks for the ride."

"Nice to have a seasoned sailor onboard," said Rich.

Ella stood on her toes to kiss Davis's cheek. "I wish you'd leave your phone turned on so I could call."

"I'll call you when I can," said Davis, pulling her to him with his free arm and kissing her quickly in front of the crew.

Ella smiled and nodded, knowing he would never call—he never did. He'd just show up one day, like a straying cat having had his belly-full of adventure.

"Good luck with the tug sale."

20

"Fair winds and calm seas." Then she added in a whisper, "Just come back."

"Are you anchoring here tonight?" Davis asked Rich as he pushed off.

"No, behind Whale Cay. A few less miles to cover tomorrow."

Ella waved goodbye as the men motored through a maze of smaller boats anchored inside the shallow harbor, watching until they were no longer visible. Each time he left she felt the same unease: she'd never see him again. With Davis it was like trusting a feral animal to come back from a hunt. Yet he always did.

But earlier this morning as she watched him dress, she'd sensed something might have changed between them. He seemed distant. And when he'd buckled the belt to his jeans, giving it a slight tug to set the hook, it had felt like a door closing.

"I have something I need you to keep for me, Ella." He went to his jacket hanging from the ship's clock on the bulkhead and pulled out a book, *The Essential Rumi*. "Remember the quote you liked so much?" he said, handing her the book. "It's in here."

"I'll take good care of it for you," she said, reassured by the gesture. "How long will you be gone?" Ella took the book, opened it to the page he had tagged and read aloud, "You were born with wings, you are not meant for crawling."

"So don't," he said, brushing a strand of hair away from her face.

"How long?" she asked again.

He leaned over her, first kissing the side of her neck, then cupping her breasts in his hands, kissing each one, lingering on her erect nipples. The moment had the softness of a dream, and the love she had felt before returned.

"Maybe a month," said Davis. "Don't lose that book. Okay?"

She slid out of the bunk, her hair, long and flowing, framing the slight build of her naked body.

"I won't."

He'd pulled Ella into him and kissed her, slipping his hand between her legs, stopping the flow of her questions. His vague answers had bothered her, but she hadn't pressed him any further.

"Jake!" Rich hollered, startling Ella from her thoughts. "Give me a hand with these lines. Make ready to raise the anchor when Carlos returns."

"Aye, aye, captain." Jake answered with enthusiasm brought on by the nearness of land.

*****

That night *Grace* lay at anchor in the lee of Whale Cay at the southern end of the Berry Islands. To please the crew, Ella made hamburgers and roasted potatoes. It was as close to comfort food as you could get on a boat. After dinner she cleaned the galley while listening to Rich and Carlos show off, telling sea stories to Jake, some real and some not so much. She missed Davis's voice in the mix, although he seldom told stories about himself.

Ella made an early night of it and tucked into her bunk to read *The Essential Rumi.* Whatever importance the book held for Davis, it also held for her. Entrusting her with it was his promise to return.

*****

In the hazy light of dawn, with seas as smooth as glass, they pulled up anchor and motored dead to windward on the last leg of the trip. By late afternoon they arrived in Nassau Harbor and cleared customs.

It was the end of the trip for Ella. After spending a day and a half helping Rich prepare the boat for the owner's arrival, she sat below packing her duffel. In a quiet moment, she took in the beauty and romance of *Grace.* The mahogany interior and burnished brass fittings were from another time. She breathed in the fragrance of the aged wood and dampness of the hull, and listened to the voice of the boat creaking and moaning as its weight shifted in the water.

Sensing someone behind her, Ella turned to see Rich standing in the doorway, hands shoved deep into his pockets.

"What's up?" said Ella.

Rich shrugged. "Came to see how you were doing."

She saw that he had changed into clean clothes, as he did without exception on arriving in port. Ella knew that he could have encountered hurricane force winds, hanging on for days by his fingertips, and yet he'd arrive with combed hair and clean clothes.

"I'm saying my farewell to *Grace*," Ella said, stuffing the last of her belongings into her duffel. "I'm grateful that the owners of these old girls are willing to miss out on all the fun."

"Not many people would have called the other night fun."

"You have to love sailing," she smiled up at him, "*and* have trust in the captain."

Rich nodded. "You flying back to Lauderdale tonight, or tomorrow?"

"Not sure. I spotted some friends at the Yacht Haven when we came in. Sam and Nikki on *Wanderlust*—do you know them?"

Rich nodded.

"Yeah," she laughed, "I think everyone knows them. Thought I'd go see if they're sailing back, maybe catch a ride."

"Looks like you'll have calmer weather," said Rich. "Mind if I walk with you? I was going to pick up some fruit from the mango man at the end of the dock."

*****

Nassau's public dock was charged with the excitement of adventure. A collision of music filled the air as Ella walked with Rich past boats blaring Latin jazz and reggae. Bare-chested men in shorts, gathered on the dock, boasted of sailing adventures while nursing breakfast beers, and well-oiled women in skimpy, colorful bikinis perched on the decks of yachts, working on the perfect shade of tan.

Rich and Ella navigated the obstacle course of tangled water hoses, piles of supplies and crews making boats ready for all points of the Caribbean. Some cruisers would leave this gateway to adventure; others would be stuck at the starting line, hanging onto the island of New Providence like a life raft after making the Gulf Stream crossing into Nassau's harbor. For some of them, the sailing season would pass, and maybe another, then eventually their owners would hire a crew like Rich's to sail their boat back to a mainland yacht broker.

At the end of the dock an old native man sat on a wooden crate under a tattered umbrella, selling mangos and a few avocados. He had the patient expression of an islander and the stately posture of a man of importance.

Rich gave the man a nod of familiarity. He was a prominent fixture and by some island code of seniority, he held this prime location unchallenged. He stood up, dialed a number on his cell phone and began speaking patois—the private language of the islanders with its musical singsong phrases. Ella turned, watching the man track Rich, his conversation slowing as they passed.

"Have you given any more thought to my offer?" said Rich.

"It's not something I would ever do, Rich. I couldn't jeopardize what I've been working this hard for—and, in a way, so has my dad. I need this restaurant." She looked back at the mango man, who had turned his attention to a customer. She lowered her voice. "Besides, the slightest possibility of going to prison terrifies me—it would be a living hell."

"I can't tell you there isn't risk." Rich waited until a hansom cab filled with rowdy tourists passed by. "I can say, these are people I've worked with for a number of years without a hitch." He stood with his hands shoved in his pockets. "Well. If you change your mind, you have my number. One more thing."

"What?"

Rich looked down for moment, as if trying to choose his words, and then held his eyes on her. "I've never known Davis to be with anyone. Be careful."

Ella nodded, smiling. "You could say the same about me. Davis and I are two of a kind, both lone wolves."

"None of it's my business." Rich folded his arms. "I guess I'll see you next delivery—unless you want to join Carlos and me for a bite out around seven."

"I'd love to, but I'm hoping to save airfare and catch a sail back."

Rich stood smiling at her.

"I know," Ella laughed. "If I took you up on your offer I wouldn't have to worry about every dime." She gave him a one-armed hug, her duffle hanging from the other shoulder. "Thanks for the sail, Rich."

"See you soon, Ella."

Ella gave him a wave and turned to walk past the native marketplace filled with palm frond hats, colorful t-shirts and coconuts carved to look like monkeys. She turned around to look for Rich. He was still standing in the same spot, arms folded, watching her walk away.

CHAPTER 3

Between the southern tip of Great Abaco and the northern shores of Eleuthera Island, a fitful wind blew on the summer waters of the Northeast Providence Channel before settling in for the night with a gentle eight-knot breeze. Millions of stars and a slice of moon lit up the night sky and cast their glow onto the sea.

Offshore Eleuthera's shallow, jagged reef known as the Devil's Backbone, Davis pushed back the hood of his jacket and deftly brought the nose of the thirty-five-foot sloop through the eye of the wind. With perfect timing, he flipped the starboard jib sheet off its winch and trimmed the sails for a close reach that would clear the southern shore of Little Bahama Bank, setting a course back to Florida's Jupiter Inlet.

Below, Jonathan Sterling Hammond rested in a light sleep, on the edge of wakefulness, lulled by the rhythmic movement of being underway—until it changed. Now fully awake, he listened carefully to the sound of his boat, the *D'Élite*, changing course.

Crawling over bales of weed and out of the cave of the quarter berth, he emerged on deck to stand in the cockpit and slowly turned to take in the sea around them.

"Are we changing course, Davis?"

"To clear Eluethera, then we'll have a straight shot back." Davis answered in a clipped tone, glancing at Jon in his pressed pants and nautical flag belt.

Jon had boasted of his sailing experience aboard his father's yacht but he was never the captain, never out on the water alone. He was slightly more adept at sailing than the owner of a chauffeured car was at driving. One thing Jon did have going for him, though, was a boat and enough cash to invest in a load.

"Did *Grace's* crew ask why you wanted to be dropped off at Great Harbour?"

"Delivering a boat to Venezuela."

"They believe you?"

"Why wouldn't they?"

Jon shrugged and lifted his face to get a read on the wind. "You think this is all the wind we'll get? I just wish we could go faster. Maybe we should start the engine."

"No," Davis said flatly.

"I'm not at all comfortable being this close to Devil's Backbone at night, especially with all this weed onboard. Those reefs are infamous for sinking boats."

"Relax, go below and get some sleep. You're on watch in an hour. We'll be clear of the rocks by then."

"I'll relax when we finally get this stuff unloaded. I bet we're less than a half-mile offshore." Jon took in the dark waters behind them, where they had picked up a load of weed in the lee of the remote Man Island. "We should run the engine until we get farther out." He stared incredulously at Davis. "Aren't you worried? I can clearly see the lights of Spanish Wells."

"Sound of an engine draws attention." Davis peered at him from under the brush of his eyebrows, his aquiline nose accentuating the fierceness of his expression. "You're getting on my nerves. It's after three, nobody's coming after us, and we're not going on the rocks. Get some sleep."

*****

"My God, I'm a smuggler," Jon said to himself, grinning as he brushed off the bottoms of his feet before sliding back into his berth.

His luck had finally changed when his stepbrother, Sam, called with an unexpected offer, a lucrative dope deal that required investing the remainder of his cash and a few weeks of his time. It would replace the lost trust money from his failed real estate venture, and grant him the chance to walk back into his family's life still a man of means, with his father being none the wiser.

Jon lay dozing when suddenly a thunderous impact jarred the boat violently, knocking him out of his bunk.

"Davis! We hit the goddamn reef!" Jon screamed, struggling to his feet to look out the porthole. A white hull was pressing against his boat. He turned toward the companionway stairs but froze at the rapid firing of a semi-automatic rifle into *D'Élite*'s topsides. *Pirates!* The boat rocked from the weight of men boarding and he dropped to the cabin sole.

He crouched beside the stairwell, listening to Davis's angry shouts. He was unarmed. His pistol, along with Davis's, was tucked in a cubbyhole at the companionway—easy access, Davis had said, in case of emergency. But to get to it now, he'd have to show himself.

Jon scooted along the cabin sole to where he could see the silhouette of a man blocking the companionway. He was shouting commands at Davis, who responded in kind. With what little Spanish Jon understood, he knew they were here to steal their load. A rapid spray of gunfire sent him ducking for cover, then the boat rocked sharply, followed by a heavy splash. Jon listened for Davis's voice—nothing, just the sound of men clambering around on deck, lowering the sails. He pulled his mariner's knife from the sheath that hung from his belt, gripped it in his trembling hand and held it

28

out in front of him. The blade was short and wide, no match for men with guns—and any attempt to fight them might just get him killed. He sheathed it again.

"Come out, little rabbit, come out of your hole," a husky voice with a thick Spanish accent boomed into the hollow of the cabin. "We know you down there." The thickset man stood guard at the companionway with his legs spread in the ready stance of a combat soldier, holding his rifle close to his chest. He turned to the others and called out orders in Spanish, sending one of the men forward to guard the hatch. They needn't have bothered. Jon wasn't about to abandon ship in the middle of the night, in the shark-infested waters of Devil's Backbone.

"Your friend is waiting for you," the masked pirate taunted Jon, leaning in so he could see him.

Jon froze, crunched beside the steps, trying to understand the rapid Spanish the men spoke. He looked back at the quarter berth where he could have hidden behind the bagged storm jib, cursing Davis. How else would they have known he was here?

"Pronto!" The man barked angrily.

"Yes, yes, I'm coming."

A hulk of a man kicked the hatch back with his boot. There were three of them, dressed in camouflage clothes, pants tucked into military-style boots, faces masked by balaclavas. Their boat, tied alongside, banged against Jon's sloop with every roll of the waves. The sight of the men staring down at him through masks made him shudder with horror.

"What do you want?" Jon took one uncertain step at a time up the companionway, hugging his shaking shoulders, stretching to look for Davis. "Davis? Where is he?"

"A pretty boy. *Maricon!* You don't look like much of a smuggler. Maybe you are friend's play toy?"

29

Jon tightened his grip, trying to control the trembling that would expose his fear. He stumbled to keep his balance while the pirates adeptly moved with each pitch of the boat.

He turned toward the bow, then to the sport fisher. "Where's Davis? My friend—what have you done with him?" His trembling voice betrayed the panic running through him.

"Your lover went for swim. I think he headed that way." The man's eyes brightened as he thumbed downward over the water.

"You threw him overboard?" Jon spun around, rushing to the side. "DAVIS!" The husky one shoved him back with the butt of his rifle. "He'll drown! I can't see him." Jon's voice rose to a screech. "For God's sake, HELP him! There are sharks in these waters."

The men laughed at the wealthy misfit dressed in his crisp pants and popped-collar polo shirt. Jon would have looked more at home at a yacht club.

"Too late. Besides, he had holes in him. He's no good anymore," the pirate laughed.

"What! You shot him?"

"He pissed me off. Don't worry, you get new lover."

"He's not—PLEASE! He may still be alive! We've got to look for him!" Jon took a step forward but the pirate lifted his rifle, blocking his way. Jon stole a look down at the growing wet spot on the front of his pants.

"Please." Jon's trembling gave way to tears and he began to sob. "Please, take what you want, there's no need to hurt me. I won't give you any trouble. Please!"

"If you do, you join your friend." The laugh had gone out of the pirate's voice. "Encerrarlo en el baño."

Jon strained to look over his shoulder at the dark waters surrounding him. A jab in the back pushed him toward the companionway. Someone flipped on the spreader lights, spotlighting the men like actors on a stage with a backdrop of the black sea.

30

"Ha! Look at this smuggler," laughed one of the men, and the others joined in. "He pees himself!"

"Below, *poco chica!*"

The pirate on the transom fired rounds into the air as he walked toward Jon. "*Vámanos!*"

Jon jumped at the sound, ducking his head. Then came another jab and his back arched as he tumbled down the stairs, landing on his knees. One of the men followed and kicked him in the stomach.

"Get up!" Grabbing Jon by the collar, he tossed him into the head and jammed the door closed. "Now you can piss yourself all you want," the man laughed.

Jon lay on the floor, shaking, clinging to his knees, then flipped up the toilet seat in time to vomit. After, he curled as far behind the toilet as he could squeeze. On the other side of the locked door, the men grunted and laughed as they lifted the forty-pound bales onto the deck. The boat rocked as they clumped back and forth, offloading the weed onto their powerboat. One of the men released another spray of bullets, triggering rounds of laughter.

Then, for a time, everything went quiet aside from the creaking sounds of the drifting boat and the bumping noise of the sport fisher tied alongside. The eerie calm was finally broken by the pirate's heavy footsteps clambering below to rummage through the cupboards. The footsteps retreated, the boat rocked once more as the pirate stepped off, then the engines of the sport fisher gunned and it was gone.

Long minutes went by before Jon pulled himself upright to look out the porthole. There was no sign of the pirates. He pushed at the jammed door without success. Holding tightly to his bruised ribs, he braced himself on the toilet and kicked at the door panel until it broke away. He reached through the splintered wood and shoved the wedged boat hook away, opening the shredded door. The load was gone—except for a single bale sitting in the middle of the salon.

"Something wrong with this one, assholes? Why not take it all?" he yelled.

He crawled to the steps and peeked out, then crept up to the cockpit, scanning the deck and the sea around him. He was alone: just him, the blackness, and the endless sea, far from home, with only a few distant pinholes of light from a scattering of settlements along the northern Eleuthera shore. He found the spotlight and screamed again for Davis, wincing with every cry. Holding onto his painful side, he called louder and louder, sweeping the spotlight's beam over the vast emptiness.

"DAVIS! DAVIS!" The sound of his voice was pathetic as he grew hoarse, and he stopped. It had been too long; the hammerheads and tiger sharks that frequented these waters would have picked up on the scent of blood carried along by the current, sensed the vibrations of panic from the heart of a drowning man, and raced to their meal. The feeding frenzy would have begun. It was too late.

"Someone help me," he cried. He reached for the VHF radio to call the Coast Guard, then looked down at the lone bale sitting in the middle of the salon. "Clever," he said, releasing the transmit button and slamming the microphone back on its cradle. He slumped to his knees amid the wreckage and started to sob.

"Fucking uncivilized animals. Fuck!" he screamed. "Fuck, fuck, fuck!" The boat slapped back and forth in the waves, the slack rigging banging loudly. The lights of Spanish Wells faded into the night as the current carried *D'Élite* away from the shores of Eleuthera. He sat, unable to move, until the discomfort of his urine-soaked clothes forced him to get up and change his pants.

"Start the engine. Set the sails. Get under way, check the charts, set your course—what course?" he mumbled to himself as he worked to put the boat right. Once underway, he set the boat's autopilot on a course away from the reefs and went below. Still shaking, he was able to light the lamp on the third try and began studying the charts. Davis had marked them clearly, with compass headings and notes on current drift. He was going to be all right for now, even though he'd never sailed these waters before and he'd never sailed alone. The weather was fair and the night began to fade with the early morning light.

"Call Sam. I need to call Sam." Jon stumbled over to the navigation station and pulled out the sat phone, turning it on and punching in his PIN before dialing out. He climbed on deck for a clear view of the sky, wondering which of the stars could actually be the satellite.

CHAPTER 4

Nassau was a foreign land compared to Rhode Island, but Ella liked it. Full of color and music, it was an island of contradiction, of drunken fun and shady deals, where innocence had every right to be lost yet still glinted in the eyes of the natives.

She walked along Bay Street, lined with island cottages painted in brilliant Junkanoo colors and the pink-and-white Georgian-style buildings from colonial times when the Bahamas had been a jewel in the British Crown. A soft, warm sea breeze blew across the island, mixed with the scent of tropical flowers, and carried the sound of the Goombay rhythms of the island's music.

Nassau had always been a sailor's town, and its history had been entwined with piracy since Blackbeard's era. The island had kept pace with the times, and modern pirates focused on drugs and offshore banking. In town, Ella easily spotted them among the tourists and locals as they swaggered with the arrogance of those who live above the common fray.

As she made her way along the waterfront, her thoughts turned again to Rich's offer and she felt a twinge of rebellious pride in being invited into the underworld of smuggling. She let herself fantasize about earning a chunk of money for a few days of sailing, and imagined naming her restaurant Anne Bonney's Table after the famous female pirate. But she knew she'd never cross that line. She had been raised in a community built on hard work and Christian morals; even though she and her father had never attended church after her mother's death, the values had been ingrained in her.

Where Bay Street turned into East Bay, the houses and storefronts gave way to marinas. Another half mile up the road she reached Yacht Haven, where Sam and Nikki's boat was berthed. On this side of Nassau, the tourists thinned out, revealing the face of local commerce, a glimpse of island life that stood on its own.

In the marina's parking lot a fisherman had set up a modest conch stand painted in lively colors. A battered seine net spool that he used for a table was crowded with conch shells and limes. She stopped to watch him handle his knife. With rhythmic ease, he chopped the conch meat, peppers and onions for the salad he sold.

"You buy, miss?" He was a middle-aged man of little means, yet his smile was as open as a boy's, lifting his entire face and brightening his eyes. "Very fresh, right off boat."

Ella looked at the rust-bucket of a skiff docked behind him, then at the cooler he sat on. Its faded paint was peeled from the salt air and sun.

"Today's?" she asked.

"Yes, ma'am! Out at daybreak." He stood up, opened the old cooler and waved his hand across his offering with a show of pride. It was clean and packed with ice.

"Okay," Ella smiled. "Enough for three."

*****

Sam and Nikki's boat was docked where the live-aboards and locals berthed, away from the action of downtown and noisy public docks. *Wanderlust* was the sailboat of her dreams: a Morgan 44, with classic lines and a warm teak interior, well outfitted for blue-water cruising. It took plenty of money to own and maintain a boat like this. Sam and Nikki apparently had it, for the varnish was deep

35

and flawless, the stainless polished, all a step above shipshape. The places you could go, she thought.

"Ahoy, *Wanderlust!*" Ella called out.

Nikki popped up from below deck dressed in a micro-bikini. "Oh, my God, Ella! Hop aboard! It's been, like, forever since I've seen you." Nikki, reliably perky, ducked her head below. "Hey, Sam. You'll never guess who just showed up."

Sam emerged from below, throwing a t-shirt at Nikki.

"Hey, Ella."

"Christ, Sam, it's just Ella." Nikki shot him an annoyed look and pulled on the t-shirt, re-fluffing her hair. Sam had a point; Nikki's bathing suits had gotten so small that Ella wondered why she even bothered wearing one.

On the docks, they were the beautiful couple everyone wanted to know—Nikki with her blonde, curly hair worn short and loose, and her petite, curvy body that was in a constant tease of falling out of her clothes; and Sam with his dark good looks and toned muscles, ever eager to pour you a drink.

Ella had met Sam and Nikki when she first sailed into Fort Lauderdale's Las Olas Marina. They had taken her under their wing, introducing her to the regulars. She had been grateful for their friendship, but they'd had little in common besides sailing. Sam and Nikki's crowd were jovial drinkers who talked nonsense until they passed out. Like a lot of people in the islands, they had a hardcore commitment to fun.

Nikki came up from the galley with a pitcher of Mai Tais in one hand and a fifth of Mount Gay Rum in the other. "Would you like an added splash?"

"No, I'll just have water. It's a little early for me." Ella watched as Nikki poured a healthy shot into Sam's drink and hers. "I brought conch salad from the fisherman in the parking lot."

"Oh, we get it from him all the time, don't we, baby?" Nikki twisted to look back at Sam. "That guy could use some help with his presentation. Speaking of presentation, you know I could help you with your restaurant. I wouldn't charge you—I'd do it for fun."

"Thanks, Nikki. When that time comes, any help would be a gift," said Ella.

Nikki brought out cheese and crackers and the three of them sat in the teak cockpit under the awning, dipping into the conch salad and catching up. Nikki was like a boisterous, misbehaving cousin who added color to the family palette, and with her meandering stream of chatter she allowed little chance for Sam to comment. Sam didn't seem to care; he was only partially listening, off somewhere else in his mind. Ella wondered how Nikki gathered so much local gossip, since she never took a moment to listen. As they talked, Ella's thoughts drifted to the risk Rich was taking. How profoundly his life would be altered, friendships and the innocent world of everyday life would be taken from him, if things went wrong.

"Are you sailing back to Fort Lauderdale?" asked Ella.

"No," Nikki responded. "Right now, here's where fun is. There's so much going on all the time, the outdoor markets, casino, and spas. We talked about sailing to Martinique with another boat, but they went on ahead."

It had been a long shot, Ella thought, and she glanced around at the other boats in the marina, looking for the busyness that accompanies a voyage. She could see that Nikki and Sam's idea of fun had changed. When she first met them, they were charged by adventure, studying charts and travel books on the islands of the Lesser Antilles. Now, their well-manicured boat sat at the dock and gathered admirers. And if Nassau was anything like their Fort Lauderdale scene, Nikki was the main attraction.

"Yeah, cruising can be boring. Then there's the freakin' squalls." Ella poked around for the real story.

"I know!" Nikki's eyebrows rose, wide-eyed as a child. "Our sail over from Fort Lauderdale was horrible. I spent the whole time below in my bunk, hanging on. It was absolutely violent out there. Thank God Sam got us here in one piece."

"Hence the luxury resorts and charming Europeans," Sam mumbled.

Ella looked over at Sam, sensing something had changed between him and Nikki. Would they last as a couple, she wondered, now that their tastes in adventure had taken different paths?

"Do you know of anyone sailing back to the mainland?" said Ella. "I was hoping to catch a ride."

"I don't," said Nikki. "Why don't you just fly? When I go back, I'm going to. I'm through with that nightmare crossing."

"How was your sail over?" said Sam.

"A bit rough—we got hit by a rogue wave, then nearly lost a crew member. It was a good thing we had Davis onboard."

"You sailed over with Davis?" said Nikki.

"Yeah. We dropped him off at Great Harbour, Berry Island. He was picking up a delivery to Venezuela."

"Just awful what happened to him," said Nikki. The exuberance had drained from her and Sam looked away.

"Happened to him—what do you mean?"

"Oh, you haven't heard?" Nikki said. "Sam doesn't want to talk about it, but you were friends."

"Heard what, Nikki?" Ella shot a glance at Sam.

"Sam?" Nikki prodded, but he slumped against the cabin side, ignoring her. "Ella, Davis is dead."

"What are you talking about, Nikki?" Ella shot up and backed away in the cramped cockpit.

"It's true, Ella." Nikki looked down at her hands.

"No, it's not."

"I wish it wasn't. He was a good man."

"Nikki," Ella raised her voice. "It's not true. We just dropped him off a few days ago. What day was that, Sunday? Today is Tuesday. He's on a delivery."

"Davis was sailing through the Northeast Providence Channel with Jon Hammond when they were boarded by pirates," said Nikki. "It's just horrible. It must have been absolutely frightening."

"Misinformation, Nikki," Ella said in anger. It was like Nikki to carelessly get it wrong. "He was sailing down to Venezuela, nowhere near the Providence Channel."

"It's true, Ella," said Sam. "The pirates came at them in the night. They must have been outnumbered."

"Pirates?" Ella looked to Sam. "He wouldn't have let that happen. You're mistaken." A shock of tears flooded her eyes. "You've got to be. Who...who told you this?"

"Jon called me on his sat phone," said Sam.

"Who is Jon?"

"Sam's stepbrother," said Nikki.

"I didn't know you had a brother." Ella looked to Sam. She slipped down to the seat, feeling lightheaded. "This has got to be a mistake."

"It's true." Nikki took a sip of her drink, then put it down. "Awful."

"He was on a delivery to Venezuela." Ella lowered her head into her hands, feeling breathless.

"Don't know about that," said Sam. "The satellite coverage was weak, Jon kept breaking up."

"Then maybe you misunderstood him." She wiped her face and turned to Sam. "Is Davis with him?"

"No, Ella, I understood him," Sam said flatly. "Apparently, Davis was already gone by the time Jon made it on deck."

"Gone?"

"Overboard," said Nikki.

"Oh, God," Ella heaved, forcing back the tears. "He drowned?" she whispered.

"Gunshot," said Sam.

She felt suddenly cold and started to shake. She looked to Nikki. "Could I have that drink? Please."

Nikki poured a hefty three fingers of rum and handed it to Ella, resting her hand on her shoulder. "I'm so sorry, Ella. I didn't know you were that close."

"We've been together a year." Ella inched away until Nikki removed her hand. She finished the rum in one toss, its warmth blunting the sharp pangs of the news, and tried hard not to believe that the man she loved no longer existed.

"How come Jon made it?" Ella lifted her head, clutching her hands to stop them from shaking.

"Don't know anything about that," said Sam.

"I should have gone with him. I should have insisted," cried Ella. I tried, she thought. I should have tried harder. He might still be alive if only I had.

"Then you'd be dead too," said Sam.

Ella glanced over from Sam to Nikki; for once, Nikki had little to say. "What happened to Jon?"

"He's pretty shaken," said Sam. "He's sailing back to Florida."

Nikki sat swirling the ice in her drink, then took a sip. "I wish I could tell you..."

"Nikki!" Sam hissed. He was becoming visibly agitated, turning his ring around and around on his finger.

"Tell me what?" Ella lifted her eyes to Nikki, then to Sam.

"Tell you it wasn't true," said Sam.

"Can I get you another drink, Ella?" Nikki's voice had lost it's shrill and she finished off her drink and poured another.

"No, thanks." Ella put down her glass. "This has got to be a mistake. He's okay. Davis is okay—somewhere." She pulled up her legs and wrapped her arms around them, resting her forehead on her knees. "Has it been reported?"

"Don't know. We just heard," Nikki stumbled. "Sorry, Ella, we just don't know any more than that."

The three of them sat in silence, each staring off in their own direction. Tears streamed down Ella's face. She closed her eyes and softly rubbed her forehead to calm the storm in her heart. "Where does Jon keep his boat?"

"Probably back at New River, the city marina along Riverwalk," said Nikki.

"When do you think he'll be back?" Ella asked without lifting her head.

"Give it some time, Ella!" said Sam. His curt, dismissive tone cut into her heart.

"What do you mean?" She shot back angrily. She shoved her salad aside and picked up a pack of matches from the cockpit table, agitatedly flipping it in her hands.

"I meant give Jon some time," Sam said, watching the matches.

"I don't care if he is in shock, I have to talk to him."

"He might just sail back to Connecticut —I doubt if he'll stick around."

"I know you need to protect your brother, Sam, but I have a right to know what happened to Davis. I love him."

"Ella, I'm sorry, but you can't bring Davis back."

Ella bent over, resting her arms on her knees. She felt physically ill, every muscle in her body aching, her mind caught in a stunned limbo. Laughter from another boat broke through the heaviness and she felt a flash of anger. How could that be, she thought, how could anyone be laughing?

Ella read the matchbook cover through a blur of tears. "La Tasca, Havana, Cuba." Flipping the match cover open and closed, she asked, "Have you been there?"

"A very short trip," said Sam. "I flew in for a weekend to see an old friend."

"I didn't go," Nikki quickly added.

Ella wiped her face with both hands and tried to catch her breath.

41

"I'm going to get a beer," said Sam. "Nikki, Ella, you want one?"

"Not for me." Ella needed to get off this boat before the dam of emotion broke and she'd be stuck in the chill of their company. Sam's brusqueness felt like a one-two punch after the news about Davis.

Sam grabbed the bottle of rum and slipped below deck before Nikki could answer. With him out of sight, Nikki snapped the pack of matches from Ella's hand and pretended to fling them over the side, confusing Ella with a mischievous smile.

"I need to be alone." Ella stood to leave. "I'm going to walk over to Paradise for a swim." She was glad she hadn't asked to spend the night. She could always go back to *Grace*.

"Looks like it's going to rain," said Nikki.

Ella looked up; she hadn't noticed the dark clouds crowding the sky. "Doesn't matter." Nothing matters, she thought bleakly.

"Why don't you come back for dinner?" Nikki asked half-heartedly.

Ella shook her head. "I'm lousy company right now. Anyhow, I think I'm upsetting both of you. I'll see you stateside." She grabbed her duffel and threw it over her shoulder.

"Ella, I'm sorry, really." Nikki stood up to give her a cursory hug. "We should be back at River Bend Marina in a few weeks. I'll call you."

Ella didn't know exactly what Nikki was apologizing for—Davis's death or their domestic tension. Nikki was always apologizing, sensing that once again she had put her foot in her perfectly painted mouth.

"Hauling out?" Ella asked, trying for normal conversation.

"No, Sam's having some new electronics installed. You know men and their toys."

"Thanks for the drink, Nikki." Ella bent down to look for Sam in the main salon. "Looks like Sam disappeared."

"He's pretty upset about Davis too."

"Yeah. Well, tell him I said good-bye. Take care, Nikki."

Ella had walked a few paces from their boat when she heard Sam's angry shouts rising against Nikki's high, defensive voice. He was telling her to keep her big mouth shut.

CHAPTER 5

Ella made her way along the dock feeling as though she were in a free-falling elevator dropping down an endless shaft. Davis was gone. Another of her life links cut, setting her adrift in a world with only a scattering of casual friends.

A soft summer tropical rain began to dapple the hot streets, releasing the scent of wet cement. It brought Ella back to when she had first smelled that smell, in the summer streets of her childhood, walking with a parent holding her hand on either side—a complete family unit. For a fleeting moment in time, she had been whole.

She needed to rein herself back in, and took shelter in an outdoor bar. It wasn't yet noon, but all the stools were taken by tourists and locals sitting side-by-side, in the one place where they mixed on common ground. She stepped up to the bar and ordered a double shot of Clan MacGregor. Wedged between the stools, she tossed back the scotch and shivered as the biting warmth ran down her throat, spreading throughout her chest, dulling the crushing pain of grief.

The rain picked up and began to hit hard on the tin roof of the flimsy shack, pounding out a deafening rhythm that pulled her back into the present. People came crushing in off the street, laughing, excited by the downpour and holding bags or clothing over their heads in a futile attempt to stay dry. Rain was good for business. The bar filled up and more people squeezed past her in soaked clothes and dripping hair. Ella ducked under a man's arm as he reached for his Bahama Mama Shooter.

"Smile, sweetheart, you're in the islands."

The last thing she wanted now was to feel anything. She pressed past him, squeezing her way out into the open where she could at last breathe.

Dark clouds scudded across the island and shafts of sunlight broke through, shining down on the deserted, shimmering streets. Ella crossed over the Atlantis Bridge to Paradise Island and headed for a private resort beach. She walked along, horrified at the thought of Davis dying alone, struggling for breath as he sank into the dark waters. She prayed to an unfamiliar god to wake her from this nightmare, offering her service, anything, just to make it not be true.

Her thoughts wandered to a better time, when they were together on the *Gina Marie*—her private sanctuary until he walked into her life. She had prepared his favorite dish, a Brazilian stew, and he played calypso rhythms on his guitar, his deep, rough voice singing the words to "Chan Chan," making her melt with joy. She remembered clearly his beautiful Cuban face with eyes so intense they seemed at times more animal than man, and his kisses—slow and lingering, with a simmering passion that broke down the barriers Ella was so practiced at retaining. She was hooked and in love, and she had felt it was mutual. He was the love of her life. *He was*—the words choked her.

*****

Ignoring the 'No Public Access' sign, Ella walked along the path to the beach, threw down her duffel at the water's edge and waded into the shallows in her shorts and t-shirt. When she was waist deep, she dove in and swam along the white, sandy bottom. The warm salt water soothed her, easing her anger, and she began to cry. She came up for air choking on her tears and, with her back to the shore, faced the open sea. The sound of the waves drowned out her heaving sobs, so deep and old she felt they would never end. She cried for the loss of Davis, for the loss of her father, and of her mother so long ago. The agony of her loneliness burst out of her and she slapped and punched the water's surface until her hand began to burn.

"God damn you!" she screamed, uncertain of who she was cursing, a god she didn't believe in, or Davis for getting himself killed. She came down as hard as she could with both hands, smacking the water. The next wave knocked her off her feet and she struggled to stand.

Slowly, she began to calm down and catch her breath. She turned to see if anyone had heard her, but the people on the beach were in their own world, busy building sand castles and reading magazines. She trudged toward shore, weighted by her soaked clothes, the incoming waves pushing and the undertow pulling at her until she stumbled out onto the sand. She had drifted south with the current and walked back up the beach to retrieve her bag.

A native boy in his teens walked along the water's edge toward her. When he reached her bag, he casually scooped it up and threw it over his shoulder. Ella's anger had found a home. She leaned into her walk, positioning herself on the side where he carried her bag. Once alongside him, she turned abruptly, grabbed her bag with one hand and, with the other, slugged the kid square in the temple, knocking him down. He lay in the sand, stunned, staring up at her. She glanced in the bag and saw her wallet and passport were still there.

"Don't mess with me," she hissed "Not today."

In a snap, the boy leapt to his feet and ran down the beach, kicking up a rooster tail of sand. Ella rubbed her bruised knuckles.

Dripping wet, she slogged through the sand back to the access path, keeping her eyes down and ignoring the furtive glances of beachcombers.

She needed to see Jon, she thought, hear what he had to say, but she knew it was true. The worst was always true. Everyone she'd ever cared about had died and left her alone.

*****

Rich was lying stretched out on the aft deck when Ella returned to *Grace*. His topsiders were kicked off to the side and his head was propped with a folded cushion at the perfect angle to study the rigging through the ship's three-thousand-dollar pair of Swarovski binoculars. A smile came across his face as Ella approached, and he quickly got to his feet.

"Is it raining harder in town?" He extended his hand, offering her help onboard.

Ella looked down at her wet jersey clinging to her skin, then up at Rich. "No, I went for a swim." She ignored his hand and hopped onboard, dropped her duffle onto the deck and slumped on the cabin top.

"Rich," Ella took a breath. "Davis is dead." The moment the words left her mouth, a damn of tears broke.

"What?" Rich pulled a rumpled cloth from his pocket and handed it to Ella.

"He's dead. An awful, horrible..."

Rich took a step back. "Who told you this?"

"Sam and Nikki." Ella wiped her face. "Nikki said Davis and Jon were sailing through the Northeast Providence Channel when pirates attacked them."

"Who's Jon?"

"Jon Hammond. Do you know him?"

"Sam's brother. I've met him," said Rich. "But I wouldn't believe anything Nikki said."

"Yeah, I know." Ella paused. "But Sam confirmed it."

"Not too sure I'd believe anything from him, either." Rich leaned in, giving her shoulder a gentle squeeze.

Ella looked up at him, hoping that he'd tell her it was mistaken information from unreliable people.

"What'd they say happened?" said Rich.

"It was Davis's watch. Jon was below when the pirates attacked. It was night. I just can't believe Davis wouldn't have heard them coming. I need to talk to Jon."

"How'd they find out?"

"Jon called Sam on his sat phone but the signal was weak—that's all the information they could get."

"What boat were they on?"

"Jon's," said Ella.

"He has a Pearson 35," said Rich, shaking his head. "Were they able to put up a fight?"

"All Sam said was," Ella hesitated, "Davis was shot and he fell overboard."

"God. It's hard to believe. We were just with him a few days ago."

"It's too horrible. I just can't." Ella's voice choked up and she looked away. Rich put his arm around Ella, softly rubbing her shoulder until she pulled away, wiping her face.

"He was supposed to be delivering a boat to Venezuela." Her voice was distant and she lowered her head, sinking into unspeakable sadness.

"Davis does a lot of favors for people," said Rich. "He might have been helping Jon bring his boat to some yacht club in the Abacos." Rich rubbed the back of his neck and looked out across the marina. "Probably more like Cape Eluethera Resort."

It seemed a possible explanation, Ella thought.

"It wouldn't have been out of his way if he were headed to Venezuela." Rich ran his hands through his hair and sat down next

48

to her. "The delivery crew might have agreed to pick him up there. Jon would have needed someone like Davis to get him through Current Cut. It's treacherous. Do you know where Jon is now?"

"Nikki said he was sailing back to Fort Lauderdale." Ella sat up, wiping her face with Rich's cloth, and then stopped, giving it a quick sniff and used her sleeve instead. "I'm not sure. Sam said he might have sailed home to Connecticut."

"He's not experienced enough to sail a boat to Connecticut."

"I thought he sailed down here."

"He bought his boat in Miami," said Rich. "I'll look him up when I get back."

"Nikki said he berths at the city docks on New River. I can talk to him. I might get there before you."

"I know where he keeps his boat. I don't want you..." Rich stopped.

"You don't want me to what?"

"Wait for me, okay? This could be a mistake or it could be dangerous. Just let me find out."

"Why would it be dangerous?"

Rich shrugged. "Don't know."

"I need to know what happened, Rich." Ella swiped away a tear. "He might be alive and in trouble."

"That's a possibility, I suppose. It's hard to imagine him getting caught off guard. He would've heard them coming. Maybe it was a boat feigning a breakdown." Rich rested his arms on his knees and hung his head between his shoulders. "This isn't good."

"No, it's not; opposite end of the world from good."

"Probably best to stay away from Sam and Nikki until I talk to Jon," said Rich.

"Why?"

"Maybe no reason. I've just never trusted those two."

"Really? I thought they were just players."

"Probably that, too." Rich looked up to the darkening sky. The cloud deck that had been hugging the island had dropped lower, and the light breeze had calmed to a whisper. The water turned a silvery shade of mercury and a sullen mist began to fall.

"Better close up the boat."

"I'll help." Ella grabbed her duffel and began taking in the cockpit cushions.

"Look, I'm supposed to meet Carlos for dinner at Mama Lyddy's Place. Why don't you join us?"

"Let me guess, conch fritters?" Ella forced a smile and tried handing Rich his cloth.

"You can hang on to it."

"It smells like Brasso." She handed it back. "Where's Jake?"

"He's in town getting a taste of island life before he flies home tonight." Rich stuffed the cloth in his back pocket. "Have dinner with us, Ella. You shouldn't be alone tonight."

"I'll be okay, but thanks. I think I'll tuck in. I'm going to try for an early flight back to Lauderdale."

"Sure?" Rich gave it one more try. "Best conch fritters on the island."

Ella considered it for a moment. She was leaving early in the morning and Rich probably wouldn't get back until late.

"I'd better not. I'm not fit to be out in public." She took a step in the direction of her cabin, then turned, realizing she wouldn't see him before she left. "Thanks, Rich, for everything."

"I'll see Jon first thing when I get back to Lauderdale. I can't use the phone on something like this, Ella."

"Why? What do you think is going on?"

"Just being cautious."

"Wish I could be there when you talk to him."

"I'll tell you everything he has to say. I promise."

CHAPTER 6

Ella had flown back to Fort Lauderdale, where the *Gina Marie* sat tied to a rickety dock behind a private house. She called it home, and for now, it suited her: the dock rent in this upriver neighborhood was cheap and the owners of the property were never around. She tossed her duffle below deck and opened the ports to air out the boat before riding off on her rusty Bickerton bike to the Las Olas Post Office to see if today was her big payday.

She'd been away for five days, but only two pieces of mail lay in her post office box—an indication of how little she was plugged into the world. No insurance or utility bills: not even the cable and credit card companies were interested in her. Of the two, one was a hand-addressed letter from Simone, her elderly neighbor in Middleton, Rhode Island, no doubt repeating her offer of a place to stay if Ella returned, which would reignite her longing for a home that was no longer there. Ella tucked the letter under her arm and walked outside, ripping open the manila envelope containing the report from the marine surveyor of her father's tugboat. She leaned against a mailbox and felt the thrill of rising expectations as she leafed through the report, looking for the bottom line.

But her dream slipped away with every careful word of the marine surveyor, a friend of her late father's, explaining the failed survey and why the sale of her father's tugboat had fallen through.

And worse, why it would never sell. She read it twice, but the facts remained the same: corroded fasteners, dry rot in the planking and ribs, an engine that needed replacing. Her father had sacrificed the tug's repairs to help pay for her education. She slowly slid down the front of the mailbox to the sidewalk, squatting on her heels and folding in like a flower closing for the night, burying her head in her arms. Oh, God—now what?

Weeks before, while signing Mr. Conti's contract for a bayside property in the middle Florida Keys, Ella had thought *this is what winning feels like.* Her years at culinary school and nights as a line chef, the dishes she crafted and menus she planned, were all for this moment. One of her father's crew had suggested the tugboat could sell for three hundred thousand dollars. Knowing her luck, she had cut her expectations in half: a hundred and fifty thousand would be plenty. She wasn't prepared for nothing—*zero dollars.*

She had had this one chance at a promising future. Now what was left? Scrambling to put together a paltry income, crewing on deliveries, cooking for people who normally lived on Spaghetti-os and breakfast cereal, living at the margin of life in a cramped boat behind some rich stranger's home? She began to sob. The restaurant was the dream that gave her life purpose; now all she felt was hopeless and alone. Would she ever win?

A woman reached over her to drop a letter into the mailbox. Ella shot her a look of annoyance and then stood to get out of the way, wiping away tears with the back of her sleeve. She crushed the mail into her bike bag and pedaled home, past houses of maddening wealth that lined the canals, to the refuge of her boat.

Ella sat at the bow of the *Gina Marie* for longer than she knew, staring numbly at the New River drifting by, carrying an occasional palm frond or coconut bobbing in its current. Finally, she picked up the manila envelope and pulled out the report. She started to read once more, then stopped, stretched her arm over the water, and let the pages unfold, flapping like a white flag of surrender between her pressed fingers until the wind tugged them free.

She got to her feet, steadying against the forestay, and watched the pages swirl above the river until they were caught in the slipstream of a passing yacht and run over by the launch it towed. A few stubborn sheets floated on the surface until the paper fibers became sodden and sank, ghosting below the water's surface before they, too, disappeared.

The ring of her cell phone startled her out of her trance. It was Mr. Conti, calling again for the promised down payment. Just great. Timing couldn't be better, she thought, tensing with each ring, delaying the inevitable. Once he knew she was broke the deal would be off, the deposit lost, and her dream crushed. The stabbing rings continued until the call went to message. At least I have the *Gina Marie*, she thought. She knew she'd never sell the *Gina Marie*; it would be like selling her father. She'd have to figure out another way—later. Right now all she wanted to do was retreat to her galley, to immerse herself in something she could control.

She began pulling out the ingredients for a Moroccan pastilla she had been refining for her restaurant—though it now seemed pointless. Maybe her salty tears falling into the mix would be her secret ingredient. She whacked the side of the knife's blade, crushing a pile of garlic onto the cutting board, then began mincing cloves as she mulled over ways to save her dream. She wished she had taken Davis up on his offer of a loan. Now Davis was gone, and no one else was going to lend her money: no family to borrow from or co-sign for her, no credit rating, since she had never borrowed money, no investor willing to take the risk, and the worst of all, no luck.

*****

Gina Marie's small cabin filled with the smells of cinnamon, almonds and chicken. Ella knew from the perfect mingling of aromas that the pie was ready and she pulled it from the oven and

53

placed it on a rack to cool. It had baked lopsided, as if it had been traveling at a high speed and come to an abrupt stop. She slammed the oven door of the gimbaled stove, not realizing the latch that locked it in place was open. The sharp edge of the oven swung back, cutting a gash in her leg that sent a stream of blood down her calf. She fought back with a barefoot kick to the oven door, then reeled in pain onto the cabin sole.

"Goddamn it!" she cried, folding in, resting her forehead on her knees. "Oh, Davis, I wish..." She leaned back against the bulkhead and looked long at the empty companionway, holding a paper towel to her bloody leg. "I wish you were here."

She slid down until she was lying flat on the cabin sole, her tears streaming across her temples and dampening her hair. She thought long about something Davis had said: "You make your own luck." It sounded like a frivolous cliché—until now. By not letting possibilities pass you by, she thought.

I'm not a quitter; she told herself, this is where I want to stay, I'm not going back to Rhode Island—I'll get the restaurant. Since Davis's death, a reoccurring thought had nagged at Ella to return to Rhode Island, but she wanted more from life than an easy familiarity. She did have the money from the sale of her family home: thirty-five thousand, after the first and second mortgage were paid off. Was it foolish to open on so little funds, possibly as a take-out while remodeling the restaurant? Would she make enough to keep it going? Twenty-five thousand dollars more would give her a fighting chance at success. The thought of Rich's offer had just crossed her mind when he called.

"There's not a lot to report about Jon," Rich began.

Ella sat up, clearing her voice. "Can I come by?"

"You okay?" Rich asked.

"Yeah, I was peeling onions."

"You want me to come to you?"

"No. I need to get out of here. Besides, I'd like to see your boat."

"Sure. I'm here all afternoon."

"Thanks, Rich." Ella paused, looking at her Moroccan pastilla. "Do you like chicken pie?"

CHAPTER 7

Ella wrapped the chicken pie in a bath towel, propped it in the basket of her bike, and pedaled the twenty-minute ride to the neighborhood where Rich's boat was docked behind a private home. The broad streets were lined with royal palms and manicured yards landscaped with exotic tropical plants. Ella parked her bike at the gate and walked along the property line, past the Eichler home with its wall of glass hedged in flowering red hibiscus. Rich must be doing okay for himself if he could afford to dock here, she thought, as she crossed the carpet of grass as deep and thick as a Cape Cod sand dune.

She stopped at the sight of Rich's island schooner, *Caroline*, wallowing alongside the bulkhead in sharp contrast to the sleek luxury yachts that shared the canal. Their gleaming chrome and deep varnish were like a pretty girl with nothing to say, compared to this old sea dog. Ella could only imagine the leagues of adventure that had passed under the schooner's keel, wearing smooth her rough edges.

Rich waved from the cockpit, gripping a wrench. He looked freshly showered, his damp hair pulled back into a low ponytail and his wrinkled white t-shirt tucked into khaki pants with cuffs rolled up above his ankles. He crouched barefoot beside a jammed mainsail winch.

"Ahoy, *Caroline!*" Ella called out, surveying the uneven pinewood planks of her hull, the thick coat of chalky white paint and the powder blue trim that softened her overall ruggedness. She was heavy and wide, with a graceful wineglass transom.

"Hey there, Ella, come aboard."

"Where did you find this boat? Looks like it's out of a Winslow Homer painting." Ella climbed onboard, holding her pie.

"She's from Man-O-War Cay in the Abacos. You're right, she does look like one of Homer's sponge boats."

"She's beautiful."

"That she is," Rich said, clearing away his tools, making way for Ella. "She used to haul cargo and mail for inter-island deliveries."

"How does she sail?"

"Slowly, like an old work boat. I only sail her to research sites, and I tow my skiff along to get around. Thanks for bringing the chicken pie."

"It's a Moroccan pastilla. They're not usually lopsided. My stove misbehaved." She handed it to him.

"It looks like a pastry. I've never had one." Rich leaned over to sniff the pie, wiping his hands on his pants before taking it. "Cinnamon?"

"It's part savory, part sweet."

"Are you hungry? Do you want to eat?"

"It's for you, for later. It's just a small thank you for, well, for everything. I'd love some water, though."

Ella followed Rich below deck, ducking under the low, rough-hewn beam of the companionway, getting the first musty whiff of the old wooden boat. Rich hunched in the cramped space, the overhead beams too low for his five-foot, eleven inches. The boat had been built in the forties for the island people, who stood a little over five feet tall.

"Headroom's the one drawback. You get used to it. She's rough," Rich looked long at Ella, "but it suits me."

"My father used to say, you can't love a thoroughbred like you can a farm horse."

"I agree with him."

There was no doubt that *Caroline* was a workhorse. Ella stood below deck in the living and working quarters of a bachelor scientist. Numerous well-worn notebooks were piled high in a corner of the salon, an Olympus microscope sat bolted to the navigation table, and test tubes and flasks were pushed off to the side of the galley counter in what looked like an attempt to make ready for company. She wondered how many hours he spent down here researching his insects, reminding her of her own hours of solitude crafting her dishes.

"You really are a scientist." She opened a cupboard and grabbed a glass, but Rich reached around her and snatched it from her hand.

"Yeah. Ah, not that glass."

Ella looked down at the dried-up worm lying in the bottom and turned back to see the cupboard was filled with jars of various insects. "Oh, nice."

"I was cleaning up a little before you came. Here's a mug."

She warily eyed the mug Rich was trying to hand her.

"How about a paper cup?" he asked.

"Sure, I'd love a paper cup." Ella smiled, glancing sideways around the galley. "So this is your lab?"

"Lab, home. Yeah. Compact, but it works."

"Why are you so interested in bugs?"

"They're fantastically successful as a species, more so than us."

"Lately that doesn't seem like much of an accomplishment."

Rich pulled out a plate of prawns from the icebox and squeezed half a lemon over them. "Why don't we go up top before the gulls start helping themselves to the chips I set out.

58

Ella followed Rich on deck, not the least bit hungry, and sat at the helm holding onto the wheel, waiting to ask what she'd come to ask.

"So, what did Jon have to say?"

"They were on a drug run and with pretty high-grade weed." Rich lost his smile as he told Ella what he had learned.

"Davis *was* running drugs?"

Rich nodded.

"Did you know he was involved in that?"

"Yeah. There are a whole lot of folks down here who do occasional runs for a financial bump. But I've suspected for a while that Davis was doing it more than occasionally."

"I never knew." Ella wondered how many other people with unfunded dreams, like hers, were lured by the easy money of the drug world.

"You're new down here. After awhile, you can pick out the people who do runs. They're more relaxed about money than their supposed livelihood should permit."

Ella thought about how distant Davis had been the morning they dropped him off at Great Harbour. She wondered, if the Venezuelan delivery was a lie, what else had he lied about?

"How'd it happen?"

"Someone must have tipped off these guys. They knew exactly where and when, and probably what. It was an expensive load. They had picked up the bales at three a.m. and were sailing back in the Northeast Providence Channel. Davis was on watch and Jon was below in his bunk. Couple of hours later, as they were clearing Spanish Wells, three men on a sport fisher rammed their boat. Jon said it hit them so hard it knocked him out of his bunk. Before he could get on deck he heard machine gun fire. He didn't know they had killed Davis until they forced him on deck and Davis was gone. He never saw him again. He must have been terrified that he would be next."

"But he wasn't." Ella couldn't stifle her resentment.

"Thing I can't fathom is why they left one bale sitting in plain sight. Jon thinks it was to keep him from calling for help. Kind of expensive insurance: depending on its quality, one bale could be worth at least sixty thousand on the street."

"Sixty THOUSAND? For something that's legal to grow these days?"

"The laws vary by state, and federally it's illegal. Besides, most of what's grown here is commercial grade. The premium stuff still gets smuggled in."

"Why didn't they just kill Jon?" she said bitterly. "That's what these people do, right?"

"Don't know. Maybe killing Davis was an accident."

"There was no way he could have helped Davis?" Ella asked.

"Ella, Jon's not to blame. He wouldn't have had a prayer against these guys. If you ever meet him you'll see. He's a preppy. I doubt he's ever hit anything but a punching bag at his club's gym—if that."

"Then why the hell was he even there?"

Out of habit, Ella pressed a prawn, testing it for freshness.

"He needed money." Rich shrugged. "Sam hooked him up with Davis, and Jon trusted things would go all right."

"It never occurred to me that Davis was into smuggling; he didn't even smoke grass. Sam does, but I never suspected him either. Now I understand why he was so weird in Nassau. Seems as though I was unaware of a lot," she added ruefully. "I didn't even know he had a brother until Nikki mentioned him."

Ella stared at the prawn before finally biting into it. The sweet, briny taste was a nice distraction. She flicked the fin into the river, and then turned to Rich. "Aren't you afraid of being attacked by pirates on one of your runs?"

"No. I wouldn't go with fewer than four crew. I don't know why Davis would chance a run with just Jon, unless there wasn't enough profit to split four ways. My guess is if the pirates knew about the run, they knew they were short-handed."

"How about Sam, have you worked with him?"

"No. I'd never trust him," Rich said. "And I can't understand why Davis did."

"Why don't you trust him?"

"Gut feeling."

"You're pretty careful, aren't you?" Ella looked around at Rich's boat. The old girl was well maintained.

"Have to be."

Ella nodded, knowing she was here for more than one reason, still uncertain if grief had clouded her judgment. But Rich had figured out a way: he was a scientist funding his own research and living the life he wanted. She leaned back against the cockpit coaming and crossed her arms, hanging onto her shoulders as if she were bracing against the cold.

"You know the thing I keep coming back to?" said Rich. "I've known Davis a long time, the way you know someone when you sail together, their weaknesses and strengths. He would have heard them coming. He wouldn't have gone down without a fight. And why didn't he yell out a warning to Jon?"

"What do you think happened?"

"Not sure. Jon was asleep." Rich leaned forward, wringing his hands. "Maybe they picked Davis off from a distance and he didn't have a chance; maybe he recognized them—someone he knew—and thought he was safe."

"Can I talk to Jon?"

"He won't see *anyone*. When I stopped by his boat, it was battened down during the hottest part of day. I wasn't sure he was onboard until I looked through the port. When he finally cracked opened the hatch, he told me to go away."

"Maybe Jon's a coward," said Ella, "not wanting to admit he hid below, leaving Davis to fend for himself."

"That was my first thought," said Rich.

"I need to talk to him."

"I don't want *you* talking to Jon, or anyone, about this."

"I can't let this go. I can't. I need to find out who's responsible."

"If you were to discover who it was—then what? Be smart, Ella, let it go."

She knew Rich was right. But she wanted someone to pay for Davis's nightmare death, and for taking him from her.

"We may never know, Ella. That's the way things work in the drug world. You have no protection if you start snooping around. If you're determined to find out who killed Davis, you may just end up dead. Hundreds of people get murdered every year in this business."

"And yet *you* go on drug runs?"

"I know the people I'm dealing with. Have been for years. I don't take chances with unknown suppliers. Maybe that's what Davis did, he got greedy."

"Smart." Ella thought how sensible Rich was. "So they can just get away with killing someone."

"Down here? Yes, they can," said Rich. "I tell you what, I've got someone who may know. And if he doesn't, he'll find out. It serves his interest to find out. But, Ella, promise me you won't ask around on your own. You don't know who may be involved."

Ella reached over and rubbed Rich's arm, "Alright. I promise." The minute she touched him she knew it was a mistake.

Rich turned and slowly pulled her into him, holding her tightly until her tears began to fall onto his shoulder. He kissed the back of her neck softly and with an exhale she let go, burying her face in his chest like a child, wanting not to move, to stay like this forever, cradled in a comforting embrace.

"Thank you, Rich." Ella rested her head against his chest and wiped away the tears.

"Ella," Rich's voice was low and wanting.

She lifted her head and felt the warmth of his breath. His hand softly cradled her face and he kissed her lips and the tear-moist skin under her eyes. She felt herself going where she'd promised she wouldn't go, melting into him, becoming vulnerable again. She pulled away.

"I'm ..." She couldn't tell Rich she was in pieces, barely holding it together. She needed him to trust her. "I'm sorry."

"Thoughtless; it's me who should be sorry." Rich gave her arm a gentle squeeze, then looked up.

A small skiff with a one-stroke outboard had motored close to *Caroline*. The boatman signaled his praise, giving *Caroline* a thumbs-up, and Rich gave him a nod of thanks.

"You okay?" Rich said, turning back to her.

Ella got to her feet and hooked her arm around the shroud, giving her something to hold on to. "No, not really. On top of everything else, my father's tug is worthless—I'm broke." She watched the skiff motor along the canal's bulkhead, the carefree boatman waving to people onshore as he passed.

"You got the surveyor's report?"

"Yeah. My dad must have used the money for tug repairs on my tuition. Ironic, isn't it? I may even have to pay to bring it to salvage."

"I'm sorry to hear that, Ella."

"Unless I can find an investor or partner, I'll lose the restaurant."

"I wish I had it to lend you. I'm making this run because I need the money."

"Thanks, I never expected you to," said Ella. But he could help her in another way, she thought, the way he had helped himself—if she had the guts. And why not? She was as smart, vigilant and experienced a sailor as he was.

"Maybe the seller would give you terms?"

"Mr. Conti will carry the loan, but I need start-up funds. And without a co-signer, no banks will lend me the money."

Just this once, she thought, and asked, "How dangerous is the trip you're planning?"

"There's risk, Ella. If there wasn't everyone would be doing it. Why are you asking?"

She felt a surge of fear swell in her throat as she stepped across a line, having mistaken her ambitions for her needs.

"Look, Rich, I'll regret it if I don't do everything I can to secure this property. Waterfront at this price doesn't come up in the Keys that often. It couldn't be more perfect. It's exactly what I had imagined, what I dreamed of." She held his gaze and smiled. "What would I have to do?"

"Are you sure Davis's death isn't affecting your decision? Loss can make for rash decisions. Maybe you should give this some time."

"His death *has* affected my decision. Absolutely. He would have helped me, somehow." She saw the uncertainty in his eyes. "I'm on my own now, Rich. I can't lose both Davis and the restaurant. I'll be left with nothing."

Rich looked away, out over the river, long enough for Ella to expect he would turn her down.

"You said you worked with these people for a long time. Tell me about it," she asked.

Rich nodded, "Unlike Davis and Jon, there will be four of us, and we'll be sailing a fifty-three-foot sloop, working with people I know—that being said, there is always a risk. I have to know you're sure about this, Ella. Otherwise, I need to find someone else."

"I understand. I've sailed with you enough, Rich, to trust you won't get us caught. If you feel good about this run, that's good enough for me. Besides, you're a scientist and I'm betting you've considered every angle."

"True, but you can't control whether the Coast Guard or a random pirate boat takes interest in you, or the possibility of someone talking or getting greedy. On the supplier end, for the most part, we're dealing with people you've never seen in your life, people who are third-world hungry, worn down by generations of poverty and desperate for relief.

"On the bright side," Rich added, "the group I'm with has a longstanding working relationship, and over the years it's all run pretty smoothly. It's your call."

"What's changed?" Ella's voice was strained.

"What do you mean?"

"When you asked me on *Grace*, you were hoping I'd go. Now, you sound like you're warning me off."

"You've been through a lot, Ella."

"Oh, I see, you don't think I can handle it. I'm tougher than I look, Rich. Remember, I was raised by a tugboat captain."

Rich gave her a warm, admiring smile, "Okay, Ella."

Ella looked to the sound of a nearby yacht starting its diesel, then turned back to Rich. "So am I in? I need to know soon."

"As far as I'm concerned, you are. You in a hurry?"

"The property owner keeps calling. I can't take his call until I'm able to promise him payment."

"You'll have to meet the boss's approval," said Rich. "But I don't see a problem. He's always taken my suggestions for crew."

Rich had thrown her a life ring, but instead of bringing relief, it exchanged one worry for another. Until now, it had been unthinkable for her to do something outside the law. Maybe the footloose style of the tropics was settling into her bones, or maybe it was just plain desperation.

"Can you tell me what you're smuggling, and when?"

"High-quality weed. We leave approximately in a week for an at-sea pickup, delivering to a port in Florida."

"And the pay? Is it twenty or twenty-five thousand?"

"I can get you the twenty-five for a three-day sail and some prep time. I know it's not everything you need."

"It's enough to get started." Barely enough, she thought. "Where's the pick-up? Approximately?"

"Not far. A full day's sail from Marathon Key."

Ella tried to calculate where that might be, happy that it ruled out the pirate sailing grounds of Haiti and Jamaica.

"Absolute silence," Rich said. "Not a word to anyone."

"I have no one left to tell," said Ella. "You won't regret it, Rich."

"I know. I have to say, Ella, I've never met a woman quite like you."

"I'll take that as a compliment."

"Was meant to be," Rich nodded. "You want a beer?"

"No, thanks. I should go. Look, earlier... you need to understand," Ella paused, choosing her words. "I'm still struggling to accept he's gone, but I will get through this, just like I did when I lost my folks. In the meantime, I'll be the best damn crew you could have."

"I have no doubt, on both counts." He leaned over and gave her shoulder a gentle squeeze. "I'll call you after I talk to the boss." His phone rang and he turned away to see the caller I.D. "I need to get this."

"Right. See you later." Ella stepped off *Caroline* and sat on the grass, taking her time to put on her shoes and straining to listen in on Rich's side of the phone call.

"Rico, thanks for returning my call. Can you do a little work for me? You know *Wanderlust*, Sam and Nikki's boat? Nikki, the pretty blonde who talks a lot." Rich laughed. "Yes, Miss little bikini."

Ella kept her eye on Rich; he still had his back to her. She shook out the other shoe, slowly put it on, and tied the lace.

"I need photos of anyone visiting them. What? When did they leave?" Rich listened for what seemed like minutes to Ella. "Why is

66

Mr. Pascal asking about me? Yeah. Well don't tell him anything. I'll settle with you the same way as always. Thanks, Rico."

Ella jumped up and stepped onboard. "I forgot my towel. Thanks for everything, Rich."

She walked back across the great lawn, turning to wave good-bye to Rich, wondering who Rico and Mr. Pascal were, and thinking they must be in Nassau, where *Wanderlust* had been docked. But what intrigued her most was why Rich was spying on Sam and Nikki.

Ella unlocked her bike and pushed off, heading back home, uncertain if she had just made a bold move or a foolish one. Yet a bold move is what it would take, not playing it safe, if she didn't want a life as a line cook waiting for luck to come her way.

CHAPTER 8

Babs had made enough money moving weed over the years to retire to a comfortable, simple life aboard her bungalow-style houseboat. She was the only live-aboard at Palmas Marina on Grassy Key, a small, Lower Florida Key that most people drove through without noticing. It was a quiet, tucked-away home to a dozen fishing boats and a few skiffs that could make it into the shallow inlet without hitting bottom.

In the cool light of the morning, she sipped coffee on her upper deck and watched a red Jeep slowly roll up the drive. She put down her cup when she saw Sam slip out and soundlessly close the door behind him. She stole inside and watched from the edge of the sliding glass door to see which boat he boarded. She had met him on past deals, and she didn't like him. She didn't trust people with the practiced manners of the upper class who came down here to make quick money; by either greed or stupidity, they always brought trouble. When she saw Sam step aboard a banged-up sport fisher at the end of the guest dock, she picked up her phone and dialed a number.

*****

68

Sam paced inside the cabin of his fishing boat with the edginess of a caged animal. He paused to stare out the window, dropped down on the settee with his fists shoved deep into his pockets, then popped back up again. The man he was waiting for was late.

A thickset, middle-aged Cuban sat on the aft deck with his eyes at half-mast, taking in the morning sun. He leaned back in the fighting chair, pulling long, slow drags from a fat joint.

"Miguel, come inside," said Sam. "You look like an advertisement for High Times."

"High Times?" Smoke floated out of Miguel's mouth as he spoke.

"It's a magazine," said Sam.

"You worry too much, man. You hide inside, people gonna think we suspicious-looking."

"That fat cow on the houseboat has been watching us, so put out the fucking joint." Sam stood in the salon, staring out the window. "Where the fuck is he?"

"He's not coming, he's sending his *associate*. I already told you." Miguel smiled, watching Sam squirm. "Why you in this business if you got no cojones?"

"I pulled it off, didn't I? But this, this is no way to do business—you show up on time. It's about respect." Sam tapped a Marlboro from his pack and lit it, inhaling long and deep. "This is fucked up."

"Smoke a joint instead, man. Help you relax."

"Idiot, I don't want to get high, I want my money. Christ, you don't think anyone on the dock can smell that shit?" Sam ripped the joint out of Miguel's hand and tossed it over the side.

"Fuck man, what are you doing?"

Sam moved to the other side of the salon's doorway and scanned the parking lot. "Does anyone know if Jon made it back okay?"

"Why wouldn't he?" Miguel pulled out his stash, saw Sam eyeing him and stuffed it back in his pocket.

"He's not the best sailor." Sam took another long draw with his eyes on the parking lot.

"You brothers have a lot in common. Not best sailor, not best tough guy. Why are you down here?"

"Money, like everyone else."

"If I did that to my brother, oh man, I'd be dead. At least we left your brother something."

"That might have been a mistake. And it's stepbrother," Sam corrected. "Pathetic weasel." Sam took another long draw, watching the parking lot, then flicked his cigarette into the water. "He's here."

A chocolate brown Mercedes 450SL, vintage cool, pulled into the marina parking lot and a man in his late forties stepped out. He looked more like a deliveryman than someone who could afford an expensive luxury car. Clutching a satchel under his arm, he tapped the bulge in his right jacket pocket as he headed up the dock.

"That's right, asshole," said Sam, watching him walk up to the boat. "Show us where your gun is. Christ, I'm dealing with amateurs."

Sam turned to his first mate. "Pack up, Miguel. We're leaving as soon as we're through here."

CHAPTER 9

Ella had heeded Rich's warning not to keep the boss waiting, and more, to be on her toes. He had described Falco Leon as a tough guy from New Jersey who made it to the top in the drug trade through a keen ability to read people. Falco paid close attention to other's demeanor: just their walk could tell him their level of confidence and strength, and with only a brief conversation, he'd know if they could be trusted. Right now, getting Falco's approval was what stood between Ella and her one chance at securing funding for her restaurant, and she left more than enough time to get to the meeting.

From the back of the cab, she looked out at the strip malls and small homes of the upriver, middle class neighborhood where her boat was docked. The closer to the ocean they drove, the larger the houses became, with lush landscaping and luxury cars parked in the drive. Finally, they passed through the gates of Harbor Beach Estate.

Winding through the affluent neighborhood reminded Ella of growing up in Rhode Island in a tiny two-bedroom cottage surrounded by century old stone mansions, the homes of the yachting class. She knew very well what it meant to be poor. Each breakdown of her father's tug would empty their savings account for repairs, leaving only enough for the bare essentials. Living in a cold house during long winters, when his work was sparse and the heating oil bill was high, she had longed for a more comfortable existence.

"A strong moral compass is more valuable than wealth," her father had often said. It was his rationalization for accepting endless hard work and struggle. But Ella wasn't willing to accept she couldn't have both. She wanted a big life.

These people didn't get where they are without taking chances, she thought. How many ways did they cheat the system to get ahead? Was what she was about to do any different?

"Just this once, Dad," she whispered. "I promise."

Ella straightened her top, brushed off her pants, and peeked at herself in the driver's rearview mirror. She thought of taking off Davis's Constellation Maritime cap, but it helped offset the long, feminine braid down her back. It had been a prized possession of Davis's, his lucky hat that he had left behind aboard *Grace*. She could use some luck now. She thought of that morning, the passionate goodbye that had caused him to forget it, and felt a pang of remorse—might it have kept him alive? It had been something of his to hang onto until his return. Now it was all she had of him.

She arrived early to the Villa del Mar, an out-of-the-way resort nestled in this exclusive neighborhood of Fort Lauderdale, a quiet retreat concealed by palm trees and ferns that opened up to an expansive private beach in view of the Port Everglades Inlet. It was a favorite of the old-money families who avoided the flashy new hotels lining Florida's Gold Coast, and a perfect meeting place for anyone requiring privacy.

She stepped out of the cab under the vigilant scrutiny of the hotel staff, avoiding their eyes, passing quickly through the lobby and the lingering linen-clad clientele who rightfully belonged. She had dressed simply in her best clothes that were neither fashionable nor new, but hung well on her tanned and toned body. She straightened her back and walked sure-footed down the hotel's lush, fern-lined path to the outside bar.

Rich and Falco sat at the cabana closest to the bar, shaded under the palm-thatched roof, drinking espresso. Falco was a slight-built man in his mid-fifties. His facial features, too big for his frame, would have appeared comical if it weren't for his striking air of power. The high, curved bridge of his nose resembled an eagle's beak and his brown eyes, underscored by dark circles and bags, set deep below a ledge of shaggy eyebrow, were brazen and cold, assessing everyone and everything.

Rich had instructed Ella to take a seat at the outside bar facing the ocean and wait for him to call her over. She ordered an orange juice and held the cold glass to her forehead to cool off. The beach was nearly empty and so was the bar, except for two hulking men wearing sunglasses and quietly drinking colas. It was the hottest part of the day in the hottest month, and Ella guessed most people were indoors.

She waited and watched, careful not to slump on the backless stool, covertly assessing Falco under the cabana. He sat back in his beach chair, his leg hiked over his knee, looking more Cuban than Italian in his white linen Havanera shirt, white pants and leather sandals. Only the dent in his thick black hair, made by the Dolphins baseball cap tucked at his side, marred his impeccable grooming. He sipped from his demitasse, keeping his eyes on Ella. She calmly turned away, clutching her hands below the countertop to stop them from shaking.

Fifteen minutes went by, but it felt like thirty, her only thoughts looping in a mantra: stay cool, calm and collected. Finally, Rich waved her over and a flush of adrenaline ran through her. She paid for her juice and started across the hot expanse to meet them. Falco looked over the top of his sunglasses, scrutinizing her like one of Rich's bugs. Rich had advised her to hold her ground with Falco but never show aggression. She took long, unhurried strides and with a smile, touched the bill of Davis's cap to greet them.

"Hi." Ella turned to Falco. He didn't get up but sat stolid, like the Godfather. She wondered if he would offer his hand to be kissed. He leaned back in his chair and fixed his deep-set eyes on her.

Ella glanced at Rich, waiting to be introduced, but Rich didn't move. It was clear she was on her own. She extended her hand to Falco.

"I'm Ella."

She leaned in further, her hand hanging in mid air. At last, he reached up and shook it firmly, holding on with a slight grip, silently watching her. She looked him in the eyes and gave him a small smile before pulling her hand free. He returned it with a grin, and she guessed he approved.

"Davis's cap?"

"You recognize it?"

"So, why are you here?" Falco asked, ignoring her question.

"Money," Ella said directly, without hesitation, looking back at Falco with a steady gaze.

He nodded slowly. "I hear you're a skilled sailor."

"I've been sailing all my life."

Falco's phone rang, but he continued to study Ella and she held his eyes. After the fourth ring he looked at the caller I.D., then answered.

"I'm listening."

She strained without success to hear what the fast, clipped voice of the female caller was saying.

"When?" Falco stood up and signaled to his men. "Who's onboard?"

The men stood up and paid their bill. Their biceps, the size of dumbbells, stretched the sleeves of their t-shirts.

"If he leaves, follow him. I think I know where he's going, but don't lose him. I'll have my men ready at Islamorada to take over."

Falco's voice tightened. "What? Keep me posted." He grabbed his cap off the chair and turned to Rich. "It's fucking payback day."

"Is it what you thought?" said Rich.

"He's dirty." Falco tapped his shirt pocket and fingered the oily wrapper of his Camacho cigar. "We're going ahead. I'll have two guys stop by to use your Whaler. Leave your phone on."

Ella jumped back to make way as Falco strode past and the two gorillas followed in his wake.

*****

"What did Falco say?" Ella wiped her hands on a towel as she poked her head up from the galley. "Am I going?" She had been listening in on Rich's phone conversation, while making grilled cheese sandwiches to repay him for the ride back to *Gina Marie* from Villa del Mar.

"It just got complicated." Rich ran his hand through his hair. "I don't think you should do this run. There will probably be other trips."

"I heard you say, 'she won't.' Were you talking about me?"

"They're going to torch Sam's boat tonight."

"What?" Ella gasped and took a step up the companionway. "Why?"

"Sam was involved with the attack on Davis and Jon."

Ella rushed up the steps. "Sam killed Davis?"

"We don't know who killed Davis, but Sam was spotted leaving the pirate boat with what Falco believes was his payoff. We've learned that the boat belongs to Sam."

"That bastard, that fucking sleaze! Davis was his friend." Ella sat down clenching the dishtowel. "It's hard to believe. That murdering son of a bitch. He has to pay for this." She looked up at Rich. Her mounting anger made her tremble. "I knew something was off about Sam and Nikki, but I never imagined…" She thought about

75

Sam's numerous trips; he wasn't affluent, he was a thieving murderer. "Where was he? Where did Falco see him?"

"Grassy Key."

"So he *is* here." Ella stared off across the canal, her anger rising. "Cold-hearted scum."

Rich rested his hand on Ella's shoulder, and after a moment, she covered it with hers until she smelled the sandwiches burning and went below to turn off the gas.

"She won't what?" Ella asked again when she came back on deck. "What else did Falco say? What won't I do?"

Rich arched his back, taking in the fore and aft bend of the mast, then took hold of the backstay and gave it a shake. "Your rigging needs tightening. I could help you tune it."

"You're not answering my question." Ella didn't bother looking up. "Won't do what, Rich?"

"Help burn Sam's boat," said Rich. "You're being tested."

Ella stood up. "Oh, yes I will—with pleasure."

"Ella."

"I've seen him at Davis's house; what kind of evil is he to kill his friend and steal his brother's money? That explains why he was so tense when I saw them in Nassau. It would have been right after he killed Davis. I can't believe he could look me in the eye." Ella slammed both fists on the cabin top. "I could kill him. Was Nikki in on it, too?"

Rich hunched his shoulders. "Listen, Ella, there's never just one solution to a problem. You don't have to go tonight. You could find an investor for your restaurant, or get a loan."

"Try and stop me. I'm going all right. I want that bastard to pay for what he's done. I know how much he loves his *Wanderlust*." Seething, she sat down, pulled her knees to her chest and buried her face for a moment. Lifting her head, she asked, "Where will Sam be?"

"Probably onboard."

76

"So, they're going to kill him?"

"No. They'll pull him off, but my guess is he'll see his boat burn."

"Poor beautiful, *Wanderlust*. It'll be heart wrenching to see her burn."

"Falco wants to make sure you have what it takes," Rich said.

Ella looked up at Rich, "Oh, believe me, I'll exceed his expectations."

"Think about it, Ella, please."

"Don't need to. Sam's getting off easy. Losing his boat is nowhere near enough for taking Davis's life, but it's a start." She stood and went below for a second try at the grilled cheese. But mostly, she needed to be alone with her rage.

CHAPTER 10

Ten o'clock at night and it was still hot. Wakes from passing boats slapped against *Gina Marie's* hull as if on an empty drum, adding to Ella's restlessness and defying her need to sleep. Quieting her mind was like trying to cage a wild beast. Her thoughts were a buzzing mix of fear for the trial by fire that lay ahead and burning rage against Sam for taking Davis's life. This won't change me, she thought. I won't let it. Sam brought this on himself. She turned on her side and flipped her pillow, trying vainly for a cool place to lay her head.

At some point, Ella fell off to sleep and was awakened at midnight by her alarm. It was time to get ready. She pulled on her only black pants, the ones she had saved for a dinner out or a meeting with the culinary school's administrator, then slipped on a black pullover and considered Davis's cap. Bringing him along seemed like a good idea, until it came to her that the scorpion symbol could be easily recognized. She grabbed a black watch cap from her locker and stuffed it in her bag. She didn't hesitate; she knew if she did, she would never go. Climbing out the main hatch, she pulled it closed, locked it and left.

She pedaled down empty streets to Rich's boat. At one in the morning on a weeknight, the houses along the way were dark;

apparently, all the respectable people were asleep in their beds. She'd never broken a law in her life—not so much as a driving violation—but in less than an hour she would be a criminal.

She locked her bike to a palm tree and studied the shadows of the yard before skirting the lawn toward Rich's boat. His light was on, but no one was on deck. The Boston Whaler, a thirteen-foot open runabout, was tied off the transom and sitting ready with hanks of rope, duct tape and a couple of red gas cans—a toolkit for revenge.

Ella knocked quietly on *Caroline's* hull and Rich slid open the main cabin hatch. The welcoming smile she had come to expect was missing, making it obvious he disapproved of her coming along. He waved her onboard.

Below deck a fair, thin, boyish man sat tucked up against the side of the settee with his arms tightly crossed at his chest. He wore a strained look and his teeth, clenching rhythmically, telegraphed his fear.

"Ella, this is Jon," said Rich.

Jon gave a slight nod, barely looking at her. His black clothes swallowed him up, reducing him to a boy playing at espionage. He had pulled his watch cap down to his eyebrows and his black turtleneck and chinos covered the rest, leaving only the delicate features of his face and his soft, smooth hands exposed.

The sight of Jon unsettled Ella. By the looks of him, she knew that whatever Davis had faced that night, he'd faced it alone. Why would Davis have chosen this man for the drug run? *Did* Davis choose him? It made no sense. The Northeast Providence Channel could be smooth sailing unless a Northern was blowing, but those waters were home to pirates looking for easy money, and sailing through with a load of expensive weed was dangerous. She had never known Davis to have poor judgment.

"You were with Davis…?" She couldn't finish her sentence.

"I was." Jon looked briefly at Ella. "I understand you were his girl." He turned back to rubbing the sides of his thumbs and mumbled, "Sorry for your loss."

"Thanks. Sorry for you, too, for what you had to go through." *Were his girl*—the cold finality of those words made her wish she hadn't brought up Davis. A sudden feeling of claustrophobia crowded in on her in the small quarters of Rich's cabin. One of the last people to see Davis alive was sitting in front of her, and the reality of it all felt suddenly raw.

"I was nearly killed," Jon said.

"Do you remember hearing or seeing another boat?" she asked.

"No. Only lights from Spanish Wells."

"Did you hear gunfire before you were rammed?" Ella pressed on.

"I wouldn't know." Jon shot her a look that told her he wanted to be anywhere but here. "It was Davis's watch, after all. I was asleep." His agitation seemed to reach his legs and his foot began to jiggle.

She could see what Rich was talking about. Useless.

"He must have fallen asleep at the wheel," said Jon. "Sam said Davis was the best. More like the best at losing my money to those thugs. I told Davis we should start the engine, that we were sailing too close to the Devil's Backbone. But no, he wouldn't listen to me."

Ella clenched her jaw. "Lucky for you Falco wants to teach your brother a lesson," she said. "So you don't have to."

Jon uncrossed his hands from his lap and began pushing back a cuticle. "Stepbrother," he corrected. "He *needs* to be taught a lesson. And I need my money returned to me. Falco said I'd get it back." He looked up at Ella, and then Rich. "All of it."

"I doubt he said that," said Rich.

"Don't worry, I'll pay for your efforts tonight." Jon looked over at Ella. "Although I'm not sure why we need you."

"I'll accept that offer," Ella said, ignoring the cut. "Tonight, I'm here for Davis. And after tonight, I hope Sam's life turns into one miserable hell."

"He's always been miserable," said Jon. "But his misery will be considerably worse after he loses his prized boat." He spoke with his chin slightly raised, vocal chords stretched, with the signature tone of the upper class.

"So, is it just the three of us?" Ella asked.

"Four. Two of Falco's men will be here shortly," said Rich. "I'm not going."

"You're not going?" Ella swung around. "I thought..."

"Never was. I've got no horse in this race and I'm caught up on my favors with Falco. I'm lending my launch. That's all."

"Oh." Ella leaned back against the stairs. She hadn't realized her courage wasn't fully her own. She'd been playing at it; and now, without Rich, she felt like an imposter. Who did she think she was, doing vengeful things with people she didn't know?

"Who are the other men?" she asked.

"Falco's muscle," Rich said. "They're ex-military, like a lot of guys in the drug trade. They've acquired a taste for the adrenalin rush—and, of course, the money."

"They wouldn't..." Ella stopped.

Jon spoke up. "For God's sake, they're not going to kill Sam! Although I wouldn't mind if they did."

"That's not what's happening here," Rich broke in sharply. "Jon, you're going as lookout. Ella, you'll help handle the Whaler when it's time to move Sam's boat out of the marina. Your father was a tug man, you should know how."

"Yes. Obviously I would know how," she said with more than a little sarcasm.

"Besides, Falco wants you on the Whaler."

"Why?"

"He needs to know you won't break under pressure."

"I thought I'd already proven that on the passage to Nassau."

"Why?" Jon looked up at Ella. "Why are you being tested?"

Ella shook her head and turned to Rich for an answer.

"It's a private matter," said Rich.

Her attention shifted from Rich to the display case behind him: a collection of soft-winged, colorful butterflies pinned to a specimen board. A sudden rap on the hull startled her: Falco's men had arrived. Rich slid open the hatch and waved to the men standing alongside his boat.

"Tie her in the same spot when you get back," Rich said, referring to his Whaler. "Go on up," he directed Jon, then caught Ella by the arm. "You can still back out," he pleaded.

"I need to do this, Rich," she said. "I just wish you were coming."

"You know the quote from Confucius? 'Before you embark on a journey of revenge, dig two graves.'"

She eased her arm from Rich's grip. "They're already dug."

"Well, you've got my number." Rich stepped aside. "Call if you get in serious trouble."

Ella waited for Jon as he carefully hung onto the lifeline, lowering his toes to the grass. She studied Manny and Neil with apprehension. The two six-foot tall henchmen in dark clothes and watch caps had the athletic readiness of the military-trained.

"Okay Jon, you've got lookout duty," said Manny. "You know River Bend Marina?"

"Yes, of course," he replied.

"What's the color and make of your ride?"

"Black BMW sedan."

"BMW? Probably a shiny late model," Manny sneered as he studied Jon. "People notice a car like that. Tuck in someplace where you can see the target and the marina. Be discreet. You understand discreet?"

"Well, of course," Jon sniffed.

"Here's a number." Manny handed Jon a slip of paper. "Call if you need to alert us. After the boat burns, the phone goes in the drink and don't put the number in your phone book. Shred that paper, and for fuck's sake don't toss it in the yard; chuck it out the window when you're on the road. Now, go straight there." Manny started walking away, then turned back again. "And don't smoke. It's an easy giveaway for a lookout."

"Shall I come back here to collect my money?" said Jon.

"Tomorrow. Someone will contact you," said Manny.

"I prefer to get it tonight. I'll meet you back here, at Rich's boat."

Manny paused for a moment. "In the street. Don't get out of your car. Get going!"

Ella saw how closely Manny watched Jon as he huffed away. After tonight, Manny will have earned himself a favor from Falco, she thought. He was dealing with novices, and novices were dangerous.

Manny must have thought of another crucial point, because he suddenly bolted in quick, long strides across the lawn and grabbed Jon's shoulder the way you would a child whose attention you wanted. Even in the dark, Ella could sense Jon's annoyance.

Manny returned shaking his head. "Feather merchant," he said to Neil. "Little fuck better not blow the operation."

Neil stared after Jon with his hands on his hips. "You told him to haul ass out of there when she blows?"

"Yep. Let's hope he's not a complete idiot." He turned to Ella. "Don't get in the way."

"Just tell me what you want me to do," she shot back.

Manny took a long look at her, "I heard your father was a tug man."

"Yeah, he was, and I'm a sailor."

"Okay, jump in."

Ella got into the Whaler, taking the bow seat, and looked for Rich, but he had stayed below.

"Can you whistle?" said Manny.

"Yeah. Why?"

"Let's hear it."

Ella wet her lips, tucked them back with two fingers and blew, bringing Rich up on deck. It was a skill her father had taught her in case she was ever in trouble.

"Softer," Manny said, giving Rich an all-okay wave. "Once we get there, you'll stay with the Whaler. If you need to get our attention for anything, some movement around the marina or a boat coming down the river, give one quiet whistle we can hear. For God's sake, don't wake the whole goddamn marina. I don't want to be dodging cops."

CHAPTER 11

Wanderlust sat in the haul-out slip at River Bend Marina, a backwater basin along the New River that berthed mid-sized workboats, cruisers in for repairs and a few live-aboard boaters looking for cheap rent.

Sam sat up in his bunk, unable to sleep. His 9mm Beretta rested next to him on Nikki's pillow and the black satchel full of cash laid propped open at his side. He pulled out a banded pack of hundred-dollar bills and fanned through them, then pressed them to his lips and burst out laughing. Grabbing handfuls of the bundled hundreds, he tossed them into the air and flopped back onto his pillow, the money raining down on him.

"Jon, you arrogant dipshit. Whatever will daddy say now that you've lost all your money?" Sam's laugh slowly calmed to a deep satisfied chuckle. *"Again,"* he said, smiling to himself.

Sam's packed bags sat ready by the main hatch. In a few hours he'd be on the six o'clock flight to Nassau to meet up with Nikki. From there, they would venture to ports unknown—Nikki favored the French Riviera, and Sam the Greek Isles. A pre-paid work order to place *Wanderlust* in dry storage lay on the marina's desk. He'd come back for his boat when things calmed down. Wherever they landed, they had enough money to last them for a year or more of high living until Sam figured out his next scheme.

He stretched out on his bunk, feeling the weight of a pack in his hand. All those years of living in his wealthy stepfather's house, Jon getting the royal treatment—the "real" son—and Sam treated like an unworthy guest that everyone wished would leave. Now it was Sam's world, and Jon's turn to get the short end of the stick. He smiled, fanning one pack after another—hundred dollar bills, all the way to the bottom of the pile.

Sam looked up from the money to voices outside. He tucked his Beretta in the back of his pants and slipped out of the v-berth and into the main salon, peering out the port and starboard portholes. Unsatisfied, he unlocked and pushed back the main hatch, poking his head out to see two men walking back from the showers with towels hanging from their necks. Cool night air rushed into the stuffy cabin and Sam left the hatch open and went below.

The ship's clock struck ten and still no call from Nikki. Once more, Sam checked his phone, deleting Jon's message—'URGENT! We need to talk, bro!'—and listened to the last message Nikki had left the day before.

"You know, Sam, Jon must know it was you." Nikki's voice had an edge that made him wince.

He hit redial, pacing the salon, peering out the ports with the phone to his ear until the call went to her voicemail. Where the hell was she? He stuffed the phone into his pocket and gazed down at the money, stroking it like a beloved pet before stuffing it back into the satchel. He checked his alarm clock, turned out the light and collapsed onto the bunk, falling fast asleep in the cool night air.

CHAPTER 12

The sound of the Whaler's engine cut into the quiet of the night as Ella and Falco's men motored up the south fork of the New River. She sat at the bow, where the apparent wind brought relief from the thick heat but did nothing to calm her nerves. She glanced back at the men, trained in military combat and over qualified for this mission, and thought of Rich's warning about the consequence of revenge. Nevertheless, she had a responsibility to the man she loved —someone had to avenge his death.

They moved along the riverbank at the root level of the banyan trees, passing the palatial homes that lined the broad banks this close to the ocean. The garage of any one of these homes would cost more than what Ella was struggling to make, she mused, possibly more than what the whole crew would get paid for risking their freedom on the upcoming drug run.

Further up, where the river narrowed, the homes were modest, dinghies replaced the yachts, and eventually the private docks disappeared and the banks of the river were lined with apartments. At half-past one they arrived at River Bend Marina. Manny cut back the throttle and stood to survey the area—all was quiet. He spotted Sam's boat and inched the Whaler toward the entrance and cut the engine, gliding silently into the marina. Neil signaled Ella into position and they grabbed the first piling. Securing a line around it, they pushed off and Neil panned out the line as the Whaler floated the short distance to the haul-out slip where *Wanderlust* was berthed. "Catch the hull," he whispered to Ella, but she was already standing ready with bumpers out to cushion any possible contact with Sam's boat. Neil tied a line to *Wanderlust's* stern.

Manny shined his flashlight onto the boat. "No trip lines. Amateur," he whispered. He waved Neil aboard and signaled Ella to keep watch. Neil slipped under the lifeline, letting the boat settle to his weight before he moved to its center. Then, Manny boarded, as quiet and lithe as a cat.

Ella hung onto *Wanderlust*, scanning the marina for any movement while keeping the two hulls apart. Sam would have to be dead drunk not to be alarmed by something hitting his boat, and she bet that wasn't the case tonight. She tried to spot Jon's car. Nothing. She worried that he was so well hidden he'd be useless, unable to see anything. Is this how he was the night Davis died, safely hidden away? She studied the darkness, her eyes following the outline of the boatyard sheds and docks, then to the boats themselves, through the web of rigging and masts. To her relief, all the boats were dark, and she saw no one.

It was a hot Florida night, and the air was still this far inland. Sam had left the hatches open, putting his comfort before common sense and making their mission easier: the bolt cutters they had brought along were unnecessary. Ella had expected Sam to race on deck when the boat dipped under the men's weight. She feared gunfire, a raucous skirmish that would awaken the marina, one that could result in her getting shot, but Sam was apparently still sound asleep. This is all his doing, she thought. In a short while he will lose everything, a casualty of his own little war. And she was here to help it along, and to see him get what's coming to him.

Manny and Neil slid below deck with the stealth of men trained to be invisible, quiet as a held breath. Ella heard a brief scuffle from

88

below, then nothing. A moment later Manny pressed up through the companionway with Sam flung over his shoulder. A strip of duct tape covered Sam's mouth. He was out cold. Neil followed, carrying a satchel under his arm.

Ella hadn't seen Sam since Nassau, when she had still considered him a friend. Now here he was, hanging over Manny's shoulder like a rag doll ready to be thrown off his prized boat.

Ella caught her breath. "He looks dead."

Manny shook his head and whispered, "KO'd. Neil slugged him."

"Shhh!" Neil signaled Ella to pull *Wanderlust* closer to the dock so they could land Sam. She grabbed the satchel from Neil.

"Careful," he whispered.

Ella felt the weight of the money. She wanted to look inside the bag and see what a pile of cash looked like, but instead she tucked it under the seat. The men hauled Sam off the boat and laid him on the dock. Manny leaned over Sam, tying his hands to a cleat.

"What if he rolls over?" Ella said softly, worried that Sam would fail to see the spectacle of his boat in flames.

Manny nodded, tied Sam's feet to a cleat across the finger dock, and motioned to Neil to cast off the lines. Onboard *Wanderlust*, the two men heaved on the line they'd attached to the piling, pulling hand over hand until *Wanderlust* was out of the haul-out slip and into the entrance of the marina. Ella floated alongside in the Whaler, looking back at Sam, her hatred for the unconscious lump on the dock hardening.

When they reached the other side of the basin, they released the line from the piling and tied it to the stern of the Whaler. Ella started the Whaler's engine and towed *Wanderlust* into the clear on the New River. Then she handed the men the two cans of gas.

Manny's phone vibrated. Jon was doing his job. A light had come on at the far end of the boatyard. The men dropped to a squat, and Manny trained his binoculars on the marina. Ella followed their cue, cutting the Whaler's engine and squatting down.

"Local taking a piss." Manny crouched motionless, holding the binoculars steady. "He's gone below." He waited a few beats, then gave the all clear.

Ella sat alone in the launch, flushed with fear from the close call. She looked back to see Sam lying unconscious on the dock, unaware he was in the midst of losing his boat. A pang of regret shot through her, but she quickly shook it off. *You make your own luck.* Davis was right, but this time it had a whole different meaning. Sam had made his own luck, and in memory of Davis, she hoped that from now on it would be of the worst kind.

Wanderlust floated down river. Ella stood in the Whaler, hanging on and keeping the getaway boat close for Manny and Neil. The men poured the gasoline below and above deck carefully, as if they were watering a plant, avoiding the splash of gas on their shoes and clothing. Droplets of gas bounced off the deck, stinging Ella's face; the fumes were burning her nostrils, the smell coating her mouth and leaving an acrid taste of petroleum. The men climbed onto the Whaler and she flopped into her seat at the bow, feeling light-headed and sick from the vapors. She grabbed the gunnels of the boat and vomited over the side.

"Here," Neil said.

Ella sat up expecting a cloth to wipe her mouth, but Neil was handing her a Molotov cocktail from the Whaler's storage box. It was time. Neil held his lighter at the ready. Ella wiped her mouth with her sleeve and for a moment the three of them paused, looking at each other.

"Move further away before she tosses that thing," Manny said. "I don't want to get hit by the back draft." When they were thirty feet away, Neil turned to Ella and lit the rag wick.

Ella held out the cocktail to give back to Neil, but he didn't take it.

"It's your throw. You'd better hurry."

She shook her head and tried to hand it to Manny.

"Falco's orders," said Manny. "Hurry! Before you blow us up."

The Whaler rocked when she stood. Her legs shook and she nearly lost her balance. She drew her arm back. *Wanderlust* looked beautiful floating among the reflections.

"NOW!" said Neil.

Ella gave it all she had, a show of willingness, but aimed to miss. The bottle bounced off *Wanderlust*'s bow.

"Ok, I've got it." Manny stood up and, with the arching throw of a quarterback, heaved two lit gas bombs at *Wanderlust* in quick succession, landing one on deck and dropping the other down the hatch. The glass bottles shattered on impact and the flaming gas swallowed up the deck, flowing below, feeding on cushions, wood and Sam's personal belongings, creating a ball of blinding fire. Ella could hear the whoosh of the fire sucking in air, the crackle of combustion, and felt instant heat radiating from the raging flames. She sat back down, watching the boat become engulfed in a violent, erupting fireball.

"Time to move out," Neil said, steering the Whaler to the blind side of the river.

"Where's the bottle that missed?" said Manny. "We need to be sure it sank."

Ella pointed to the bobbing bottle floating along the riverbank behind *Wanderlust*. Neil circled back, letting Manny grab the bottle and remove the cloth. Satisfied it was sinking, they headed down river hugging the bank, out of view from the marina.

Ella sat at the bow facing aft with a clear view of *Wanderlust* burning, knowing her anger had missed its real target. Boats were alive to her, they had a soul, and Sam and Nikki's boat was a beautiful example of the nautical craftsmanship her father had taught her to admire. Now *Wanderlust*'s deep varnish was curling under the heat, the fine carpentry of the Burma teak in flames, while the real scum lay safely curled up on the dock.

A billowing black cloud filled the night sky as flames lapped at the mast, climbing to the top and outward along its spreaders, giving shape to a burning cross. My baptism of fire, Ella told herself. My God, what's next?

The fire found its way to the fuel tank and, with a thundering explosion, burst the tank wide open, scattering sparks and flaming shards into the air and finishing off what was left of *Wanderlust*, while the three of them slipped away downriver, unnoticed.

The great boom had rocked the air, rattling windows, setting off car alarms and howling dogs. Ella's anxiety mounted as lights went on and people spilled out onto their lawns and decks in nightgowns and underwear, shouting in excited voices and pointing at the ruin of *Wanderlust*. She listened to the fading cries as they motored farther downriver. Before they rounded the bend, she saw Sam on the dock kicking and thrashing, trying to get free of the ropes while his boat burned in front of him. Neil gunned the engine when they rounded a bend in the river, and the boat accelerated and began to plane.

Ella sat in a miserable gloom, smelling of gas, not feeling victorious or vindicated, as she had expected. She had earned Falco's approval and a ticket to fast money, but was Davis's spirit somehow set free with this act of retribution? Right now, all she wanted was a hot, comforting bath instead of what she'd get: a cold shower on the deck of her boat.

"How much money's in the satchel?" Ella wanted to know what Davis's death and now this act of revenge, sending someone's life up in smoke, was worth.

"Don't know, probably a couple hundred thousand guessing from the weight of it," Manny answered. "Not about money. You don't piss off Falco." Manny spoke in a loud, harsh whisper over the whine of the old two-stroke outboard. "This business can get ugly real fast. Falco's right; stamp it out before it gets out of hand."

"*Can* get ugly?" Ella said in disbelief.

"Miss, this is nowhere near ugly," Manny said. "Korengal Valley, getting ambushed by Jihadis, that's ugly." Manny looked away for a moment. "IEDs. Man cut in half by a fifty-caliber machine gun. That's ugly. You have no idea."

Ella registered the grim pride in his voice. "I guess I don't," she conceded. "Korengal Valley? In Iraq?"

"Jesus," Neil shook his head. "Afghanistan, The Valley of Death. Manny and I spent two tours there."

Neil reached into his pocket and held up a piece of paper for Manny to see. "He had an airline ticket: Nassau, six a.m. flight. It was on his bunk."

"Give it to Falco. He'll want to know who's waiting in Nassau," Manny said.

"Probably Nikki, his wife," Ella added quietly. The noise of the outboard made it difficult to be heard without yelling, but she knew how voices traveled over water. He'll be missing his flight, she thought.

Manny reached under the seat and tugged out the satchel. Unzipping it, he pulled out a pack of hundred dollar bills and handed it to Ella.

"Your cut."

"It's Jon's money." She doubted a big handful of hundreds was what Jon had in mind when he said he would pay her for her efforts.

"Doesn't matter. You earned it," Manny said, shoving the money into her hands. "You did your part tonight, aside from that lousy pitch."

"Okay. I'll take it." Ella felt the weight of the small bundle, fanning through the bills "How many are in here?"

Neil twisted around to look. "Don't know, maybe fifty."

"Five thousand?" This is how it's done, she told herself, fanning the pack of bills a second time, watching the tight-lipped smile of Benjamin Franklin flip by like something she'd seen in a movie. She wondered about Manny's and Neil's cut, and how small a pile would finally find its way to Jon. He'll end up with what he deserves, she thought. He'd done nothing to help Davis, and he had hidden in the safety of his BMW and watched as others had taken his revenge for him.

"So I passed the test?" Ella could see Manny didn't understand. "Will you tell Falco that I did okay?"

"Sure," Manny nodded.

This is how people like me get ahead, she thought grimly. Pretty soon I'll be flipping through five times this. She stuffed the pack in her pocket and zipped it closed, patting it to make sure it was secure.

CHAPTER 13

Sam awakened slowly from the knockout and raised his cheek off the rough planks. The slip where *Wanderlust* had been berthed was empty. He struggled to get up but his hands and feet were tied to the dock, bound like a calf ready for branding, unnoticed, in a dark corner of the boatyard. People were shouting and running toward the river and he could hear distant sirens approaching. He tugged at the ropes and twisted his neck as far as he could, squinting at the spectacle of flames on the water lighting up the night sky. He strained until he finally saw that it was *Wanderlust* that was burning. The duct tape muffled his screams as he frantically tried to break free. He scraped his cheek against the dock to peel back the tape, ignoring the splinters of wood gouging into his face.

"Over here!" someone yelled, and in a moment people were running toward him.

"What the hell?" A tall man in his mid thirties, wearing rumpled boxer shorts and t-shirt, bent down to peel off the tape and untie the ropes. "Are you hurt?"

Someone took Sam's arm and helped him up.

"No." Sam tugged off the rest of the ropes. "That's my boat!"

"Figured as much. Hell of a boat to lose."

"What happened?" A young woman pushed her way into the gathering crowd of awakened boaters. "We need to have a night watchman or something. My boat's all I got."

"Who'd you piss off?" asked the man who had untied Sam.

"I don't know. I was asleep, a noise woke me and I was slugged. That's all I know."

"Your face is bleeding." The young woman held out a tissue, but he ignored it.

Stunned, he stared at his boat and rubbed his jaw, which was beginning to swell. The attention of the onlookers shifted to the arriving fire engines and police cars, and people drifted off to answer questions and watch the firemen work; a few remained by his side to offer support. Panic overtook him and he turned away from *Wanderlust* to look along the dock and in the water, pressing past the crowd to scan the riverbank, but he didn't find what he was looking for: the black satchel.

"I'll go get a cop." The young woman took off in the direction of the first responders.

"I'm okay," Sam said. "Really, I'm good." He felt his pockets. His car keys, wallet and phone were still there, but he was barefoot.

"I'm going to get some shoes out of my car."

"I'll get them for you, you should rest."

"No! But thanks. I need to use the head anyway."

Sam rushed into the shadows, skirting the edge of the boatyard. He looked back at the Good Samaritan who was now waving the cops over to where Sam had been tied, wanting to show them the evidence. Sam quickened his pace. When he got to his car, he turned to look at *Wanderlust*. Flames had engulfed the mast piercing through the rolling black smoke, and the portholes were alight from the blaze down below. Two fire engines had parked on the edge of the riverbank and the firemen had jumped into action, grappling with hoses that spewed water and foam at the flames in a solid arch. But it wasn't making a difference. It was too late.

"Someone's going to pay for this," Sam muttered under his breath. "This is war."

He slipped into his Jeep and took one last glance in his rearview mirror; *Wanderlust*'s mast toppled over, leaving a fiery trail into the water. He slammed his foot on the gas and sped out of the marina. He had a good idea of who might be involved.

It was nearly three in the morning, and the streets of Fort Lauderdale were empty except for the cars parked in front of the numerous topless bars along the strip malls. Sam drove in a blind rage toward Jon's boat. His face was bleeding, his jaw hurt like hell, and he had just lost the money *and* his boat. He slammed his hand hard against the steering wheel. "Where the fuck are you, Nikki?" he screamed.

*****

The New River Municipal Marina was a dimly lit, ungated boat basin on the palm-lined river walk of downtown Fort Lauderdale with curbside access to the boats. Sam pulled up beside Jon's boat, *D'Élite*. The lights were on in the cabin. He sat clutching the steering wheel, car idling, then finally pulled the keys out of the ignition. He checked his image in the rearview mirror, cleaning up the blood on his face, and ran his hands through his hair.

Growing up, Sam and Jon had always been at odds. And even though Sam was stronger in sports and achieved honors in his studies, Jon could rely on the powerful backing of his father. But tonight Jon was a long way from home, and daddy wouldn't be too happy with what his favorite had just done.

Sam stepped out of his Jeep, stretched his neck to each side, and shook his shoulders loose like a boxer heading into the ring. He knocked on the side of *D'Élite*'s cabin. The hatch was wide open. When there was no response, he knocked again. "Jon? You awake? It's Sam." Still no reply. He boarded and went below. "Jon? Do you know where Nicki is? She's not answering her phone. Jon? You awake?"

Jon lay face down on the cabin sole, his arms tucked in along his sides, the pockets of his pants turned out. "Jon, you all right? Still rolling out of your bed, man?"

He bent down, turning Jon over to shake him awake. Jon's head flopped to the side with an unnatural looseness and his eyes were locked in a lifeless stare. His neck had been snapped.

"Jesus Christ!" Sam fell back, kicking frantically against the cabin sole to gain distance from the body. "Holy crap! Fuck!" He spun around, scanning every part of the boat to be sure the murderer wasn't still there, but he was alone with the body. Jon's wallet lay open and emptied on the cabin sole, along with his cell phone. The boat had been trashed, his belongings tossed by someone searching for something worth murdering for.

"You stupid fuck. Why in the hell'd you choose this marina? Fucking idiot. It's wide open."

Sam got to his feet and started his own search of every locker and cubbyhole, but neither his satchel nor the bale was there. He picked a partial bud off the cabin sole, taking a sniff and looking at the sparse trail of leaves leading up the companionway steps.

"FUCK!" he screamed and flung the bud at the bulkhead. "Fuck. Fuck. Fuck!"

He leaned against the stairwell, vacantly staring at Jon—the snob who'd always made it a point to tell Sam that, no matter what he did, he'd always have the blood of a commoner running through his veins.

Sam picked Jon's phone off the cabin sole and checked the call log. Nikki had called an hour ago. He jabbed 'call back'.

"Jon! What's up?" Nikki's voice was bright.

"It's Sam. Jon's dead, Nikki. Where the hell have you been?"

"What do you mean, Jon's dead?"

"I'm at his boat. Looks like his neck was broken."

"Did you do it?" she asked accusingly.

"Fuck no, Nikki, of course not! Where have you been? Where are you?"

"I'm in Nassau, like we planned. I'm staying at the Palm Hotel."

"Like hell you are. I called. They said you hadn't checked in."

"Jon's dead? Are you sure? Did you call 911?"

"Nikki, he's cold. He's probably been dead for hours. Why were you calling him?'

"Well, I couldn't get hold of you."

"Bullshit. You think I don't check my phone?" Sam waited for a reply that didn't come. "Nikki, uh, our boat's been burned."

"What? Why?"

"My guess, retaliation. I was sure Jon had to be involved; that's why I'm here. Fuck, Nikki! This is not the way it was supposed to play out." He recounted his tragic night, but was met with silence on the other end. "Nikki, are you still there?"

"Of course," she said faintly. "Did you see anyone leaving Jon's boat?"

"No, I didn't even see the guy that slugged me."

"How could you even think Jon was capable of pulling this off?" Nikki asked.

"Who else had a reason?"

"That boat was the nicest thing you had."

"Don't you even care if I'm all right?"

"Of course I care, Sam, but you wouldn't be calling me if you weren't."

"I wish you were here, Nikki. I need you, honey."

"Oh, Sam, why don't you get on a plane and meet me? We'll figure out what to do when you get here."

"Where's here, Nikki? I have no idea where you are." Sam's voice tightened and he slumped down to the cabin sole by Jon's feet, tears welling in his eyes. "Stupid fuck was never very bright."

He sat holding the phone to his ear with Nikki quiet on the other end.

"Another thing, Nik," Sam's voice lowered. "The money's gone. I'm going to get it back, Nik, I promise. Jon must have had it, but someone beat me to it. His boat's been trashed. Whoever killed him took it."

"Well, Sam, that's not 'another thing,' that *is* the thing. How are you going to get it back? Stand in the middle of the street and scream until someone brings it to you? It's gone, Sam. You'll never get it back."

"Don't, Nikki. Don't start." His voice cracked and he cleared his throat before he went on. "I need you right now, Nik. I've lost everything and my brother is dead."

"Stepbrother," she corrected. "He was never a brother to you. Remember? Pull yourself together, Sam."

Gone were her usual terms of endearment: Sammy, love, babe, honey, all the names she used that made him believe she loved him.

"So, who's your new lover, Nikki?"

"Sam, don't be ridiculous. It's late. I'm going to hang up now."

"Nikki, please."

"Look, Sam, you know the cops are going to link this to you. So whatever you do next, be smart about it. If I were you, I'd call 911 for poor Jon before he gets too ripe. But for God's sake, do it from a pay phone. Toss Jon's phone in the river, it's got my number on it. And wipe your prints off whatever you've touched. You need to get out of there."

"Nikki, listen. I've got another trip coming up. I was going to tell you in Nassau. I'm sure to make a bundle on it. I'll get another boat. We'll still do everything we said we'd do."

"Sure we will, Sam. Call me tomorrow," Nikki said, and hung up.

CHAPTER 14

Ella sat on her hands, surrounded by the hair salon's chrome and mirrors, draped in a black nylon cape with her head tilted forward, watching twelve-inch strands of her hair float to the floor— hair that had been with her when she and her father sailed the Narragansett Bay, with her when she entered The Culinary Academy. Hair that Davis had run his fingers through.

"You know you could have donated that." It was a woman wearing Cole Haan pumps the color of pewter and standing too close to Ella's chair.

Ella lifted her head. The woman was in her mid-thirties, her pinched face framed by a fan of foiled hair. She leaned in toward Ella with her manicured hands set on her hips, her bony elbows pushed out, giving the black nylon cape the shape of a bat.

"It's a shameful waste when there are people who could use that hair, like kids with cancer."

"Too late," the hairdresser said brusquely, tilting Ella's head back down.

"You should have asked her."

The hairdresser had. But to Ella, it was asking too much. She couldn't explain her reluctance, but she wasn't ready to let a stranger take a part of her. It took courage to do what needed to be

101

done, to shed the girl in her to make way for the woman. When she hesitated, the hairdresser took her silence as a 'no' and had let the clipped hair fall to the floor.

Ella had chosen the fashionable Cristophe Salon because she wanted the best. Until now, the only person to have cut her hair other than herself had been her mother. It was one of the last fading memories she had of her. Now, this bat of a woman, too wealthy to work and driven by causes stood in judgment of her. She tilted her head up and studied her for a moment, biting back resentment at the intrusion. The hairdresser moved her head back into position, checking the evenness of her cut and Ella turned her gaze to the floor, watching the pewter pumps step over her hair and clomp away.

"Samantha," the hairdresser called after her, "Cici will pour you a glass of champagne." The other patrons stole glances over the tops of their magazines, then shifted their eyes back to the page, devouring tips on how to stay young at thirty.

Ella had avoided looking at herself until the cut was finished so she could minimize the emotional reaction she knew would come. After nearly an hour of washing, cutting, moussing and blow-drying, the hairdresser spun the chair to face the mirror.

"What do you think?" she asked, glowing with pride at the hand she had played in Ella's transformation.

Ella was momentarily stunned. The reflection in the mirror wasn't her. The loose waves of the bob framed her face, lending her a look of confidence. But it left bare her neck and she felt exposed. She looked to the hair lying on the floor that had been her lifelong comfort.

"A new you! I hope you have something special planned."

Ella shot her a guilty glance, and then forced a smile, handing her cash from her earnings the night before. Walking to the door, catching her reflection in the mirrors as she passed, she tried to become acquainted with "the new Ella." Gone was the feminine softness of her long, flowing hair, and the woman that Davis had loved. The new Ella had the look of a woman capable of taking care of herself, of going after what she wanted. She threw her shoulders back and shook her head unrestrainedly. Instead of the regret she had expected, she felt light and relieved.

Outside the salon, she was bending to unlock her bike when her phone rang. It was Mr. Conti, again. This time she answered it.

"I know I've been hard to reach. I sent you a cashier's check for $500 this morning. You should have it tomorrow."

She paused, listening to his concern. "It's a good faith payment." She stood up, holding onto her bike lock. "The rest is coming in a little over a week. I do have it. But by our agreement, that installment isn't due for another two weeks." Ella listened to Conti voicing his misgivings and tried to clamp her lock to the bike frame. "Mr. Conti, I know you have to sell your property. You *are* selling it —to me."

A young man walked up, took the lock from her hand and clamped it onto the frame. Ella stared down at him with one hand gripping the handlebar, afraid he was about to steal her rusty bike. "I am the right person, Mr. Conti. I'll give my whole life to it." Ella covered the phone and looked at the man. "I'm trying to have a private conversation."

"Out here?" The man lifted his hands to indicate the busy sidewalk.

She put up her hand to silence him, shooting him a look of disapproval. "Yes. I'll have it in two weeks. Please cash the check." The young man was beginning to annoy her, and she turned her back to him. "I promise," she said, and snapped the phone shut.

Ella turned around; the man was still there. She bent down and checked her lock.

"I used to have a bike like that," he said.

"Really?" Ella stood up and was within inches of him but didn't move away—and neither did he. He was good looking in a clean-cut, decent kind of way with an easy smile. "Really?" she said again, and took a step back. She doubted if anyone had a rusty, folding British bike like hers. "It's kind of a rare bike." She held her eye on him. "Never lead with a lie."

"What?"

"When you're trying to pick up a woman, never lead with a lie. We *always* know."

"Thanks for the advice." It was his turn to take a step back. "My family's folding bike was a Bickerton portable that we carried aboard our boat on Lake Michigan."

"Oh. I guess we don't always know," Ella said with a smile. "Nothing seems real here in Florida."

"I'm beginning to see that. My name's Marc Eton."

"French?"

"French Canadian. Marcel Eton," he said in a French accent.

"Ella Morgan. American, one hundred percent." Ella reached out to shake his hand.

"You're not from here?" Marc asked.

"No." Ella wondered when to end this conversation, but he had a calming effect on her. "I sailed down from Rhode Island last year."

"Offshore?"

"From Rhode Island to Virginia with a friend, then picked up the Intracoastal and made the rest of the trip solo." She proudly placed a slight emphasis on the word 'solo'.

"I figured you were a sailor with that kind of bike. Are you still solo?"

Caught in her own trap, Ella smiled.

"Pretty courageous trip to make alone," he said.

"It's what I needed to do. The courage was faked." It was an easy confession for her to make to a stranger.

"I get that. Would you like to get a cup of coffee?" he asked abruptly.

"So you like rude women?"

"Just people that speak their mind."

She took her time answering, stuffing her wallet into the bike's travel bag. Here it was again, the impulse to say yes, where she never would have before. She had taken up residence in a foreign body: someone else's body, someone else's mind. He looked sweet, Ella thought, like someone from Middleton, her hometown—a wholesome Midwest sailor, probably from a good family by the calm confidence he showed. She was so far from wholesome right now that spending a bit of time with him would feel like a vacation, reminding her of the life she hoped to regain one day.

She had a few hours before meeting Rich and his crew at the Villa del Mar. What harm would there be in taking one last hour in the world of normal people before she ventured on into the darkness of the drug world?

"Sure. I'd love a cup of coffee."

They stood together scanning up and down the street.

"There's a café up there." Marc pointed to a place with sidewalk tables.

A line of people waited outside the door. Crowded, Ella thought. After being in the salon for an hour, she had had enough of public places. The cup of coffee now seemed complicated and awkward.

"Well, maybe some other time."

"I make a good cup of coffee," Marc offered.

Ella considered it. He had the uncanny familiarity of an old friend who was ignorant of the mess she was in. "You live close by?"

"Yeah. I have a place on the canal."

"Okay, I have a little time," said Ella.

"La vie est belle."

"I don't speak French."

"Life is beautiful," Marc said.

They walked and talked about growing up sailing, he on Lake Michigan and she on the bay in Rhode Island. She pushed her bike along, her heart pounding in her chest and awkwardness nagging at her edges, unsure she could go through with this tough woman part she'd begun to play. Life is beautiful. If only that were true for her.

Ella felt relieved when they arrived at his apartment complex tucked in alongside the canal, thankful it wasn't some shabby, rent-by-the-week motel. The jalousie windows, red tile roof, and small pool centered in the lush palm and fern landscaping were typical of vintage Fort Lauderdale style.

Marc's place was on the ground floor facing the canal with a privacy hedge of white oleander. As they walked up to his door, he put his hand on her shoulder, and his touch dispelled her tough woman persona completely, leaving her vulnerable.

"Look, I'm sorry, I..." she said turning away from him.

He unlocked the door and took her hand, leading her inside.

"Maybe some other time."

But he leaned in and kissed her neck, then her lips, wrapping his arms around her, pulling her toward him. Softly, quietly, gently, as in a dream, he kissed her until she began to return his touch, giving in to the rising desire until they lay on his bed, their warm naked bodies pressed into each other. His hands lacked the calluses that Davis had, and his smooth skin was unblemished by weather and time. He pushed himself inside her and her body shivered with pleasure, releasing a wave of emotion that sent tears streaming from the corners of her eyes.

She lay with her head resting on his chest, listening to him breathe, his arm cradling her, as natural as if they were a couple, until she slipped into an easy sleep.

She woke with Marc asleep at her side and peeked over at his bedside clock: an hour had passed. She was careful not to rouse him, slipping slowly out of bed and quietly pulling on her clothes. She picked up her shoes to leave and then turned back to the bed. She thought of the complications a conversation would bring and decided not to wake him. She knew little of him, other than that he was a man from Michigan who sailed the lake and whose family owned a folding bike. She knew he was nice. She had been lucky. On her way out the door, she turned over a piece of mail on his kitchen counter and wrote: 'Dear Marcel, thank you for the comfort you gave. Ella.'

Once outside, Ella sat on the grass pulling on her shoes, looking at his apartment so as to remember it, and then pushed off on her bike. She chose a route on the quieter back streets, along the New River. She sensed a shift in the weather, and a gust of wind rattled the palm fronds and moved grey-bottomed, cumulus clouds across the sky. The wind ruffled her hair as she rode, and she felt a new coolness on the back of her bare neck. The weight of her hair pulling at her scalp for all those years was gone. She felt light and free as the first drops of rain tickled her face.

On the road ahead, police were directing traffic to a single lane. Yellow crime-scene tape marked off a sailboat and half the street. Police cars and several emergency vehicles were parked in hurried disarray. Ella slowed her bike and stood up on the pedals, stretching to see as she glided along. There they were, with their flashing lights, taking charge as they must have last night at Sam's burning boat, taking statements from the mingling live-aboards. The sight of uniformed authority kindled fear in her that someone might have seen them last night, or noticed an unfamiliar car leaving the scene. An alert boater with a memory for numbers might have taken down the license plate of Jon's car as he rolled out of the marina. Or the weakling Jon might have bragged to someone about getting his money back. The thought of being handcuffed and pushed into the back of a squad car made her drop to the bike seat and peddle like hell, turning down the first side street she came to.

CHAPTER 15

The first hint of winter was riding in on the cool northern breeze, and muted sunlight cast long, lavender shadows on beaches nearly empty of tourists. Offshore, a flock of brown pelicans headed north, cruising inches above the waves in v-formation with their heads tucked back on their shoulders. Ella turned to watch, then looked beyond the birds to the shoreline that disappeared into the morning haze and thought with longing of her hometown. This morning's pre-run meeting at the Villa del Mar with all the players would set in motion something that was a far cry from the values she had learned there. Keep walking, her father would have said, tugging her back to her senses. But his tugboat hadn't sold, and she was on the threshold of a great thing. She couldn't turn down a chance to make the money she needed, money that could bring relief and a promise for her future. Just this once, she thought, and turned inland from the shore, just a few days of sailing. It'll be fine.

She wound her way through the grove of Royal Palms toward Villa del Mar, her heart beating at fear's pace. She paused at the outer edge of the property and spotted Rich and Falco sitting quietly alone under a cabana. She waited, hoping the others would arrive. When after a few minutes they hadn't, she threw back her shoulders and joined them.

"Good morning," said Ella, and in a move to show her independence, she took a seat away from Rich. "Looks like more rains..."

"So where's this Burke guy?" Falco interrupted, glancing stone-faced at Ella.

Rich stood and walked to where he had a view of the restaurant, and then returned. His face narrowed into a frown when he looked at Ella, and he shook his head. Ella instinctively reached for her hair and her hand landed on the bare skin of her neck.

Rich turned to Falco. "He's coming."

"You look like a boy," Falco said to Ella, then twisted to glance over his shoulder at Rich. "Do we need Burke?"

"We need everyone," Rich said. "Give him a couple of minutes."

"No I don't," Ella said to Falco. "I can get a wig for the trip," she offered.

"We're leaving tonight." Rich sat down, resting his elbows on his knees.

"Tonight? There's a storm coming in."

"Doesn't matter, may even work to our benefit. Here he is," said Rich.

Ella followed Falco's gaze and turned to see Burke stepping out of the lobby holding a cup of coffee and a croissant. He was nearly six feet tall with blond, close-cropped hair, and mirrored sunglasses concealed his eyes. Ella watched uneasily as Burke took long, slow strides through the sand, holding his coffee away from his pressed white shirt.

"You're late," said Falco.

Burke lifted the croissant in his hand. "You should try these. Almost like in Paris—buttery crisp outside, cottony inside." He spoke with an Eastern European accent. Ella watched quietly as Falco examined him.

"Shut up and sit down," Falco said at last.

Burke had the swagger of defiance and Ella could see by his manner that he was unaccustomed to taking orders. So, it's not going to be all nice and easy, she thought.

"He'll be fine," said Rich, as if he had read her thoughts. "Sit down, Burke."

Falco narrowed his dark eyes at Burke, watching him pull up a chair in front of Ella.

"You're blocking me," said Ella.

"Sorry, I didn't know woman was pirate too. Maybe you cook for us?" he laughed.

"See?" Ella smiled at Rich. "He knows I'm a woman."

"Sorry, Missy." Burke inched his chair out of her way.

She saw Falco take notice of Burke's teasing smile. If she didn't play it right, Burke would have them thinking a female crew member was asking for trouble—an unwanted risk on a drug run. Okay, mister, I'm onto you. "The name's Ella," she said, broadening her smile.

Rich moved on, ignoring their exchange. "All right, this is how it's going to go." He sketched out the run, giving their departure time, and pointedly leaving out the pick-up's destination. "Beside being damn good sailors, you each have your own expertise. Burke, you're our engine man. Ella will be cook and part of the cruising couple ruse, and Carlos brings his rigging skills."

"Exactly where we go?" Burke interrupted.

"After what's happened to Davis and Jon, Falco and I are keeping the coordinates to ourselves. All I'll say is, it's a one-day sail from the Lower Keys."

"Why? What happened to these men?" Burke asked.

Falco leaned back in his chair and hiked his leg over his knee, watching and listening.

"A friend, Davis, was killed—murdered." Rich's voice was flat and steely.

"Murdered? Where?"

"Northern Eleuthera," said Rich.

"Who did this?"

"We took care of him," said Falco coldly.

Ella looked away, toward the water. The cloud deck had lowered and the fine drizzle turned to rain, beating at the surface of the sea. The morning light had become a mournful gray, reminding her that the sea was Davis's grave.

"We don't know if he was acting alone." Rich glanced at Falco, who answered with a faint nod. "But Falco and I have good reason to believe he wasn't working with any of our people."

Ella turned back to listen and wondered, how reliable a source could be in this business?

Burke nodded. "Whoever doing this be stupid come after us. We be prepared," he said. "Where's Carlos?"

"He needed to take care of his family before he left."

Falco pulled a cigar from his shirt pocket and rolled it between his fingers, drawing in its scent as he passed it under his formidable nose. He held it like a prop—a king and his pleasures—and locked his gaze on Ella. His dark eyes, shadowed in circles, bore into her. She acknowledged him with a slight smile of confidence and turned back to Rich.

"Why the sudden change of plans? I thought we were going next week," said Ella.

"Wasn't sudden. We just didn't tell you," said Falco.

"Gives everyone less time to talk." Rich hunched over, his arms resting on his knees and his fingers intertwined in a knot. "Mouths shut. Clear?"

"That always case," said Burke.

"This time it's paramount," said Rich.

They all sat listening as Rich discussed some of the details, but after only a few minutes Falco got up to leave. "I've taken care of things on the supply end—there shouldn't be any problems. But keep in mind: it's an important load. I'll see you in Marathon."

Rich stood, towering over Falco by a foot, and they walked out of earshot to talk. A bodyguard ran out of nowhere with an umbrella to shield his boss from the rain. Falco pulled out his cigar again and patted his pockets for a lighter until Rich snapped a flame with his and lit it for him. It wasn't lost on Ella that Rich didn't smoke. Falco turned away, puffing clouds from his cigar, and lifted his eyes to Ella. She thought she saw a faint shrug of his shoulders when he turned back to Rich. Had she blown it, leaving her one chance lying on the hair salon floor?

*****

"Everything okay?" Ella asked Rich when he returned.

"Of course."

"Good," Ella smiled. "So, what else is going to happen with Sam?"

"Sam involved?" Burke let out a laugh. "Little coward hiding in hole right now."

"Burke's right. We don't need to spend any more time on Sam. He's been warned. Just remember, Sam's not the only rat out there." Rich sat down. "Here's the thing. We've worked with these people a lot over the years, but this trip is different. It's the last one. Falco says we're covered, but still, the end of a relationship is when all the goodwill starts to break down. We need to stay sharp; we can't afford any fuckups. A lot of people would love to get their hands on this load: twenty bales of Jamaican High-Grade, over-the-top premium and very expensive."

"Why, is this the last run?" Ella was becoming uneasy. But if Rich didn't feel good about this trip, he wouldn't be going—or would he?

"Our sources won't be able to supply us anymore. The cartels are shutting out the small-timers."

"Corporate politics enter drug world." Burke slumped back in the beach chair and folded his arms over his chest.

"It's been happening for a long, long time," said Rich.

"Where we meet delivery boat?" asked Burke.

"Like I said, you'll know once we're underway."

Ella listened, keeping her worries to herself so as not to appear weak or unreliable. But it was becoming clear to her that the dangers of getting caught by the Coast Guard or DEA were only half the worry: there were other smugglers, and the cartel. She could still back out. What was worse, she asked herself—giving up her chance, or taking the risks? She looked at Rich, strong and capable, a man in charge. But could she trust him with her life?

"Who are investors?" Burke prodded.

"There are three, but you don't need to know them and they don't need to know you," Rich said, seeming eager to get on with it. "But one of them is a Coastie helicopter pilot; he'll be looking out for us on our sail back to the Keys. Any questions?"

"Nice security to have," Ella said. "But, how well do they patrol the Keys?"

"They're closely watched, no doubt about it. There's the Coast Guard, Sheriff's patrol boats, and Citizen Watch. That's why we're coming in on Labor Day, one of the busiest days on the water with boozed-up boaters keeping the patrol boats distracted. We have air coverage looking out for us, but it doesn't eliminate surprises.

"Hard-and-fast rule: after you get paid, spending has to be discrete." Rich looked at Burke. "No new cars, and no gold chains. People talk, and the Feds listen to chatter around the docks. Remember, we're in this thing together."

"Like Danny guy at Summerfield's," said Burke. "One day he broke, next he driving 450SL, buying drinks for everyone."

"Notice he's not around anymore?" Rich leaned forward and rubbed his hands together. "Okay, here's the gig. We have the use of an investor's Swan 53. It's a beautiful boat, a dream to sail. His family's coming early October to sail down the Keys. They don't know about his side ventures, so the boat has to be cleaned and aired out when we get back."

Rich was in command, and he knew the ins and outs of the drug trade from apparent years of experience. It wasn't the Rich Ella thought she had known, not the delivery captain or the up and up scientist, but another man she never seen.

Rich got up from his chair. "Pier 66 gas dock at midnight, don't be late," he said. "I don't want to wait for you. We'll go over the charts once we're all onboard. Remember, this is a three-day trip, a night pick-up at sea. Pack for foul weather: as you can see, there's a front moving down on us."

"What about food?" Ella got to her feet. "I need to get a grocery list together."

"I'll take care of it," said Rich. "We don't have much time. Okay, everyone, I'll see you tonight."

"I'd like to do the shopping. How will you know what to get?"

"I'll get the basics that always work," said Rich.

"Can you at least get real butter, olive oil, and some garlic? And greens would be nice."

"It's not that kind of trip, Ella," said Rich.

CHAPTER 16

With its high-rises, highways and hustle, Ella could almost forget that south Florida was sub-tropical until she smelled the air after a storm, when the fragrance of gardenia blossoms, orange trees and fertile, moist soil scented the humid breeze.

It was close to midnight when she walked the near-empty, storm-strewn streets along the Intracoastal, her duffle bag slung over her shoulder, stepping over the downed palm fronds and busted coconuts that had fallen from the towering palm trees. She headed toward Pier 66 Marina's brightly lit gas dock, its muted reflections cast long over the night-black water.

Ella could see Carlos and Burke facing in opposite directions a distance apart, waiting for Rich to motor down the Intracoastal Waterway. After meeting Burke, Ella had wondered how the two of them would get along. Like Burke, Carlos had a forceful personality; maybe that's why Rich had chosen them, what was needed in this world. From their stances, she guessed they had little to say to one another. This is going to be a difficult sail, she thought: four people in tight quarters for several days, with two of them vying for dominance. She had learned from past deliveries to stay out of the way of Alphas.

She lingered in the shadows and scooted atop a dock box to wait, savoring the last moments she'd have to herself. The scent of Burke's cigarette drifted down to her, and she heard Carlos brusquely remind him that they were at a fuel dock. Burke flicked his cigarette into the water as Carlos shook his head and walked further away.

There was no sign of Rich, and no sound other than the wind. Ella's mind wandered to the still-warm memory of Marc, but it wouldn't settle there. She was just a crew member on someone's expensive yacht, sailing to, who knew where, not yet a full-fledged criminal. She was becoming one, though—slowly, by degrees, starting with the burning of Sam's boat. And in a few days, the process would be complete. Her transformation would likely go unnoticed: Florida had a wild side and smuggling was in its blood.

A breeze of eighteen knots remained from the storm, snapping at a small white Bimini top behind Ella, beating out the rhythm of a drum roll. Ella pulled her knees to her chest, worrying as she had each time she left the *Gina Marie* unattended; everything she owned, and all she had left of her father, was onboard. If this run went bad and she got caught, even the twenty-thousand-pound tensile strength steel padlock wouldn't stop the feds from confiscating her boat. She had no grounds to carelessly think that it was her time to be lucky.

The rhythmic churning of *Merlin's* diesel broke through the rustling wind: it was time. She slid off the box and hurried toward the fuel dock as the fifty-three-foot sloop emerged out of the darkness. Carlos and Burke moved to hold *Merlin* off from the quay, but Carlos stopped at the sight of Ella.

"What the hell's she doing here?" asked Carlos.

"You not know we have woman pirate coming?" Burke laughed.

Carlos wasn't smiling.

Merlin glided toward the dock and Rich threw the engine into reverse, slowing her forward motion and jockeying her to rest alongside. His competence, and the sight of the Swan's fine lines, settled Ella's nerves. These people knew what they were doing.

"We're not tying up," Rich called over the engine noise. "We're shoving right off."

Burke jumped onboard but Carlos stood in Ella's way, blocking her from boarding.

"Something going on, Carlos?" Rich asked.

"You think it smart to bring her along?"

"You missed the meeting with Falco," said Rich. He looked up and down the empty dock. "Get aboard, we need to get underway." He motioned to Ella. "Come on, Ella."

"Hi, Honey," Ella chirped as she hopped onboard, pulling off her knit cap and fluffing her hair.

"Fuck!" said Carlos.

"Just a joke," said Ella.

"Not funny." Carlos shook his head in protest. "Don't feel right about woman onboard," he protested. "This is not a yacht delivery."

"Get onboard, Carlos or we're going without you," Rich snapped.

"Christ, Carlos, that stupid superstition is so old it's laughable," said Ella. "I promise not to whistle and I didn't bring bananas."

"Bananas?" said Burke.

"They're bad luck," Rich said. "You coming, Carlos?" He engaged *Merlin's* diesel and opened up the throttle.

Carlos shoved *Merlin* away from the dock and jumped aboard, keeping his eyes lowered.

"All cell phones off—all the way off," commanded Rich. "We need complete phone silence."

"For how long?" Burke said, pulling out his phone.

"The whole damn trip. Carlos, Ella, yours too. We can't risk being tracked."

"Already off," said Ella. She threw her duffle into the salon and took a lookout position on the bow, as far away from Carlos as she could get. She had been worried about Burke, thinking of him as the brute. Carlos's objection was a surprise; they had sailed well together on several deliveries.

Rich sounded the ship's horn, signaling the 17th Street Bridge to open and allow them to pass. Once through, they motored along the Intracoastal, past the berthed container ships of Port Everglades and out the inlet into the black night of the Gulf Stream, riding the tide that pulled them out to sea.

"Where should I stow my stuff?" Ella asked Rich.

"Forward port cabin."

"Nice. Cozy," Burke said.

"I can take a quarter berth," said Ella.

"Woman don't belong on run," said Burke.

"So it seems." Ella glanced over at Carlos.

"Burke, put a lid on it," said Rich.

"You know," Ella said, as she headed below with her duffle, "fuck that quarter berth. I'll take the cozy cabin."

"She's as good a sailor as any man I've sailed with," said Rich. "As you damn well know, Carlos."

"Let me guess." Ella stopped in the companionway. "Women are only good for cooking and screwing."

"Cleaning," said Burke.

"I wouldn't have guessed that would be one of your concerns," Ella snapped back without a thought to keeping the peace.

"Having her onboard might just save our necks when we sail back with the load. If the Coasties saw your sorry asses they'd board us in a heartbeat," Rich said. "Time to raise the sails. Ella, take the helm."

Ella smiled, turning back to take the wheel. They were motoring south, hugging the shore where the Gulf Stream ran at its slowest, countering the northern flow. Rich gave the order to head up and Ella brought the bow into the wind. The men heaved, and the billowing mainsail rode up the seventy-foot mast, wind buffeting the canvas at its edges. Once the halyard was secured, Ella fell off, allowing the wind to fill the sails. She switched off the spreader lights and shut down the diesel. It chunked to a stop, leaving them to the quiet of the night. To Ella, there was nothing sweeter than this: all that remained was the simple dynamics of sailing the wind, the sound of the hull cutting through the water, and an occasional flap of the sail while the crew sat silently, surrounded by the black pool of the ocean, and watched the lights of land recede into darkness. It was the beginning of September; the hurricane season was nearly over, the trade winds were steady and the family crowd had headed back home. It was a good time to be on the water.

*****

Daybreak brought winds at eighteen knots, which likely would stay that way until nightfall. Ella had risen with the sun and was making the crew's breakfast, hips braced against the counter with the help of a galley strap, knees bending like springs to the rise and fall of the boat in the rolling sea. When the boat dropped hard off a wave, sending her apple cobbler airborne in the gimbaled stove and sloshing the batter out of the pan, she gave in to simplifying the menu.

She wanted nothing more than to have this trip go smoothly, but it was getting off to a ragged start—first with Carlos, and now Burke. If she let Burke run over her, there would be no end to it, but if she fought back it would affect everyone onboard. She knew her cooking sometimes had the magic of bringing people together; hopefully this would be one of those times.

Rich's grumbles preceded him as he emerged from his cabin, lumbering and groggy, on his way to relieve Carlos from his watch. He looked more boy than man, and Ella stifled an urge to hug him good morning. Instead, she handed him his coffee as he passed through the galley, stopping briefly at the navigation table to check the charts and GPS.

"We should be near Key Largo," he finally said. "Good coffee, Ella." He stuck his head out the hatch. "Carlos, look like Key Largo to you?"

"Yep. Alligator Reef Light off the bow at one o'clock and French Reef at three o'clock," Carlos called.

"We're making good time," said Rich. "I'll be up in a minute to relieve you."

He ducked back below, taking in Ella. "Can't get used to your short hair."

Ella reached for the strands on her head, looking away and feeling self-conscious. "Do you want some eggs?"

"In a bit." Rich paused before heading on deck. "Looks nice, Ella." But his tone was more sympathetic than complimentary.

"It'll grow." Ella surrendered a smile and then handed up Carlos's coffee. "Milk and three sugars, right, Carlos?"

Carlos briefly lifted his eyes, taking the cup. "Thanks."

*****

Ella stood in the companionway, taking a break from preparing breakfast and watching Carlos pull out his graphite pole and collection of spinners and lures. A few gulls hovered in *Merlin's* draft with a sharp eye on his fishing pole, then abruptly dipped their wings and returned to the tide line to hunt their breakfast.

"What you catch on small pole?" Burke's tone was mocking as he pushed past Ella to come on deck.

"Your dinner." Carlos settled into the cockpit. "Size doesn't matter; it's a high-strength graphite rod."

"Not what I heard," Burke laughed.

Ella braced against the companionway with a tray of coffee and warm apple cobbler that now looked more like bread pudding. "I could use a hand here."

"Smell good, Ella. I have two sugars in coffee," Burke said, grabbing the tray.

"That's fascinating, Burke." Ella turned back, heading below to clean up her galley, and left Burke holding the tray.

"You suppose be cook," Burke shouted after her.

"Cook, Burke, not your personal galley slave."

Burke settled against the back of the cabin and lit a cigarette.

"Could you move to the port side with that cigarette, Burke? The smoke's coming below," Ella complained.

"Right, you Americans all so clean-living now, no flavor left in your safe lives."

"I heard emphysema is a lot of fun—you get your own oxygen tank." Ella stopped and shot Burke a look. "Are you going to be this much fun the whole trip?"

"Maybe."

Carlos's fishing pole briefly arched from a hit, then straightened.

"Rich, you want another cup of coffee?" Ella asked.

"Sweet." Burke drew the word out between clenched teeth that held his burning cigarette. He glanced from Rich to Ella, smiling, turning a pack of matches around and around in his hand. The black pack with its red type caught Ella's eye and she glimpsed the words "La Tasca."

"Helmsman always gets waited on, Burke," she said, keeping an eye on the matchbook. "But we'll make that an exception when it's your watch."

Burke laughed, tucking the matches in his pants pocket before flicking his cigarette over the side.

Why him? Ella wondered. Rich could have chosen from so many able sailors who would have been willing to take a risk for a healthy chunk of cash. Burke seemed dangerous, but maybe he was the real thing, a real smuggler—unlike her, a visiting amateur on an adventure into the underworld.

Carlos's rod dipped again and this time the hook held. The line sang as the fish ran it out, and Carlos worked at teasing it in. Their boredom interrupted, Rich and Burke shifted toward him, cheering with the enthusiasm of punters at a horse track, until the line went limp and they relaxed back into their seats.

"He'll be back. I got him interested now," said Carlos.

Burke propped his feet on the seat across from him, sipping his coffee. "Man, bad business about Sam's boat."

"Heard about that," Carlos said. "Pissed somebody off."

Rich remained silent, and down in the galley Ella took her cue from him and said nothing.

"Man, somebody had it in for those two," Burke pushed on.

"Don't know why anyone would have it in for Nikki," said Carlos. "She's a nice lady."

"He doesn't mean Nikki," said Rich. "He means Sam and Jon, his brother."

Ella looked up, startled. "Why? What's up with Jon?"

"Up?" Burke let out a nervous laugh. "More like down. Fucker's dead."

"What? Dead?" Ella stiffened. "You sure?"

"Yeah, got his neck snapped," said Burke. "You know Jon?"

"No, not really," Ella said. "Just that he's Sam's brother." She felt a sudden wave of fear and dropped to a companionway stair. Someone knew what they had done.

Rich had the helm, but his eyes were on Burke. "How'd you hear, Burke?"

"Someone at boatyard."

"I heard about it on the morning news," said Rich. "Didn't mention how he died, just that they found him on his boat."

Ella shuddered, distressed at the news of Jon, fearing it was an act of retaliation and terrified that she could be next. She had biked past the New River Municipal not knowing it was where Jon berthed his boat or that his death was the reason for all the police cars. Who would do this, she wondered. Was it Sam? She turned to Rich, but he avoided her eyes. Why hadn't he told her? Was he trying to protect her, or was he protecting his own interests by not scaring her off this run?

Carlos's line buzzed out as another fish snagged the hook. "See? What'd I tell you?" He pulled the rod back against the tension of the line, reeling in, letting it run out, playing it.

"God, what hell is this?" Ella sat down in the cockpit. "First Davis, now Jon—who's doing this? I had no idea Florida was so dangerous."

"You don't know hell until you live war in Serbia. *That* is hell!" Burke said.

Rich held his stare on Burke. "Paper said it looked like a robbery."

"They know what was taken?" asked Burke.

"Didn't say. His boat was ransacked, that's all." Rich turned his gaze to Ella. "I doubt it was any more than that."

Ella wasn't convinced. She looked at Rich, Burke and Carlos—three battle-tested, capable seamen. Perhaps this life was only for men like them.

"I never liked that marina," Carlos said. "Too open. Downtown has real scum hanging around."

His fishing pole arched and shivered under the weight of the fighting fish. He pulled the pole back, working the line, reeling in a pompano that fought to get free.

"Burke, grab that net."

Ella joined the others, leaning over the side to watch. Carlos held the reel close to his chest, the muscles in his arms and neck taut as he pulled the fish alongside the boat.

"Now, Burke! Net him!" shouted Carlos.

Burke hung over the lifeline and scooped up the battling fish. The twenty-inch pompano arched and flapped, a rainbow of shimmering colors, beating itself against the deck, its mouth opening and closing as it suffocated in the air. Carlos took the butt end of his knife and whacked it hard on the head, killing it.

"Excellent!" said Burke. "Now catch one for rest of you."

CHAPTER 17

Sam stood in his room on the sixth floor of the Comfort Inn Oceanside in Deerfield Beach, his forehead pressed against the window, staring blankly out at the Atlantic Ocean. He'd been standing that way so long, his head had begun to hurt from the weight of his body leaning into the glass. A "Do Not Disturb" sign hung from the room's doorknob. The room was beginning to pile up with take-out containers and room-service trays. Several newspapers lay tangled in the covers of the unmade bed, folded to articles about *Wanderlust* burning. None covered the death of Jonathan Sterling Hamilton: for the sake of the tourist trade, most local papers kept murder out of their news. But now, on the third day of waiting, at two in the afternoon, Sam's cell phone finally rang.

"Hello?" Sam took a step back from the window, his face tightening into a fist as he listened. "Where've you been, man? I've been going fucking nuts stuck in this room waiting for you."

The voice coming over the line dropped to a no-nonsense level, cutting off his complaint.

"No I couldn't. The cell coverage in Deerfield sucks. Soon as I step out the door it drops all the bars." He turned on his heels and began to pace, stepping over the clutter on the floor. "Boat's ready, man. Guys too."

Sam stopped to listen, running his hand through his hair, then said, "Of course I didn't talk to the cops. They're not going to be a problem. I left before they got there."

Sam clenched his jaw, fuming. The man was treating him like an amateur.

"I'm the fuckin' victim here. It was *my* boat that got burned, *my* brother murdered."

He turned to look out the window. "Right. Right. Tomorrow. Noon." He grabbed a pen and paper and quickly wrote down a number.

"I'm *not* going to be fucking late. I'm going stir-crazy here."

Sam hung up the phone and collapsed into a chair. Ten seconds hadn't gone by before he sprang back up, pulled on a clean shirt, grabbed his room key and headed to the Deerfield Pier.

The deal was on. He was back in play.

*****

In the middle of the afternoon, JB's On The Beach was empty except for a barman replenishing his inventory and a dark-haired, shapely waitress setting tables for the evening crowd. Sam had been here once before, the day he'd met Nikki. He'd been driving back to Fort Lauderdale from a business meeting in Boca Raton and had stopped in for lunch. She had been here, eating alone, something he would later find out she hated. She was beautiful, and she looked at Sam as if he were the most important man she'd ever seen. He invited her to join him, and she did. They had been together, or in daily contact, ever since—until now.

"You still serving?"

The waitress shot a look over her shoulder. "Sit anywhere," she said.

Sam grabbed a menu on his way to a window seat, glancing at the side table he'd shared with Nikki two years ago. He looked briefly at the menu, then snapped it closed.

"Start with something from the bar?" she asked, straightening the tables as she walked over to him. She had an open smile that said she hadn't been a waitress very long.

"Any dark German beers?"

"Aventinus?" She stumbled with the pronunciation and pushed back a strand of hair from her face.

Sam grinned, glancing at the name tag perched on her breast. "That'll work, Cindi. And I'll have the filet mignon, medium rare, baked potatoes with sour cream—got any chives?"

She nodded. "Vegetable?'

"Whatever, sweetheart."

"I see you're a man of good taste. You here all alone?"

"All alone," Sam smiled. "Just looking forward to a long, slow meal."

"Alright-y, mister." She grabbed the menu off the table and met Sam's smile. "Coming right *up*."

Sam pulled off his wedding ring as he watched her walk away, her ass round as two soft peaches pulling at the stretch of her mini as she weaved and twisted her way back through the tables. He turned to the window and looked out across the beach, eyeing the hot girls in bikinis, barely covering their shaved, tight bodies, giving him a throbbing hard-on. Women like Nikki—exciting and slightly vulgar.

From the corner of his eye he glimpsed a familiar motion and turned to see Nikki walking from the beach with that lovely sway of hers. She was carrying her beach bag, and tied around her slim waist was the flowered scarf he had bought for her on their trip to Martinique. Her rhythmic walk turned heads as she passed. He sat, momentarily stunned, before jumping up and running out of the restaurant, but when he got outside, she was gone. He searched in every direction, in doorways and stores, peeking inside parked cars as he ran past, but she had vanished.

When he returned to the restaurant, the foam on his beer had gone flat. He chugged it and ordered his steak wrapped to go.

"Change your mind?" said Cindi.

"It got changed for me."

"If you find you'd like company later on, I get off at nine."

Sam nodded and raced out the door. He camped out on a park bench that had a view of the road, parking lot and beach and sat there, blind to the bikinis passing by, eating the steak with his hands and dipping the cold baked potato in the plastic container of sour cream.

"Nice, Nikki. After two years, at the first sign of trouble—you're gone. Bitch."

He tossed the end of his potato at an attentive gull. It was a mistake: now, he had a flock gathering. "One mishap. Who you with now, Nikki?" he shouted, kicking the gulls away.

Two teenage girls kept their eyes on Sam, moving to the far side of the sidewalk as they passed.

"I'm on the fucking phone," he yelled at them. But he wasn't. He got up to leave, flinging the rest of his steak at the birds. For the last three days he'd wanted nothing more than to leave Deerfield Beach; now it would be agonizing to go.

He pulled his wedding ring out of his pocket, turned it around in his hand and finally put it back on. "I'm doing all this for you, Nikki."

*****

Sam woke, still in his clothes, with the morning light flooding his room. He'd left the drapes open after a night of searching bars and restaurants, walking the streets calling out Nikki's name. Useless, if she didn't want to be found.

He took a long shower, his last for at least a week, and packed his bags before walking down to the beach to look for her one more time. He went back to the same bench with his coffee and perched on the backrest, watching. In the distance, he saw a blonde with a slight build walking along the shore, and he ran across the sands—but it wasn't her. He had postponed leaving long enough. He took a sip of cold coffee and then tossed it. It was time to go.

At nine o'clock, he packed up his Jeep and drove along the beach and down side streets, combing the area, slowing to look at another woman who wasn't her. Now he was late. Turning onto Highway A1A, he headed to Marathon, staying within the speed limit and keeping an eye out for the Fort Lauderdale Police. He flipped on his stealth radar detector with its voice alert and took to the surface roads until he passed Fort Lauderdale's city limits.

"I'll get it all back, Nikki. You'll see. I'll get it all back and more." He picked up the Overseas Highway and headed to where the others would be waiting for him aboard his sport fisher.

CHAPTER 18

At mid-afternoon, the crew of *Merlin* sailed into Marathon and dropped anchor in the protected waters of Boot Key Harbor. The clouds over Lower Florida folded like piled whipped cream, deepening into darker shades of steel grey over the scattered whitecaps. With the increasing wind, *Merlin* tugged at her anchor like a stallion pulling at its reins. It was an irritating motion for Ella, who was already on edge. The relentless testing of the anchor's grip on the sandy bottom had her fearing it could slip its hold, grounding them in the shallows, forcing them to wait for the next flood tide to float them free and causing them to miss their pickup at Cay Sal Bank.

Ella stood in the galley listening to the storm warnings on the VHF radio while she minced garlic for a hearty meal she was preparing before they set out in the morning.

Strong cold front to move through South Florida tonight and tomorrow. Small craft advisory in effect for all waters, with northwest winds of twenty to thirty knots, gusting up to thirty percent. Seas reaching fifteen feet with long swells.

She knew it was going to be a nasty crossing. The Gulf Stream gained speed squeezing between Florida and Cuba, and this norther would be hitting it head on. Sailing into Cay Sal Bank wouldn't be any picnic, either. She had studied the chart, seen the Bank's outlying rocks and islets, and knew they would be treacherous in stormy seas. She looked to Rich, bent over the chart, working his calculations.

He lifted his head, taking in the broadcast. "Sounds like we're in for it—nothing to do but be prepared."

"We knew it was coming," Carlos said, starting up the steps. "I'll go over the rigging again."

"Good. Burke, check the engine and make sure everything is tight. Ella, make a pile of sandwiches, enough to get us through the crossing." Rich rolled up the chart that he had marked, stuffed it in his duffle and headed up top. "I'm going ashore to see Falco."

"I'll go with you," Burke said, following him on deck.

"No. I'm going alone."

"What if you fall overboard? How we find Falco?"

Ella stopped in mid-cut when she heard the words 'fall overboard' and took a step up the companionway to listen. She watched Rich pull the dinghy up to the transom and toss in his duffle.

"I wait outside." Burke's tone was demanding.

"Keep it up, Burke and you'll be the one over the side," said Carlos.

"I want to see channel."

"We're leaving at five a.m., and there's a storm coming in. I need you to secure the boat." Rich's tone made clear that it was an order, not a request.

"When will you be back?" asked Ella.

"Before dark. I'll have dinner with Falco." He pumped the fuel bulb and pulled on the outboard's starter cord, but the engine was cold.

"Need to open tank vent." Burke stood over him with folded arms and shifted his weight uneasily.

Rich ignored him and, on his third try, the outboard started. He pushed off from *Merlin*, pointing the dinghy toward Marathon Key.

Unaware she was twisting her dishtowel into a knot, Ella watched Rich motor away. Great, he was leaving her behind with two thugs. She picked up the binoculars and held them steady on the dinghy. Burke stood at her side, watching until Rich turned west down a canal and out of sight, then pushed past her to go below.

Carlos strapped into the bosun's chair and began pulling himself up the mast, checking the rigging as he went. Ella sat down at the helm and watched the lowering clouds move in. The breeze carried the scent of fall, and she wondered idly if it had travelled the distance from New England.

"Bur —" The wind sheared off the end of Carlos's words. "I need nee— nose pli—. Needle nose pliers!"

Ella finally caught his words and went below to get Burke. She wasn't prepared for what she saw. Burke was standing in her cabin with a pair of her underwear held to his face, nodding to what was being said on the phone in his other hand. At that moment Ella found the word for the underlying energy she'd sensed about him: *predator*. She strained, unable to hear the whispered words that made him smile, until she had had enough.

"Burke! Get the hell out of my cabin!"

With a leering smile, Burke gave Ella the once over. "Just want to see how first class travels." He dropped her underwear and pocketed his phone.

"Stay out of my things, you creep."

Burke brushed by her, pressing his body against hers, as if smelling her underwear had created an intimacy between them.

Ella pushed him off, angry that she had to put up with this creep. "Carlos needs a pair of needle nose pliers."

"No problem."

*****

Ella was back in the galley cooking when Burke tromped down the stairs. He pulled the staircase away from the companionway to get at the engine, leaving her penned in. She kept her back to him and tried to ignore his grunting and Serbian curses as he leaned over the engine, clanging wrenches against metal. She wondered how long he'd be there, how long until Carlos was down from the mast, how long until Rich returned.

At first, she thought Burke had lost his balance and fallen into her from the jerking motion of the boat. But he stayed pressed into her back with an arm on either side, trapping her, as he reached for the paper towels with both hands. She could feel his breath on her bare neck and she shrank from him, trying to make herself small, then ducked out under his arms.

"You belong in a cage." Ella stepped away.

Burke's eyes widened and he pressed his face close to hers as he wiped the grease from his hands. "Why? You think I'm some wild animal?" he said, smiling. He shoved the soiled towels into her hands and then grabbed a slice of ham, popping it in his mouth.

Ella looked up at the open hatch.

"He can't hear you," Burke smiled.

"I grew up around tug men, Burke. I know how to play hardball if I have to," she said, tossing the towels in the garbage.

Like it or not, she thought, I signed up for this. She considered retreating to her cabin until Burke finished with the engine or Carlos returned to the deck, but instead pulled out her ten-inch cook's knife and thrust the blade into an onion in rapid chops.

"Ella, make me a cup of coffee."

She kept chopping, louder and faster, drowning out Burke's voice.

Burke gave up, switched on the radio to a local channel and stuck his head back in the engine compartment. The sound was a welcome distraction, the announcer's voice spiking with enthusiasm until he came to the weather report and dropped into a somber tone.

"Marathonians, I'd stay in tomorrow. We have a nasty Northeast front coming through with winds up to thirty miles an hour kicking those waves up pretty high. Fish are going to be hiding under a rock and I'd suggest you do the same."

A thud on the deck announced Carlos's return. Ella put down her knife and started to her cabin, thought better of it and took the knife with her.

*****

It was nearly sundown when Ella heard Rich motoring back. She looked out the galley porthole wondering why the last-minute meeting, and what had they talked about for the past few hours. Falco hadn't struck her as someone you could shoot the breeze with. Was Rich picking up the co-ordinates for their rendezvous, or had something gone wrong?

After the men lashed the dinghy on deck, Carlos and Burke went to their cabins and Rich returned to the navigation table, where he unrolled the chart and slipped it under the plastic sleeve for tomorrow's sail.

"How did it go?" Ella asked. "Everything okay?" She had finished cleaning the galley and slid in beside him.

"Yeah, all's good." Rich gave her a reassuring smile.

Why all the secrecy, she wondered? Security, or was it to keep in place the hierarchy of power? She checked to see if Burke's door was completely closed and then spoke in a voice just within hearing. "Rich, I caught Burke in my cabin while you were gone."

"What was he doing?"

"He was smelling my clothes—actually, my underwear."

Rich let out a laugh and rubbed his forehead. "Your underwear? I'll tell him to stay out of your cabin."

"I did. There's something seriously wrong with that guy."

"Just try to stay away from him. We only have a couple of days onboard."

"Little hard to do on a boat." Ella looked over at Rich. "He was on his phone with this stupid grin on his face."

"He was talking on the phone?" Rich sat up, turning to Ella.

"Yeah."

"What was he saying?"

"I couldn't make it out, his voice was muffled."

"Why didn't you tell me?"

"I am telling you."

"You do remember the order for complete phone silence."

"It wasn't me using the phone."

"I know." Rich scooted Ella out of the booth ahead of him, nearly landing her onto the cabin sole.

She got out of his way, watching him charge Burke's door, banging on it with his fist.

"Burke! Open up."

Carlos opened his door. "What's up, boss?"

"Open up, damn it!"

"What, man?" Burke called through his closed door.

"Open the door."

"We sinking or something?" Burke cracked the door and peered out. "What emergency?"

"Give me your phone."

"Why?"

"Hand it over," Rich demanded.

Burke grabbed his phone from behind the door and shoved it into Rich's hand.

"Everyone. Hand them over," he said. "Ella, your phone. Carlos, yours too. I should have done this in Lauderdale."

"What's up, man?" Carlos asked.

"Who were you talking to, Burke?" asked Rich.

"My girl." Burke's eyes shifted to Ella. "Private."

"Not today." Rich's voice flared. "Does she know about this trip?"

"Delivering boat. That's all. I tell her nothing but I go and come back soon."

"I'll turn off my phone." Carlos pulled his out and began powering it down when Rich snatched it from his hands.

Carlos took a step toward Rich with fight in his eyes. "Hand it back, man."

"Later. You'll get it back at the end of the trip," Rich said. "We're about to pick up a load worth several million, for Christ's sake! The GPS in a Smart phone can be tracked; someone right now could be sitting at a computer plotting our position."

"I need to keep in touch with my wife," Carlos backed down. "My little girl is not well."

"Sorry to hear that, but there's nothing you can do about it out here. I'll keep all phones until we're through with this run. No exceptions."

When Ella returned with her phone, Rich was hitting 'call back' on the last number Burke had dialed. She could hear it ring, and then a women's voice answered. Rich snapped the phone closed and glared at Burke.

"She my girl, now," Burke said. "Take my phone, man. I don't care—just give back to me."

"Did she give you anything to take along?" Rich kept his eye on Burke. "Anything at all?"

"No. You think she plant bug on me?"

Rich stared down at Burke's phone, shutting it off. "Of all the women, Burke. You know Sam's the rat."

"She not with Sam. She waiting for me."

"Nikki?' Ella exclaimed in surprise.

"If anything goes wrong on this trip you're going to be one sorry bastard," said Carlos.

Burke's angry eyes flashed at Ella before he slammed his door closed.

"Is Nikki his girlfriend?" Ella asked.

"Sorry, boss. But if you don't trust him," Carlos said in a harsh whisper, "now's the time to get rid of him. After we leave, that's it."

"Who's the girl?" Ella asked again.

"Yes, that was Nikki," Rich said, looking over at Ella, then turned back to Carlos. "I don't want to pull him off over personal shit. Besides, he's a great engine man and we may need him."

*****

Two hours before sunrise, with drizzle weeping from the clouds, Ella stood on the bow holding the spotlight on the anchor line and signaling to Rich at the helm while Burke and Carlos hauled in the anchor and lashed it on deck. As they motored out she aimed the light on the first channel marker for Rich to get his direction, then on the boats resting at anchor along the way. Rich had ordered complete silence in hope of slipping out unnoticed.

At least they were going out on a flood tide, Ella thought. It seemed like a good omen, considering *Merlin's* deep draft in these shallow waters. The channel narrowed with unexpected bends, and the local charts warned of shoaling on its southerly side. Rich pushed the throttle as they passed Boot Key's shield of mangroves and into the full force of the wind that pressed them to heel under bare poles. Ella could hear waves rolling in from the Straits of Florida and hitting the outer reef, but she couldn't see them. She wouldn't have seen her own hand if it hadn't held the flashlight.

From the cockpit, Carlos shone a light on the marker they had just passed, showing they were snaking sideways with the current. Rich corrected, keeping the boat centered in the channel until they entered the black waters of the Gulf Stream. They raised the sails and set *Merlin* on a course for Deadman Cays on the northwest side of the Cay Sal Bank—an atoll sixty miles south of Marathon Key, the

137

westernmost point of the Bahamas and just thirty miles north of Cuba. A high concentration of blue holes made it a popular dive spot, but at night the secluded northeast tip was a perfect site for a drop.

Ella wedged herself in the galley, making breakfast and listening to the men talk on deck. When the coffee was brewed, she handed each their mug fixed just the way they liked it.

"Women are distraction in dangerous situation," Burke shared with Carlos.

"I'm a sailor first, Burke." Ella popped up from below with a plate of warm, tortilla-wrapped sausages. "And from what I've seen so far, a better one than you."

"We see about that," said Burke.

"Have one, Burke. It's not a dangerous situation yet." Ella caught Carlos's smile as she handed Burke the plate.

*****

Before long the small islets of the middle Keys disappeared behind the rolling waves and lowering clouds, leaving them alone in a starless, moonless night. The Stream poured out of the Gulf of Mexico in a four-knot current, butting against the brisk northeast wind and slapping the waves into peaks, their white tops scudding off in streaks over the black water. *Merlin* sailed at a good clip under her first reef, taking on constant spray across her bow.

"What do you think, Captain, seven hours at this speed?" Carlos shouted over the wind.

"Hopefully less to get to the Bank, and maybe a couple more hours southeast to Dog Rocks," Rich yelled back. "If we're lucky— before dark. Weather report says it should clear by evening."

"I hope they're right. Hate to pick up a load in this shit." Carlos lit up the sails with the spotlight. "We need to flatten the main."

"That could be trouble," Ella said, pointing to a spider web of lightning crackling from cloud to cloud, revealing a boiling storm mounting in the distance. "Does anyone want something more to eat before this storm hits?" She ducked quickly, dodging a sheet of spray. "I made a pile of sandwiches."

"What you got?" Carlos asked.

"Well, there's turkey with cranberry sauce, egg salad with a hint of curry, and roast beef with a horseradish sauce," Ella smiled. "Or we have that box of Oreos that Rich brought."

"I'll have the roast beef, toasted bun with side of fries," Carlos said, picking up on her playfulness.

"And of course, au jus from the spice-rubbed roast," Ella bantered. "How about you, Rich? I could scrape out the filling in your Oreos and put in egg salad? A little extra nutrition there?"

"What?" Rich sat at the helm, too far away to hear.

"I said, I'll bring you a sandwich," she yelled back.

"Stop with all the food talk," Burke said.

Ella looked over at Burke. He was curled up against the cabin like a child, the hood of his rain jacket cinched so tightly that she could barely see his ashen face.

"A little green around the gills, Burke?" She wondered if the breakfast sausage had been a good idea. "I'll get you something for that."

"Get the latest on the weather," Rich shouted.

The first rumble of thunder was loud enough to startle Burke from his slump. Ella took a long look at the sky before she ducked below. She switched the VHF to the weather channel and listened as it looped through the reports for South Florida and the Florida Straits, then stuck her head out the companionway.

"They're reporting a vigorous squall line building in the north, should pass over sometime tonight," she hollered to Rich. "Radar shows it's heading right for us."

Rich nodded and said something she couldn't hear. A racket of sound was coming from below deck: everything that could move was moving. The contents of drawers banged as they shifted from side to side, cans and bottles clanged against each other and the hull moaned from the strain on the rigging as they rode the waves.

Ella stumbled through the boat with a hand on the overhead, dodging the swinging hammock of fruit as she passed. Being below deck during a storm was like being blindfolded on a rollercoaster: you never knew when the floor was going to drop out from under you. She checked the bilge to make sure the pump was working, then tightened the screw dogs on the portholes. The submerged starboard ports were seeping under pressure from the rushing river of water as the hull heeled forty-five degrees into the sea.

Ella dug the sandwiches from the icebox, stuffed them into her pockets along with a jar of pickled ginger, and went back on deck. "Here you go, Burke," she said, handing him the ginger. "Eat it slowly. It should calm your stomach." She braced against the companionway for a moment, considering him. Even the best of sailors get seasick, but it was remarkable how easily it had robbed him of his arrogance.

Merlin dropped off a wave and Ella grabbed onto the cabin top, turning her back to the wall of sea that shot across the boat and hit hard into the cockpit. She made her way to the men, steadying herself against the compass pedestal and pulling the sandwiches from her pocket. Carlos stood at the helm in his yellow slicker and life vest, water dripping off the end of his nose.

"They're a little squashed. I can take the wheel while you eat, Carlos."

"I'll relieve him after I eat," Rich said. "I don't think you want to steer in this weather."

"Why not? I've sailed in worse and on smaller boats." Rich's protectiveness was annoying, undermining what she was here for. This trip wasn't just about the money; it was also to prove to herself she could go it alone. "Did I ever tell you about the time I rounded the Horn on the back of a killer whale?" A smile came across her face, and she said, "I'll take my watch like everyone else."

"I wouldn't doubt it, Ella," Rich said. "OK, You're up after Carlos."

The crew sat silent in the dark, gauging the crests, watching for the one that could overtake them. Carlos worked *Merlin's* path over mounting swells that picked up the hull, carrying her along before dropping her to slip-slide down the backside, and then a moment's pause as she stalled in the troughs before the next wave came, again and again.

The first light of dawn broke through the night sky in soft shades of orange, revealing storm clouds dropping a curtain of rain. High-altitude winds had shorn the tops of the clouds to the shape of an anvil pointing directly at *Merlin*. They were doing a solid nine knots; at this speed, they could make Deadman Cays by early afternoon, and Dog Rocks easily before sundown—an altogether exciting ride as long as the weather didn't worsen.

Ella sat facing aft, huddled against the coaming with her legs drawn up to her yellow parka, her life vest and GPS locator in place and one hand tightly gripping the cockpit coaming. From the protective cave of her hood, she had been tracking the running lights of a ship on its way to the Gulf of Mexico until it suddenly disappeared. She stood up to see what had blocked her view. A wave, taller than *Merlin's* mast, was rushing toward them.

"Guys! Ten-o'clock!" Ella stabbed at the air toward the port bow. "Huge goddamn wave!"

"Oh fuck!" Rich hollered. "Carlos, I'll take the wheel. Ella, get below." He started the diesel to help maintain forward momentum, picking his path between waves and pointing the bow toward the monster barreling down on them.

"I'm good here!" Ella had tucked herself in close to the cabin and was hanging on with both hands. "I'm already tethered to the lifeline. You guys need to do the same."

"Burke, put the boards in and lock down the hatches!" Carlos shouted down into the cabin. "Pronto! We're getting pooped by this one." He pulled the hatch closed and tethered his vest to the lifeline. "Just don't let the bow get buried!" Carlos yelled at Rich.

"We're going to need some fucking luck. This could flip us." Rich looked over at Ella. "Wish you'd get below."

"Too late," Ella said. She kept her eye on Rich gripping the wheel, trying to keep upright with one knee pressed to the deck and the other foot braced against a cleat. *Merlin* slipped down and down, sinking into the oncoming wave's trough that sucked in the water before it, raising a wall of water on all sides. The boat stalled in the canyon and then, with a mighty heave, the hull began to lift with uncontrollable speed, heeling onto her side, mast nearly parallel to the water, sails kissing the waves. They were close to going under as the leading edge of the wave poured over the boat.

Water came at Ella from all sides and she clenched the handholds in a struggle to hang on. When *Merlin* shuddered free, she could see Carlos wedged in the flooded cockpit and Rich braced against the wheel. The boat floundered as the wind pushed them into the rolling seas; one more ounce of wave power and *Merlin* would have rolled three hundred and sixty degrees, dragging the crew under with her.

Merlin recovered with her mast intact but the rigging a tangled mess. The sails spilled the water they had captured, but the main was useless until they could straighten out the lines. Rich steadied his footing and pushed the engine to full power, trying to gain control.

That's when it began to pour.

"Jeezus Christ! Could it get any wetter?" Ella yelled.

"That was fun—one big fuckin' wave." Rich was grinning. "Everyone okay?"

"Good spotting, Ella," Carlos said.

"It's getting light. We should be able to see them coming." When she stood, the cold puddle of water that had gathered in her hood streamed down the inside of her jacket. She shook off the discomfort and stared hard at the sea, looking for disproportionate waves. In the gauzy light of dawn it was difficult to see where the sea ended and sky began.

"We're getting out of the middle of the Stream, so the sea should start to calm down, " Rich said.

Carlos shoved back the hatch. "Burke, you okay?"

"What the fuck was that?"

"Get on deck, we need to free the main," said Carlos.

"We under water?"

"Hell, yes!" Rich yelled. "Keep watch. Waves like that could snap our mast."

"That fuck things up." Burke turned, taking in the sea.

"Let's shorten the main down to the last reef," Rich said. "Ella, take the helm and head her up."

Gripping the wheel, Ella forced the boat to head up and course through the waves. The wind howled and whipped through the rigging, pounding the sails while the sea boiled around them. She watched for Rich's hand signals as the men struggled to set the rigging and free the sails to stabilize the boat. Even though they were tethered to jack lines, she feared someone being struck by the swinging boom and knocked overboard.

When all was set right, Rich took the helm to get a sense of the sail trim. Ella climbed up onto the boom, clung tightly to the mast and scanned the water. Rich had called it: the sea was becoming less angry, and she guessed by the drop in the wind that the squall was passing.

"I don't see another one," Ella reported back to the cockpit. "Maybe that was our one piece of bad luck."

"Don't believe in luck," said Carlos. "Any luck you have is what you make."

Familiar words, Davis's words, Ella thought, looking back at Carlos. She went below for a towel and came up wiping her face. "So you *don't* believe a woman onboard is bad luck?"

"What?"

"Nothing—here's a towel."

Burke sat hunched over, blocking the wind with his back, his hood cinched tightly around his face and a cigarette hanging from his mouth. "Sea could calm down now and make me happy." He was thumbing the flint wheel of his lighter, trying to strike a light. "Fuck." Burke flung the lighter over the side.

"Ocean's not a garbage can, Burke," said Rich.

"American made junk," he said digging into his pockets.

"Probably made in China," Ella said. She stood alongside Rich at the helm watching Burk search his pockets and wondering what Nikki saw in the brute. At last he pulled out a black and red pack of La Tasca matches and curled over, protecting his cigarette from the wind and rain, striking one after another in cupped wet hands until he lit his damp cigarette.

"So you and Nikki are a couple?" Ella leaned into Burke to ask.

Burke nodded, exhaling a cloud of smoke at Ella, making her back away.

"You get those matches together in Cuba? I saw some like them on Sam and Nikki's boat."

Carlos had been coiling up the main sheet, but turned to look at Burke's matches on hearing his homeland mentioned.

"Sam's boat, not Nikki's. Why you ask questions all the time?"

"Just piecing something together," said Ella.

"You nosey."

Ella twisted so she could watch Burke's face. "Does Nikki know who killed Davis?"

"Wouldn't know," said Burke.

"Maybe that's why she's with you. Maybe she's afraid of Sam."

"She well-hidden."

"So, she *is* afraid."

"Stay out my business," Burke warned. "Nikki happy. She needed man who can deliver."

144

Deliver what? Ella wondered. What was Nikki really doing with Burke? If she had Nikki pegged, it was about money, not sex. Ella shivered from the chill and considered changing into dry clothes, but there were still sheets of spray blowing across the boat and she only had one spare set. She took a seat out of the wind instead, leaned against the cabin and stole a look at Rich, who had been listening, looking displeased. She guessed that he too was putting pieces of the puzzle together.

"Did you see Davis when you two were in Cuba?"

Burke didn't answer and turned his back to Ella.

"You knew Davis?" Ella persisted.

"I met him once." Burke stood up abruptly, threw his cigarette over the side and went below.

"Stop," Rich mouthed to Ella, then called after Burke, "Burke, next time you throw a cigarette over the side it's going to cost you."

"Really? What you gonna do?" Burke turned back.

"How about a grand a butt. Doesn't make up for all the fish you're killing."

"You can't do that. I get my pay as agreed," Burke argued. "How much is grand?"

"It's my run, I'll do as I see fit."

"Grand's a thousand dollars." Ella watched Burke disappear below deck and then lowered her head to Rich. "I think he knows what happened to Davis."

Rich turned and flashed Ella a quick look. "Wait until we're back and paid to get your answers. That's an order."

He was right: you don't fuel grievances at sea. Ella nodded and leaned back, worried that once in port, Burke would be gone, along with any chance of finding out what he knew.

They had come through the worst of the storm. Rain had calmed the rough seas, flattening the wave tops and making for a smoother sail. By noon, they had made good time and were leaving the Gulf

Stream's axis for calmer waters strewn with spindrift from the passing storm.

"We're about twenty miles from the Cays," said Rich. "The current has driven us farther east."

"That's handy," said Carlos. "Drop us off at Dog Rocks."

Rich took out the Swarovski binoculars and scanned the horizon. "We're looking for the Cay Sal lighthouse. It's abandoned, so there's no light, but it's sixty feet tall. We should be able to spot it off the nose at thirty degrees." Rich handed the helm over to Ella and went below to study the charts.

"Head up as close to a hundred and ten degrees as you can," he yelled from below. "See if we can avoid tacking."

Ella sailed close-hauled, looking for fresh ripples on the water's surface that would indicate a gust heading their way. When she pushed back the hood of her parka to feel the wind direction on her face, an icy finger of water rolled down her arm and along her side, invading her only remaining dry spot and sending a chill through her damp bones.

The front was moving south toward Cuba, leaving them shrouded in a gossamer veil of moisture, diffusing the light into a hazy grey. The clouds on its backside rolled off like coiled fists ready to punish some other poor mariner. She could see Cuba's Sierra Maestra mountain range on the horizon.

Before them, the ragged, razor-edged coral of the islets of Cay Sal Bank were becoming visible. Ella wasn't expecting what she saw. The site looked too exposed for picking up bales of marijuana with a street value of several million dollars, even under the cover of night. The islands frightened her with their uncivilized rawness. They looked like a place where anything could happen, a godforsaken place at the end of the world. Her mind turned to the savage deaths of Davis and Jon. Here she was, in a place she didn't belong and fearing the same fate—all because she was determined to get the restaurant. Any lingering notion that this trip was like an ordinary boat delivery had vanished. She braced for what might come, feeling in her gut that she had made a dangerous choice.

CHAPTER 19

Offshore the Cuban archipelago, *Merlin* held fast at anchor along the ragged rocks of the Damas Cays, where the chart was marked 'Dangerous Shoals'. The more protected anchorage, a quarter-mile north at Dog Rocks, was their rendezvous point. With still six hours to wait, Rich preferred to hang back where he would have a view of the arriving mother ship—or any unwanted company.

The storm had passed, leaving only billowing clouds drifting south over the island of Cuba in the fading light of the magenta sky, and the calming waters swelled in shimmering shades of mercurial blue.

Ella worked below deck, restoring order and mopping up the saltwater that had rushed in from their knockdown at sea. "Rich, where are we going to store—" she popped her head out of the hatch and whispered, "the bales?"

"Salon and the quarter berth. Get rope ready. We'll secure them in case we're hit with another squall."

The men were on deck hauling dive tanks and flippers out of the lazarette in an attempt to disguise *Merlin* as a pleasure boat. The Cay Sal Bank was patrolled by Coast Guard helicopters looking for smugglers and raft riders from Cuba trying to make it to Key West.

All it would take was a Coast Guard pilot becoming curious to bring their whole operation down.

Ella heard Rich call for flags and she handed Carlos the US ensign and the Bahamas courtesy flag.

"It's unlikely the air patrol will come out after that storm, at least not until tomorrow," said Rich. "We may have hit some luck."

"What?" Ella said, coming up from below. "What about your Coast Guard friend who's looking out for us?"

Rich slipped the binocular strap over his head. "He's stationed in Marathon. I don't know anyone at Guantanamo Bay."

"Oh, I thought..." The thin veil of safety that Ella believed they had didn't exist. She tilted her head back, searching the sky, but saw only a few gulls diving in the shoals for their evening meal.

"This is where you supposed to lay on deck in your bikini," said Burke.

"Oh dear, I forgot my bikini." Ella shot Burke a look of faux dismay. "Or did you see one among my things?"

"Ignore him." Rich stood facing south, focusing the binoculars on the waters between them and the Cuban shoreline.

Ella joined him on the cabin top and scanned the northeastern rim of the atoll. "See anything?"

"No, but we need to stay sharp, watch for any craft—boat, airplane—or sign of people on the islets," Rich said.

"Do you expect trouble?" Once again, she thought about his secret meeting with Falco.

"Always—in this business, you're a fool if you don't." Rich turned to the rest of the crew. "We're taking shifts. I want eyes on the water at all times."

Rich checked his watch. "We'll do one-hour rotations. Burke, Ella, Carlos, then me. The final hour, I want all hands on deck. The binoculars are Swarovski's—treat them with respect."

"I thought I recognized *Grace's* binoculars," said Ella.

"I rescued them from idiots," he grinned.

"Oh, I see," she smiled, keeping her eyes on the water.

"They were lying under a rusty chain at the bottom of the lazarette." He turned back to Carlos and Burke. "We'll haul anchor at half past midnight. Get some rest; we won't get another chance at sleep until past daybreak. Burke, you're on first watch."

Rich handed Burke the binoculars, then stretched out in the cockpit. Burke straddled the boom, binoculars hanging from his neck, and lit up the stub of a joint.

"Will you be able to spot anything stoned?" said Ella.

"Do you good to get little stoned, loosen you up," Burke said.

"Yeah, then I could be a shithead like you. I think I'll pass."

"Burke," Rich raised up on his elbows. "I've told you twice to stop smoking that shit. Dope fucks with your judgment."

"I got it," said Burke. "No worry." He took one last drag and flicked the butt over the side before heading to the bow.

*****

Ella scanned the sky and the rocks of Dumas Cay that took on the menacing shape of a serpent's spine, a sleeping dragon below the surface, armored plates protruding above the darkening waters. If only I could draw a blanket of cloud over us to keep us hidden, she thought. She went below to check the radar, zooming in on the nearby rocks. The radar picked up movement on the far side, but she couldn't tell if it was flotsam carried along on the tide or a slow moving boat.

"Rich," Ella called up from below. "There's movement on the radar—not sure what it is."

"Where?" Rich rushed down the hatch. "Did you mark it?"

"Yeah. Definitely something, it's leaving a trail. How about I go up the mast to take a look? I have good night vision."

"So do the Swarovski's. Okay." Rich went on deck, ordering Burke to retrieve the bosun's chair from the locker. "There's movement on the radar."

"You going up mast?" said Burke.

"No, Ella is."

"I'll haul her."

"As long as you promise not to drop me," said Ella.

She kicked off from the mast as Burke cranked the winch, hoisting her up.

"That's good," Ella shouted at the halfway mark, but Burke kept cranking. "Stop! Burke!" Christ, she thought, looking up and seeing she was nearly at the masthead. Will this son of a bitch ever leave me alone?

Carlos craned his neck to watch. "Burke, cut the crap."

Rich took over, tying off the halyard. He turned to Burke, who was leaning against the boom. "You can be a real asshole."

"I know," he said, grinning up at Ella.

The sea still moved in long swells from the day's storm, and seventy feet above deck the mast swayed dramatically. Ella wrapped her legs around the mast to steady herself and scanned the islets. At the northeastern tip of Dog Rocks, she caught a white flash through the binoculars. She tried to hold them steady, but the mast's movement made it difficult and she was becoming nauseous. Beyond the rocks there was a wink of light and she grabbed the stay to pull herself around. A white fishing boat was moving slowly along the shoal. She looked down and waved at Rich, then pointed to where she saw the small boat.

She took one more full circle around and then called out to be lowered.

"White hull; may be a fishing boat." Ella handed Rich the binoculars. "Looks like it's heading west."

Rich climbed on the boom and focused the light-gathering binoculars. "Got them. Looks like a thirty-footer without a bow pulpit, has radar, possibly three outboards, can't see who's onboard."

He jumped down, checked his watch and pulled a field notebook from his hip pocket, jotting down the description, time and position. "What in the hell are they doing out there?" He looked up from his pad. "We need to watch where they're going, track them on radar."

"I'll take a look." Carlos grabbed the binoculars out of Rich's hands. "I don't think we need to worry, they look like Cuban fishermen. Storms trigger a feed—it's a good time to fish."

"Seems unlikely a Cuban fishing boat would have three outboards."

"One or two probably don't work, boss."

"We worry about everyone out here," said Rich. He went below to check the radar, then came on deck and lay down to rest. "They're heading towards Deadman Cays. Burke, tell me their position in ten minutes."

Ella stood near Carlos, keeping her eyes on the water. "Have you done runs before, Carlos?" She wanted to hear stories to soothe her unease, hopeful stories of smooth runs where crews walked away relatively wealthy.

"Yeah, a few. Has to feel right, like this one."

Ella looked over at Rich, who shrugged a smile and then closed his eyes.

"He plans things out carefully," Carlos said, nodding toward Rich.

"How did you get started in this business?" Ella prodded.

"My family left Cuba when I was young and moved to Colombia where there was plenty of talk of quick fortunes. When I was sixteen I got a job working for a grower, running bales all night down the dock to a shrimp boat. Hard work, they were heavy, but I got paid two thousand dollars—big pile of cash to help my family. Got me hooked on fast money for a while."

"A while?" Burke laughed. "You still hooked, man." By now Burke had slid off the boom and was hanging over it like a rag doll.

"I quit for a time," said Carlos. He eyed Burke warily. "Burke, do your damn job."

"I'm focused in, man."

"Maybe you should focus out," said Ella as she scanned the sea. There was no sign of the boat they'd been watching. "What's the radar show, Burke?"

"I just checked—half way across the bank, on a heading to Deadman," Burke said.

"They're either familiar with these waters or they're stupid. There are shoals everywhere," said Ella. She turned back to Carlos while he was in the mood to talk. "Why did you quit? Did something happen?"

"I got married, had a little girl, moved to US—was worried about getting busted by ICE, getting deported. It's just a matter of time really for me—and my family." Carlos began to sound agitated. "I'm not going back without money. So I start again, smarter this time."

"How so?"

Carlos shrugged his shoulders and turned away, ending the conversation.

"Me, I love money," Burke said, looking through the binoculars for a moment and then climbing onto the boom again. "You nobody without money."

"Yeah, that's how the money fever starts," said Rich.

"Thought you were asleep, man," Carlos said.

"Never totally asleep on a run."

"Now cook's turn to do job," said Burke.

"I'm on it." Ella went below, reluctantly opening the cans of Dinty Moore Beef Stew that Rich had bought. She cringed at its faint dog food odor as she heated it over the flame, toasted bread as a side and served it.

After dinner she went to the bow, looking for any sign of boats, then headed down to the galley to clean up. Her Wusthof knife bag lay opened on the counter, and a knife was missing. She was up the ladder in two steps.

"Who took my paring knife?"

"I needed to cut water hose," Burke said.

"A water hose!" Ella cried. "Out of my knife case?"

"What the big deal?"

"You had no right. You'll ruin the edge."

"Don't get huffy upset."

"Where is it?"

"Right here." Burke sat in the light of the lantern holding the knife by the point over the dark water and taking a long drag of weed. "You want it?" he said through exhale of smoke.

Rich lifted his head off the cushion to look. "Give the knife back, Burke."

"I don't know. This too much fun."

From the galley, Ella grabbed one of the ship's knives and tested the tip for sharpness. "Sure you want to go there?" The knife handle rested in her palm, and she found its balance before stepping up the companionway.

Burke laughed, waving her paring knife over the water. Ella pulled back her arm. With a round, smooth swing, she flipped her wrist and released the knife, sticking it into the deck, barely missing Burke's foot.

"Whoa!" Burke lurched to the side. "Woman, you nuts?"

She had a second one waiting in her hand. "Next one, I'll land it in the middle of your fucking foot. You won't walk on it for at least a month."

"Stop fucking around, Burke, or you'll find yourself marooned on those rocks." Rich stood up and grabbed the knife out of Burke's hand.

"I'll row you over there myself," added Carlos.

Rich pulled the other out of the deck and handed both of them to Ella.

Ella looked up at him. "They were a gift from my father."

"The knives or the skill to throw them?" Rich asked.

"Both."

Burke shrugged his shoulders. "How do I know father give knives?"

Carlos smiled. "You know how to take care of yourself, Ella."

"I'm learning."

"Burke, hand over your stash," Rich said.

"It calms me, man."

"No, it doesn't. It turns you into an asshole. Hand it over."

Burke dug into his pocket and handed a bag to Rich.

"All of it."

He fished a couple of joints from his shirt pocket and handed them over. "Now you have weed *and* phone."

"You'll get them back," Rich said.

"How about a truce, Burke?" said Ella. "You leave me alone and I promise not to poison your food."

"Okay. You a tough woman."

"Good. All right," Ella said with a forced smile.

"I know not to piss off cook—we be friends."

"Let's just start with civil."

*****

Ella stood her watch on the foredeck away from the cabin light, looking out at the dark waters and listening hard for any sound that didn't belong. A shooting star streaked across from the north and without hesitation she made a wish: please get me through this alive. A lucky star, she thought, this trip could have been far more dangerous with a full crew like Burke.

She wondered from which direction the mother ship would arrive. Would they have their running lights on, or would they come in dark, under the cover of night? She thought about Davis, mysterious Davis—it had been part of his appeal, but she was just now realizing how little she'd known about him. How many times, she wondered, had he been in this spot, waiting for a load? Had he, too, been nervous?

"You doing okay?" Rich joined her at the bow.

"Yeah. I'm fine," said Ella. "What kind of boat is the mother ship?"

"Could be a number of different kinds, from a rust bucket trawler to a multimillion-dollar yacht. You never know. With this group, I'd say a rust bucket."

"Why? Are they poor?"

"Not hardly, just smart. A fishing boat draws less attention. Plus, if things go south—which in our case they won't—they can abandon it with minimum loss."

"If things go south?"

"We'll be okay. Nervous?"

"A bit." She looked up at the stars. "I've never seen the Milky Way this clearly."

"Some cultures believed it to be the River of Souls, a stopping-off place before they joined the sacred river beyond."

"River of Souls?" said Ella. "I wonder if they found it comforting, believing they could see the spirit of someone they had lost."

"It's hard to know if it were meant to comfort or control. I'd find it haunting."

"Not me." Ella looked up, heartened by the thought of Davis and her father among the stars. She stood up and scanned the waters. Her watch was nearly over, leaving just three more hours of waiting.

"You never said what you were going to do with your money."

"Fund my research," said Rich.

"It's that important to you, to take these chances?"

"Yeah, it's what I love. Striders are a bellwether of a changing environment. But until I gather more data, the powers that be won't be convinced. Meanwhile all the expense comes out of my pocket."

They were all trying to finance their dreams by smuggling a drug that gave people a passing euphoria. What harm's in that? Ella thought.

Rich lifted the binoculars to the rocks, adjusting the focus. "You know how to handle a gun?"

The question caught Ella off guard, but she recovered with a quick nod. "Somewhat. Target practice a few times with Davis—a revolver and an automatic."

"You should have one on you tonight when we pick up the load."

"Do you think we'll need them?"

"Come back to the cockpit."

Ella walked aft, toward the flat lighting of the oil lamp that shone like a campfire on the men's faces. She guessed they were too restless to sleep. They sat in the cockpit breaking down and cleaning their arms while trading tales of powerful guns they had fired. Two machine guns lay on the seat next to Carlos, handguns and boxes of ammunition on either side of Burke, oil rags and cleaning rods scattered about between them.

"You probably haven't shot one of these before." Rich picked up an AK-47.

"No." The assault rifle looked menacing, meant for one thing: to kill.

"You should know how it works."

Carlos stopped cleaning his gun, watching Ella's hesitation. "She doesn't need to know."

"Everyone does. Even if you can't shoot it, you sure as hell need to look like you can."

The rifles looked battle worn; one clip had been wrapped in duct tape and the wood of the butt stock was banged up. Ella wondered if Rich had had to use them before.

"It's insurance." Rich looked at Carlos and Burke, then turned back to Ella. "Hold it like this." He tucked the butt of the gun against his shoulder, cradling the stock in the palm of his hand.

Ella looked to Carlos, but he was back working on his pistol. Whatever made her think that this could possibly be easy? An AK47?

"Listen up, Ella. It's fairly simple to use. Here's the safety. Push up to keep it on, down for firing."

"Taking safety off, hardest part," said Burke.

"Why?" asked Ella.

"Means you gonna shoot," said Burke.

She recoiled, taking another step into the quicksand, sinking further into a world she had meant only to visit briefly. Rich pushed the gun at her, grabbing her hand and placing it in a palm-up position to hold the stock.

"Here, you try. It's not loaded. When you pull the trigger, it's going to have some kick, so be sure you seat it firmly against your shoulder and have a good stance. The cartridges will pop out to the right. Don't let that throw you off."

"It's heavy."

"Seven pounds."

"Fires forty rounds a minute." Carlos's voice was energetic, like a kid approaching a carnival gate. "But this gun is not for you. You spray the bullets, you could hit anyone."

"Carlos, I think it's your watch," Rich said pointedly.

"I'm on it." He stood up, grabbed the binoculars and headed to the bow.

"Keep your ears sharp, too, Carlos," said Rich.

"Always, boss."

Davis had insisted that Ella learn how to defend herself while living alone onboard *Gina Marie*. He had given her a small Smith and Wesson twenty-two-caliber pistol to keep onboard. She had stowed it unloaded at the back of a drawer.

"Maybe I should show Ella how to use pistol?" Burke grinned.

"No need. I know how."

"What, a pellet gun?" Burke's taunting tone was back.

"We've called a truce, remember?"

"What you learn on?"

"Smith & Wesson and a Walther."

Davis had taken her out to the undeveloped part of Tamiami Trail and set up cans for shooting practice. He'd stood behind her with his arms wrapped around her, his guiding hands showing her the maximum grip control, his head resting next to hers as he taught her to line up the sights, kissing her neck to throw her off. Ella had felt the weapon's potential and even then, part of the thrill had been that it frightened her.

Rich laughed. "Okay, Annie Oakley, here's a Smith and Wesson SD 9mm. It's a semi-automatic with a standard clip that holds sixteen rounds. I only have one clip for it, so if you have to shoot, don't forget to count."

So there was a possibility. "Sixteen rounds—okay. Is it loaded?"

"Yeah. Here, let me release the magazine. I don't want you firing it now."

"Where's the safety?"

"There isn't one. It has a stiff trigger that serves the same purpose."

She held the Smith & Wesson on her lap, turning it over, feeling its weight, then lifted it to look down the sights. She shoved the full magazine in, then released it. Burke took the gun from her hands and carefully went over its features.

"I think I've got it." She released the magazine and stuffed the gun in one pocket of her parka and the magazine in the other, along with a box of cartridges.

She looked over at Burke, who was back to cleaning his gun again. Whatever they faced tonight, they needed to do it as a team. She would make more of an effort to see the solid side of him that Rich knew. Burke had survived the Balkan Wars growing up. He had earned the right to be a little crazy.

*****

The glow from the lights of Havana relieved the weight of the darkness, but the sound of the waves against the rocks played tricks with Ella's ears. At times, it seemed louder and closer, as though *Merlin* was dragging her anchor, bringing them nearer to the rocks. This is the worst of it, she thought, listening for the arrival of the mother ship and keeping watch on these little spits of land stuck in the middle of the Caribbean Sea, one cup of coffee after another, waiting.

She went to her cabin, locked the door and climbed into her bunk. Curling into a ball and pulling the covers over her head, she lay with the comforting memory of Davis's shoulder —how she had rested her head there until he lifted his arm, inviting her into the secure world of a man who knew what was right, knew the way through life. She lay with the ache of missing him until she drifted off.

CHAPTER 20

A sharp knock on the door jarred Ella out of a nightmare. She had been sailing *Merlin* alone in dark and remote waters when she hit a reef and started sinking. She had scrambled up the mast, holding on as the boat capsized, leaving her perched inches above shark-infested waters.

She shot up, looking around the pitch-black cabin, remembering where she was.

"It's time, Ella," said Rich.

"I'm up," she rasped and waited for her heart to slow its wild racing before she pulled back the covers. The metallic taste of adrenaline coated her mouth, the smell filling her nostrils. She slid out of the bunk, rubbed her face with her hands and ran her fingers through her hair, ruffling herself awake. After a rough sail and only a few hours sleep she felt deeply exhausted, yet the hardest part was just beginning.

Rich had called for a blackout in their final hours of waiting. She stumbled out of her cabin in the dark, feeling her way into the main salon. A faint light came from the companionway, where the night was lit by a multitude of stars.

Ella could hear that the men were already on deck. "Rich, any sign of the boat we saw last night?"

"None. Carlos went up the mast for a look."

"Good. Can I turn on a light to make the coffee?"

"One. Use the small galley lamp."

After putting on the kettle for coffee, she leaned over the sink, splashing cold water on her face to clear the fog from her mind, then headed onto *Merlin's* deck—their own tiny island, floating on the night sea. She scanned the waters, looking deeply into the blackness for the shape of a boat, but still there was no sign of the mother ship.

The men were taking down the dive flag, stowing the cockpit cushions and clearing the deck of anything that would get in the way. She could see their shadowy forms in watch caps, sheathed knives hanging from their belts. They were already armed. Carlos wore his gun holstered, and from the look of Burke's bunched-up shirt, his was tucked into the back of his pants. Ella guessed Rich's gun was in his pocket.

"Would anyone like some food?" Her question hit her as oddly normal.

"No time. Just coffee—make it fast." Rich spoke in a low voice. "Quietly Ella, we need to listen for the boat."

Ella set the tray of strong-brewed coffee on the cockpit seat and went below to get ready. Eight bells sounded on the ship's clock, signifying the beginning of the midnight watch, and with each strike her heart beat faster. She pulled the gun from her duffel and stared at the hefty, cold metal in her hand, then brought it up and peered down its sights like Davis had taught her. She dropped her arm and, trying to imitate the speed of a trained gunman, raised the gun and took aim. But her hand trembled and she caught her reflection in the mirror on the back of the cabin door. She refused the fear she saw in her eyes and threw back her shoulders, looking more determined than brave.

She stuffed the gun in her fleece pocket, zipped it and looked around the cabin to see if there was anything else she might need, settling on her father's mariner's knife. She clipped it onto her belt and turned out the light. She was as ready as she would ever be.

On deck, the three men looked like sentries standing their posts: Burke at the bow, Carlos amidships and Rich on the transom, all listening and watching for the first sign of the boat.

Rich turned to Ella and studied her. "Got your gun?"

Ella patted her right pocket.

"Magazine loaded?"

Ella nodded. *Christ!* She'd forgotten it. What was wrong with her?

"Carlos, Burke," Rich said, calling the men to the cockpit. "We'll pull up anchor in a few minutes. These guys always run on time. You know the drill. Above all remain cool, keep your hands out of your pockets and no fast movements that can be construed as aggressive. Ella, once the bales start coming over, I want you to go below. We'll toss them down the companionway and you move them to the side. We'll need to work fast."

Ella nodded.

"We'll worry about stowing them later."

"We work in dark?" said Burke.

"No, unless they object," said Rich. "We'll light the lantern. Spreader lights cast too broad a light; we can't assume no one is watching. Another thing: they'll tie up to us, and they'll want to have quick release." Rich rubbed his hands together, and Ella took it as a sign he too was nervous.

"Do you know these men?" asked Ella.

"I don't know who's coming," Rich answered. "But they have more reason to be afraid of us—most likely they'll be loaded for a second delivery tonight. These people have a hair trigger. They're used to working with the cartels, so stay alert and don't give them any excuse to pull out their guns."

"Like what? asked Ella.

"If they think you're going for a gun," said Carlos. "I'll put out the bumpers."

"Both sides," said Rich.

"I'll give you a hand with those." Ella tied off the starboard bumpers, starring warily into the night.

"When we pull up to their boat, Burke, I want you amidships; and Carlos, you're on the transom with me. Ella, stay near the companionway. Everyone, keep an eye on the water for that sport fisher and any other boats. We don't want any surprises."

When Rich started *Merlin's* engine, Ella ran down to her cabin. The magazine sat on her bunk in clear view. She pulled the gun out, slammed the magazine into place and shoved it back in her pocket. What else had she forgotten? She took one last look around, then rushed back on deck.

Carlos and Burke had stowed the anchor and chain. Now underway, Rich motored along his plotted course toward Dog Rocks at a close but careful distance from the edge of the ragged shoal.

"Sixty feet, fifty-eight," Ella called out readings from the depth sounder.

"Just tell me if it gets below forty," said Rich.

Ella steadied herself in the companionway, her fatigue having been swept away by adrenalin; she diligently watched the depth sounder and the sea. Beyond the chug of *Merlin's* diesel and the rigging's restless slapping against the metal mast, she could hear the faint sound of waves breaking on the nearby shoal.

"Rich, boat running dark, five o'clock." Burke had spotted the white bow wave breaking through the darkness.

Ella turned around, straining to make out the shape of a fishing trawler moving along the eastern side of the bank, coming up from the direction of Cuba and gliding toward them like a ghost ship.

"Take the helm, Ella."

"What's our heading?" she asked. A flutter rose from her stomach and lodged in her throat.

"Three hundred-thirty degrees. Keep it slow," said Rich.

Rich took the binoculars from Burke and adjusted the focus. "It's them."

The men gathered on the aft deck and cockpit watching the trawler draw near. Rich signaled with the ship's spotlight, a long and short flash. The trawler returned in kind.

Rich was right: they had come in an old fishing trawler. The rust-stained white hull lumbered through the small chop with a cloud of smoke fanning from its transom. As it came into view, Ella could see the old workboat was running low in the water, laden with its load. Battered tires hung from the rail, skipping on the water's surface and banging into the topsides. The double rigging stood tall and a net filled with cargo hung from the arm of the aft davit. Two men stood alongside the pilothouse; at least one more was at the wheel inside.

Burke began pacing the deck, smoking and mumbling in Serbian, and Carlos stood still, watching, steadying himself with a grip on the backstay.

"Looks like they were lucky to make it out this far," said Ella.

When they were within a hundred yards, Rich flashed two long and one short with the spotlight, requesting them to approach on the starboard, but the trawler was heading for their port side and Carlos obligingly retied the boom.

"Ella, stand ready in the companionway." Rich said, taking back the helm.

"Looks like guns out already," said Burke.

"It's to be expected," said Rich.

"Where? I don't see them," said Ella.

"Way they stand," Burke said. "Combat ready."

Out of reflex, Ella turned and looked at the two rifles sitting within easy grasp on the starboard cockpit cushions. One wrong move from any one of them could trigger an exchange of gunfire—

and she could be dead. She backed down a step into the companionway.

The chugging diesel grew louder as the trawler drew closer out of the night, close enough for Ella to make out two of the men, their faces hidden in the caves of hooded sweatshirts. She looked hard at the figures and saw that what she had assumed were boat hooks were machine guns held tightly across their chests. They stood silent, one thin and one barrel-chested, studying the crew of *Merlin* as the space between the boats lessened.

The thick diesel smoke from the rust bucket blew across *Merlin's* transom, worsening the already low visibility. Ella worried something was wrong and it was why they had chosen to raft upwind. She studied the trawler from bow to stern, then scanned the waters around *Merlin*.

"Here we go. Keep cool. Keep your hands out of your pockets," said Rich.

One of the hooded men shouted out, "Diablo?"

"Negocio, amigo!" Rich responded with the code.

Satisfied, the crew gestured for *Merlin* to come closer. Rich sidled *Merlin* up to the trawler. The waves pushed the manicured yacht's topsides into the rusted, rough-planked workboat. *Merlin's* bumpers pressed against the tires, dampening the blow. The barrel-chested man tossed a noose over *Merlin's* main winch and tied the line off on the trawler's cleat.

"Veinte?" he said, putting up both hands with fingers spread open and signaling twice, indicating twenty bales.

"Sí, veinte," Rich yelled over the sound of the two diesel engines and gave a thumbs-up.

The thinner man swung his machine gun around to his back, picked a bale from the cargo netting and threw it onto *Merlin's* deck. The forty-pound bale teetered on the edge of the rail and Burke lunged, grabbing it before it fell into the water. He turned to the trawler, but Rich caught him before he spoke.

"Keep calm, Burke," said Rich. "Ella, light the lantern."

A pale glow cast onto *Merlin's* deck, spilling over onto the trawler and making the men more visible. She expected them to protest, but they didn't. Instead, the barrel-shaped man pulled out a cigar and leaned back against the pilothouse to wait. When he flicked his lighter, Ella could see his mustached smile beneath the hood, and the glint of metal in his teeth lit by the flame as he puffed on his cigar. She was glad he was a boat away.

Burke had squatted down to watch Rich cut open the bale and pull out a dark-brown bud. Rich took his time, breaking it apart and breathing in its aromatic scent, then handed it over to Burke.

"Looks like good shit, man," said Burke.

"It's what we wanted." Rich stood and gave a thumbs-up, accepting the rest of the load.

"Cuidadoso, amigos," Carlos yelled for caution.

"Americanos delicados." The thin man laughed and turned on the winch, lifting the netted load off the deck. The other man stuck his cigar in his mouth and prepared to guide it.

"ALTO!" screamed Rich, pointing to the arm of the davit heading for *Merlin's* backstay.

"Parada!" A tall, dark-skinned man rushed out of the pilothouse holding a machine gun, pointing at *Merlin*. "Parada! Parada!" He came across the deck in long strides, shouting orders in Spanish and pointing to *Merlin's* rigging with the tip of his gun. The cigar smoker looked at *Merlin's* backstay for the first time and snubbed out his cigar, carefully placing it in his pocket.

"Pronto!" said the captain.

Ella hadn't seen the impending disaster of damaged rigging and a dumped load. Only Rich had, saving them from a night of searching the seas for lost bales.

The captain stayed on deck, standing guard. The men dropped the netted load back onto the deck and laid down their guns. Picking up bales with the strength of men who had done a lifetime of manual labor, they aimlessly tossed them onto *Merlin's* deck as if they were cheap bags of cotton.

"Shit," Burke yelled.

"Shut up," said Rich. "Ella, get ready below."

More bales flew across, landing with a thud on the deck and tumbling precariously close to the edge. Carlos caught one from falling off the stern and shouted in Spanish at the trawler's crew. Another landed in the companionway, close enough to Ella to make her wonder if they were aiming for her. The load was already bought and paid for. If one went over the side, it would be Falco's, and his investor's, loss.

"Adiós, pequeño conejo," the thin man laughed and the other joined in, amused by *Merlin's* crew scrambling to keep the bales on deck.

Ella was relieved to be below. She grabbed the bales the men tossed down and muscled them to the side. When the bales stopped coming, she stood on the lower step, barely visible, watching the man in charge. He seemed more threatening than the other two; it probably wouldn't take much for him to use his gun. He carried his authority like a club—just like Falco. When the last bale landed on *Merlin's* deck, the leader waited for his crew to retrieve their guns before returning to the pilothouse. The trawler's diesel coughed and choked when it engaged, spewing a cloud of white smoke as it pulled away, obscuring their departure. Then the trawler was gone, disappearing into the darkness like the ghost ship it was.

"Are they always so careless?" Ella shivered in relief, watching them go.

"Just the deck hands," said Rich.

"They probably been sampling the product," said Carlos.

"The pilot had it under control," Rich said. "I have no doubt that if a bale had landed in the water, he would have pushed one of his men over the side to retrieve it."

Burke stared after the trawler. "White smoke means water in fuel. Don't understand why use boat with cracked head."

"I don't know," Rich said. "Let's get these packed away and get the hell out of here." He held the binoculars, taking a long look at the sea, and then set a course toward the Cay Sal Lighthouse until they were ready to hoist the sails.

Ella joined Carlos and Burke below to double bag and tape the bales, preventing the powerful marijuana scent from permeating the interior. The heavy fragrance hung in the air like a thick fog. Ella covered her mouth, breathing into her hand while she opened ports and hatches to let in fresh air before helping. Jockeying forty-pound bales around was strenuous work and she put her back into it, keeping up with Carlos and Burke.

"Ella, now you buy restaurant." Burke pocketed a bud from a split in the bale before he sleeved it. "And Carlos be hero to family."

Ella smiled over at Carlos, but he had turned away. "And Burke, now you can be powerful," said Ella.

"Already powerful." Burke pulled out his rolling papers to make a joint.

Carlos stopped to watch Burke, and a flicker of disgust crossed his face. Ella thought he was about to stop him but Carlos just turned back to the bale he was taping.

"Carlos, Rich said this is his last trip," said Ella. "Is it yours as well?"

"Maybe last for him," Burke said. "There are other runs, other captains."

"What about you, Carlos? Do you have another trip planned?"

"Let's finish this job before we start talking about another," Carlos said.

"Why you want to know?" said Burke.

"I'd be interested in going again. Aside from the men with machine guns throwing forty pound bales at you, it's not that different than a boat delivery." Her words surprised her. What had happened to "just this once"?

"Stop talking and get the rest of these bagged," said Carlos.

Ella looked up from taping a bale. Carlos's sharp words cut into her sense of relief, reminding her of the urgency of their task, which was both criminal and dangerous. Be careful, she thought. Do something once and you're just a visitor; twice, and you start to become it—a smuggler. She kept her mouth shut and worked faster until all the bales were bagged.

"Take the wheel, Ella," Rich ordered when she came on deck. "Keep her on a two-seventy heading so we'll clear the rocks."

Ella took the helm. The wind on her face was calming, but they were only halfway there: they still had had sixty nautical miles between them and Marathon Key. She stood as lookout on the cockpit seat, holding onto the shroud, steering *Merlin* with her foot and listening to the men below. They grunted under the task of pressing bales into the berths and any storage locker they would fit, banging their heads and straining their already tired muscles. Rich worked in silence while Burke cursed in Serbian and Carlos in Spanish.

She thought of the men on the trawler heading back to Cuba and wondered how dangerous they really had been. Was she just lucky they'd had no reason to kill them? Or were they men from a poor country, proud like Carlos, returning home as successful providers for their families? She pictured the Cuban's gnarly face lit by his lighter, the metallic tooth gleaming behind a crooked smile. Could a man like that belong to anyone?

But Ella was intrigued by the third man, the force, the leader. What is it that makes someone powerful, she wondered. It was more than intelligence, more than physique or gender. Was he born with a drive to be in control of his world, or was it something he'd earned along the way from the hard choices he was willing to make?

Rich came on deck. "See anything?"

"Happily, nothing to report," said Ella. "The wind's picking up. We'll have a good sail back."

"Carlos, Burke, let's get the sails up," Rich said. "We'll change course once at Cay Sal Lighthouse to 305 degrees, aim for Marathon. The four-knot current will push us north to overshoot by a few miles. By daybreak, we can adjust our course to sail down the coast to Marathon. It'll look like we're coming from Miami."

"Fine by me," Carlos nodded.

"Keep alert, people," said Rich. "We're not out of it yet."

CHAPTER 21

Time slowed to a crawl on the darkest, longest night that Ella could remember. Bone-tired, she stretched out on the cockpit seat with her head against a folded cushion so she could watch the following sea. Her senses were dulled by lack of sleep, and she slipped into a kind of trance as she slid down the backside of the adrenalin rush from the encounter with the Cubans. She was drifting toward sleep, in the easy rhythm of sailing in moderate winds, when a faint mechanical sound made her sit up. Straining to hear past the laboring noises of the hull and rig, she turned her head, searching for the sound, and listened until she caught the familiar rhythmic drone.

"Do you hear that, Carlos?" Ella rose to her feet, steadying herself with a grip on the mainsheet. "Off the port beam." She pointed to the southwest. "It sounded like a motor." She looked hard, trying to draw a shape out of the night. "I can't see anything."

Carlos stood up at the helm, twisting away from the wind to listen. "I don't hear it." He looked south toward Cuba.

"I do," said Ella. "I'll get Rich and Burke."

"Burke's asleep. Rich is going over the charts." He pushed back the sleeve of his jacket and checked his watch. "We're changing course soon. Rich will be up in a minute."

172

Ella went to the transom and held onto the backstay, cupping her ear with her hand to catch the sound. "You can't hear that, Carlos?"

Carlos faced the stern and listened. "No. Wind can play tricks with your ears. Might be distant thunder. I've seen lightning flashes up ahead."

Ella turned toward the northern sky. She hadn't noticed lightning, just the pitch black. She peered into the void, unable to distinguish between sky and sea. She might as well have been blind. She raised her gaze higher off the water, worried that the wall of blackness was the hull of a massive freighter bearing down on them.

There it was again, clearer, a sound too high-pitched for a freighter. A worse fear overtook her: pirates were coming for their load, as they had for Davis's.

"It's not coming from the north, and it's not thunder," said Ella.

"Rich," Carlos pressed into the companionway and called down to where the captain sat hunched over the chart, "I'm not hearing it, but Ella says she hears an engine."

Rich looked up. "What?" He threw down his pencil and rushed up top. "What direction?"

"About nine o'clock, from Cay Sal Lighthouse," Ella pointed. "Can you hear it?"

Rich charged below, barely touching the steps, and checked the radar. A small echo trail had entered the edge of the display and was heading toward them.

"Burke. Get up! We've got company," Rich barked. "Carlos, get your gun."

"Already have it." He patted his holster.

Ella followed Rich, taking in shallow breaths as she went below. Despite their efforts, the skunky odor of marijuana hung in the air. If it were the Coast Guard, they'd smell it right away. She leaned over Rich and studied the radar screen. "Looks like they're coming right at us."

"And fast," said Rich. "Get your gun, Ella. Make sure it's loaded. Burke!"

Burke opened his cabin door in crumpled clothes, squinting with sleep. "What's up, man?"

"Trouble. We've got a boat coming at us." Rich pushed past on his way back up top. "Carlos, let's tack and see if they follow. Ella, watch the radar," Rich shouted over his shoulder. "I want to know if they change course. Burke, get your ass up here. And bring the rifles!"

Burke raced up on Rich's heels, grabbing the rifles and ammunition out of the locker as he passed.

"Helm's alee!" Carlos shouted, passing *Merlin's* nose through the wind, putting her on a heading back to Dog Rocks. Rich and Burke worked the sheets, setting the sails for a beam reach.

"Ella, what do you see?" yelled Rich.

"They're staying their course. Doesn't look like they're following us."

A sigh of relief passed through the crew.

The blip tacked. "They're changing course!" Ella screamed. "They're tracking us!"

"Pirates or Coast Guard?" said Burke.

"Don't know," said Rich. "At two in the morning, I'm betting pirates—FUCK!" He ran his hands through his hair and turned around, assessing the boat. "Turn off all lights, including the running lights. Carlos, head her up to forty degrees. Burke, man the genoa."

Ella stayed glued to the radar screen, trembling, her eyes filling with tears. *This can't be happening.* "I think we should head downwind," she screamed. "They cut the corner. They're gaining on us."

"Start the engine, boss. Give us more speed," said Burke.

174

"Right. Full throttle, Carlos." Rich dropped below. The radar screen showed the afterglow of the boat's trail as they turned to keep up with *Merlin*.

"Carlos, put her on a heading of one-forty. It's a faster point of sail, angles us away from them." Rich watched the boat's delayed reaction on the radar, mimicking their moves. "They definitely have radar."

"We're never going to outrun them," said Ella.

"I know," said Rich. "Everyone armed?"

Burke lifted his shirt to show his Glock. Ella ran to her cabin and grabbed her 9mm, releasing the magazine to check it. This time she knew it was fully loaded. She slapped the magazine back in with the palm of her hand, sending a jolt of fear through her, knowing she was probably going to use it. She pulled back the slide to load a bullet into the chamber and shoved the gun in her pocket. Stark reality fired her with a new sense of purpose. She wanted nothing more than to do her part and not let the others down.

She heard Rich call to take down the sails: they must be getting close. She felt her resolve begin to slip; she couldn't breath. A fleeting thought of crawling into the storage space under her bunk passed through her mind, but she pushed it away, pulled on her watch cap and raced on deck.

"Ella. You've got the helm," said Rich.

"Heading up!" Ella called out as she brought the nose of the boat into the wind.

With the men in position, Carlos released the halyards. They grabbed the flapping mainsail by fistfuls, yanking it down at breakneck speed and bunching it into heaps between the lazy jacks while Burke furled the genoa.

"Clear the deck!" Rich commanded. The men quickly coiled the lines and threw the cushions below.

"Think it's the Coast Guard?" said Ella.

"No. They'd have announced themselves by now," said Rich.

Ella faced south toward the sound of the approaching boat and slipped her hand into her pocket, gripping the cold metal of the gun, trying to suppress the panic running through her and anxiously scanning the pitch black sea. The racing engine grew louder as it gained on them, and her pounding heart kept time. Davis flashed in her mind, sinking hundreds of feet into a dark watery grave. Oh God, please, she prayed, not me too.

"Fucking hell, we're sitting ducks on this boat," said Rich.

His apparent fear heightened Ella's. Did they stand a chance against pirates? How many were coming? How well armed?

"What are we going to do, Rich?" said Ella.

Rich stopped, looking over his crew. "I say fight. As I see it, it's fight or surrender the load, and I'm not willing to give it up. A lot of fucking money's at stake here."

"Our lives are at stake," snapped Carlos. "If we fight, they won't think twice about killing us."

"We get them onboard, then we fight." Burke looked at Rich. "Okay with that?"

Rich turned to Ella. "How about it, Ella?"

"Are they're going to kill us?" She caught her breath. "How good are you guys?"

"Depends how many there are," said Rich. "We'll need you to cover us. Can we count on you to use your weapon?"

"I'll do what I have to," said Ella. "Either way, we're fucked. We might as well put up a fight."

"There's a better chance we'll survive if we don't," said Carlos. "I have a family."

Ella shivered in fear, listening to Rich, watching the anger grow on his face as the sound of the boat grew closer.

"We all have reason to live, Carlos," said Rich. "And we'll damn well fight for it."

"In war, always be first to fire," said Burke. "If we surrender they kill us anyway."

Ella nodded, trying to get a grip on the terror shooting through her.

"Fight it is," said Rich. "Unless of course it's the Coast Guard, then we're screwed." Everyone looked at Rich, then out across the water.

"Let's move," Rich ordered. "Burke, check the rifles. Make sure they're fully loaded. Carlos, get the tender's paddles out; might come in handy." Rich threw open the lazarette, pulling out a hunk of chain and a boat hook. "Wish I had a bat."

"I'll take one of these AK-47," said Burke.

Rich tossed him an extra magazine, stuffed one in his back pocket and dropped below, kicking cushions aside on his way to check the radar. Rushing back on deck, he braced himself, fixing his eyes on the spot where he expected the boat to break through the night. "We should be able to see them soon. The radar has them right off our port beam. Weapons ready, everyone."

"What if we tie off the boom to starboard?" said Ella. "Force them to come at us portside. At least we'd have some control."

"Ella, you think like soldier," said Burke, pulling the boom over and securing it. Carlos joined Burke in tugging down the sail to create a block.

"Why do we have to let them board?" cried Ella.

"Pretend to surrender," said Burke.

"So they don't pick us off like fish in a bucket," said Carlos. "Powerboat can out maneuver us."

"I'll take the wheel. Carlos, get behind the mast," Rich ordered, "Burke, behind the sail and lie absolutely flat, don't let anything show above the gunwale. I don't want them seeing you until they're on deck."

"I can't see through sail."

"I'll call to you when it's time. Ella, cover us from below."

"Just don't shoot me," said Burke.

"You loaded?" Rich asked her.

Ella tapped her pocket. "All sixteen bullets and some spares."

"Okay. Keep it ready," Rich said. "We all need to watch each other's backs."

"Be careful, Rich," said Ella. "You'll be the only one out in the open."

Ella looked up at the sky. Dawn was still an hour away. Would the moonless night work to their advantage? She dropped below, searching for anything she could use as a weapon, and pulled out the galley knives and the flat-bottomed skillet. Unhooking the fire extinguisher, she put it in the sink to use as a club.

All that was left to do was wait—the hunted, waiting for the predator to strike. She stood with one fist clenched and the other gripping the gun, glaring at the bales tucked into the salon's berth. This is what we're risking our lives for, she thought.

She took a step up the companionway. "Rich, I'd be willing to throw over a couple of bales—when they get close enough to see."

"Won't be enough. If they know where we are, they know how much we've got."

"Rich right," said Burke. "We fight for whole load."

Ella turned to look at Carlos standing by the mast with an AK-47 hanging off his shoulder. She watched him pull the 9mm Ruger from his hip holster, check its chamber, then tap his knife to be sure it was there. She felt for her father's knife, then the gun in her pocket. She could think of no way out of what was about to happen. Her racing heart made her feel dizzy and panic caught in her throat.

"Can't see anything. Fucking black like hell." Burke grabbed the binoculars from the companionway and scanned the sea off the port side.

Ella checked the radar screen. "We should see them by now," she called out.

"Over there!" Burke shouted. "Five o'clock."

Ella ran to the steps, a rush of fear shooting through her as she saw the emerging shape of a boat.

Rich grabbed the binoculars. "Shit! Fucking pirates, coming straight at us and fast. Stay cool, remember, we want them onboard."

Carlos looked at Burke and hissed, "Listen to Rich—stay cool."

"Burke, get down. Everyone in position," said Rich. "Don't get knocked overboard. Chances are you won't make it back on."

Out of the blackness, the deep V of the sport fisher's bow sliced through the water, kicking up a bow wave as it roared at them.

Ella crouched on the top step. "Looks like the boat we saw behind Dog Rocks. Vultures. They've been waiting for us to pick up the load."

"Get below, Ella. I don't want them to see you." Rich turned back toward the boat. "Hang on."

The sport fisher came at them wide, circling *Merlin* and throwing wake on top of wave. *Merlin* rolled and rocked, and everyone fought to keep their footing. Ella wedged herself by a porthole, trying to glimpse the boat as it sped past. She counted four pirates: one at the wheel, and three holding machine guns leveled at *Merlin*. The tallest one, wearing a red headband tied over his ski mask, braced against the transom and fired a burst of warning shots into the air. Now they were coming straight at them, full bore. Ella tried to brace herself. At the last instant, they turned sharply to smack flat into *Merlin's* topsides.

The explosive impact knocked Ella off her feet, throwing her against the salon table. A sharp pain shot through her side as she struggled to regain her footing. She hung onto the companionway runners and peered out to see Rich still at the helm.

The sport fisher turned, coming back to plow into *Merlin* once again, ricocheting off her topsides like a massive bumper car. The man with the headband stood on the bow, ready to board, along with another man whose red dreadlocks fluttered in the wind like flames shooting from under the baseball cap pulled low over his face.

179

Rich turned the wheel hard to starboard and shoved the engine to full throttle, pivoting *Merlin's* transom off the powerboat and sending its bow further away, trying to force them to board amidships.

The pirates circled aft of *Merlin,* coming around her portside and shining a blinding high-beam spotlight across her deck, momentarily catching Ella before she could duck below.

Burke came up from behind the boom and raised his gun, taking aim at the light.

"Burke, stay down, damn it," Rich hollered.

"They'll fucking kill us!" The spotlight lit up Burke's face. His eyes looked wild; it wasn't hard to believe he had taken lives before to save his own. He tried to steady himself against the boom, then took the shot. He missed the light, but hit the pirate holding it. The man fell to the deck crying out in Spanish and dropping the light. It rolled along the deck, its beam sweeping over the pirate boat and into the sky like an errant searchlight.

Ella rushed to the porthole, straining to see, and caught a glimpse of the helmsman. He wore no mask and in a brief instant as the light passed over him, she saw that he was white and shorter than the others.

A gunman on the fly bridge retaliated with a spray of bullets, throwing Burke back with a slug to his left shoulder. Rich dove for the cockpit well and Carlos pulled back behind the mast while Ella watched from below. She could see the masked gunman dressed in black with a triple magazine bandolier crisscrossing his chest.

The sport fisher turned off and sped away into the dark night.

"Burke, how bad you hit?" Rich rushed to his side.

"Shoulder. Hurts like shit."

Ella grabbed a towel from the galley. "Burke, here!"

Burke stuffed it under his shirt and pressed hard to slow the bleeding.

"They're coming back!" Rich yelled. "Everyone get down and hang on. Carlos, it's up to you and me. You take the bow. I'll take mid-ship."

Without a helmsman *Merlin* pitched violently in the waves and the crew struggled to keep their balance.

"I can fight," said Burke. "Not first time I shot."

"I'll fight," said Ella.

"Stay down, Ella. Wait until it's time," Rich commanded. "You hear me?"

"How will I know?"

"You'll know."

The pirates came back at *Merlin* with wild screams and thundering guns, smacking once more into her topsides. Burke was thrown to the deck. Rich gripped a hunk of chain in his left hand and the boat hook in the other as he braced against the boom. Carlos stood hugging the mast.

"My God, are they trying to sink us?" Ella cried.

The helmsman threw the engines in reverse and the boat hovered aside *Merlin*. The tall pirate in the headband stared down from the fly bridge with his rifle trained on Rich.

"Drop your weapons and we let you live." His voice was raspy, with a thick Spanish accent. He sprayed another burst of bullets into the night above *Merlin*.

Ella tucked back into the galley, covering her ears at the loud cracking of gunfire. The helmsman revved his engines and pushed against *Merlin*.

"Pronto, amigos. You out-gunned. Out-powered, too," he laughed.

Carlos dropped the AK-47, pulled his Ruger from his holster and slowly laid it on the deck.

"Smart, amigo. Now you." He motioned his gun at Rich and Burke.

Rich let the chain fall from his hand and tossed down the boat hook.

"Do as they say," Rich whispered to Burke. "We need to get them onboard."

"No time to be stupid," ordered the pirate. "Or you want your mast full of holes? Maybe I chop it down with my machine gun."

Ella could see Rich and Burke from where she hid. She heard the dull thud of Burke's Glock hit the deck and watched as Rich lifted his shirt to show he was unarmed. His Walther was still in his pocket, but it was no match for the machine guns pointed at him. Was this it? Were they surrendering? Ella wiped the sweat from her palm and clenched the gun.

The helmsman gunned the sport fisher into *Merlin's* hull, pushing her to take the waves on her beam and causing her to rock. The wounded man with the dreadlocks leaned against the fishing boat's cabin, rifle held ready to fire. The pirate in black dropped his rifle and pulled out a pistol, then he and the man in the headband jumped onto *Merlin's* bow.

Crouching below, Ella followed their footsteps across the deck, deep pounding sounds like a war drum, as they moved toward Carlos. The forward hatch was still open and she hurried to close it, scrambling over the pile of cushions. She was too late. The men rushed Carlos.

She raised her gun to shoot, but what happened next came too quickly. The pirate in the headband landed a powerful uppercut and Carlos crumpled to the deck, unconscious. The one in black moved toward the hatch, and she backed into the head and peered around the corner. When he poked his head below, she pulled back. As they rushed the cockpit, she slipped out of hiding and edged toward the companionway.

The pirates came at Rich and Burke. With the speed of a serpent's strike, Burke kicked the pirate with the headband, slinging his good arm around the man's neck in a chokehold. Rich dove at

182

the man in black, throwing him to the deck and sending his gun skittering across the cockpit. He was slighter in build than Rich, but moved with the agility of a practiced fighter.

Ella lifted her gun and peered down the sights but couldn't get a clear shot. She stood rigid, listening to the bangs and crashes as Rich and Burke fought the pirates, unable to see who was winning. Waves cracked the boats together and the wind slapped at the loose rigging, snapping it against the mast. Curses, smacks of flesh, thuds of bodies falling hard.

She ran to Carlos at the forward hatch. "Carlos, Carlos! Get up." Carlos rolled to his side—dazed, he reached for his Beretta, and began firing on the pirate boat. The pirate at its helm fired back, spraying the foredeck and pinning Carlos behind *Merlin's* cabin top.

"Oh, fuck!" She looked back at the companionway. She had to act now.

Stuffing her gun into her pants, she dropped to the cabin sole and crawled toward the companionway. She pulled the gun out and sat trembling, holding it with both hands. It might be possible to shoot one of them, she thought, but would she be quick enough to shoot the other without getting shot?

She slid along the cabin's bulkhead and looked out the porthole. The helmsman on the sport fisher looked dwarfed by the machine gun he held, but he was in command of his weapon, spraying another round of bullets at Carlos, keeping him pinned down. The pirates were overtaking them.

Ella crept toward the edge of the companionway, trying to see around the corner. Burke fought wildly with his feet. His blood-soaked arm hung limp at his side, his good hand held tight to the backstay as he delivered a kick to the pirate's chest, sending him reeling backward. He came at Burke again, and this time Burke landed a one-two kick to the thigh and stomach of his opponent, knocking the man down. She watched as Rich took a heavy blow, knocking him off his balance. He stumbled to the edge of the boat.

"Alto!" the man aboard the sport fisher shouted, firing off a rapid round from his machine gun, the bullets pinging as they ricocheted off the mast. "Alto!"

Burke gripped the backstay, waiting for his opponent to get up. Ella could see he was struggling. In a moment it might be too late, they could be overtaken and all killed. Rich slipped his hand into his pocket, trying for his gun. The pirate saw it, too, and slugged him to the deck. The gun fell from Rich's pocket and slid out of reach as he suffered another blow.

Ella shoved her gun in her pocket and flipped on the binnacle light, dimly illuminating the cockpit, enough for her to see. She rushed on deck, grabbed the boat hook and swung it like a club at the pirate, striking him across the back. He fell off Rich and into the cockpit well. She stood over him ready to strike again.

"Alto! Ahora!" Another burst of gunfire ripped into the night. Ella ducked, grabbing a look at the gunman. His cap was missing and his dreadlocks flailed in the wind—a wild, modern-day Blackbeard. Ella knew he wouldn't be able to get a clear shot and guessed he wouldn't try. She looked down at the assailant. His black ski mask was twisted, covering his eyes. He jerked it around to where he could see, exposing his fierce, frightening eyes. She raised the boat hook once more, bringing it down hard across his chest as he tried to get up. The masked man writhed in pain and grabbed hold of the boat hook, twisting it out of her hands. Ella watched in horror as his free hand pulled out a gun. She took a step back.

Rich made a lunge for his Walther, but the boat took another hard wave and it slid further away. The masked man swung his gun at Rich, then at Ella as he got to his feet. He fired at Rich and missed.

"Like hell!" Ella ripped the gun from her pocket and fired. Her bullet struck him in the side, throwing him to the deck.

"Ella!" the pirate screamed.

She stepped back from the man clenched in pain at her feet. *How did he know my name?*

"TIO!" The helmsman on the sport fisher fired into the air, then took aim at *Merlin* and fired again, missing Ella.

Ella pointed her gun at the wounded man's head. "Drop your weapon or I'll fucking finish off your Tío!"

Carlos crawled along the cabin's side to help Burke. Before he got there, the pirate slugged Burke to his knees and fired on Ella.

"Ella!" Rich tackled her from the side, taking the shot across his back.

Carlos knocked the gun out of the pirate's hand, taking aim at his head, and forced him to the deck with a kick to the stomach.

"Now drop it, or I'll put a bullet in both your heads," screamed Carlos. The pirate at his feet sat up, raising his hands above his head. Burke scooped up his gun from the deck, holding him at gunpoint, and Rich grabbed the gun from the man Ella had shot.

Ella got to her feet. Holding her gun on the wounded man, she reached down and pulled off his mask. Stumbling back, she dropped her gun. "Oh God, what have I done?" *It was Davis.*

Breathing laboriously, Davis curled to his side, then onto his knees, gripping the cabin top and struggling to get up. Ella instinctively moved to help him, then stopped cold.

"You're supposed to be dead!"

"Don't shoot." Davis raised a hand to the helmsman on the sport fisher. "No dispares!" he repeated, but his voice faltered.

Stunned, Ella braced herself against the boom and stared at the blood oozing between Davis's fingers as he clasped his side.

"You fucking lying bastard. Why?" Backing away, she cried, "How could you?"

Davis tried to get up, slipping in his own blood.

"Paco." His voice was weak. The pirate moved to help him, lifting him up. Together they made their way out of the cockpit and toward the bow of the sport fisher.

Ella moved toward Davis, reaching out and touching his shoulder. He didn't turn to her touch but moved on, leaving her hand empty. She fought the urge to grab hold of him.

"Get him the fuck off my boat." Rich swiped up the assault rifle and held it on Davis and the tall pirate.

"Man, you one nasty prick," said Burke. "Piece of shit."

Davis slumped, hanging onto a stanchion, then turned to Ella and grabbed her arm, jerking her toward him.

"Rumi book I gave you." He spoke in a breathless rasp. "Look inside the cover, Ella. Please, I have a son. Help him."

She clutched his arm, unable to speak, then Davis pulled away, leaving a bloody handprint on her sleeve.

"Socorro." Davis raised his head slightly to Paco. The tall pirate lifted him back up.

"You cold bastard. None of it was real, was it?" Ella's voice shook with rage, making it difficult for her to speak. "I'm such a damn fool."

"Sácame de este barco," Davis hissed at Paco, his voice now barely audible.

"Was it you who killed Jon?" Ella shouted.

Davis turned slightly, bent over in pain, looking at no one.

"I didn't..." he slumped into the pirate's arms. The pirate braced him with his shoulder.

Ella roiled with anger. The man she had loved was a heartless stranger, a predator who hunted them down to steal their load.

"You're nothing but a murdering, low-life pirate—a fucking lying thief." Ella turned back for the gun she'd dropped and snapped it up. "Maybe I should just finish you off. Then I'd know you'd stay dead."

"Ella, NO!" Rich grabbed the gun out of her hand. "Don't even think about it. If Davis dies, we die."

Rich pointed his gun at the man who was tracking Ella from the sport fisher. "Throw your weapons over the side or we shoot your Tío. Now! And believe me, it won't be hard to do."

"It's over," Carlos shouted. "Está terminado!" He held his weapon on Davis and the pirate Paco. "Do as he says or Tio dies."

The men waited for a nod from Davis before tossing their rifles into the sea.

Ella turned away while the rest of *Merlin's* crew watched with guns trained on Davis and Paco as they struggled to board the sport fisher.

"Ayuda!" Paco shouted. The helmsman jumped down and together they hoisted Davis through the tangle of lifelines and guardrails. For a moment, it looked as if he might fall between the boats.

Ella turned her back. It would be easy to take pity on him, as you would a wounded animal trying to reach safety. But her face remained hard, and she never turned to see if he made it. The sport fisher backed away from *Merlin*, pivoted to point its bow southeast and took off.

The four of them stood, shot, bruised and stunned on *Merlin's* aft deck. Ella finally turned to watch, her chin jutted out in scorn, as the sport fisher retreated toward the lights of Havana and was swallowed by the night. The hum of the engine grew fainter until only the sound of the sea lapping against *Merlin's* hull remained.

CHAPTER 22

Merlin rolled in the waves in an aggravating motion without sails to steady her, or a helmsman to course her through. Ella grabbed for the wheel and it calmed her trembling hands. The anger in her was consuming and she needed to move. She threw the engine into gear, putting the boat back on course to Marathon, and getting them out of this hell as fast as she could. A fragment of sound from Davis's boat came off the port quarter, catching her ear and she turned, staring into the black void.

"How'd he know we were here?" she asked.

"I haven't figured that out," said Rich. "Not yet, anyway."

Burke clung to the backstay with his gun drawn, aiming at no one. At last, his knees buckled and he collapsed to the deck.

"We need to get Burke below," said Rich. "There's an IT Clamp in the first aid kit."

Ella tied off the helm and went below to the medicine cabinet. When she closed its door she saw her pain reflected in the mirror. She shut her eyes, dropped to sit on the toilet lid and started shaking and weeping, her lips quivering. "I hate you, you fucking cold bastard. I hate you, so deeply. I hate you." She rocked herself slowly until the heaving stopped and she sat staring blankly at the bulkhead.

"Ella!" Rich hollered. "Did you find the clamp?"

"Yeah." Ella shook her head and stood up. "Coming," she called, wiping her face with her sleeve.

"How's this thing work?" she said, handing Rich the clamp.

Rich ripped open the package and quickly clamped Burke's wound before he had time to protest.

"God! Fuckin' shit!" Burke cried in pain. "What fuck you do to me?"

"Oh," Ella winced. "That looked like it hurt."

"Stopping the blood flow so you won't bleed to death," said Rich.

"I have more holes," Burke groaned, referring to the piercing pins that held the clamp in place.

"Hang in there, Burke," Rich said. "We'll clean your wound as soon as we get the sails up. We need to be ready in case they come back."

Rich leaned into the cabin and checked the radar screen and then ordered Ella to head up so they could raise the sails. The crew was bruised inside and out, she thought. She could see Rich's bloody back through his torn shirt, Burke curled in pain; of the three men, only Carlos had come out of the attack unharmed.

"You no fuckin' help," Burke sneered at Carlos. "Maybe I slug you, see how easy you knock out."

"Sorry, boss," said Carlos. "He hit me square on."

"You were there when we needed you."

Rich reached over and held Ella's shoulder. "You okay at the wheel while Carlos and I go over the boat for damages?" He looked as though he wanted to say something more, but didn't, instead he gave her shoulder a squeeze.

Ella nodded. "It's where I prefer to be." What she most needed most right now was renewed courage to rise out of this hell, and sailing could give her that.

"Carlos," Rich called, "check the bilge and see if we're taking on water. I'll inspect the topsides."

Rich shined the spotlight on the hull. The deep fiberglass finish was gouged and a few worrisome cracks ran below the waterline. He examined the boom and the mast, searching for where bullets had struck. "Appears to be only superficial damage—nothing structural."

"Bilge is dry," Carlos reported.

"Can we please get out of here?" said Ella.

Rich and Carlos hoisted and set the sails, and *Merlin* was sailing again, heading strong along a course back to Marathon, bringing Ella some relief. She felt for the direction of the wind on her face, pulled in the mainsheet and adjusted the genoa to a balanced trim. Sailing brought her back to a world that made sense.

"Burke, let me take a look at your wound," said Carlos.

"NO! Ella, look after me," Burke said.

Ella nodded and handed the helm over to Carlos.

"We'll sail close-hauled," said Rich. "Carlos, point up as high as you can on a starboard tack. We've got a decent wind and with the speed of the Gulf current we'll make good time."

"Can we turn off stinkin' engine?" said Burke.

"After we get to the center of the Stream. We need to get out of here as fast as possible," said Rich.

"Do you think they'll come back?" said Ella.

"Don't know, but pirates aren't our only worry. There's the law. I want to be well positioned at daybreak. We don't want it to appear like we're coming from Cuba."

"Your Coast Guard friend won't be any help until we get close to Marathon," said Ella.

"That's right. We still need to worry about the stations in Key West and Miami."

Ella couldn't stop shivering. She rubbed her arms to calm her nerves and lifted her gaze to the sky. There was no end to danger until they were finally on land. She looked back at Cuba. Lights were coming on in the coastal villages as the fishermen, honest, hard-working men just like her father, got up before dawn to labor all day for their families.

"Let me look at your shoulder, Burke." Ella pulled back Burke's blood-soaked shirt. "Christ." In the grip of the IT Clamp, the flesh on his shoulder was shredded and a circle of purple bruised skin surrounded a deep, red-black hole. "Let's get you below. You can use my bunk. It's more comfortable."

"Finally, I get good bunk. No. I don't go below; make a bloody mess. I need fresh air, where I see everything." He lay back in the cockpit.

"You've got a point," Ella spoke softly. "I'll get some warm water to clean this up."

"You have tea bag?"

"You want tea?"

"No, teabag on wound will help stop bleeding. Has to be black."

"Is that a field dressing?" Ella opened the first aid kit; it was well stocked with painkillers and up-to-date antibiotics. "I think we've got enough of the real thing, Burke. Besides, it looks like the clamp is working."

Rich brought up cushions and blankets, tucking Burke in to keep him warm and elevating his shoulder. "You in much pain?" Rich asked.

"Roll me a joint, man."

"I can do that." Carlos looked over at Rich.

"Sure, man, you've earned it," Rich relented.

Rich propped Burke up and Ella pulled off his shirt. "It looks like the bullet went right through." She cleaned the wound gently. "Does this hurt?"

"Go ahead, has to be done."

"It needs to be stitched," said Ella.

"Falco can do that when we get to Marathon," said Rich.

Ella washed away the blood, rinsing the cloth in the pan until the water turned red.

"Are they still showing up on radar?" Ella lifted her head to Rich.

"They're on a heading of two hundred," he said. "That would take them to Matanzas. It's a lot closer than trying for Havana."

Ella looked back toward Cuba. "What if I killed him?"

Burke bent forward so Ella could clean the blood off his back. "Ella, I would have done same. More. Finish bastard off."

She wrung out the blood-soaked cloth. "But taking a life, any life —I can't live with that." She shook off her welling tears. "I aimed for his arm, I had the shot, but he moved, or the boat moved. I don't know. He'll probably die. Who knows what help he'll get, if it'll be soon enough."

"They attacked us, Ella, and if you hadn't shot him, we might all be dead." Rich stood watch on the cabin top. "Man, I never saw this one coming. Never took him for a pirate."

Carlos finished rolling the joint, lit it and handed it to Burke. "Here you go, man."

"Thanks." He inhaled a long drag and started to lie back down.

"Not yet, Burke. This may sting." Ella sprayed his wound with an antibacterial dressing.

"Ko ti sisa!" yelled Burke. "You kill me."

She stopped and pulled back.

"Sorry, Ella, I mean nothing. You a good woman."

Heaviness filled Ella's heart like cold lead and her body was going numb from her heart outward. She wrapped the gauze around Burke's shoulder, looped it under his arm and helped him lie down, tucking him in with all the gentleness she could muster.

"It's okay, Burke. We need to keep an eye on this. I think we should clean it again in a few hours."

"Maybe Davis had Jon killed," said Burke. "Did you put in tea bag?"

"I don't know about putting tea bags on a bullet wound. Besides, the clamp is working; the bleeding is slowing down.

"Ella," Rich said, "that wasn't the Davis we knew."

"Knew?" she said ruefully. "I saw what I wanted to see." A man she respected as much as her father. "He's not fooling anyone now."

Ella looked up at the sails. They were well trimmed, flat against the wind. "Do you think they intended to kill us all?" Only now had the thought occurred to her: Davis could have taken her life.

"I think they were willing," said Rich.

"His own friends? Me?"

"I don't think Davis was supposed to come onboard," said Carlos. "I think he was taking the place of the guy Burke shot."

"Oh, so he'd send one of his men to kill me?" She shot a look at him. "Not that it matters anymore."

"Davis couldn't have known you were onboard, Ella," said Rich.

"Their spotlight caught me. After the first impact I stuck my head above deck to see. It was just an instant, but I think they saw me." She turned to Burke. "You okay? You need anything?"

Holding a lung full of smoke, Burke shook his head.

"He needs water," said Rich. "He's bled a lot. He'll get dehydrated quickly."

Ella stood and took a sweeping look at the surrounding night, then went below.

"Check the radar while you're down there," said Rich.

"Already have. They're out of range, but there's a new trail coming from west-northwest. It's in the middle of the shipping lane."

"With one half-dead and one wounded, I doubt they'll be back," said Carlos.

"Keep a sharp eye," said Rich. "They put this game into play and that means they have people to disappoint. It's possible they have a backup crew."

Rich got up. His bloodstained shirt stuck to the skin where the bullet had grazed his back. He followed Ella below. "Could you look at this for me?"

193

"Sure."

"You okay?"

Ella nodded. "Will be." Her lips tightened. "I may have killed him, orphaned his son. Part of me hopes he dies, but that's not who I am. I didn't sign up for murder."

"Sooner or later, everyone in this business gets caught up in things they thought they'd never do. You saved my life—all of our lives."

Ella unbuttoned his shirt, pushing it back off his shoulders. Dried blood glued the fabric to his back.

"What a mess."

She gently inched his shirt free, let it drop and dabbed the wound with warm water. The bullet had ripped across the surface of his muscle. One instant of luck had saved him; a moment earlier, a slight turn, and he could have been shot through the heart.

"I'll need to clean it before I dress it."

She started to turn away, but Rich took her in his arms and pulled her in. His kiss carried the heat and power of surviving a battle, but Ella pulled away and out of his arms. "Let me clean this up for you. It's going to sting."

She dressed his wound, taking her time with gentle care and searching for something inside her as she worked, some part of her that could feel—but it wasn't there.

"Your face isn't in much better shape." She wiped the blood from the cuts and the split lip that was beginning to swell. "That shot was meant for me."

Rich nodded. "I'm just grateful it missed."

He paused at the companionway before going on deck. Ella had her back to him, putting away the first-aid kit. She turned to watch him leave. It felt like her heart had died, and all she could think was that it was too late. And that was okay for now. Anything was better than feeling.

*****

194

Burke lay stretched out on the cockpit seat, swathed in blankets, his head and shoulder elevated. Ella noticed the strained look on his face was only slightly eased by the joint he had smoked. The painkillers clearly hadn't kicked in yet.

"When I..." Ella paused. "When Davis was shot, one of the guys called out, 'Tío'. He said it twice. He was calling to Davis."

"Uncle," said Carlos.

"A family of smugglers?" said Rich. "Interesting."

"You spell it T-í-o?" asked Ella.

Carlos nodded.

"It's time to change course," said Rich. "Carlos, put her on a heading of fifteen degrees. We'll hold that until sunrise."

They were making good time in a moderate breeze and well positioned to ride the axis of the Gulf Stream. Ella looked up at a clearing in the clouds to see Polaris high off their bow, a beacon in the night. You could always count on Polaris to guide you, her father had told her; it's always there.

"Carlos, go ahead and cut the engine," said Rich.

The racket had strained Ella's already worn nerves, and it was a relief to hear only the sounds of the boat making her way under sail. Lightning in the north brought welcome respite from the dark. She sat upright in the cockpit, listening, and when she was satisfied that she heard nothing more than *Merlin* and the sea around them, she relaxed.

"We're doubling up on our watches until dawn," said Rich "I'll stand watch with Carlos. Burke, you're in sickbay. Ella, try and get some rest. You're on in two hours."

Without light, Ella had to feel her way along the cabin in uneven steps, the sole lifting, then falling away beneath her as *Merlin* rode the waves. With outstretched hands she followed along the edge of the salon table to the bulkhead that led to her cabin. Once inside, she tried to close the door but her jeans pocket caught on the door handle and a surge of rage coursed through her. She ripped free her pocket and slammed the door shut.

In the pitch black, the cabin felt smaller, the sides closer, the overhead lower. She reached for the bulkhead to steady herself and climbed into her bunk, then pulled the blanket over her head and closed her eyes, feeling the rhythm of the heeling boat as it plowed through the sea.

Two hours before her watch sleep wouldn't come; she hadn't expected it to. She lay listening to the deep groans of the hull and an occasional voice filtering through from on deck. Her heart felt crushed by hatred, and she seethed with anger at the betrayal from a man she thought she knew. Never again would she be so naive, she promised herself. Never, never again.

CHAPTER 23

In the faint light of predawn, Sam drove the sport fisher at full throttle across Nicholás Channel toward Archipiélago de Sabana— the hundreds of cays and islets scattered like pearls on Cuba's northern shore—to a cay on its outer reaches. Cayo Cruz del Padre was thirty miles south of Cay Sal Bank, a good hour's ride on rough seas.

"Think he'll make it, Paco?" Sam called down from the fly bridge. The tall, sinewy Cuban was cradling Davis in his arms, bracing against the motion of the boat. Davis's eyes were clenched in pain and his body, covered in blood, jerked with the pounding of the boat.

"He'll make it," said Paco. He gripped the handrail and wedged his body against Davis. "Hang in there, man, we're almost at Dr. Ts."

Sam turned to watch the breaking waves off their starboard quarter. The Gulf current was hitting them broadside, driving them closer to the shoals. He navigated the rolling swells while keeping an eye out for patrol boats. But at four in the morning, it was at once too early and too late for the Cuban and U.S. Coast Guard boats that cruised these waters along the international line, looking for drug smugglers and Balseros—the Cuban raft people—trying to escape.

197

Sam labored in the tight following seas, turning his head forward and aft, checking his position relative to the shoals and trying to gauge the waves that threatened to swamp the cockpit. He gunned the throttle and eased off again, working each wave as the boat dropped into the trough before climbing its way out. It was dangerous to run before the sea, but it was the fastest, most direct route, and Davis was running out of time.

Sam was running out of time, too. He needed to go back for Falco's load, this time leaving nothing to chance. He had buyers lined up, but most of all, he needed the money to get Nikki back.

The Cuban with the dreadlocks held tightly to the cockpit seat and struggled to keep his wounded leg up to slow the bleeding.

"Tomás," Paco shouted through the engine noise. He took off his headband and handed it over. "Tie it off with this. How bad is it?"

"It went clean through the side," said Tomás. "It'll be okay."

"I need to show Sam the inlet. Hang on to Davis." Paco slipped out from under Davis. "Keep him still."

"He's not looking so good."

"Don't say that, man. He can hear you," Paco snapped. "He's going to make it."

Tomás scooted into Paco's place, but the boat suddenly dropped in a trough, knocking him to the cockpit floor. Paco threw his leg up to block Davis from falling.

"Don't let him fall, man!"

Paco held onto Davis. Tomás fell again, slipping on the blood that pooled under his feet. He wrestled against the violent motion of the boat and into position to hold Davis.

"Keep talking to him," Paco urged.

"What should I say?"

"He's your uncle, man," said Paco. "Talk to him about his son, doesn't matter. He needs to stay awake."

Paco climbed up to the fly bridge. The pitching of the boat was more aggressive higher up, and he slid repeatedly on the wet metal steps.

"Is he still alive?" Sam asked, his hands clamping the wheel in a white-knuckled grip. He was soaked from the bow spray that came in sheets whenever they rammed the backside of a wave.

"Barely."

"How do we know the doctor's there?" Sam asked nervously.

"He's always there," Paco said, ducking a wall of spray. "That's his problem. He can't leave."

"Why not?"

"Shouldn't be much longer," Paco said, ignoring Sam's question. "There's the Cayo Cruz light on your left. See it?"

The seven-second light was a skeletal tower, a century-old lighthouse that marked the northernmost point of Cuba.

"Yeah. Ten o'clock."

"That's it. Keep it there."

"How come we didn't know Ella was onboard?" asked Sam. "Two months of planning—buyers are going to be pissed."

"We should've gone in shooting," said Paco. "You take someone's load, you fuckin' kill them. Davis went soft."

"We've got to go back."

Sam ducked quickly, giving his back to the slap of water coming over the bow. The salt was beginning to burn his eyes and crust on his jacket. "Drop off Davis and finish what we started. This time we won't be shooting AKs at the sky." Sam's voice was strained. "We don't have time to waste, man. We've got to act now."

"Pay attention," said Paco. "We'll talk later. It gets dangerous here."

Paco started down the steps. "Sam."

"Yeah," Sam shot a look over his shoulder.

"Next time you yell out my name on a hit," Paco said evenly, "I'll fucking shoot you."

199

"That wasn't me, it was Davis," said Sam, but Paco was gone.

As the sea floor rose, so did the height of the waves. They lifted the sport fisher and rolled beneath her. Sam muscled the boat, keeping her on course. He was used to the deep keel of a sailboat that didn't slip across the water's surface like a sled.

"Go faster," Tomás shouted up to Sam.

"Any faster and we'll bury the nose in the back of a wave."

"Just drive the fucking boat," said Paco.

"I don't think Tio can hear me anymore," said Tomás. "His eyes are staying closed."

Paco slid down the ladder from the fly bridge and shoved Tomás to the side. He applied pressure on the wound and Davis's eyes flickered like a light about to burn out. The bleeding was slowing— or maybe Davis was running out of blood—but it had been an hour since he was shot; that he was still alive meant the bullet had missed a vital organ.

"Davis, I'm here for you, man, like always." Paco held him in his arms. "You got to fight for your son; Topo needs you, man." Paco's eyes shone with an angry fire as he pleaded with Davis. "I know you're strong enough. Listen to me, man, we're almost there."

They were running on the eastward side of the reef where the height of the waves grew, rushing the sport fisher down the slope from the crest to the trough with increasing speed. Sam shot a look at Davis, checking he was secured, and opened the throttle, powering through a wave, frantically trying to keep the boat from yawing to one side and broaching.

"Over there!" Paco shouted, pointing to bleach bottles marking the entrance to the inlet. "Keep them on your portside, the shoals come out far here."

"Where's the searchlight?"

"It fell overboard when Tomás got shot."

"I can barely make out the inlet."

"Go slowly, man," said Paco. "After we pass this point it opens up, then fucking step on it."

Night gave way to dawn as they motored through the narrow channel that widened into calmer waters in the lee of the cay. Sam pushed the throttle wide open and planed the boat, its wake cutting a clear path across the inlet.

Streaks of light broke through the clouds lighting a solitary home recessed among the mangroves. Smoke drifted up from its stovepipe marking the doctor's thatched-roof house. It was as isolated from civilization as this cay was from the main island, and as Cuba was from the rest of the world. Paco pointed to an uneven wooden dock shored up by rocks, its railing made of driftwood. The whole of it listed toward the doctor's shiny new speedboat sitting at an angle, indicating it was on the hard.

"Put her on the other side, on the end," said Paco. "Dr. T. always docks his boat too close to shore. It's shallow, and the tide is going out."

A small, barefoot boy, about six years old, stood watching from the shore. His fists were shoved deep into his pockets, and the same curly mass of black hair as his father's hung to his shoulders.

Paco looked down at Davis. "Your son is here, Davis. Topo's come to greet you."

Davis's eyes opened slightly and he strained to look at Paco.

"Don't call him Topo." It was the first Davis had spoken since the shooting. His words came out coarse and faint. "Nicholás, after his grandfather."

"You got it, man," Paco smiled.

Sam pulled back the throttle on his approach and the boat surfed in on its own wake. A dim shape of a woman, followed by a hunched dog, came down the rickety dock that swayed with their every step. She greeted them with a broad wave and the shawl she clutched slipped off her shoulders, revealing her long, black hair. She had the golden skin and broad features of the Taino Indians, descendants of Amazon Basin tribes. She stopped at the end of the dock and the dog settled at her feet.

Sam threw the engine in reverse as they reached the dock, slowing the boat's forward motion.

"Paco, what is wrong that you come so quickly?" the woman called.

"It's Davis. He's been shot," Paco said looking toward the boy, who had started down the dock.

She turned back to the boy, "Topo, I need you to stay there."

She boarded the boat before it had come to a full stop. A woman of fifty-some years, she had the poise of a priestess.

"Shot where?"

"Near his stomach," said Paco. "Is Sully awake?"

"No. He still sleeps."

"It's bad, Siani." Paco's voice was low. "We need Sully, now!"

"How long have his eyes been closed?" she asked.

"Since we passed the lighthouse," said Tomás.

"Davis, it's Siani." She leaned over him until her face was close to his mouth. "He still breathes, but his exhale is longer than his breath in. We need to hurry. Paco, run, wake Sully. We'll bring Davis in."

"Tomás got hit, too," said Paco. "I'll carry Davis."

Siani turned to look at Sam. "Who do you bring with you?"

"Sam. I'm a friend of Davis," said Sam.

"You have to stop bringing us trouble, Paco." Siani held a hard, wary gaze on Sam.

"We don't have time for that." Paco looked down at Davis. "He's is in danger, Siani. Tomás, go wake Sully. Hurry. Sam, help me with Davis."

"He is upstairs," said Siani. "Topo, go with him. Tell Sully your papa has been hurt."

"Papa?" Topo started down the dock.

"Topo, you must go now. Run, wake Sully." Siani's harsh tone sent him running toward the house, Tomás limping behind.

*****

Topo had already reached the sleeping loft by the time Tomás came clumping up the stairs. Sully sat bolt upright in bed. His grey hair, wild and coming loose from his ponytail, stood out like straw to the sides. He pulled out a pistol from under his pillow and aimed at Tomás.

"Hands up, you little fuck."

"Don't shoot, Sully. It's me, Tomás."

Sully reached to the side table for his glasses and put them on, all the while keeping his aim on Tomás. "What the hell are you doing here?"

"It's Papa!" Topo was at the bedside tugging Sully's arm.

"Alright, Topo. Stop pulling on me." Sully pried his small fingers from his arm.

"Siani says Papa's hurt."

"Go see to your dad, Topo. Go!" Sully's voice, a smooth baritone, back when he was a surgeon practicing in Boston, had been etched raw by years of hard liquor and tobacco.

Topo stood at the top of the stairs, watching Sully scoot himself out of bed.

"Go." Sully waved the gun at him, sending him running down the stairs.

"You need to hurry," said Tomás.

"There is nothing I *need* to do, Tomás. What's wrong with him?"

"Gun shot." Tomás was becoming agitated. "Please, Sully, it looks pretty bad."

"No such thing as a good-looking gunshot wound."

"I'll get you some coffee."

Downstairs, Paco and Sam carried pails of water from the cistern to the fire grate outside. Siani sat on the floor next to Davis cradling his wrists in her lap, trying first one and then the other, her eyes closed as her fingers searched for his pulse.

"His liver and kidneys are weak. His heart is tired." She gently brushed his hair to the side. "You have really hurt yourself this time. Just stay with us, Davis. We are helping you."

On the veranda, herbs hung drying from the overhead beams in an array of green, gold and deep red tones, herbs that had helped heal the numerous people who came to Siani. She passed her hands over the different plants, choosing and crumbling leaves between her fingers, smelling for the aroma that would signal the right blend.

"Topo, come here." The boy moved quickly, eager to help, and grabbed the bowl and pestle from her hands. "Gently crush these herbs into a fine powder." She turned to Tomás. "Did you give Davis anything to drink?"

"No. Didn't think of it."

"Good."

Sully walked down from the upper floor in heavy steps, wearing only the khakis that he had slept in. His old, wrinkled face stood in contrast to the smooth, tanned belly that hung over the top of his pants. His watery blue eyes, set in a field of pink, suggested the torments and conflicts of a compromised life. Long ago he had been a respected American neurosurgeon. Now the cartel claimed what was left, making him one of theirs and nicknaming him "El Sastre," The Tailor.

He walked barefoot over to the table with labored breath, picked up the gnawed butt of a hundred-dollar Cohiba Behike with the gold profile of a Taino sorcerer on its band and struck a match to it. From the looks of the mostly full box of cigars and a crystal decanter of Maxima rum, the cartel had just paid a visit.

"Where's my coffee?" Sully grumbled.

"Tea brewing," Siani motioned to the open kitchen. "It is better to clear your head."

"I want coffee, damn it." Sully exhaled and peered through a cloud of cigar smoke at his wife sitting next to Davis. "How is he?"

Siani wiped the sweat from Davis forehead. "His skin is cool to the touch. He's gone into shock," said Siani. "I am preparing herbs. You need to get ready."

Sully took the cup of tea Tomás had been trying to hand him and sat down, staring at Davis from across the room.

"Qué hubo, Sully? Help him," yelled Paco. "He's dying."

"He shouldn't have gotten himself shot. No wonder he's dying."

"His son can hear what you say," said Siani.

"Siani," Paco pleaded.

"Sullivan." Siani said impatiently. "Topo needs his father."

"Why? He's never around. He's already abandoned the boy." Sully didn't look like he was about to help anyone.

"Davis is like a son to me." Siani rose and stood over Sully, her voice pressing down on him with all her force. "Go wash up. I'll make you something stronger to drink. Hurry, Sully."

"You fix him," Sully said, unwilling to budge.

"Sully! I am not a great surgeon like you. I will clean up the poison in his body. But first you have to sew him back together. Please hurry, we can't bring him back from the dead."

Siani watched him leave the room. The sad resignation on her face made it clear that she had been with him long enough to watch the man she loved and admired slowly destroy himself.

"How long has it been since he used his knives?" asked Paco.

"Bailey!" Sully bellowed from the sleeping loft. "I removed a tumor on his neck. "

Sam had been pacing in the background with his hands shoved deep into his pockets. He stopped to listen.

"He's been bleating about it ever since," Sully laughed.

"Their goat," Paco said to Sam.

"A goat? This is a lot more serious than a fucking goat."

"Unless you only have one goat," said Tomás.

205

"Quickly, help me prepare the table for Davis." Siani removed the strips of palm fronds and a basket she had been weaving, while Sam cleared Sully's side of the table, tossing off the ashtrays, liquor bottles, soiled glasses, and a stack of novels bookmarked at various points of lost interest. Once the table was cleared, Siani laid down a plastic tarp to protect it and, over that, a clean sheet.

Siani had added her mix of herbs to the steaming water and their green medicinal aroma filled the room. She leaned over the simmering pot with eyes closed, taking the measure of the brew as she fanned the scent toward her. She picked a handful of dark red leaves and crushed them between her fingers into a powder, adding them to the pot. When she was satisfied with the aroma, she dropped Sully's instruments in for a moment to sterilize them, then added patches of cloth to absorb the medicine. After a few minutes she picked the cloths out, placing them in a bowl to sit until they were cool enough to lay over Davis's wound.

Sully came back down the steps in the same rumpled pants, wearing the top of tattered green scrubs. He sat off to the side drinking his tea and watched his wife and the men lay Davis on the table. Finally, he stood, his brow beaded in sweat, and poured a healthy splash of rum into his tea.

"Tie him down. Use a sheet. I don't want him moving when I'm mucking around in his guts. God, I hate a gut wound."

Sam watched Sully pull a vial of morphine from the cold box. It looked like he had plenty, another indication of the cartel's influence.

"Tomás, get another lantern over the table. I can't see shit." The rum had revived Sully and he began barking orders. "The rest of you, get the hell out."

Sam followed the others outside to wait in the shade of the palm trees.

"Stay close, Paco, I may need you," Sully called after them. "Take Barney with you."

At the mention of his name, the dog got up and followed the men outside.

Sully studied the wound and looked over at Siani washing her hands. "We'll have to go digging for the fuckin' bullet."

"His body is weaker than last time," Siani whispered. "He is getting too old for this kind of life." She leaned over Davis and kissed him lightly on the forehead. "You are strong, Davis. You will make it through."

"This wound is worse." Sully drew the morphine into a syringe. "Much worse."

*****

Paco sat stretched out on the chaise lounge, his bony arms crossed behind his head. His long, skinny body looked accustomed to missing meals. Barney settled by his side with a deep sigh.

Sam took a seat next to Paco. "Now's the time, man. We need to go. We've gotta go back out there before they get too far away. Davis can't help us now."

"Watch what you say," said Paco. "Nicholás, come sit by me."

Topo stood watching his father through the screen.

"Topo!" Paco called out. "Topo, come sit with me."

Topo stood, shaking his head.

"You know Topo means gopher?" said Paco. "Sully gave you that name."

"What's a gopher?" asked Topo.

"A little furry animal that lives under the ground."

Topo shrugged his shoulders.

"Tomorrow we start calling you Nicholás, like your papa wants, the name of your grandfather. Today you are still Topo." Paco took hold of the boy's arm and sat him down next to him. "We'll wait." He turned to Sam. "He'll make it."

"Even if he makes it, he won't be in any shape and we need to move, now." Sam shot a quick look at Topo. "Better for the kid; he'd have Davis's cut."

"We wait." Paco spoke in a brusque finality, his voice raspy from fatigue.

Sam leaned over and scooped a handful of sand, letting it sift through his fingers, and then tossed the remaining grains aside. "What's Sully doing in a place like this?"

"He was big-time surgeon in the states," said Tomás. "Killed someone important on the operating table, long time ago. Pissed the family off. Now he's the cartel's doc, El Sastre."

"Tomás, if you want to keep that reckless tongue in your head, shut the fuck up," Paco hissed.

"He already knows, man." Tomás took a long drag off his joint and offered it to Paco.

"Don't smoke that shit around the kid," said Paco.

Sam reached for it, then declined.

Paco turned to Sam, his deep-set eyes staring out over the high cheekbones of his worn face. "You forget about this place. Once we leave, it never existed. You straight on that?"

"Believe me, I wish I'd never seen it. Only reason I'm here is because everything's gone to shit."

*****

It had been well over an hour since Sully and Siani had begun working on Davis. The roosters had started their morning racket, greeting the rising sun. The dog got up, stretched its back and went out to see what the roosters were crowing about. Sam stood up and began to pace. Topo got up and went to the doorway to check on his father.

Paco sat up in his chair, watching Sam with the sharp, appraising eye of an animal. The poverty of Jamaica had taught Paco survival skills that ruled out nothing and showed in the deep anger of his hardened face, framed by his wiry Medusa hair. He studied Sam, a man of white privilege.

"It's only because of Davis that you are here," said Paco.

Tomás sat on one chair, his foot propped up on another. He had cleaned his wound and was now wrapping it with a strip of cloth. He straightened up and looked at Paco, then at Sam. Something had changed.

"We should go now," said Sam. "They're sailing, maybe at six knots, my boat goes four times that speed. We can still catch them."

"No. Not going to happen." Paco's tone had chilled. He slumped back in his chair, lacing his fingers together across his stomach, and trained his deep-set eyes on Sam. "Like your boat. How good is its engine?"

"Great. It's a Cummins; I had it overhauled last year. We're wasting time." Sam pleaded with Paco. "We're too close to let this get away."

"By the time you catch up, they'll be in U.S. waters," said Paco. "Getting caught with a load—there's no buying your way out. It's over for you, man."

"They're nowhere near U.S. waters," said Sam. "We can catch them."

"There's no 'we'. You need to refuel, that's an hour in the wrong direction, easy." Paco's hand slid over the gun in his pocket.

"Sully must have fuel for his boat." Sam walked over to a storage shed and looked inside.

"No."

"Look, it could take me years to replace what I had with Davis. I need this load."

"Go yourself, we're not stopping you," Paco grinned. "It's your fuckin' boat."

"What's left of it," Tomás sputtered an exhale of smoke at Sam.

"Tomás, what do you say?" Sam pressed on. "We have fuel enough to catch them, then we could siphon their fuel. Lot of fucking money for the taking."

"Paco's right. We don't have an American family to come save us," said Tomás.

"Neither do I, not anymore." Sam's stepfather despised incompetence as much as he did criminals. "I'll go it alone if I have to."

"This run's trashed," said Tomás. "You acting desperate. That's messed up, man. Always bad luck."

Sam came to rest against a palm tree and snuck a furtive glance at Topo, who stood quietly watching his father through the netting that edged the porch.

"Where does Davis spend most of his time—here with his son?"

"In the Keys," said Tómas.

Sam nodded, looking out to his boat. "Have either of you been to his house?"

"Never been to States, man—not even close," said Tomás.

"Why you ask?" said Paco.

"No reason, just passing the time."

"Smoke a joint, man, listen to the birds." Paco pulled out a pack of Gitanes and stuck one in the corner of his mouth, looking amused by the sight of the white man squirming. "It's a beautiful morning." He lit his cigarette and blew a cloud of smoke at Sam.

"If this is over, I need to get back."

"To that sexy woman of yours? She will be disappointed, you coming back with no money."

"How do you know about her?"

"I know all, man," Paco laughed, taking another drag. "We'll wait to see what happens with Davis. Remember Davis? Your friend?"

"It'll be too late then," said Sam.

Paco's eyes tracked Sam as he walked to the entrance of the common room where Davis lay. Sam pulled back the curtain of mosquito netting. He let it drop and stepped back from the heavy scent of incense mingled with blood and the medicinal brew of steaming herbs drifting from the fire pit. He watched Siani leaning over Davis, applying a solution from a bowl she was holding. Sully had moved away from the table, taken off his bloody apron and gloves and thrown them on top of the blood-soaked rags in the pail on the floor.

"How is he, Doc?" Sam asked. Sully didn't answer; instead he brushed past him on his way out to the yard to speak to Paco.

"He stands a chance. Siani will do her magic. When she is finished, his body will want to live." Sully gave a half-convincing smile at Topo. "Tomás, take the pails out back to the pit and burn the rags."

"Let me finish tending to Davis." Siani looked up at Sam standing in the doorway. "In a moment you can help Paco move him to a bed."

She covered Davis's wound in a warm poultice and when the dressing was complete, Sam and Paco moved him to a bed in the corner of the common room. His inert body, made quiet by morphine, looked small and fragile—a formidable man whose power had drained away with his blood.

"Let him sleep. If he can make it through today, he might stand a chance," said Sully.

Sully joined the men in the yard, heaving a deep sigh as he stretched out on a chaise. "Your boat looks like it crashed through a reef. What the hell happened to it?"

"Unforeseeable bad luck," said Sam.

"There isn't any other kind." Sully struck a match, pulled a stub of a cigar from his pocket and puffed at it until it was lit. He leaned back, looking at Sam, then turned his gaze to the boat. "Looks like it's sitting high in the water. Doesn't look like it's carrying much."

"Not carrying anything," said Paco. "Don't worry, Sully, We have money to pay for Davis."

"I'm more worried about what's going to become of Topo," said Sully.

Sam looked over at Davis's son. Topo was still standing outside the netting and watching over his father, his long arms hanging by his side.

"How long have you been living out here?" Sam asked.

"Long enough to forget. Why?" Sully turned to consider Sam.

"Kind of isolated."

"I prefer to be alienated from the ordinary. But there's always someone finding us, like you. You look like a man in the wrong place."

Sully stiffly twisted in his seat. The aroma of eggs cooking drifted from the kitchen. "Smells like breakfast." He got up and looked over at Paco, holding him in his gaze. Paco looked down and nodded.

Sam caught the exchange. He turned and looked past the shrubs and palms and the chicken-scattered beach to where his boat was docked, then followed the men inside. The table where Davis had lain was now cleared, the tarp removed, and only a few drops of blood remained on the wooden floor. Siani had put on a fresh tablecloth and returned the basket of fruit to the table.

He walked over to where Davis lay, bending down to look at him. His eyes were closed; he looked peaceful. "So, you think he'll make it?" Sam said.

"Leave him alone," Sully growled.

Sully's tone made Sam straighten up. He took in the room. Siani was busy setting out papaya and cassava bread. Paco sat on a stool staring out at the inlet and Topo leaned against him, watching his father from across the room. Sully and Tomás stood together, their eyes locked on Sam.

"You mind if I use your bathroom?" Again, no one answered. "Where's the bathroom?" Sam said louder.

Only Siani looked up. "Around back."

"Paco, go with him," said Sully. "Show him where it is."

Siani turned around from her stove. "Sullivan, he can find it on his own. Paco, sit down, let's enjoy our food." Paco stood to watch Sam leave the room, his eyes following him as he rounded the side of the house.

Sam opened the outhouse door and banged it closed, then saw the boy, standing, watching him. The boy backed away and bolted to the house. Sam raced for the path that ran along the tree line next to the house and led to the water. At the last tree he froze. The hundred feet to the dock was wide open. He took a deep breath and sprinted as fast as he could across the sand.

He ran to the rickety dock. Ducking at the sound of gunfire, he flipped the lines from the boat cleats and jumped in. Paco was running down from the house with a pistol in his hand, his long legs kicking up a rooster tail of sand, with Tomás limping behind. Sam started the engines and threw the gear into reverse. Sully's boat, docked on the other side, was now hard aground; they had no way to chase him. He spun the bow around to face the inlet and took off at full throttle, bringing his boat up on a plane, skimming across the water's surface. Paco fired in rapid succession and a hail of bullets ripped into the water on either side.

Sam looked back. Paco, Tomás and Sully stood at the water's edge with Davis's son behind them, pointing to the dock. Sully turned and slammed his fist into Paco's face, knocking him to the sand, and stalked back toward the house.

CHAPTER 24

All that remained was to wait for this trip to end. Ella lay in her bunk listening to Rich and Carlos talk in the galley. She sat up when she caught a fragment of what Rich said: "This time they'd be willing to kill for it." She slumped back down, knowing who he meant. Carlos replied, but she didn't strain to hear what he said. She didn't want to know. Fear had worn her out.

Dawn was breaking, and in the dim light she could see blood on her shirt from Davis's hand. She pulled it off and threw it on the cabin sole, then fell back onto her pillow. She was unable to think and lay motionless, letting the tears trickle from the corners of her eyes to run across her temples. The horror of shooting Davis kept stabbing at her, and she knew her heart could only break so many times before it barred itself from feeling. Was this how she would feel from now on? Dead? Dead heart? Dead dreams?

She rolled onto her side, curling up, and clung to a memory of her father. She had climbed up in his lap, nestled her head in his arms and begun to cry. It was after her mother had died, and she'd had a consuming fear her father would die too. He'd touched her hair in soft, calming strokes. "It's a waste of time to be afraid," he'd said with a smile.

She was only eight, and the idea seemed foreign to her. As if you had a choice to be afraid! But the deeper meaning had slowly come

214

to her. Even though tonight she had earned this despair, she knew she would let Davis go in a final act of self-defense. Unlike the loss of her parents, whom she carried in her heart, tonight was about dying a little, allowing numbness to take hold, and facing the truth about Davis.

His last whispered words came back to her, and Ella slid her hand under her pillow for the book he had given her before he'd left: *The Essential Rumi*. She had kept it close, reading it again and again, and it had given voice to what she'd thought was his love. Now, at the touch of it, she recalled his betrayal. She wanted to get rid of it, toss it out the porthole. But the memory of Davis's grip on her arm, as he'd pulled her in to utter his labored words, was strong. "Rumi—inside the cover."

She flicked on her flashlight and studied the red, marbleized pattern of the jacket. The protective plastic cover was taped to the inside flap. She peeled it back and a folded paper slipped onto her lap. It was a map of Davis's yard, drawn in his careful hand and clearly marked, obviously meant for her to read.

Ella studied it, not noticing anything significant until her eye was drawn to foliage under a tree: among the carefully drawn leaves of ivy was a small X. She had heard stories of smugglers burying their money, but this was right out of Treasure Island. How like Davis to be old school, he barely used his cell phone.

"Please, I have a son," Davis had said. "Help him." But what could she do about that—if anything? How would she even find him? And in any case, why would she owe Davis this favor? She carefully folded the map, returned it to its hiding place, resealed the tape and vowed to reexamine it when she returned to Florida.

She fell back onto her pillow and thought about the private world of the man she had loved for the past year: a father, husband, and uncle. She had stayed at his home in the Keys. There'd been no family photos, nor any belongings but his own. No feminine touches that a wife might have made. No toys or other evidence of a son. So, where were his wife and son? Were they hidden? If so, why? It's not my concern, she thought. But her mind kept working at the puzzle.

The pirate had called out "Tio" to Davis. She lifted up onto her elbows. She had seen that word, "Tio," along with a string of numbers, written on the inside cover of the La Tasca matchbook on Sam and Nikki's boat in Nassau. She tried to remember the numbers. They hadn't been written like a phone number. So what were they?

She recalled the last four digits because of the zeros: 0100. Could it have been military time, the way her father had called out the hour? Suddenly it fell into place: 0100 had been their scheduled time to pick up the load; the other numbers must have been the date. *Sam was in on tonight's ambush.* She thought about the driver of the boat: he'd had Sam's build. The bastard had been onboard. She remembered that Burke, too, had had a La Tasca matchbook. She'd left Burke's bloody shirt in the sink and now she went to it, searching the pockets and pulling out the matchbook. She held her breath and opened the cover. It was blank. She tossed the matches on the counter and went to find Rich.

*****

The mist had turned into a lazy rain, forming smooth puddles, red with the blood that remained on deck. The lowering slate sky, backlit by an occasional flash of lightning, glowed as from exploding bombs in a distant war. In the light of dawn, Rich sat with his arms draped over the wheel, a look of deep concern on his tired face that said everything there was to say.

"Anything?" Ella asked from the second step of the companionway.

"All's quiet," said Rich. "Did you check the radar?"

"Clear. You want the awning up?

"No. I want to be able to see."

216

Carlos and Burke sat quietly in their respective corners of the cockpit. Ella slowly turned full circle—they were alone on the water. She looked down. It was now light enough to make out the blood-streaked path where Davis had pulled himself along. Drops of reddish-brown blood spattered the cockpit and Rich's legs and shoes. A spray of bullets had splintered the teak toe rail and cracked the fiberglass in a number of places on the cabin sides, one of them close to where she had been standing. Seeing the damage, she knew that last night she had come close to dying. She crossed the cockpit and lifted the lid of the lazarette, pulling out the deck bucket.

"I'll get that." Carlos unfolded out of his corner, patting the right pocket of his slicker that hung unevenly from the weight of his gun. He tossed the rope-tethered bucket off the transom and it caught with a jerk, filling it with water. The wind had blown back his hood, and Ella could see the thick muscles in his neck tighten as he hauled the laden bucket in. He splashed water on the bloody deck as casually as he had washed away the remains of the fish he caught and clubbed to death. Blood from Davis, Burke and Rich streamed together, spilling through the scuppers and over the side.

"My guess, if they were coming back they would have by now. It's starting to get light," said Rich. "But that doesn't mean we can drop our guard."

The cool breeze hit Ella's face when she turned toward the bow, away from the jagged silhouettes of the Cuban mountains sinking slowly into the southern horizon, reminding her of the night's horror. She felt trapped on this pod of a boat, surrounded by water and hours out from the Keys. She wanted nothing more than to run as fast and far away from this as she could—but this run had been a means to an end; its wreckage would be something she'd have to learn to live with.

She was grateful for the comforting blanket of clouds warding off the invasive glare of the rising sun. She looked back at Cuba, knowing it would always be a reminder of how she'd been fooled.

But then in the distance, a flash of white caught her eye. She grabbed Rich's binoculars and stood up on the cockpit seat. A powerboat was pounding across the water at a reckless speed, rolling side to side with the waves on its beam, heading southwest toward the Lower Keys.

"Can you check on Burke?" Rich said.

Ella shot a look over her shoulder. "He's asleep." When she turned back, the boat was gone. "I saw a power boat."

"Where?" Rich shot up. "What kind?"

"A sport fisher, seven o'clock, heading toward the Lower Keys, I think."

Carlos grabbed the binoculars out of Ella's hands and rushed to the cabin top. "You think you saw a boat?"

"No, Carlos. I know I saw a boat. I'm not sure exactly where it was heading."

A white fishing boat appeared for a moment riding high on a wave, then dropped behind the rolling seas. Carlos waited through the rise and fall of the waves, trying to catch another look before going below to check the radar.

"Were you seeing the stern or the beam?" said Rich.

"More on the starboard quarter," said Ella. "That's why I thought they were heading to the Lower Keys. In a hurry, too, by the way they were flying over the water."

Carlos rushed up from below in a rage. "They're heading to Marathon."

"At least they're not coming at us," said Ella. "What are you thinking, Rich?"

"Thinking that I don't believe in coincidence. Another sport fisher driving recklessly across the waves?" said Rich. "Take the wheel, Ella; I want to check their path."

Burke propped himself up on one elbow to look toward the mainland. "Fuck. Why they going past us?"

"Hurrying to rip someone else off," said Carlos. He lifted himself onto the boom for a better view and braced against the mast.

"I wonder who?" With one hand on the wheel, Ella twisted around to look for the boat.

"What'd you see?" asked Burke.

"Nothing," said Carlos, dropping to the cabin top.

"They can't do anything to us now," said Ella, trying to reassure herself. "Besides it's Labor Day. There'll be boats everywhere soon."

"Labor Day make easier for them," said Burke. "Remember why we coming back today? Coast Guard busy fishing drunks out of water."

"I think it's them." Rich took back the helm looking tired and nearly out of fight. "Their path has them coming from somewhere near Matanzas, Cuba, on a heading to Marathon. So why are they passing us by?"

"Maybe they're headed for Davis's home in Marathon." Ella shivered from the cool breeze—or was it the thought that Davis really had a treasure that could fall into the hands of his accomplices?

"Let's just stay alert and get this thing done," said Rich.

"Ella." Burke pulled himself up and slumped against the cabin side.

"What?"

"Can you get my gun and something to eat? Bring my oil rag?"

"Not your slave, Burke." Ella gave Burke a soft smile, relieved to see him coming back to life. She lifted up his blanket. He had bled through his bandages and would be useless in another fight.

"Sorry about Davis," Burke said.

"Davis is the one who's sorry. If he lives to be sorry." There was blood on her fingertips when she pulled her hand away.

"I don't think he knew you onboard," said Burke. "When he saw you, threw off his game. That's why we still alive."

"Doesn't matter anymore. Seems as though people say or do whatever it takes to get what they want: pretend to be a lover, show a kindness, or just fucking shoot someone. Whatever works." Ella felt Burke's forehead and the sides of his face. "You've got a fever."

"Not everyone is like that," Rich said quietly.

"Yeah, but how can you *ever* know?" Ella looked over at Burke for a moment, then went below to run cold water on a washcloth and collect towels, fresh bandages and a clean shirt. Back on deck, she gently wiped the blood from Burke's back, redressed his wounds and helped him on with his shirt.

"Thanks Ella," said Rich. "We can't let that get infected. If he needs to go to the hospital, the gunshot wound will get reported."

"I'll keep an eye on it." Ella pressed the damp washcloth on the back of Burke's neck to help bring down his fever. "Did anyone know Davis had a son?" she asked.

"Did he?" Rich looked back over his shoulder, scanning the waters. "He never mentioned it to me."

"What about a wife, or the boy's mother—where is she?" said Ella.

"Know nothing about a wife," said Carlos. "I heard he had a boy somewhere. He never talked about himself."

"Not often," said Ella. But there were nights on her boat, after sharing a meal she had prepared for him, after they made love in her bunk, when they were fed body and soul and were sitting out on her aft deck, that Davis's wall had started to give way. Bit by bit, she had watched and listened to his stories, gathering clues to who this rugged, seasoned sailor was and never once suspecting he was a man pursuing wealth at all costs. She would never get caught like that again.

Down in the galley, she sliced cheese and onions for grilled sandwiches. Her practiced knife skills gave way to crude, angry chops, and she slapped the sandwiches together. How could Davis have lied to her so completely? What a fool she'd been not to see it.

And now, like a recurring nightmare, the demons he'd unleashed were a threat to them all. Her anger swelled and she grabbed the knife by its tip and flung it at the bulkhead, sinking it deep into the wood with a solid thump. She picked up another and aimed at a bale of weed, tossing it even harder. Grabbing a third, she tossed it with everything she had, burying it in the bale alongside the other. She slid slowly down to the cabin sole and stayed there, staring at the bulkhead until she smelled the butter burning in the pan. She reached up over her head and blindly turned off the flame, then sat for a while, jostled by the rhythm of the boat, and tried to shake off the wave of anger. Slowly, she forced herself up and began disassembling the sandwiches to make them over again.

Rich came racing below. "Something's burning."

"Was. I had the heat up too high." Ella stood to face Rich. "I think you need to let out the main a little. *Merlin's* heeling too far; it makes for a slower sail."

"I will." Rich looked at the knife stuck in the bulkhead and pulled it out. Ella walked over and pulled the other two knives out of the bales.

"Well, at this point, a few more holes in the boat don't really matter," said Rich.

"What are you going to do about that?"

"I know the yardman at River Bend. He'll help us out."

At the word 'us,' Ella realized that once back in Lauderdale she wouldn't be able to just hit land and run for it. The boat needed to be taken care of.

"I guess we'll all have to contribute."

"We'll see what Falco wants to do about it."

"At least we still have the load."

"Exactly."

Rich caught sight of the chaos of bread and cheese on the cutting board. "In time, Ella." He leaned in to give her a one-arm hug, but she moved away.

"It's not time that heals." She looked up at Rich. "People say that, but I've learned it's not true. You actually have to do the hard work yourself."

Rich turned to head up the companionway, but Ella caught his sleeve. She needed a private moment with him. "Rich, you heard one of the pirates calling out "Tio" when Davis was hit."

Bone-tired agitation showed on his face and he stepped back into the salon. "Yeah, I heard."

"When I went to see Sam and Nikki in Nassau, I saw a matchbook on their boat from La Tasca in Havana. The word Tio was written on the inside of the cover, along with some numbers. At the time I didn't know or care what the numbers meant. But when Sam became irritated watching me handling the matchbook, I guessed that they were important. Now, I think I know why. The numbers were the date and time for our pickup. I think Sam and Davis have been partners all along."

"You think Sam was in on this?"

"It adds up. When the pirate dropped the spotlight, it rolled, lighting up the man at the wheel for a split second. He wasn't Cuban; he was short and white. I couldn't tell who it was, but I can guess."

"What were the numbers?'

"There was a string of them. I just remember the last four, 0100."

"Our pickup time—makes sense. After all, he was in on stealing Jon's load." Rich stood with one hand against the bulkhead and the other on his hip, his head hanging down wearily. He looked up. "We've got the load. Let's just finish this thing."

Carlos shoved his face below. "Cap, I think we need to change course. Time to head toward the Keys."

"I'll be right up, Carlos."

He turned to Ella. "We'll leave this matter for Falco. I think we can relax a little bit. It's daylight, the Coast Guard will have their hands full. We're halfway to Falco's and tonight we'll get paid. The pickup crew will have plenty of well-armed men. Tomorrow, we'll sail *Merlin* back to Lauderdale and it'll all be over."

Rich bent over the radar screen. "They're definitely heading for Marathon."

"If it's Sam, he's probably going to Grassy Key."

"It's a fool's move to go where Falco's men can find him," said Rich.

Ella wished they would find him, before Sam looted Davis's treasure. Whatever Davis had buried, he wanted her to find. She turned back to the cutting board. "I'm making grilled cheese. Sound good?"

"When wouldn't it?"

She caught Rich's glance at the charred mess on the cutting board.

"I'm remaking them."

$$*****$$

It was Ella's watch and she adjusted the trim of *Merlin's* sails with every small wind change, sailing her smartly on a broad reach at eight knots against the Gulf Stream. No one, aside from Burke, who lay in a pain-pill-induced fog, had slept in the past two days. Steering *Merlin* helped focus her mind, and she mulled over the sequence of events, starting with the theft of Jon's load. Something wasn't adding up.

She leaned into Rich. "That was a clever move Davis and Sam pulled on Jon," she said. "He never saw anything. They had him locked inside the head. He never saw Davis not-die, never saw them steal his load."

"Sailing offshore Eleuthera at that hour of the night, anyone would believe they were hit by pirates," said Rich. "Who would have guessed it was his own brother?"

"Who killed Jon?" Ella asked, "If it wasn't Davis?"

"You crazy you believe Davis." Burke lay resting with his eyes closed.

"The pain pills must be working, you were sleeping for a good hour," Rich said.

"Feel like shit." Burke tried to lift his head up.

"Hang in there, Burke. We're nearly there," said Rich.

"Nearly?" Ella raised her eyebrows, but Rich's scowl told her to back off.

"Maybe Sam killed Jon and took his money," said Carlos.

"Killed his own brother, then stole his money from him a second time? I helped Jon get that money back," said Ella. "If that hadn't happened, he'd be alive."

"Jon was way out of his element," said Rich. "He should never have been there."

"Like me," Ella mumbled under her breath.

"Sam didn't kill Jon," said Burke. "He found him dead. He called Nikki, scared shitless. Nikki told me."

"Can't trust Nikki," said Carlos. "She might have killed Jon."

"Shut your mouth about Nikki." Burke tried to sit up but grimaced from the shock of pain and settled back. "Nikki's okay."

Ella looked over at Carlos, thinking he had more to say. "Carlos, do you know Nikki?"

"Nikki gets around," he smirked.

If Burke had his strength, Ella thought, Carlos would be swimming for shore right now.

"I'm not ruling it out, but I have my doubts that Davis killed Jon," said Rich.

"I don't think he killed Jon, either," said Ella. "He would have done it earlier, when they stole Jon's load."

"Then who did it?" said Burke.

Carlos reached into the lazarette and pulled out his fishing pole and tackle box. Everyone tracked his movements; it was a welcomed distraction.

"Could be random thief," said Burke.

"I don't believe in coincidences," said Rich. "Not in the drug trade. It's one place everything really does happen for a reason."

"It's history," Ella said. "Does it really matter anymore?"

"Oh, it matters," said Rich. "We need to make sure that rat is dealt with."

"Only if you keep playing at this game." Ella turned to Rich. "Are you?"

"Probably not," said Rich.

A lot different than the 'no' he had said before, she thought, rubbing the chill from her arms. She hadn't been warm or dry since they left Fort Lauderdale over two days ago.

Burke tried twisting to his side to talk to Ella. "You tell Davis about this trip?"

"Just when we were playing nice together," she glared back at him. "Davis was dead then, remember? But somebody told them the date and time."

"What about you, Burke, and you, Carlos? Any slips about this trip?" Rich looked hard at his crew. Carlos leaned back against the coaming, tying a Bagley jig on his line.

Burke just shook his head. "I don't create enemies. I've known too much trouble."

"You're not creating trouble going after Sam's girl?" said Carlos.

"She already done with him. I didn't steal her."

"It's possible the leak came from someone on the other end, maybe crew on the mother ship," said Rich. "The last run is when everything starts falling apart. People grab what they can before moving on." He turned away from the others to look off across the water. "Falco's going to go out of his mind with this."

Ella worried over what this failed attack might have set into motion. Davis may have died. Would they be coming after them to settle the score, kill them in the middle of the night as they had most likely killed Jon? Would she ever feel safe again?

CHAPTER 25

Falco hung the binoculars around his neck, double-locked the gate to his beach house and picked his way along a path lined with sea-grape. After ten years in the Keys, he still looked straight out of Long Island in his freshly pressed casual wear, having never adopted the island's relaxed dress style that he considered sloppy.

Labor Day had brought out the crowds, a parade of boisterous families coming to stake out their patch of beach, hauling colorful umbrellas and baskets overflowing with food and alcohol. Falco avoided them, taking the overgrown trail that led to the inlet, passing through a small grove of Australian pines with their bleached, knuckled roots spreading out like bony fingers clutching the sands. He stopped at the inlet and looked at the water level eddying on the inland side of the channel marker—the tide had turned, the water was falling. He continued along the water's edge, carefully stepping over the muck of the wrack line until he reached the beach.

Falco raised his head to the whumping of a Coast Guard helicopter moving swiftly across a darkening sky. He watched, shuffling the change in his pocket, searching the holiday-crowded waters for *Merlin* with the intensity of someone who stood to lose a small fortune.

He pulled out a Camacho cigar and lit it. Taking a few puffs, he kept his eye on the orange helicopter banking away from shore. He checked his watch, turned and walked back to his house on a spit off Marathon Key, a two-story hurricane-proof fortress obscured by rows of Royal palms that stood like sentries.

*****

It was a morning of collective restlessness aboard *Merlin*, the crew still uneasy about how the run might end. Ella and Rich listened below to the Coast Guard VHF channel with eyes on the radar screen, which showed growing clusters of small vessels along the coastline and inlet.

Merlin's VHF radio crackled with the first Labor Day distress call: "Mayday, mayday, Coast Guard Marathon." The panicked voice reported a party boat spewing black smoke. People were jumping into the water and no one was wearing life vests. Holiday boaters were streaming to the scene, creating more confusion, and the Coast Guard broadcasted an order to clear the area. The day was just beginning.

Rich's face brightened. "Beautiful! Just what we need: the perfect distraction."

They were now close enough to land that the offshore breeze carried the moist, sweet scent of tropical soil. Ella made her way forward, dodging sheets of spray and holding onto a shroud, then the handrail, lifeline, mast and finally the forestay, like a monkey swinging from vine to vine. She reached the bow and held firmly to the pulpit, noting the cloud of black smoke that pinpointed Marathon Key. She stood wedged between the forestay and the jib's luff, watching the bump of land slowly grow into the shoreline of Florida, acting as Rich's eyes, pointing the way through the crowded waters.

It was nerve-wracking weaving among the yachts and speedboats, falling off slightly to miss a windsurfer, heading up to dodge a flock of jet skis flying recklessly across their path. Soon, they would be at the channel's entrance; this would all be over and she could go back to feeling herself again—whoever that was. Her self-image had always been in the hands of someone else: her father's little girl, Davis's lover—borrowed identities, not hers to own. That's over, she thought. This voyage was proof that she was taking charge of her life.

Ella looked up at the sky. The mix of grey-green and black clouds boiled in a rolling tumble over her head. The tip of a waterspout formed and wagged its tail toward the water, then sucked back into the cloud, teasing like a child sticking out its tongue.

"Copter coming from Vaca Key," Carlos shouted.

Against the steely sky, the orange Coast Guard helicopter stopped short, keeping its distance from the whirling spout; it dipped to the right, circling once in the same rotation as the spout, then veered toward land.

"That's our 'good-to-go.'" Rich gave a quick wave to the retreating helicopter. "All we have to do is not run aground and we're home free."

"Good job, man, on the Coast Guard," said Carlos. "Is your friend based out of Vaca Key?"

Rich glanced at Carlos, pointedly ignoring his question.

Burke watched the sky from his cocoon of blankets. "I don't think we done with funnel."

Ella tossed the extra cushions below and was picking up empty water bottles when she realized she was smiling. Rich's and Burke's faces had relaxed, too. Carlos's fishing line had begun to sing out again and he stood with his back to her, reeling in a fish. Everyone was on the edge of relief, without having quite earned it yet.

The funnel reappeared, like the finger of God poking through the clouds, frightening the boaters with its power to flip their small boats. En masse, they began making a run to safety, crossing each other's paths and creating chaos. The funnel had cleared a path for *Merlin*, but it left them exposed as they raced toward the small private inlet that led to Falco's.

Ella stood tall at the mast, ready to drop the main on Rich's command. She could make out the people on the beach, some gathering their belongings, a few standing at the shore taking in the weather's show, while others remained stubbornly planted on their blankets. If the waterspout moved to land, they would be piling into their cars, blasting their horns for others to get out of their way.

She faced into the wind blowing warm and dry off the land, and felt like a proud warrior returning with the spoils of war. She studied the people on the beach growing larger and clearer the closer in they sailed. Which of them would do what she had in order to change their life, she wondered: if they had the chance, would they have the courage? She turned to check on the spout and saw the familiar orange of the Coast Guard cutter coming from Boot Key.

"Coasties at nine o'clock," Ella said, making her way to the cockpit.

"Time to hang below, guys," ordered Rich. "Carlos, give Burke a hand."

Ella stood behind Rich at the wheel, holding onto his shoulders, playing the happy couple. It seemed they had been gone a lifetime.

"Was this the toughest run you've ever been on?"

"Never had to defend a load before," Rich answered. "Ripped off once at Deadman Cays when I was still too naïve to realize that the Cuban pirates patrolled their neighboring waters. But I haven't been double-crossed until now."

"Well, we survived, load intact," said Ella, "and now we get paid."

"We were lucky, Ella." Rich turned to look at her. "But that kind of luck doesn't happen twice."

229

Ella gave his shoulders a squeeze. "I know." She picked up the binoculars, focusing on the rollers kicking up at the inlet, and then trained them on the cutter. The Coast Guard was trying to assist a small powerboat that was dead in the water. The Guardsmen had their backs to *Merlin* as she passed four hundred yards off their beam.

"Thank God for lunatics on small boats," said Ella.

"Don't jinx it. We still have to get past the sand bar at the mouth of the inlet. Go stand watch at the bow." Rich leaned into the companionway and ordered the men to move to the forepeak, shifting their weight forward.

"Sailing in will help lift the hull over the bar," said Rich. "Once we get into the channel, it's a pretty consistent twelve feet."

Merlin was doing a solid six knots, her keel only inches above the rising bottom. She bumped the sand bar with a gentle kiss and Ella spun around with a nervous glance, only to see Rich smiling at the wheel. *Merlin* lifted to a breaking wave, surfing her sleek, powerful hull over the bar and into the channel.

"Depth at twelve feet," Rich shouted. "Drop the main."

Ella let go of the halyard, dropping the sail into the lazy jacks, and Rich threw off the jib sheet. The sound of the flapping sails and rigging, the jib halyard zinging through the winch as they glided into the calm waters of the channel, made a climatic finale to the dangerous leg of the trip.

"What a team." Ella returned Rich's smile as she made her way back to the helm and slid in behind, wrapping her arms around him. "We made it." Her words came out in a breath as she rested her head lightly on his shoulder, avoiding his wounded back. Rich reached around and held tightly to her shoulder, giving it a gentle squeeze before taking his hand away.

Ella called out the diminishing depths as Rich slowly motored *Merlin* against the outgoing tide, careful to stay in the middle of the mangrove-lined channel.

"There it is. That's Falco's house."

Ella pulled away from Rich and looked up. "It's a fort."

The two-story cement structure had few windows facing the western channel. A six-foot cement wall enclosed the property, with a high security gate at its entrance.

"It looks like something an investment banker would own."

"In a way, he is an investment banker," said Rich. "Get ready to dock."

"He got all that with drug money?" said Ella.

"I don't know his business, but probably."

"Wow."

Ella kept her eye on the house as she moved aft to get the dock lines from the lazarette. The property sat along a private inlet that led out into the Gulf in easy range of the islands of the Bahamas and Lesser Antilles. The land had been cut away and dredged, making a private waterway. Ella imagined a scaled-down version with *Gina Marie* berthed at her dock and a white sandy beach for early morning walks and afternoon swims—an expensive dream for a novice restaurateur.

"Topsides are so banged up, it's pointless to put out bumpers." Ella said, making ready the lines.

Rich shook his head. "Tie them on anyway. We don't want to make matters worse. Someone is going to have to pay top dollar to get her back in shape, and fast."

"Who?" asked Ella.

"Yet to be determined. Falco isn't known for his generosity"

Rich dropped the engine back into neutral, letting *Merlin* glide the remaining distance, then put her in reverse to stop the forward motion of the twenty-four-ton boat, landing *Merlin* neatly at dockside.

"One thing, Ella. When we get inside, don't talk to Falco. You can say hello and goodbye. Otherwise, keep quiet."

"Why?"

"Respect. You're not his equal. No one is."
"Wow. How do you get power like that?"
"You can be sure no one gave it to him."

CHAPTER 26

Ella stepped off *Merlin* onto solid ground with unsteady legs after spending three days at sea. She faced the boat, studying the evidence of the hell they had been through: deep cracks ran down the topsides to below the waterline; chunks of fiberglass had cracked away, exposing the inner layers of construction. They were lucky they hadn't sunk.

Rich jumped off the boat and shot a waved salute at Falco watching from the second-story wall of windows.

Ella looked up at him staring down, his arms folded across his chest. From his look of annoyance, she guessed the extensive repairs would come out of his pocket.

"It's worse than I thought," Rich said, looking over the hull.

"Do you think we can sail her to Fort Lauderdale like this?"

"She's not leaking, but man, that's going to be one expensive repair. Come on, we need to get inside. He doesn't like anyone hanging around outdoors."

"We're surrounded by walls," said Ella.

"Satellite coverage." Rich thumbed at the sky. "Let's move."

Burke threw his good arm over Rich's shoulder and Carlos steadied him on the other side, helping him off the boat. Ella waited for them at the entrance to Falco's lair, and listened to the eight-foot-high door's numerous electronic locks being released.

Once inside the foyer, she took in the marble staircase that curved upward past a crystal chandelier to the landing where Falco rested on his forearms against the brass rail like a vigilant gargoyle, watching them arrive. An overwrought gold-framed mirror took up most of the far wall, reflecting vintage Italian posters and Ella with the rest of *Merlin's* weather-beaten crew.

Rich looked up. "Load's secure." His voice echoed in the canyon of the foyer.

"I can see *Merlin's* water line. Get it all?"

"As promised, all sweet leaf."

Falco pointed his chin at Burke. "What happened to him?

"Shot."

"And *Merlin*? Looks like you hit the rocks."

"Ambushed. It got messy. Burke needs to get stitched. Hoping you could do that."

"Can't. What do you mean—ambushed?"

"A double-cross. Let's get Burke taken care of and I'll fill you in," said Rich. "I saw you stitch someone after the Andros run."

"He died."

"I didn't know that."

"I'll call someone. He's a vet, but it's all the same. Help yourselves in the kitchen. There's beer and some kind of Cuban dish my housekeeper made."

Ella looked around. For the first time, a wealthy person's home didn't intimidate her. No longer just a tug man's daughter, she had delivered the goods: she was a player in a dangerous world. She leaned against the doorway with her hands in her pockets, looking salty and tousled from three sleepless days of hard sailing and ambush. She looked up at Falco with unblinking calmness.

He took his time walking down the marbled steps, hands loosely in his pockets. When he finally reached the bottom he walked over to Burke, pulling back his shirt. "What's that?"

"An IT Clamp," said Rich. "Slows the bleeding."

"Useful," said Falco. "Take him to the guest room where he can lie down. If he's still bleeding, put something under him."

"I'm good, I don't need doc," said Burke.

"It needs to get stitched," said Falco. "I don't want this thing getting infected when he's back up in Lauderdale. This is the only doc he's allowed to see. Understand?"

Falco didn't speak to anyone but Rich. He glanced briefly at the others, assessing, not acknowledging them, then went into the downstairs study and closed the door to make the call.

"Do you think I should get him something to eat?" Ella asked Rich.

"Beer," said Burke. "Love a beer."

"Maybe you should wait, see what the vet—the doc—has to say," said Rich.

Burke's flushed face and strained watery eyes told Ella he still had a fever. She placed a cool wet washcloth on his forehead and covered him with blankets.

"Anyone Falco calls won't make him wait," said Rich.

"Try to rest," Ella said, tucking the blanket in around Burke's shoulder. She turned and followed Rich out of the guest room.

*****

In the upstairs living room, Ella, Rich and Carlos settled in for the wait: for the vet to arrive, for the load to be picked up, to get paid, to get back to their lives.

Falco walked up the stairs to join them. "Going to cost a fair amount of change in repairs."

"I know." Rich sat with his ankle hiked up across his knee, his clenched fists pushed out along the arms of the chair.

"So what happened? Did you get boarded?"

"We were attacked a half-hour after we picked up the load. They came at full-speed, ramming us hard. There was a short exchange of gunfire, Burke got hit, and then they jumped aboard."

235

"Same MO as the hit on Jon's boat," said Falco, heading to his leather swivel chair by the picture window. It was an island away from the rest of the living room. A small table stood in arm's reach, crowded with an empty espresso cup and a *Wall Street Journal* folded to an article of interest; a clutter of discarded *Barons* and *New York Times* lay on the floor. It was the only sign Ella could see that Falco lived here: the house lacked any books or personal touches that didn't appear to come from an interior decorator.

"Did you get a look at anyone?" Falco sat down, keeping his eye on Rich.

"Yeah. Davis," said Ella, unable to keep quiet.

"Davis is dead." Falco's tone was dismissive and he looked away in annoyance.

Rich shook his head at Ella to keep quiet. "He isn't—he's alive," said Rich. "He faked his death; this was his operation."

"Are you sure?"

"Hundred percent. He was onboard. I fought him. Pretty sure Sam was driving the boat."

Falco paused before he spoke, narrowing his eyes on Rich. "Why didn't you just shoot them when they came at you?"

"We didn't want to start a gunfight we'd lose. They had the maneuverability and height where they could just pick us off. We needed to get them onboard. Turned out to be the right strategy: it saved the load."

"Why are you still alive? Why didn't they just mow you down on their way in?"

"They tried—hitting us head-on at full speed." Rich's face was drawn and he looked tired of the talk. "You saw the hull. But then Davis spotted Ella and it stopped him."

"Davis's girl." Falco nodded.

"Was," said Ella, glancing at Rich. "Before I knew he was a traitor."

"Ella..." Rich shook his head.

Falco glanced at her, then to Rich. "How is it you still have the load?"

"When they boarded, it was a bloody fight. Carlos was knocked out on the foredeck. It was just Burke and me: Burke had been shot, his one arm was useless and we were losing the fight. Then Davis pulled a gun and Ella came up from below and shot him. Saved our lives."

"Ella shot Davis—her lover." Falco kept his eyes on her.

"He had on a balaclava, she didn't know it was him. The fight was over when Davis's men saw that he was badly hurt. That's why I think it was his operation."

Falco buried both hands in his hair and gripped his head. "Davis and I go back years, and the prick plays me?" He dropped his hands and turned to Rich. "Where's he now?"

"Radar showed them heading toward Cuba, possibly Matanza or one of the de Sabana Cays."

"De Sabana Cays. I bet I know where he was going."

Where? Ella wondered. Back to his Cuban family?

"Where'd he get hit?"

"Somewhere near his gut." Rich lowered his voice. "Didn't look like he was going to make it."

"If he isn't dead, he will be—I'll make sure of it," said Falco. "Unbelievable."

"Early this morning we spotted what looked to be the same boat running hard on a course to Marathon."

Ella watched Falco take in the insult of Davis's betrayal, just as she had had to. A slow burn of anger seemed to rise in him until he shot up from his chair to stand by the window.

"What kind of boat?"

"Mid-size sport fisher running on three Mercury outboards."

"Boat Sam was on at Grassy Key had three Mercs," said Falco. He shook his head and pulled out his cell phone, leaving a message for Babs to report any sighting of Sam or his boat.

"I think Davis and Sam have been teamed up for a while. Ella saw a matchbook from a club in Havana on Sam and Nikki's boat. The date and time of our pickup were written on the inside flap."

Ella avoided looking at Falco and whispered to Rich. "La Tasca."

"Cheap bar." Falco sat back down. "When was that?"

"About a month ago in Nassau," said Rich.

"Son of a bitch. We should have taken him out when we lit his boat. Prick will have cost us at least fifty grand in repairs." He checked an incoming message on his phone and pocketed it. "Then there's the business of Willie Devero taking a bullet."

"What? When?" said Rich.

"Two days ago. Not surprised. Willie made it his business to know things he shouldn't." Falco seemed amused.

"Who is Willie Devero?" Ella whispered to Rich.

"Mango Man, in Nassau," said Rich. "That would be a day before our pickup. Was he robbed?"

"No. They found him at his stand, middle of the day," said Falco. "It was an execution. My guess had been Cubans."

What information could be worth a life? Ella was beginning to see how men like Falco solved their problems, valuing loyalty over lives, and in all likelihood, money over all. But she wasn't afraid of Falco: for now, at least, she was on the right side of him.

"Sam went to Cuba a week before Jon's boat was pirated," added Carlos.

"How do you know he went to Cuba?" said Falco.

"I heard." Carlos shrugged. "Don't remember. I'm just saying Sam and Davis could be behind all of this—the killings, the robberies."

"No. Someone more methodical, even more ambitious, and they're cleaning house," said Falco. "Willie outlived his usefulness or ratted out the wrong guy." He looked thoughtfully at Carlos, then turned back to Rich.

A brief flash of alarm shone in Carlos's eyes and Ella wondered if she needed to worry. Or was the time to worry behind them?

Ella sat on the edge of the overstuffed couch, trying to find room among the crowd of pillows, quietly listening to Falco and Rich discuss the inside workings of the drug world. She held back her questions in hopes that they would continue their conversation here rather than taking it someplace private.

She gave up on the couch and stood by the window overlooking the Atlantic, still feeling the phantom movement of the boat under her feet. Looking south along the Overseas Highway toward Davis's house, she could almost see his road. She wondered if Sam, or someone aboard the sport fisher, was racing down Davis's long driveway at this very moment, with the hope of finding his treasure. I'll be back down in one day, she thought. Whatever Davis had buried in his yard must be important, and I have the map.

"I'm surprised Willie lasted this long," said Falco. "Word was he had quite a network—information going to people in the States, Jamaica, and probably Cuba as well. He really was a shit."

"A useful shit when he passed on info that served us," said Rich. "But you're right, Willie's only loyalty was to whoever paid the most."

Who could blame someone like the Mango Man, surrounded by so much wealth and by people who didn't need to work ten-hour days to just get by? The last time Ella had seen him he was standing behind his rickety fruit stand, the palm frond roof half blown away. It made sense now, she thought, his stand was his office in a world where respect for the law dropped somewhere around Palm Beach and continued falling the further south you went.

It had been only twenty minutes after Falco called in his favor to the vet when the intercom on the security system sounded. Falco buzzed the man in, and he nodded a greeting in everyone's direction as he reached the landing. He was a red-headed, sun worn man in his sixties with a satchel hanging off his shoulder. "Where is he?"

Falco didn't budge from his chair. "Downstairs," he said with an arrogant abruptness.

Ella wondered if he also owed Falco, though it was hard to imagine what favor a veterinarian would ask of him. She got up and followed him downstairs to help with Burke.

Burke didn't speak, only grunting slightly when the vet removed the clamp and saw the damage the bullet had done to Burke's shoulder. He worked quickly, giving Ella the impression he was in a hurry to leave. He cleaned and stitched the wound closed, then gave Burke a strong shot of antibiotics along with a bottle of pills and something to help him sleep. Then, after assuring her that Burke would be fine and well in a few days, he quietly left by the back door.

*****

In a cloud of steam, Ella stepped out of the glass brick shower onto the cool marble floor. The fogged mirror reflected a featureless, weather-burned face until she swabbed clear a patch with her towel. The sight of her short hair stopped her and she took into account her reflection. Her brightly shining eyes, still spirited from the high adventure, were confident. She decided she liked what she saw, the strong woman she'd become, one who knew how to take care of herself. She had started to towel-dry her hair when a noise startled her and a tall, dark shape passed outside the glass brick wall heading to the front yard, toward *Merlin*. Ella dressed quickly, tugging on jeans over her damp skin.

She cracked open the bathroom door. The hall was empty. She slipped into the hall, looked in on Burke, then crept toward the voices at the back of the house. Rich was sitting by the pool with Falco; his hair and shorts were wet from a swim and a towel was draped around his neck.

Ella slid open the glass door and called in a loud whisper. "There's someone out by *Merlin*. I can hear them."

"It's cool," said Rich.

240

"They're my men," said Falco. He was smiling, enjoying Ella's concern. "Men you'd like, who aren't afraid to shoot."

Ella straightened. Falco had just acknowledged her for the first time.

"Where's Carlos?" she asked.

"He's calling his wife," said Rich, twisting around to see her.

"So, we have our phones back?"

"No, not until we get to Lauderdale," said Rich. "Carlos walked over to the marina to use their phone. You finished with the shower?"

"Yeah." Ella moved aside to let Rich pass and paused straddling the doorway, caught in a moment of indecision. Falco sat facing the pool with his back to her. He was alone.

"What do you want, Ella?" Falco said after awhile.

She rubbed the side of her neck. A chance, she thought. She was bone-tired and hadn't thought this through, but she had done the math. Davis's treasure could be just a sentimental gift for his son, or there may not even be a treasure. Her twenty-five thousand in pay wouldn't get her far toward opening a restaurant. She stood rigid, knowing this would be her one chance alone with Falco, her one moment to secure her future. She had survived one run, she could gird up for another. And who was Falco? A man sustained on wealth and power: a drug lord with bodyguards, she thought, whose son had called him 'scary'—she'd get eaten alive. She turned to go inside.

"Ella?" Falco spoke in a low voice the texture of gravel, edged in curiosity.

Ella hesitated. Was she willing to go on alone without Rich's protection?

"A job." She heard the words leave her mouth, careless words she hadn't planned on saying, thoughts she hadn't had time to examine. She froze, staring at the back of Falco's perfectly trimmed hair, and waited. She turned to look inside, down the hall. The

241

bathroom door was still closed. She hoped Rich was taking a long, hot shower.

"How about you come down some night and make me dinner?"

"Not interested in that kind of job," said Ella.

Falco laughed and nodded. "Okay, we'll talk, Ella. What's your cell?"

She watched him pull his phone from his shirt pocket and add her number to all the others that inhabited his world.

"I won't have my phone until Lauderdale."

"I know." Falco put his phone back in his pocket and looked over his shoulder in Ella's direction. "Does Rich know you're asking me for work?"

"No. I hadn't planned on asking."

*****

Around nine o'clock, long after sunset when only the glow from the island's lights remained, a late model Mercedes sedan rolled into Falco's driveway. Ella stood tucked back from the curtain's edge at the upstairs window and watched Falco's armed guards move from the shadows, machine guns ready in their hands.

The bodyguard stepped out from the driver's seat. Though he had the bulked muscles of a gorilla, he calmly submitted to the ritual of a thorough pat down by one of Falco's men before opening the Mercedes' back door. A tall, rail-thin man emerged gripping a briefcase to his chest and stood with an air of nobility as Falco's men frisked him. The money had arrived.

When all was clear, Falco walked out of the house wearing an oversize baseball cap and a black windbreaker. He and the man with the briefcase boarded *Merlin*, and the driver went to wait in the car.

Ella kept watch from the second-story window even after the men had gone below. She passed the time studying the graceful lines of the Swan 53's design and feeling remorse for the battered boat. She glanced at Rich standing watch over *Merlin* at the far side of the window. For the first time since she had known him, she wondered if he had a girl. A handsome, capable man like him would have to, she thought. He was the one man she knew she could trust. Unlike Davis—the betraying, murderous thief.

After less than ten minutes, the buyer and Falco emerged, and moments later the Mercedes rolled quietly out of the driveway. It was Rich's cue to join Falco on *Merlin*. Ella was left alone with Carlos to wait for their pay. The money is coming, she thought. This will finally be over.

"How's your wife, Carlos?"

"Good." He took a long look at Ella. "You have family?"

"No." Ella said under her breath, keeping her gaze on *Merlin*.

"You should stay away from the window."

"They've gone." But she stepped back anyway. She didn't want Falco to see her doing something careless.

"If you're going to spy on someone, you should consider the lights behind you. You're backlit."

She retreated to the kitchen and put on the kettle for tea. She needed a lift and a distraction while she waited for Rich to return.

"I think I hear the vans." Carlos walked over to the window and looked out. "I'm going down to help them load the bales. You should stay here."

Carlos giving her orders hadn't bothered her until now and she was glad to see him go. She turned off the kitchen light and went back to the edge of the curtain. Two black SUVs with tinted windows rolled into the driveway, and Falco's men came out of hiding from the shadowed recesses of the yard. They moved toward the SUVs with weapons drawn.

Ella counted five hefty men slipping quickly out of the vans, pausing only for the mandatory pat down before they went to work unloading *Merlin* in a bucket brigade. The transfer was complete in twenty minutes, and they closed the SUV doors. As quietly as they had come, they rolled away. Falco's guards retreated back into the shadows for the night. She never saw Carlos go out to help.

Ten minutes after the vans left, Rich came into the living room carrying a manila envelope. He had already paid Carlos, and Burke would get his in the morning when he woke.

Ella sat on a kitchen stool, cradling a teacup in her hands, and watched Rich walk toward her with her pay—earnings whose value she had downsized over the course of the day. She set down her cup and took the envelope from him, feeling the heft of two hundred and fifty hundred-dollar bills. She guessed it weighed around a half pound, about the weight of a firmly packed onion and a fraction of what she remembered Jon's bag of cash had weighed the night that they had burned Sam's boat.

"Thanks, Rich."

"I hope it gets you started with your restaurant."

Ella nodded and looked up at Rich. "I'd go again."

She wished Rich would surprise her with news he had accepted one last run from Falco and wanted her to crew. But it was unlikely. If she had to go with another crew of Falco's, she would, but the thought scared her. Either way, she had made up her mind.

"Really?" Rich sounded genuinely surprised. "After all that's happened?"

"They wouldn't be stupid enough to try again."

"Don't rely on naive logic to make your decision. You don't know who you're dealing with. We haven't identified the leak; we don't know if it came from the Cuban's side or ours."

"Davis is out of the picture for a while." Ella paused and then said, "If not forever."

"It could be someone worse than Davis, much worse," Rich said sharply. "Falco will look into it. Until we know, don't hop aboard another run."

"I'd like another chance, Rich." Ella could see that he was displeased. "It's not enough."

"Never is." Rich looked hard at her, as if trying to read her mind.

Ella held up the envelope. "This is a far cry from the hundred and fifty thousand I thought I'd get for my dad's tug. Did you know sixty percent of restaurants fail in the first three years?"

"I've heard that," said Rich.

"I need to improve my odds," said Ella. "I need enough to have a fighting chance."

Rich gave Ella a stern glare. "And the whole world would open up to you?"

"Over time, I guess." Ella could see her reflection in the window; she looked tired, and she straightened her posture.

Rich crossed his arms and leaned back against the kitchen counter. "I'm getting out of this business, Ella. There are too many stateside and Canadian growers putting out weed."

"Can't you compete with them? Isn't there always room for people with a boat and the willingness to sail down?"

"I don't know the new people coming in and I don't trust them. Look, it was fast, easy money while it lasted, but now it's over. You got in on the tail end of it." Rich's tone sounded fatherly. "When your friends start stealing from you, and are willing to kill, maybe you should lower your expectations, go easy on yourself."

"Not a habit I want to acquire." Ella pulled back. "The only place I find peace, Rich, is in planning my future. I am *so* close—within reach."

"Then find a partner. Maybe there's someone at your school. There's never only one way, Ella. There's always more than one solution to any problem."

For her, the tide was always running out, never flooding, so much so that she was determined that this time she would control the outcome. It was how people like Falco got ahead.

"How much did you make on this?" She needed to know what was possible if she was going to cut a deal with Falco.

Rich didn't answer, and from the look on his face, he wasn't going to.

"Was it three or four times what I made?" said Ella. "You're set. You already have your stash of cash."

"Ella."

"Was it more?"

She caught the slight tightening of his lips, giving her a clue to how much he'd made: something over a hundred thousand.

"We were lucky Davis saw you. Otherwise, we'd all be dead. You know that, right?"

"Next time we'll be more prepared for trouble." Ella took a step back.

"Are you willing to kill for it?" Rich leaned into Ella. "That may have already happened."

"You know damn well I had no choice," Ella shot back. "There *is* a chance he's alive."

She watched as Rich pushed off from the counter and walked away.

*****

Ella was back aboard *Merlin,* sitting on her bunk and fanning through the pile of cash laid out in front of her. She picked up a packet of hundreds and took in the sharp smell of inked paper. Pulling one out of the bundle, she checked the watermark to see if it had the face of Benjamin Franklin. It was real. Fanning through the pack of bills gave her a calming sense of security. All she needed to do was double it—or more. The fact that she had earned this pile of cash in just three days was proof enough to her that she could do it again. She had the wits and the courage. She considered the packs of hundreds, a small pile that would go down quickly if she weren't careful. She thought about how Jon's money had been taken from him. She was pulled from her thoughts by the sound of creaking floorboards outside her cabin and then a knock on her door.

"Ella? You still awake?" said Rich.

"Who is it?" Ella stalled for time. Scooping up the cash and stuffing it back into the envelope, she slid it under the mattress.

"It's Rich."

Ella opened the door and poked her head out, greeting Rich with a smile.

"Saw your light on. How are you doing?" Rich whispered.

There was no need to whisper: they were the only ones onboard. Carlos had decided to stay in Falco's other guest room after Rich turned down the offer.

Ella just looked at him and shook her head.

"Look, I'm sorry. I didn't mean that the way it came out. You were nothing but courageous. You saved our lives." Rich took a step closer.

"You made a valid point," said Ella. "I'm just trying to think things through, Rich. A lot's happened."

She knew why he had come because she felt the same way: the high from having survived a battle, from being renegades with a pile of cash for their efforts. The rush from winning had to go somewhere. And he was at Ella's door. The quiet moment lingered to the edge of awkwardness.

"Be a shame to waste this freshly showered body," she smiled as she backed into her cabin, allowing him in. She slowly pulled her top over her head, leaving her firm breasts bare, nipples hard with excitement. She caught one hand in her sleeve. Rich moved into her, holding the trapped hand behind her head, and pressed against her, kissing her neck. Ella could feel his hard excitement, the thrill of his fingers running down her smooth back as she pressed her breasts into his chest. Rich's hands found the button to her jeans and ripped them open, yanking them down. She stood naked, shivering in front of him as he ran his hands over her breasts and down to her moistness. Ella leaned back and spread her legs open. She pulled him into her, aching to be filled. She had control, the power to say yes, the power to make him throbbing hard and ignite his passions.

CHAPTER 27

The hundred-ten horsepower diesel roared to life from a cold start with a knocking clatter, shaking and vibrating as it warmed up and jarring Ella from a short, but deep, sleep. She sat up naked, alone in a tumble of sheets and twisted blankets, squinting her eyes to focus on the clock. Four in the morning. It was still dark. Why so early? She fell back in protest, curling into Rich's pillow, the sheets still warm with his lingering scent.

The night with Rich had started out as a hungry passion between two warriors who survived a battle. But their exhausted bodies had soon mellowed into quiet lovemaking before they fell asleep in each other's arms. Ella lay with her arms folded around his pillow and vowed that today was the start of her new life. Tomorrow, she'd rent a car and drive back down to Marathon to see what Davis had buried in his yard.

She basked in the calm contentment of her new self-reliance. She no longer needed the protective hand of a father or lover to hold. She felt the freeing lightness of knowing she could make it on her own. The lovemaking had been proof; it had been fun, exciting, without being shackled to the need to be loved, or to own a lover.

She tossed off the covers, stood up on the bunk and poked her head through the open hatch. The night was bright with stars and only thin wisps of cloud remained. Rich stood leaning over the transom with a flashlight, checking the cooling water spitting out the exhaust pipe. A light went on in the foyer of Falco's house, the front door opened and Carlos walked out with Burke trailing slowly behind.

Ducking below deck, Ella searched for her clothes. Her underwear was caught up in the sheets at the foot of the bed, her t-shirt was bunched under a pillow and her pants sprawled across the cabin sole on Rich's side. She gathered her things, straightened the sheets and moved to her own cabin to finish dressing.

The envelope was still under her mattress where she had left it the night before. She ran her hand over it, reassuring herself that it was all still there. She had counted it too many times to do it again. But this wasn't the best place to keep it. She removed the bottom drawer from under her bunk, dropped the envelope into the hollow space and shoved the drawer back in.

*****

Rich was hunched over a chart at the navigation table reviewing their course to Fort Lauderdale when Ella emerged from her cabin.

"Good Morning." She walked past, running her fingers along his shoulder. He caught hold of her hand, pulling her into him before releasing his grip.

"Why are we leaving so early?" she asked, stepping back.

"Falco wants us out of here before daybreak. It's okay by me. I'd like to get back before dark. We have a decent wind and the Gulf Stream carrying us, so it should be only a nine-hour sail."

Carlos and Burke came onboard, both half awake. Burke settled into his spot in the cockpit and Carlos tumbled below.

"How are you, Burke?" Ella asked, straining to be heard over the engine noise.

"Like someone give me horse tranquilizer. What'd I miss?"

"Late night intrigue and a very good version of Ropa Vieja," she said. "Does it hurt?"

"Like hell." Burke held his shoulder.

"Any coffee?" said Carlos.

"I was just starting it." Ella said.

"What intrigue?" said Burke.

"Just the usual, men in black with guns boarding *Merlin*," she joked.

"Not funny."

"Is Falco awake?" asked Rich.

"Didn't see him." Carlos looked at Rich and then Ella, likely sensing something had changed between them.

"Let's shove off. We'll have our coffee under way."

"I'll get the bow line," said Burke.

"You need to stay still," said Rich. "That wound has to heal. Remember what Falco said."

Ella covered Burke with a blanket, then took his place handling the bowlines and Carlos cast off at the stern. Rich piloted *Merlin* away from Falco's dock and out into the channel.

A veil of mist rose off the water, concealing the curve of the channel's bank. Ella stood watch on the bow, straining her eyes as she peered into the haze. Carlos brought out the spotlight and shined it on the bank, but it was useless: the scattered light reflecting off the fog was like a white wall. Burke kept his eye on the depth sounder, calling out the changes as they inched their way toward the inlet.

Everyone had a job, working together for a common purpose. It was what Ella loved about sailing, and even though this adventure had turned deadly she would miss this temporary family. At the end of the day they would all return to their own lives until the next delivery, or the next drug run, when a new family would form. She was returning to a life half built, but confident she could make it on her own. Whatever part of herself she had lost on this trip, she had gained in courage.

Above the mist she could see Falco's house as they passed. In the tall slit of a window Falco stood backlit, hunched in his bathrobe, hands shoved into his pockets, alone in his fort, watching. She ventured a small wave that she thought he wouldn't see, but he nodded before he turned away.

Merlin motored out the inlet without bumping the bottom, riding higher in the water after unloading the eight hundred pounds of cargo. With the mist-shrouded island behind them, Rich set her on an east by northeast heading to pick up the Gulf Stream. A few miles out, a thick, low fog bank marked the edge of the warm current that they would ride back home.

Sometimes things do go your way, Ella thought. Sometimes you get to win, even if it's just a little.

A loose line of white pelicans flew above an empty beach swept clean of footprints by the changing tide. The tail end of the storm had pushed the towering clouds to the edge of the southwest horizon, clearing the way for fair skies. It was Ella's day, and it was as new as the rain-washed air. She leaned against the cockpit coaming, faced west and considered the darkened houses that dotted the shoreline—households asleep in their beds. She started to dream of a life that would someday be hers. With her restaurant in the Lower Keys, she'd build her own place in paradise.

Rich stood at the helm. The light breeze rippled his t-shirt against his toned chest muscles and arms that flexed as he handled the wheel. She smiled up at him, rekindling the glow from just hours before. He turned his head and smiled back, eyes bright with kindness. I'm going to have to be careful, she thought.

"I'm starving. Who'd like some breakfast?" said Ella.

"You happy," said Burke.

"Very. So what's it going to be, French toast?"

"Bacon," said Burke.

"Gone. We finished it off yesterday."

"How about potato egg dish you make?"

"Frittata? Takes too long. I'll make it for lunch. How about you, Rich?"

"I could eat." Rich smiled broadly at Ella, making Burke laugh, but Carlos shifted his attention to the horizon with an air of disapproval.

Rich's lack of restraint caught her off guard. He had tipped the others to their intimacy, revealing him to be a man who takes prizes. It's my fault, she thought. It was careless to have slept with him.

"I'll make French toast while we're still motoring out." Ella's brief look of annoyance wasn't meant just for Rich. It was a demand for respect. "What about you, Carlos?"

"Doesn't matter," Carlos mumbled.

"I thought you were a breakfast person."

"It's too early for breakfast, sun's not even up." He lifted his head, eyes shifting under his thick brow from Ella to Rich and back again.

"Well, French toast it is."

"I'll check the chart before we eat," said Rich. "Grab the wheel, Carlos." He followed Ella below deck and stood at the bottom of the stairs, watching her pull out pans and plates.

Ella turned around and met his eye. "I don't want *anyone* knowing my business."

"Sorry. I wasn't thinking. I understand why... I am sorry." Rich tried for a smile. "Will you have dinner with me tomorrow night? We should celebrate."

"I thought that's what we were doing last night." She turned her back to him.

Rich crossed his arms and leaned back into the steps. "Well, it was a bit more than that."

"Right now, Rich, I can be a friend and sometime lover, but nothing more."

"Would it be different if I said yes to another run?"

Ella turned, insulted, collecting her thoughts. "That's not the way I'm built. I lost someone I loved. I lost him in more ways than one."

"I know." Rich pulled her into him. "I'll always be your friend, Ella, and hopefully, your lover."

"Thanks." Ella let him hold her, kissing her lightly.

"I've wanted you from the first time we sailed together. Saint Lucia. You're an intelligent, beautiful woman, Ella—and a gifted sailor. How could I not?"

"Dinner sounds wonderful." She backed out of his arms, not wanting him to go on. She thought about her trip back down to the Keys. "I need to take care of something. Can we make it Friday instead?"

"What's happening tomorrow that's so important? Don't tell me you're meeting with Falco."

"God, no." Ella turned away and pulled the eggs and butter from the icebox. "I'm renting a safe deposit box and looking for a berth for *Gina Marie* in Marathon." She was making it up as she went, but it now seemed like a good idea.

"You don't have a car. I'll drive you."

"I'm getting a car. Can we make it Friday? Where should we go?"

"A place on the beach I think you'll like," said Rich. "The chef's a friend of mine, someone that might be helpful for you to know."

"That's really thoughtful of you." Ella could see Rich had bought her story, and she smiled. "Carlos is sure grumpy this morning. He get bad news from his wife?" She broke an egg into a bowl and grabbed for another.

"Didn't notice," said Rich.

"Maybe he doesn't like getting up at four in the morning," said Ella.

254

Rich leaned in and whispered into her ear. "He's jealous. He's had his eye on you."

"Yeah?" She turned into Rich's arms, an egg in her hand. He pulled her hips into him and kissed her deeply.

"Maybe he has his eye on *you*." With her free hand, she squeezed the ticklish spot she'd discovered the night before.

"Hey, stop."

"What happening down there?" said Burke. "We getting breakfast?"

"I think the crew is going to mutiny if they don't get fed," Ella said, turning back to the galley. "Isn't the captain supposed to be checking the charts?"

*****

The wind had shifted to the southeast. The crew raised the sails and Rich set *Merlin* on an easy reach. He cut the engine, providing relief from the noise, vibration, and oily stink of the diesel. The only sound now was *Merlin* sailing the calm waters in a ten-knot breeze, carried along on a four-knot current.

Ella served French toast, sliced oranges and warm maple syrup with a pot of fresh-brewed coffee. They enjoyed their breakfast stretched out in the cockpit, with even Carlos agreeing that this was the best damn French toast he had ever eaten.

"So, what are you going to do once you're back, Burke?" said Ella.

"Buy machine gun."

"Seriously?"

"Very serious," said Burke.

"You looking for another run?" Ella asked, ignoring Rich's discreet signal for her not to get involved.

"Already have one. Why?" Burke said. "You want to come?"

"No, I was just thinking how lucky you are to be alive," said Ella. "And here you are planning another run."

255

"You take when it comes. People forget about you quick down here," said Burke.

Ella thought about her conversation with Falco and wondered how long it would take for Falco to forget about her—if he hadn't already. What if he didn't call? Should she have asked for his number?

"What are you going to do, Rich?" Ella asked.

"Starting the new research project I was telling you about."

"Right, of course. The water striders in New Guinea."

"Papua New Guinea and the Solomon Islands," said Rich.

"You smuggle to study bugs?" said Burke in disbelief.

"It's what I do."

"We call you Captain Darwin," said Burke.

Carlos got up, collected the breakfast dishes and brought them below. Ella could hear the rattling bang as he tossed them into the sink.

She ignored the clatter and curled her knees to her chest. Turning back to Rich, she asked, "When?"

"Why you study them?" said Burke.

"Because they're interesting," he replied. "Their presence is an indicator of the ocean's health. The water has to be free of pollutants, or the surface tension breaks and they sink and die."

Ella leaned forward and asked again. "When?"

Rich looked up at the sails and pulled in the main slightly. "In two weeks."

"For how long?"

"Not sure. Not long." He stood up and tugged the jib sheet.

So that's it, Ella thought. Rich really didn't have plans for another run. Her future now rested on Falco.

"Will you have enough money to finance it?" Ella added, wishing she had more than a vague idea what he had been paid for the run.

"Yeah, I'm good for awhile." He wore a look of resignation, as if he had just lost her.

Ella sat quietly, looking up at Rich.

"I have a chance at a contract with the U.S. Navy," he continued.

"Navy?" said Burke. "Wow, man, you crossing over."

"Disease control. They collect data on bugs from around the world. It's just for a few weeks," he said directly to Ella.

She nodded and attempted a smile. She didn't have time to wait until his money ran out. She leaned back against the coaming, putting her disappointment aside. She glimpsed in him a lifestyle she admired: independent, full of adventure and intellectual stimulation. He might not be able to help her, but he inspired her to envision a big life where she, too, could have it all.

"What about you, Carlos? What are you going to do next?"

The question caught Carlos as he was coming up from below.

"Nothing." He turned and headed back below deck.

"I don't blame you, man," said Burke. "Carlos, you down there, man, roll me joint. Under my pillow. Careful, loaded gun under there."

*****

From the navigation station below, Rich called up the new heading to Ella at the helm. She adjusted their point of sail a few degrees to the north to follow along the string of islands that led to mainland Florida.

"You should see Alligator Reef lighthouse pretty soon." Rich came up on deck and sat to the lee of her. Keeping his voice low, he leaned into her. "Have you seen anyone touch my duffel bag under the nav table?"

"Your money bag?" she whispered.

"The very one."

"No. Why?"

"It's been moved, hundred and eighty degrees from how I stowed it."

"You sure?"

"Positive."

257

"Is anything missing?"

"Don't know, haven't counted it."

"Burke hasn't moved from his spot." She turned to look for Carlos. He was standing on the port quarter looking out across the water to the islands. "It might have slid out and Carlos shoved it back. Everything moves on a boat."

"You're probably right," said Rich. "Except we haven't been heeling more than five degrees."

"Maybe you should find a better hiding place. You know you can't trust us criminals," Ella smiled.

"Lighthouse at ten o'clock," said Burke.

"That'd be Alligator Reef Light," Carlos said, pulling back his sleeve to check his watch. He grabbed the binoculars out of Burke's hand and headed to the bow. Once there, he stood facing northwest, scanning the Keys, and taking an occasional over-the-shoulder glance back at the cockpit.

Ella looked up and around, worried that perhaps Carlos thought Sam was coming back, this time for their money. Aside from the lights of a freighter moving along the eastern horizon, she saw no other boats on the water. She curled up against the cabin side and went back to reading the dog-eared Travis McGee novel someone had left onboard, *The Deep Blue Goodbye*. If anyone went below, they'd have to pass by her. She took another sweep of the water, then returned to the tough-guy private eye who lived on a houseboat and worked only when his cash ran out.

For the third time in a half-hour, Carlos went below. Ella twisted around, pretending to look over the cabin top, and watched him move aft to his quarter berth.

There was no need to worry about Burke: the joint he had smoked had worked and he lay dozing, stretched out in the cockpit.

She lifted her eyes from her book to watch Carlos emerge from below.

"Packing my bags," Carlos said.

258

Ella looked at Rich and shrugged her shoulders. "Mind if I take a shower?"

Rich nodded his okay. "Carlos, your watch is coming up."

"Set it on auto pilot. No reason not to," said Carlos. "I still need to pack my fishing gear."

Rich shot Carlos a sideways glance. "We're still a good hour out."

Ella had gathered up her book and coffee cup and was halfway down the stairs. "Want me to take the wheel?" She could see Rich had started setting up the autopilot.

"I'll do it," Carlos said. "Just give me a couple of minutes."

"I'll be quick," Ella offered.

"Take your time," said Carlos. "We don't need to conserve water."

He was smiling, something she hadn't seen him do since they sailed *Grace* to Nassau.

*****

It was a luxury to have a hot shower on a boat. Ella soaped up her skin, washing away the scent from last night with Rich and the salt borne in the breeze and bow spray. But *Merlin's* shower was so small that she had to open the stall door to shampoo her hair. She tucked her head under the low-pressure spray, rinsing away the shampoo suds, when she thought she heard someone bang against the door.

"Rich?" She moved out from under the stream of water and listened. "Is that you?" Silence. She ducked back under the showerhead for a final rinse.

And then came a crack like thunder. She turned off the shower and opened the head's door to the sharp sound of gunfire and muffled shouts from Rich.

"RICH! What's going on?"

Merlin took a hard jibe. The wind caught the leeward side of the sail, slamming the twenty-foot boom to the limit of its range, sending a shock wave through the hull. The boat shuddered and rolled, throwing Ella onto the cabin sole. Another gunshot fired, and this time she could clearly hear Rich's angry shouts coming from the cockpit.

"Oh, Fuck!" Sam's back, she thought.

A deep, nauseating chill ran through her. Dripping wet, she crawled out of the head and pulled on her shorts and t-shirt.

"What's happening?" She rushed to the port then the starboard porthole, slipping on the varnished cabin sole in her wet feet. There was no boat that she could see. Rich sat slumped at the wheel holding his arm, blood seeping between his fingers and down his sleeve.

"STAY, ELLA! Stay down!" Rich screamed.

"Where are they?" She ran to Rich's cabin to sneak a look out the forward hatch. "Are they onboard?"

"It's Carlos!"

"Carlos? Is he shot?"

"Get your gun, Ella! NOW!"

"She can't." Carlos turned and looked down the companionway, his face cold as stone. "I've got her gun—got them all hidden away."

"What the hell's going on?" Ella dropped to the cabin sole and crawled behind the navigation table. "Burke?" From where she was hiding, she could see Burke's foot draped over the edge of the cockpit seat.

"Burke's not going to answer you." Carlos's lips spread to a grin. His eyes had darkened with cruelty.

"Rich, what's wrong with Burke?"

"Carlos shot him," Rich's voice was pained and breathless. "Shot us both."

"How bad?" She looked out to see Carlos and crouched back, pulling her knees in tightly. "Is Burke dead?"

She knew Rich kept his gun under his mattress; she needed to get to his cabin. She squatted, ready to bolt.

"No, but not looking good," said Rich.

"Carlos, what have you done? We're your friends." Ella looked around for anything she could use as a weapon. Rich's duffle lay at her side—a bag full of money, what this was all about. She could threaten to burn it.

"Friend?" Carlos laughed. "You stupid little girl. This is business. There are no friends here."

"Carlos, take the money and get the fuck off the boat," Rich commanded.

"You're through telling me what to do. You fucking people act like we were born to serve you. You think my people aren't smart— we're smarter than your pampered ass!" Carlos ducked his head below and Ella burrowed further under the table.

"Where are you, Ella?"

Rich's right hand hung blood-soaked at his side but he fumbled with his left, pulling his knife from its sheath. He took aim at Carlos's back, but his left-handed throw took a wild curve, sending the knife flying past Carlos to land below, spinning across the cabin sole toward Ella. Shaking, she stretched out and swiped up the knife.

"Looks like you missed, Boss." Carlos said in a mocking voice.

"Carlos, throw the guns over the side or I'm going to set fire to Rich's money." Ella held out a pack of hundred dollar bills. "You can take the money, take *Merlin*, leave us the dinghy."

Carlos stepped down to the first rung of the companionway steps, bending to look for her.

"Ella!" Rich screamed a warning.

"There you are." Carlos fired a shot, splintering the trim of the nav table above Ella's head. "You don't have a play, Ella. You don't have a gun." He took another step down into the cabin. "My guess, you don't even have matches."

"Carlos, don't do stupid, man!" Burke's voice was strained. "You kill us, we'll haunt you forever—I know."

Carlos swung around, took aim at Burke and fired, hitting him square in the temple. "That's not going to happen."

"Fucking bastard," cried Rich. "I'll kill you!"

Carlos turned and fired on Rich, hitting him in the leg, then turned back to Ella.

Ella could hear the thud of Rich's body falling to the deck. "NO-O!" she screamed. "Rich! Rich! Oh God, NO!"

Peering around the edge of the table, she could see Carlos's eyes flashing in the galley light, strained and wild. Terror raced through her blood so fast she couldn't breathe. She felt the weight of the knife and tried to take in its balance, but her hand was shaking so violently she could barely hang onto it. Tears blurred her vision. She'd never make the throw. Carlos's foot moved down to the next step of the companionway, and he hunched under the overhead to see into the cabin. He was coming below.

Ella dropped the money and rushed to Rich's cabin, slamming and locking the door. She could hear Carlos drop into the salon, racing to throw his shoulder into the door, a second behind her. She flipped up Rich's mattress. His gun was gone. She grabbed his flashlight, pushed open the overhead hatch and wiggled through the hatchway onto the deck just as Carlos smashed the door open.

Ella pressed behind the mast, gripping the knife and flashlight. She tried to steady herself, to overcome the choking fear, knowing she had only one chance. The autopilot had broken free and *Merlin,* having chosen her own point of sail, was headed out to sea. She peered around the edge of the mast, cursing herself for not closing the hatch. She could hear Carlos banging around below, opening drawers and lockers.

Carlos popped his head up through the forward hatch. "Ella, where'd you hide your money?" His voice was as calm as if asking for a cup of tea.

Ella sucked in further behind the mast.

"Not telling?"

She tracked Carlos's movements below deck toward the stern of the boat and slipped around the mast, trying to stay hidden.

Carlos stepped up in the companionway. "Ella, where did you hide..." he paused, rubbing his hand across his forehead, and screamed, "YOUR FUCKING MONEY?"

His voice boomed, jolting Ella, giving shape to what she was up against. It didn't matter if she told him where her money was, he'd kill her anyway. She needed him closer, close enough for a clean throw of the knife. He jumped below, pulling out the silverware drawer and flinging it across the salon, the cutlery clattering as it scattered over the cabin sole. She heard him empty the cupboard, pots and pans pinging like a steel drum as they bounced off bulkheads.

"Rich? Rich, can you hear me?" Ella looked around the mast. Only the top of his head was visible.

"Yeah." Rich's voice was hoarse and low. "I'm pretty shot up."

Carlos came up on deck, smiling and waving her knife bag. "Ah-h. The treasured knife bag, the one your dead papa gave you. This must be worth one clue. One clue, Ella? No?" He shoved Rich aside with his foot and sat down, unrolled the knife bag, pulled out the Wüsthof paring knife and flung it into the water.

"That was just the little knife, Ella. There're four more to go. Here's precious knife number two."

She heard the splash, and all the succeeding splashes that ended with the bag itself. The knives meant nothing to her now. She edged out from the protection of the mast to check on Rich. He was slumped on the cockpit deck with his head resting on the seat, his dimmed eyes watching Carlos. Blood soaked the right side of his shirt and the left leg of his pants. She pulled back behind the mast and raised her face to the sky for what might be the last moment of her life. She breathed the sea air deeply, trying to calm herself so she could think, but instead began to cry. I don't want to die, she prayed. Not like this.

Carlos stood up from his seat in the cockpit, glancing toward Islamorada. "I'm losing patience, Ella."

The thought of swimming for shore came and quickly went. They were at least a mile offshore and sailing away from land. Carlos would shoot her like a fish in a bucket. Even if she could make it in these dark waters, she'd never abandon Rich. She felt the weight of the knife in her shaking hand. She'd have to pitch it hard to do any good.

"Where's your money, Ella? Tell me and I'll let you live. Promise. I'll even let boss man live." He turned to Rich and lifted his chin with the barrel of the gun.

Rich grabbed the barrel with his good hand, trying to wrestle it away, but Carlos jerked it back and smacked him in the face.

"Rich?" She looked around the edge of the mast. Carlos was still too far away.

"Rich is taking a nap. Your money was under your mattress last night, Ella. Where'd you hide it? Tell me and I'll let you take the dinghy." He took aim at the base of the mast and shot, missing her foot by inches. A fisherman playing at wearying his catch, alternating hopeful promises with threats.

"Please, Carlos."

Carlos smiled at her and holstered his gun, his free hand twitching at his side. "She begs. That's a start."

Ella tracked him as he turned to the lazarette. She could see the slight movement of Rich's head as he, too, watched Carlos.

Carlos opened the lid, pulling out the diving weight belts. He looked at Rich, then toward the mast, before he started strapping one around Rich.

"What are you doing, Carlos?"

"Help him sink to the bottom, don't want him bobbing around on the surface. Maybe with all the sharks in these waters it won't be a problem, but success is in the details, Ella." He held up the other two belts, grinning. "Got one for each of you."

When he finished with Rich, he strapped a belt around Burke, wiping his bloody hands on Burke's shirt. Holding up the final belt for Ella to see, he said, "Unless, of course, you tell me where your money is."

"You're a cold fucking bastard. You'll burn in hell."

"Hell? I was born in hell. I live there."

Stepping over Burke, he threw the weight belt down and started up the port deck. He looked taller, bull-like with his shoulders raised, leaning into his walk.

"Carlos, please. Think about your family, your wife and daughter."

"My wife is dead. I don't have a daughter." A grin spread across his face as he pulled his gun from his holster. "You know what hell is, Ella? It's watching someone you love die a horrible death because you can't get the medicine that could save her. She's in so much agony that it's up to you to end her life. Someone you can't bear to live without. That's what your fucking country's embargo did to me and my people."

"I am not my country. Rich and I are your friends."

"Doesn't matter anymore. Dinero, Ella. Only thing of value to me: M-o-n-e-y. This deal got fucked because of you," he hissed. "I had people waiting for that load."

Ella pressed her head against the mast, begging for help: someone, God, Rich, anyone. But no one was coming. "Davis wouldn't want you to hurt me, Carlos."

"Ha! You don't know Davis." Carlos fired a shot into the air.

Ella trembled, angry that she had been so completely fooled. Carlos was a calculating, cold-hearted killer and he was good at it.

"Davis *always* did what was needed," Carlos boasted. "A businessman rising in the Banda de Hermano cartel."

"With Sam?"

"With me! Sam's a punk with a boat, expendable like that fucking old islander with the big mouth."

"And Jon?" She gripped the flashlight, unsure if she could pull off throwing both it and the knife. She slipped it into her back pocket.

"Jon? Fool with too much money and a bale he didn't know where to sell." Carlos paused, holding onto the side stay. "I just saved Jon from his miserable life," he laughed, taking another step closer.

Ella had one throw; if she missed she would die. Her whole body trembled and she tried to steady her hand. She brushed away the tears blurring her vision, wiped her sweaty palms on her pants, and set the balance of the knife in her hand.

The only thing she was aware of was the knife, the target and the metallic taste in her mouth. She felt the knife release from her fingers at the end of her arching throw, watched it tumble in the air as Carlos raised his gun, saw it sink deep into his chest, a stunned look in his eyes as he gasped for breath before he fell. For a moment there was only the distant, high-pitched buzz of adrenaline filling her ears.

She collapsed to her knees, bracing against the mast. In a breath she realized she was still alive. She looked sideways at Carlos, fearing what was next, but he lay still with the gun resting in his open hand. She crawled the few feet to him and grabbed for the barrel of his gun, but his hand closed around it. She snatched the flashlight from her pocket and smacked his wrist until the gun dropped to the deck. She swept it up, holding it on him while she patted him down. Rich's Walther was tucked into his back pocket; she retrieved it and then scuttled backward out of his range.

"Fucking knife." His eyes afire with hatred, he strained to speak in a huffing breath. "Davis will find you."

"Davis is dead." She started back to Rich but stopped, thinking about the phone call Carlos had made at Falco's. She turned to him. "Unless you know something?"

But Carlos didn't respond. Staying her distance, she saw his body had gone limp and his eyes now stared blankly out to sea.

He was gone. She looked up, turning full circle to scan the water. They were alone.

What she saw when she came to Burke made her turn away, shuddering in horror. He was shot through his temple, the exit wound leaving a spray of blood, brain and bone on the deck. Trembling, she cast her eyes to the side and stepped around him.

"Rich?"

He lay crumpled, soaked in his own blood, eyes flickering as he struggled to speak.

"Oh god, Rich."

Ella knelt beside him, unbuckling the weight belt and pulling back his blood-soaked shirt to see the wound: a ragged hole in his right upper arm.

"ITClamp?" Rich strained to sit up, then laid back down.

She shot a look at Carlos. He hadn't moved. "I'll get it."

"Tie this off." Rich held tightly to the wound on his leg, slowing the flow of blood. He looked over at Burke as Ella pulled sail ties from the lazarette. "Burke?"

"He's gone." Ella kept her head down, not wanting to look at Burke. She wrapped a sail tie around the top of Rich's leg below the groin. She tied if off tightly, then stuffed a cushion under his knee. "We need to keep it elevated," she said. "I'll get something to cover him."

She hurried below and grabbed a blanket and supplies. Returning, she laid the blanket over Burke, trying not to look at the destruction the bullet had caused, choking back grief for the savagery of his death. Anger overtook her as she thought about the vicious deceptions of Davis and now Carlos, and she raged at herself for being fooled.

She knelt at Rich's side, washing away the blood to study his wound and pressed an icepack to slow its flow. Having made up her mind on how to proceed, she acted quickly and without warning, fixing the ITClamp's needle prongs around his wound.

"Shit!" he cried. "Holy mother…"

"Your technique."

Rich nodded. His breath was labored, and he settled down flat on his back. "Best way."

Ella gave him a Vicodin, finished dressing his wounds and then covered him with a blanket. "You'll be alright, Rich," she said, stroking his hair. She leaned over him, resting her cheek against his, and held him gently for a moment.

Rich lifted his head only slightly. His eyelids were heavy and his body trembled in spasms. "Thank you."

Carlos's cough startled Ella and she slowly rose, peeking over the cabin top at where he lay unmoved. A spattering of blood spread from his mouth, but there was little from the knife lodged in his chest. *He was still alive.*

"God damn you, Carlos!" she stood up and screamed at the top of her lungs. "GOD DAMN YOU!"

She collapsed at the far end of the cockpit, staring at Carlos and worrying over what she would have to do, as *Merlin* sailed east toward the fog bank and further from land. The wind shifted around the bow, forcing the boat onto a starboard tack. The sails flapped and snapped as they caught the wind, jolting the boom to port and startling her to her feet. Carlos lay where he had fallen, his body rocking slightly with the movement of the boat. Her screams and tears had done little to help her. She took a step closer to Carlos; he looked dead.

"Ella." Rich's voice was faint. "I need to get to a hospital. We still have the dinghy?"

"Yeah, dinghy and outboard, tied off the transom." She thought of how Falco warned against going to the hospital with a gunshot wound. They'll investigate, she thought, and my life will be over. She looked around at the bullet holes in the cockpit and remembered the scraped hull. She'd have to confess to smuggling and possibly murder. All she had left was her dream. If she had to spend time in jail, maybe a very long time, she'd be ruined. She'd have nothing.

Ella looked over at Burke's body, fearing the same fate for Rich. She needed to hurry if she wanted to save him. She could secure the money and drop it over the side. Come back for it later. "I'll call the Coast Guard. They can airlift you to a hospital. We'll tell them that we were attacked by pirates."

"No. Don't—too much evidence. They'll know we had weed onboard."

"Rich, we can't risk your life. I won't."

"I've been busted before. I have a record." His voice was becoming faint.

"Busted?" More secrets, she thought. "You think you could make it into the dinghy?"

Rich nodded. "Burn the boat. Can you do that?" He lifted his head to look at Burke, then lay back down. "Can you get them below?"

Ella looked over at the blanket. Deep red stains spread across the white cotton where it touched Burke's wounds. "Carlos strapped a weight belt on Burke. I could put one on him, too."

"Easier."

"If he's dead."

"Give me the gun, I'll cover you."

Ella handed Rich his Walther. "Just don't shoot me by mistake." She bent over Rich and pushed back the hair from his face, still bruised from his fight with the pirate. "What about *Merlin's* owner?"

"Insured."

"We need to hurry. I can pack the money in plastic and drop it overboard. I'll mark a waypoint with the GPS. Anything you want me to pack?"

269

"Wallet. Toss my phone."

Ella nodded.

"Binoculars."

"Of course." Ella leaned over Rich and kissed his forehead.

"Put *Merlin* on course to nearest resort, get us close to shore," said Rich. "You can drop me off. Hurry, you need to get away before sunrise."

"We'll make it, Rich. I promise."

"Do you know what to do?" said Rich.

Ella closed her eyes briefly to the task ahead, and then looked at Rich. "No, I don't know how to kill a boat like this." It was something she would never have considered doing.

"Okay," Rich nodded slightly. "Bare the wires to the bilge pump motor, then open the propane shut off valve, extinguish the stove's pilot light, turn on all burners and open the engine's seacock, and then slit the intake hose enough for a slow stream of sea water. When the bilge pump float activates the motor, it'll spark the fuel."

"And good-bye sweet *Merlin*," said Ella.

"It'll work. Close the hatches."

"Propane sinks," said Ella.

"Better to be sure." Rich spoke slowly, the pain showing clearly on his face.

Ella felt his forehead—it was cool and clammy. "I'll hurry."

"When you're ready, set autopilot's course due east." Rich tried to lift his head and winced from a jab of pain that forced him back down. "Once I'm ashore, take the dinghy south, then scuttle it. Be smart. *Merlin's* name is on the transom. It's the only solution; our fingerprints are all over this boat."

Ella nodded, "I know."

She grabbed the binoculars and scanned the shoreline until she found a stretch of beach belonging to a small resort. Their lights were on. She set *Merlin's* autopilot for shore, then checked on

Carlos, noted the exact position of his body, and rushed below to gather their belongings.

In the ten minutes it took to sail close enough to shore, Ella had added her money to the duffel. She found Rich's wallet and his prized Swarovski binoculars, sealed them in doubled zip-lock bags and stuffed them in, then tossed his phone over the side. Using the same heavy plastic bags they had used for the bales, she double-bagged the duffle and secured it with tape. She gauged the weight to be about thirty pounds; it would have no trouble sinking. She made up a separate waterproof travel pack with her ID and cell phone, Davis's map, and three thousand in cash—enough to buy her way to safety for the next few days.

Carlos's body moved slightly, sending a spike of adrenaline through Ella. Was it the boat's movement that jostled him or was he still alive? She was too afraid to get close enough to find out. If he were any other animal she would have put him out of his misery. At a safe distance, she kept an eye on him and worked quickly to get her and Rich off the boat.

With the depth sounder reading twenty feet, Ella set *Merlin* to heave to, cutting her forward motion until it was time to disembark. She hefted the bag to the aft deck and looked down into the dark abyss. She hadn't considered the depth. She couldn't free dive that far and haul up a thirty-pound bag: it was impossible.

Suddenly, the thought came to her of tethering a buoy to the bag, like the ones she and her father had used on crab pots. This time, she would submerge the buoy on a short rope just below the water's surface.

The duffle sank quickly at the end of the thirty-foot hank of rope with its small boat fender tied at the halfway mark. It hit bottom and Ella hung onto the rope's bitter end, reconsidering. There was a possibility she'd never see it again. She turned to look back at Carlos and the bloodstained blanket covering Burke. There was only one way out of this. She let go of the rope.

271

With great care, Ella took a reading on the handheld GPS, saved the co-ordinates as a waypoint and did a visual triangulation of structures onshore, then did it all again, checking her numbers twice more for good luck. She added the GPS to the watertight money belt and strapped it on.

She stared coldly at Carlos's prone body. Having saved the worst for last, she retrieved the weight belt meant for Rich, laid it next to him, then rolled him on top of it.

"I hope you're still alive when I burn this boat. Your own personal hell for all the lives you've taken."

He hadn't moved, but she could feel the warmth from his body. It was possible he wasn't dead, but she didn't search for a pulse—she didn't want to know. She snapped the buckle closed.

It was time for them to go before Rich went into shock, before the people on these sleepy islands awoke to their safe, normal lives and spotted them motoring from *Merlin* toward shore. She tossed cushions and blankets into the dinghy to make Rich comfortable. "Rich, it's time. I need to lower you into the dinghy before I prepare *Merlin*. If something goes wrong, I don't want you trapped onboard. Can you help me?"

Rich nodded, trying to throw off the blanket, becoming angry when it was clear he was too weak.

Ella tied the dinghy alongside *Merlin's* ladder, then helped Rich into a life jacket. She attached a line to his jacket and slowly lowered him into the dinghy. Once he was in, she covered him with blankets.

"I'll be two minutes, Rich. We're almost there." She hurried below to do what she'd been rehearsing in her head, following Rich's instructions and, finally, closing the hatches. Before she stepped into the dinghy, she double-checked the autopilot's setting.

As she turned to join Rich, she stopped at the sight of Burke's covered body and tried to think of a prayer to honor her friend's passing, but words wouldn't come. She felt empty. All she could think to say as she stepped off *Merlin* was that she was sorry, and that was deeply true.

*****

Ella maneuvered through the waves, giving Rich the smoothest and fastest ride she could manage. She looked back at *Merlin*. In the pearl-grey light of morning, the boat sailed east for the middle of the Gulf Stream. The white blanket that covered Burke had blown off into the water.

As they approached shore, Ella jumped out of the dinghy and steadied it through the surf. Once she had the boat secured she ran as fast as she could toward the resort.

"Call 911!" she screamed. "A man's been shot. Hurry!"

When she was certain help was coming, she returned to see that Rich had crawled out of the boat and was lying in the sand.

"Get out of here, Ella. Now!" He tried to lift his head but it was more than he could do.

"I don't want to leave you. How will you...?"

"I'll feign amnesia. I'll call you."

Ella kissed him on the lips, and he kissed back. "Soon as possible?" She bent down and kissed him again. "Please, Rich."

"Go!"

Ella pushed the dinghy off the sands and motored quietly away. Looking back, her heart sank at the sight of Rich lying alone in the dark. But people were already running down to help, searching the beach with their flashlights.

When she had motored a half-mile south to where the bottom dropped away and the current picked up speed, she pulled the plug from the dinghy's drain and eased up on the outboard's throttle. In the cold-blue light of predawn she drifted along, slowly sinking, watching Rich's rescue. The flashing lights of an ambulance and police cars had arrived.

The water reached the dinghy's seat and Ella eased quietly into the sea without a splash that could attract a shark. She swam with strong sweeping pulls, straining to keep her head above the choppy water, trying as hard as she could to get distance from the coming explosion, turning back only briefly to see that the dinghy had sunk below the surface.

Nothing happened. She treaded water and watched *Merlin,* her sails full, her sleek hull heeling slightly in the light breeze, sailing further out to sea under the brightening sky. Could Carlos still be alive and capable of turning off the propane? The horror of him burning alive jarred her, but still she prayed for the boat to burn.

She turned toward land and saw that she had motored out further than she thought. She wasn't a strong swimmer, and the fight to save Rich's life and her own had taken all the strength she'd had. She could see *Merlin* in the distance sailing free, a ghost ship with her fingerprints on every surface. Goddamn it, burn! As she struggled toward shore, she reviewed her preparations to turn the boat into a bomb. The last thing she had done was to open the propane line. It *had* to burn.

The voice in her head repeated over and over in a silent chant: *Be brave, be strong.* Her mind shifted from fear to determination and back with the pressing thought of a shark attack. *Be brave.* She turned over and floated on her back, exhausted and cold, watching *Merlin* sail on. Shivering, she gave off the deep cry of a wounded animal. *Fucking Burn!*

A wave washed over her, then another. She coughed out the salt water. *Move, Ella, move!* She flipped back over and began to pull herself along with leaden arms and tired legs unwilling to kick, then heard the explosion. She snapped around, stretching her head high above the waves, and saw a mushroom cloud of flames and black smoke billowing from *Merlin.* Burning shreds of debris littered the sky, and startled birds scattered from the trees on Islamorada.

Finally, Ella found her luck; the current was slowly carrying her to a sandy haven. But the waves had grown on the shallow sea floor, and she tumbled toward shore like a piece of flotsam, taken in then pulled seaward by the undertow, teased with the promise of safety. She struggled to stand, but once again her weak legs lost their footing and the undertow sucked her down. She tumbled in the waves until the sea had finished with her, discarding her onto the shore.

Ella crawled from the shallows onto the beach and collapsed face down, allowing herself to sink into the cool sand. She was spent enough to sleep, but she didn't dare. Through half-opened eyes she watched as a mutt padded along the shore. Detouring over to her, he sniffed around her face, gave a strained whimper and continued along the beach. She felt grateful for the brief moment of normalcy, watching the mutt lift his leg to a clump of kelp before moving on. Rolling over, she rested on her elbows and watched *Merlin* sink lower into the water, listing heavily to starboard. A great black cloud of oily smoke billowed out of her, signaling a disaster at sea. Soon, rescue boats would be on the way. She lay back down and stared up at the sky, heartsick and broken.

I want to go home. But where was that? A wave of loneliness compressed her, reducing her to a fraction of her size, a pebble sinking to the bottom of a pond. She felt as hollow as an abandoned shell. Had she been killed, she thought bleakly, no one would have missed her.

She looked down the beach in both directions. She didn't know Islamorada. She tried to get up, lifting herself to her knees, but her legs were shaking and she sat back on her heels to gather strength. She could hear the siren of the sheriff's boat long before it raced out of Islamorada's inlet toward the burning remains of *Merlin*. Pretty soon the Coast Guard would arrive, followed by spectator boats and the curious running down the beach to watch.

It wouldn't take long for the authorities to put together the gunshot victim washed up on the beach and the burning boat at sea. Someone, eager to help with information, would tell of a young woman, a Good Samaritan, calling for help, then disappearing.

She needed to get out of sight. She got up and brushed off the sand. The sea breeze had somewhat dried her soaked clothes and salt-coated hair. She headed up the beach toward what looked like a resort before anyone came around asking questions.

CHAPTER 28

Ella stumbled along the private ocean-side path that led to Cheeca Lodge & Spa, not having the heart to look back. Behind her, she could hear the urgent blast of an air horn from the sheriff's boat, and somewhere along the Overseas Highway sirens sounded from rescue vehicles. With everyone coming to help, Rich surely would be okay.

The morning sun rose, brightening the sands of the resort's groomed beach. Pairs of white Adirondack chairs sat empty under the lazy fronds of long-legged coconut palms. It all looked so clean and peaceful, luring Ella in. She dropped into a chair and watched *Merlin*, partially obscured beneath the black smoke, as her bow lifted higher and her transom sank deeper into the water. The exploding fuel tank would have blasted a hole in the hull, allowing the water to overtake her, weighing her down and pulling her into a watery grave. Any attempt by the rescue vessels to prevent the twenty-four-ton boat from going under would be futile.

Early risers were running to the water's edge, some with binoculars raised, others chattering on cell phones. Soon there would be a crowd rubbernecking and pointing at the spectacle, unaware of the pain and loss of life that had taken place on *Merlin*.

Ella hunched forward, cradling her chin in her hands, until she could no longer watch. It was time for her to move on, but she felt as ragged and shaky as an old drunk, with about the same degree of confidence. She needed to get a room and pull herself together. She stood up, shoeless, and faced the resort, straightening her clothes, brushing off the sand and combing her fingers through her hair. No one would rent her a room in her condition. She needed new clothes, and sunglasses to cover her haunted eyes.

The Cheeca Lodge & Spa was a twenty-seven-acre Valhalla of old money, a secluded tropical playground with bungalows tucked among a thousand graceful palms. Ella had grown up living near the wealthy, listening to the way the elite spoke, studying how they moved with easy confidence: the beautiful people, who believed money made them exceptional, even if they had never earned a dime. Right now, she needed to seem one of them. She lifted her head, threw back her shoulders and ambled along the edge of the pool to the entrance.

The Luxury Boutique wouldn't open for another hour. She walked back to the poolside bar and picked up a *New York Times* and *Wall Street Journal* from a stack on the counter and ordered an orange juice. The bartender was busy setting up for the day and barely glanced up as he handed her change for a hundred-dollar bill. She found a private spot on the beach and eased into a chair for an hour of holding it together until she could collapse in the safety of a hotel room.

With her back to *Merlin*, she sat alone with her head bowed in exhaustion and worried again about Rich. She looked down at her clothes for traces of his blood. If there had been any, it had washed away on her swim to shore. She could still see Carlos's prone body and the horror of Burke's remains. She shuddered and looked over at the bar. She could use a double shot of scotch right now, but she didn't dare. She needed all that was left of her to focus on a plan—

278

what she would do today, and tomorrow, and all the tomorrows that followed.

*****

Ella had been lucky with the distracted barman, but the middle-aged sales clerk at the Luxury Boutique dropped her smile when Ella walked in. They must see all types at these resorts, she thought, especially in the Keys, where the wildness of Florida gets into people's blood. The clerk's eyes followed her around the shop, and when Ella moved out of her line of sight she would find something near her that needed attention. The clerk had mistaken her for some light-fingered local wandering in off the beach, and who could blame her? Ella looked like what she was; a castaway who'd just survived a shipwreck.

She paid cash for a garish silk blouse and skirt, jeweled sandals, a floppy-brim hat, large sunglasses and a small travel case. Minutes later, under the wary eye of the clerk, she emerged from the changing room transformed. The Louis Vuitton glasses concealed the grief in her eyes, and she held the unread newspapers prominently, signaling that she belonged. Strolling across the marble lobby, forcing a casual smile, she approached the reception desk.

"Good morning." She raised her chin. "I'd like a room."

"Good morning." The clerk gave her a welcoming smile and positioned himself at the computer. "And what name is your reservation in?"

"I'm without one. I'd like a room for one night, possibly longer." Ella gave him her best smile. "I'm visiting friends in Islamorada, but I could use a break. I've stayed here before and it was so peaceful." She glanced over her shoulder toward the beachfront and placed her copies of the *Times* and the *Journal* on the desk in front of him.

"Well, it certainly is. But our guests make reservations months, even a year in advance."

"Would you please check for me? It's after the holiday; maybe you have an early departure?" She struggled to maintain a smile.

"Certainly. That's quite something, that boat burning."

"Where?"

"See the black smoke?" The clerk pointed to *Merlin*. "It really blew. You didn't hear the explosions? There were two."

"Let's hope the wind doesn't change in our direction." Ella looked up briefly. "Any survivors?"

"So far, no. I'd be surprised if anyone could have survived *that*."

"So, do you have a room?" Ella quickly refocused the conversation.

"Looks like you're in luck. We do have a cancellation, but it's for the Superior Ocean Front King Room," The clerk paused, "at $680.00 a night, single occupancy."

"Sounds perfect. Do you mind cash? I'd give you a card, but I'd prefer it not to show on my account." Ella doubted cash would faze a clerk at an island resort.

"Of course. The Superior Ocean Front is one of my favorites. It has a spiral staircase off the balcony that leads right to the beach. I think you'll be very happy there."

Ella wondered if she'd ever be happy, anywhere, ever again.

"I just need your photo ID," he smiled. "And what name can I register your room under?"

"Ella Morgan," she said hesitantly, handing him her driver's license.

The clerk leaned over the desk. "I'll get someone to help you with your bags, Ms. Morgan."

"I can manage. I'm traveling light." Her voice began to edge toward a high-toned cadence as she regained confidence. She turned to walk away, then stopped. "I'll need a car for the rest of the week. Can you arrange one for me?" She pushed a hundred-dollar bill across the counter. "For your trouble."

"Certainly, Ms. Morgan. I'll call the concierge."

"I'll need the car at noon." She turned on her rhinestone sandals and headed toward her room. It's so much easier being rich, she thought. You don't have to do everything yourself.

*****

Ella locked the door to her room, turned on the TV, and surfed the news channels. No coverage yet on Rich or *Merlin*. From her window it looked as though most of the island was gathered on the beach and watching first hand. She left the TV on mute and picked up the phone.

"Room Service, please." There was a pause on the line as the operator transferred the call. "Yes, this is Ms. Ella Morgan. Are you still serving breakfast?"

After a shower, shampooed in lavender soaps and towel-dried in Egyptian cotton, she put on the plush resort robe and lay down on the king-sized bed. The ceiling fan in her pale yellow room caressed her with a soft breeze. By now, Rich would be in surgery and the fireboats would have doused the flames on *Merlin*—a useless effort for a sinking boat. She rested with half-opened eyes, feeling not quite of this world, and gazed out the picture window at the tops of gently swaying palms until there was a light tap at the door.

The porter rolled in a cart with eggs Florentine and Canadian bacon, a side plate of berries, a double-shot latte and fresh-pressed orange juice. The thought of food had seemed better in the abstract. Now, sitting in front of it, the smell put her stomach in a knot. She sipped the orange juice and changed the channel.

"There's still no information on who was aboard the yacht or how it caught fire," an announcer was saying. An inset at the left of the screen showed a video of *Merlin* burning and boats clustered upwind to watch. "Officials are unable to locate the boat's registered owner, Boca Raton investment broker Keith Anderson, and fear that Mr. Anderson may have been aboard. Still no word on any survivors, but a man in his mid-thirties was found early this

281

morning on the beach at Islamorada with gunshot wounds. He was taken to Mariners Hospital where he remains unconscious but is expected to recover. Police have yet to question him."

"Oh Rich, thank God you're okay," she whispered. She searched other stations, but they all had the same report. Just as she clicked off the TV, her cell phone rang. It had to be Falco. Not now, she thought. She stared at it until the ringing stopped. Maybe once she knew whether Davis had a treasure and she'd been able to retrieve the submerged duffel of money—then she'd know if she still needed Falco. Later, she thought. I'll think about it later. She pushed away her uneaten breakfast.

*****

The molded wonder of a white Cadillac made Ella feel like she was driving around in a small living room, and she wished she had asked for a compact. She pulled off the highway into Bud's Tackle & Marina on the southern tip of Islamorada Key and stepped out. The roadside marina's berths were filled with sport fishing boats and diving runabouts, and the oily smell of diesel hung in the air.

She briefly looked around for Sam's sport fisher, then headed to the bait shop. Under a sign that read 'Anglish Spoken Here' sat a little curly-haired boy clutching a small scallop shell in his filthy hands. She was drawn to his sad eyes and face covered with a layered accumulation of dirt. Seeing him made her think of Davis's son; was he now an orphan? She gently touched his shoulder for a fleeting moment before opening the screen door.

The shop was packed with fishing tackle made for catching anything from bonefish to giant tarpon, and all the necessary diving gear for exploring reefs. A tanned, middle-aged man with an agreeable face stood behind the counter. He lifted his head as she walked in, then peered out the window as though expecting a man to follow her in.

"Morning," she smiled, brushing back a strand of her hair. "My husband sent me over to reserve a boat for reef diving tomorrow at sunrise. We're staying at Cheeca Lodge."

"You have saltwater experience?" he asked skeptically.

"We both do, yes. We have a sailboat in Fort Lauderdale. He's good with engines, too," she said proudly.

The man stood looking at her, brazenly sizing her up.

"We're not dockside boat owners," she added. "We do sail our Hinckley."

It was easier than she had imagined renting a speedboat with only the simplest lie, a fancy car and a worthless credit card backed by the perception of wealth. After she paid cash for the day's rental and a dive mask, the man walked her out to the small pier that ran alongside the work shed. He gave her a quick review of the boat, handed her the keys and told her to mind the channel markers all the way out.

"There's a depth sounder on board. Keep it turned on. If you're not familiar with these waters, they get shallow real quick. If the prop gets bent, it's on you."

On their walk back to the tackle shop Ella looked for the boy. She had pulled out a twenty to give to him, but he was gone.

"Was that your boy on the steps?"

"No. Poor little kid—don't ask."

"Could you see that he gets this?" She handed him the money.

"Sure, but he'll just buy candy with it."

"I don't care." Ella took one more sweep of the docked fishing boats. "We'll have the boat back by tomorrow noon," she promised and shook his hand. Beyond him, she saw a black BMW sedan race north on the Overseas Highway. The Keys weren't short on fancy cars, but she had a feeling about this one. Falco would have to come see *Merlin* burn for himself. She put on her hat and sunglasses and walked back to her car.

*****

It was a twenty-five mile drive from Islamorada to Marathon Key. Ella floated along in the Cadillac on the single-lane road to Davis's house, wondering what she'd find. She slid her hand inside her bag and touched the cold metal of Rich's Walther.

If Davis were home, he wouldn't be alone. The thought struck her as a possibility and she pulled out her phone, autodialing his number. It rang and her throat thickened with a wave of emotion at the thought that he might be there. The call went to message, stating his phone was out of range. There was only a slim chance that he had survived, but in her mind it would make her less a killer if Carlos were the only casualty. She passed the exit to Falco's and, five minutes south, turned into Davis's long drive, a tunnel of palms and tall Banyan trees ending in a stand of mangroves at the water's edge—a secretive passage to a private person's home.

As she pulled up, she could see that something wasn't right. Davis liked order: he had a sea captain's sensibility and, for him, everything had a place. But the garage carriage doors were swung open and its contents were scattered about the drive. Rolling quietly over the gravel, she stopped and pulled out the Walther, got out of the car and stood to listen—but heard only the wind rustling through the palms. She walked lightly along the crushed-shell pathway that led to the backyard and a wooden dock on the canal. She stopped at the veranda and peeked through the wide-open French doors to his bedroom.

Davis's place had been ransacked. He'd lived as simply as a monk, but what few belongings he'd had were strewn across the floor. Drawers were pulled out and emptied of his clothing, the bookshelf turned over, and the mattress pushed halfway off its frame. Whoever had done this was gone, with or without Davis's fortune. She looked out across the small backyard to the avocado tree standing in the corner; the ground around it appeared undisturbed.

She stepped into his bedroom. It was hard to think of the Davis she had known here, hard to think of herself as the one who'd shot and possibly killed him. They had spent a lazy day making love in this room with the sea breeze drifting in through the French doors. She remembered lying here, happy and content, her legs entwined with his, watching the light shine in through palms that moved with the breeze and cast patterns onto the walls and old wooden floors. But it had been a deceptive happiness. The wealth and security he'd wanted to offer her came from smuggling drugs. And now she was a smuggler herself.

She picked up a broken framed photo of Davis that she hadn't seen before. He was standing in front of a rustic beach house holding a small boy in his arms. A native woman with long, black hair leaned in at his side, her arm resting on his shoulder, and an old black dog lay at their feet. She lifted the photo from the broken glass and turned it over. On the back were the names *Davis, Topo* and *Siani*. *Topo* had been crossed out and, in another hand, *Nicholás* was written above. She slipped it into her pocket and began to search through his scattered belongings until she found what she was looking for: a letter from Cuba, a way to find Davis's son. The return address was written in a neat hand and the colorful stamp was postmarked a year ago.

Ella opened the letter and checked the signature; it was from Siani, the woman in the photo. Stuffing it into her pocket, she picked some papers off the floor and a photo of herself fell out—one she hadn't seen before. She was smiling brightly at the helm of the first boat she'd been hired on to deliver. Davis had been the captain. It had been the beginning of their affair.

A barking dog startled her. She stuffed the photo in her pocket and moved toward the living room, spooked, peering around the corner as she went. She walked over to the edge of the front window and peeked out. No one was there, but it felt like a warning.

She grabbed a shovel from the garage. Gripping the map, she hurried down the path to the avocado tree. It turned out that she didn't need the map. The soil around the base of the tree had been freshly turned.

Shovelfuls of dirt lifted easily away until she hit something hard. She caught the sound of a boat motoring up the canal and crouched listening until it passed. Now at a quickened pace, she bent down and brushed away the dirt covering a black plastic box. When the container was unearthed, she tugged it out of the hole and onto the lawn. It was nearly two feet long, and half as wide. She brushed away the remaining soil and flipped open the top.

"Holy shit, Davis."

Two layers of hundred-dollar bills lay in neat packs, and a sealed manila envelope sat on top along with a cotton bag of coins and two gold bars stamped "Suisse 10 oz. Fine Gold".

Ella fell to her knees, breathless.

"All this, and you needed more?"

She lifted one of the gold bars and felt its weight in the palm of her hand. Shaking her head, she sat back on her heels and fanned a pack of hundreds, trying to take in the fortune Davis had accumulated. What had she meant to him, that he'd entrust her with all this—his son's inheritance?

"Guess what, you fucker," she muttered under breath, "some of this is mine."

From the looks of the soil, someone had dug here in the past few weeks, she thought. Was it Davis adding Jon's money to his hoard of cash? Or whoever tossed his house—had they found it, and were they coming back? She leapt to her feet and pushed the dirt back into the hole, layering the depressed patch of ground with fallen palm fronds, then tossed the shovel across the yard. The box was too heavy to carry. She found a hank of rope, tied it to the handle and dragged the box to the car, then heaved it into the trunk. She was looking back at the trail the box had left when she heard a vehicle coming down the long driveway. She jumped into her car and sped out.

Sam's red Jeep Cherokee barreled down the narrow drive toward her. Glare on the windshield made it difficult to see, but she figured that the blonde riding shotgun was Nikki. The Jeep was kicking up dust as it raced down the middle of the drive, leaving her no room to pass. She held her ground. At twenty feet, Sam spun his car ninety degrees in an attempt to block her, but skidded on the gravel in a cloud of dust and crashed sideways through the ferns into the tangle of mangrove roots.

Slowing to pass, Ella rolled down her window to see Nikki jump from the Jeep, looking tousled and out of control.

"Fucking asshole!" Nikki slipped on the gravel and caught her balance. "Ella, is that you?"

Sam rushed from the Jeep, red-faced with fists clenched and breathing hard like a charging bull, until he saw Ella. She stopped the car, and locked the doors, resting her left hand on the window button and her right on the Walther.

"You again." She wanted more than anything to run Sam over, but she wasn't going to be stupid—not with a tub of money in the car.

"What are you doing here?" asked Sam.

"I could ask you the same question." Ella checked herself. She needed to throw them off her trail. "I was hoping that he'd be here, and this nightmare was just a dream." She looked at Nikki, who was standing with her hands on her hips like a little girl who hadn't gotten her way in a very long time. "So, why are you here, Sam?"

Sam didn't answer, and turned to check for damage on his Jeep.

Ella took her foot off the brake and began to roll forward.

"Ella, wait!" yelled Nikki. "What did you find in there? Did you find anything?"

"You mean in Davis's home? Nice, Nikki. You've gone from ripping off loads to robbing the dead."

"Whose car is this?" Nikki twisted around to look inside Ella's car and grabbed for the handle, grimacing when she saw it was locked.

Ella had never seen Nikki without her makeup. She was always perfectly groomed, dressed in carefully chosen outfits. Now, she looked wild-eyed and desperate, thrown together and covered in a fine layer of dust.

"Why are you really here, Ella?"

"I already told you. Was it you and Sam that trashed his house?"

"Did you find it?" Nikki stood biting her lip, squatting to see into the Cadillac.

"Find what?"

"He had some money hidden. Actually, it's Sam's money."

"Why would it be Sam's?"

"They're partners. Did you get the money off the boat?"

"How would you know?" said Ella.

"Know what?"

"That he had money hidden."

"He told me."

"Why would he tell you, Nikki?"

"We partied for a couple of days." Nikki lowered her voice and glanced over her shoulder. Sam was lying on the ground, checking the Jeep's undercarriage.

"A couple of days? When?" Anger rose in Ella's voice. "When, Nikki?"

"Last week. We were getting stoned and he let it slip."

Last week was when Davis had cancelled their plans because of some business he had to take care of.

"God, who haven't you fucked?"

Nikki looked around to check if Sam had heard. "He was sweet on you, Ella."

It never was real between us, Ella thought. "You just made things easier."

"What do you mean, easier?" Nikki looked confused. "It didn't mean anything."

"Nothing means anything down here. You knew about this whole ugly double-cross, didn't you?"

"What could I have done?" Nikki's voice rose in defense.

"You could have spoken up. Saved lives. But, then, there was the money." Ella squeezed the steering wheel. She wanted to get out and slug Nikki. "Three people are dead, and one of them was supposed to be me."

"No one was supposed to get hurt."

"That's what the machine guns were for? So no one would get hurt?"

Nikki turned toward the house. "It's got to be here. Did he tell you where he hid it, Ella?"

"Try asking his son. Everyone else is dead."

"Son? He has a son?"

"Had. Davis is dead, remember?" She watched as Nikki looked away. "He is, isn't he?"

"How would I know?" Niki huffed.

"You know."

"Well, you shot him. I had nothing to do with that. You're the one who killed him."

"You and Sam deserve each other." Ella took her foot off the brake and started rolling away.

"Wait, Ella. Do you know where his money is?" Nikki kept up alongside the car. "Wait! Fifty-fifty split and I'll tell you if he's alive or not."

A slight smile flickered on Ella's face before she could stop it.

"You do, don't you? It's in the car." Nikki turned, "SAM! The money's in her car."

Ella hit the gas, kicking up gravel and dust. She glanced in the rearview mirror at Nikki running after her, screaming.

"ELLA STOP! God damn it! STOP!"

Nikki halted in the middle of the gravel lane, nearly obscured in the billowing dust, stomping her feet, her arms thrust straight at her sides, screaming with everything she had. "STOP!!!!"

Ella saw Nikki jump to the side as Sam's jeep burst through the dust cloud and raced toward her. He tried to pass in an attempt to cut her off. She stepped on it, but they were quickly coming to the end of the lane. She stretched her neck to look past the trees for crossing traffic on the Southbound A1A. A fast-approaching semi blasted its horn. Ella floored it, racing across the road. Sam slammed on his brakes but skidded over the gravel, right into the path of the truck. It hit him broadside. His tires buckled on impact and the jeep flipped and tumbled side over side, landing upside down and sliding into the mangrove swamp.

Ella pulled off the road and started to get out. Other drivers stopped. The truck driver jumped from his cab and ran to help. Nikki emerged running from the driveway, hysterically screaming for Sam. Ella got back in her car and watched. Nikki was on her knees at the Jeep, screaming Sam's name.

Ella put her car in gear and slowly pulled onto the road, taking one more glance behind her. Nikki rose, watching as she drove off, and pounded her fists in the air, screaming.

"MURDERER! I'll fucking get you for this!"

Ella rolled up the window. And now Sam, she thought, rubbing the back of her neck. It was time get out of the Keys, away from Florida—as soon as she retrieved the duffle. But first she had to trade in the Cadillac.

CHAPTER 29

Ella's wake-up call came at five in the morning, pulling her out of a deep sleep. The ring had startled her, triggering a flashback of the frenzied warning blasts from the semi's horn, the sounds of crashing metal, screams, and the rolling tumble of Sam's jeep ending wheels-up in the swamp. She rolled over and lifted the receiver to silence the call, then dropped it back in the cradle. Burying her face in the satin pillows, she waited for her heartbeat to calm. She had learned from the news that Sam hadn't survived the crash. To think that only a week ago she had considered him a friend. Now she was certain he would have killed her for Davis's money. But Rich had survived, and for that she could be thankful. If only he were with her now.

She reached for the remote, opened the curtains and saw that it was still dark, then closed them again. The final leg, she thought, staring up at the ceiling. With all the money sitting in the trunk of the car, she was tempted to leave the duffle for the fish, but the thought that most of it should go to Rich made her sit up. She could sleep in tomorrow, stay another day and open a safe deposit box. Last night, she had traded the Cadillac for a mid-size black Chrysler. In the land of thieves, its trunk wasn't the best place to stash money, but for now it was all she had.

She flopped back onto the soft, warm bedding, her tired body resisting getting up to go dive into the cold, dark ocean. She switched on the lamp and picked up the photo of Davis and his family from the bedside table. There was an ease in his face that she had never seen. He looked happy leaning into Siani and Topo, natural, like a father would. She could see now that Davis had never belonged to her, that they'd never really been a couple. But what she did have was his money, a possible address for his son —and uncertainty of what to do about any of it.

Get up! Ella told herself and kicked off the covers, switching on the coffee pot on her way to the bathroom. A long, hot shower got her blood moving again. She dressed in her old clothes, streaked with white salt crystals from yesterday's swim, and prepared for the dive, stuffing a pillowcase with towels and the hotel's plush robe. She turned the TV on low, hung out the 'Do Not Disturb' sign, grabbed her coffee and left for Bud's Tackle & Marina.

First light was beginning to blush the sky and push back the inky black night. The world looked a little more beautiful to her now that she had escaped the cold breath of death.

She parked the Chrysler behind a shed, locked it and ran along the dock to the rented runabout. She tossed in her things and checked that it had an anchor; the boat hook was missing, so she borrowed one from another boat. The engine started on the first try, and she threw off the dock lines and headed out the channel. At the last channel marker she turned north along the coastline, keeping an eye on the depth sounder as it jumped from ten to forty feet and then back again.

The only marine traffic was a ship crawling south along the horizon; otherwise the ocean was as deserted as the highway. She pushed the throttle wide open and planed across the glass-smooth water.

She had less than fifteen minutes before sunrise to find the duffel and get it aboard. Keeping her speed at twenty mph, she estimated that she would make the two miles in six minutes. She cursed herself for taking her time lying around in bed. She kept watch for other boats; scavengers would surely arrive at the crack of dawn to have first pick of *Merlin's* thousand-dollar winches and state-of-the-art gear.

She turned on her handheld GPS to let it warm up and looked for her landmarks. The eastern horizon began to brighten, casting a thin light across the water and making it easier to find her way. She passed the silhouetted, tree-lined spit of land with the two lighted radio towers that she had noted as markers. Up ahead was the Cheeca Lodge, dimly lit for morning staff, and the beach where she had washed up.

Ella pulled back the throttle and watched her GPS search for the waypoint she had saved. Its proximity alarm sounded at fifty feet from the location and she put the engine into neutral. In the near distance, orange buoys and air bags marked the site where *Merlin* had sunk. The tip of her eighty-foot mast still jutted above the surface. She had joined the many sunken ships from the past four centuries that littered the bottom along this coast.

Sharks would have taken the bodies by now. Ella couldn't think about them: she couldn't go into the water shuddering with fear, sending the telltale signals of prey in distress. She had to stay focused. She needed to get this done and get out while the scavengers and law officers were still asleep.

She slipped on the dive mask and pushed her face into the dark water, looking for the buoyed duffle and any threatening creatures looming below. She moved to the other side of the boat. Nothing. Dawn was prime feeding time for sharks; she had to hope they were farther out on the reef. She pushed up the mask and checked the GPS. The boat had drifted with the counter current, floating south past the waypoint.

The GPS was only accurate to about fifty feet. Ella moved the boat until she was spot on the waypoint, then motored north a hundred feet and lowered the anchor. The small plough would slow the boat's drift and, if it encountered shallower water, would set itself in the sandy bottom, preventing the boat from running aground.

In the brightening sky, she watched a fishing boat leave Bud's channel with another trailing close behind. She was running out of time. She held onto the gunwale, pressing her mask into the water. Where are you? The proximity alarm sounded again as the boat passed over the GPS waypoint. Still, she could see nothing. With the anchor still dangling, she motored slowly back toward the coordinates, overrunning the mark east by a hundred feet. Finally, she spotted the submerged buoy and the duffel beneath it in plain view on the sandy ocean floor.

Ella grabbed the boat hook and slipped into the water. A rush of silver flashed in front of her and circled back, stopping a few feet away. A four-foot barracuda held her in its gaze with a fearsome eye. Its deep-hinged jaw had an underbite, exposing piranha-sharp fangs that moved in a slow chewing motion. She froze, breathing heavily through the snorkel. She couldn't take the chance of climbing back aboard, afraid that it would attack her legs. She had heard of barracudas ripping chunks of flesh from divers' limbs. She waited, holding the boat hook out in front of her as a weapon.

She never saw the attack. The boat hook was ripped from her hand in a cloud of bubbles. She twisted around, searching for the barracuda, but it was gone and the shiny aluminum boat hook, bitten in half, sunk to the bottom.

Slowly she searched the waters with the limited peripheral vision the mask afforded, worrying over the shiny bits on its strap. She floated still as possible, watching, but the barracuda was gone. How easy it would be to climb back into the boat. So close, I'm so close, she thought. I can do this. She took a few breaths and then a deep one and dove for the buoy line, twisting as she descended, looking for predators. She snagged the line and came up for air, spinning around to find that the boat had drifted southwest toward the shore. It was too far away for the length of line on the buoy. She dove back down, retrieved the buoy and retied it at the surface, then swam back to get the boat.

She motored up-current to the buoy and grabbed hold of it, pulling hand over hand until the duffel reached the surface. The thirty-pound bag had seemed a lot lighter going into the water, and she struggled to get it over the gunwales.

The plastic was still intact. She ripped it off and checked the money; it was dry. She tossed the weight belt over the side, stuffed the plastic inside the duffle and zipped it closed. Pulling on the Cheeca Spa's robe, she wrapped it tightly around her, sat down in the cockpit and caught her breath, staring at the duffle while the boat drifted south.

The first-light fishermen were heading out to the reefs, and dive boats were following. Against her better judgment, Ella motored over to the orange buoys to say goodbye to *Merlin*, knowing its memory would haunt her. Waves washed over the exposed tip of the mast, the jib halyard still attached, the rigging in a tangle and the charred remains of the submerged sails rippling slowly with the current. Below, she could see the ghostly shape of *Merlin* on the bottom, her starboard quarter blown out in a ragged hole.

She looked hard into the deep for Burke's and Carlos's bodies, worrying that the weight belts were a mistake, anchoring the men to the bottom to be discovered as evidence of murder. She had been horrified by her hope for sharks to take them away, and now she saw their shadowy sway emerging from behind the edge of the hull. There was nothing of Burke that remained down there, she told herself, and turned away.

She shifted the outboard into gear and motored south toward Bud's channel, twisting around for one last glance at *Merlin's* mast. All of this destruction, she thought. For what—a chance at the good life?

She thought about Burke and their hard-earned friendship, how he had grown up surrounded by war, and she felt deep remorse that his life had to end this way.

She slowed when the first of the scavenger boats came up alongside her.

"Find anything?" the grizzled helmsman called.

"Nothing worth taking." She gave a friendly wave and pushed the throttle wide open.

*****

Ella glided the boat into its slip and tied it off, then secured the duffle in the trunk of her car. She grabbed the quarters she had brought and headed to the weathered pay phone she had spotted the day before. She cleared the booth of empty beer cans, wiped the receiver on her sleeve and dialed the Mariners Hospital's number she had memorized from her room's info packet.

"Hello. I'm calling about a man admitted yesterday. He was found wounded, lying on the beach early in the morning." She waited on hold, pulling the bathrobe in tightly around her.

"Good Morning. I'm calling to find out how the man..." She tried to remember if the news had said he was shot. "Sorry, bad connection. The man that was found on the beach yesterday morning—how is he doing?"

She paused to listen. "There were two? He was lying near some cottages, possibly in his late thirties, light brown hair. What did the other man look like?"

"No, I'm not a relative." She paused again.

"I understand. It's just... I'm the one who found him. I'd like to know if he's okay. His nurse? Sure, I'll hold."

She studied the graffiti tags and phone numbers that covered every surface of the booth. BLAH was written in black marker across the top, and she wondered whether it was a comment on the booth itself, or on a conversation someone was having.

"Yes. Thank you." Ella listened. "No. No, I'm not a relative. Yes, I understand. But I'm the one who found him. Can you tell me if he's ok or not?"

She looked back, checking on her car, listening to the nurse.

"I really don't want to... well, sure. My name's Carla Burke. Please, can you just tell me, did he live?"

"Wonderful. Thank you. And what about the other man who was found?" Ella listened quietly. "I'm sorry to hear that. Thanks for your help."

CHAPTER 30

On her second day at Cheeca Lodge, Ella rocked gently in a hammock strung between two palms at the water's edge as a warm breeze brushed over her, soft as goose down. She dangled her leg over the side, occasionally pushing off with her toes to keep the hammock in motion. She was alone on the beach; even the white sands had been raked smooth, erasing the footprints of yesterday's guests. She lazed in the luxury of the resort, untethered in time, not knowing where to go or what to do.

A Seafood Tower sat in ice on a table beside her. She was hungry, but still too shaken to eat. She picked at the lobster tail, ate a marinated mussel and warily eyed the barracuda ceviche. She had no interest in eating the predator after that morning's attack. Finally, she gave up on the food, slipped out of the hammock and headed back to her room to count the money.

*****

Behind locked doors and drawn curtains, Ella sat cross-legged on her bed and stared in disbelief at Davis's cache: two million one hundred thousand breath-taking dollars. He had clearly been hoarding money for a long time. How much would finally have been enough to make him stop risking his life and the lives of others? For someone who had grown up in aching poverty, maybe there could never be enough.

Inside the plastic tub were a pocket-sized muslin bag and an envelope. She untied the bag's drawstring and emptied its contents into her hand: ten one-ounce gold Krugerrand coins. She let them cascade from one hand to the other, captivated by their weight and the bright clinking sounds as they dropped one by one. Pressed in the bottom of the bag was a necklace made of a worn leather string laced through the natural hole of a smooth, flat beach stone. It was a simple necklace, like a child would make after a day's beachcombing. Ella wondered if Davis's son had made it for him. She slipped it into her pocket.

She tore open the small padded envelope and pulled out packets of carefully folded tissue. Unwrapping them, she found five emeralds of varying sizes and shades, and two small diamonds that sparkled in her hand. She picked out an emerald the size of a quarter and held it up to the light, marveling at its vivid green, the color of spring grass and clear as a mountain stream. She slipped it into her pocket alongside the stone necklace.

The duffle sat off to her side filled with the crew's pay, including her twenty-five thousand. She unzipped it to take out her share, then stopped at the haunting, raw memory of Burke's and Carlos's bodies. She rubbed her hands over her face, waiting for the images of blood-soaked sheets and *Merlin's* charred remains on the ocean bottom to fade.

"At least Rich survived," she said softly.

She stared at the duffle meant for Rich, then transferred ten packs of hundred dollar bills into it from Davis's box. It hardly made a dent. She added the rest of the jewels, gold coins and bars, then zipped it closed. She would take her share out of Davis's money before giving it to his son. When Rich was well, he'd have a nice surprise waiting for him, enough to fund his research for years.

This is it, she thought, looking at Davis's remaining two million dollars—a chance, a real chance. But not here, not in the Keys with Nikki seeking revenge. She'd cancel her contract with Mr. Conti and find a safer place far away from here. And then there's Falco, she thought, regretting that she'd asked him for a job.

This new wealth had saved her, sparing her from finding out how far she would have gone in its pursuit. She felt both lucky and cursed. It was wealth gained at the cost of others' lives. She could buy nearly anything she wanted, go anywhere she wanted. Yet it felt as distant and foreign to her as being told that she was an heir to royalty.

How much was rightly hers? She began dividing up the money, half for her and half for the boy. She'd worry about how to get it to him later. She'd earned it, damn it: for surviving Davis's attack, for having to kill two men to save her own life, and for watching a friend die. It was her payoff for Davis's betrayal. And for a boy in Cuba, a million dollars would easily last him a lifetime.

She remembered Siani's letter on her bedside table. She had put off reading it, not wanting to learn more about Davis's hidden life. Now, she slipped it out of its envelope and unfolded it.

Siani's tone was kind but firm, telling Davis it was time for him to be a father to his son. Nicholás needed to go to school, she said, and needed friends his own age.

His son, not theirs, Ella thought. She picked up the photo and studied Siani. She was older than Davis. Was she his mother, a friend, maybe an aunt? They had similar facial features, with high cheekbones and dark, deep-set eyes. Who was Nicholás's mother? Was she alive and, if so, where was she?

Siani was asking Davis to take his son from the island, away from Sully and all the "bad people" who came there. Who was Sully? What bad people? She was asking Davis to bring Nicholás to live with him in Florida. A request ignored, for the letter was postmarked a year ago, yet there had been no signs of a child at his

Florida home, no toys or clothes. And yet, possibly in his dying moment, Davis had begged her to do what he hadn't.

Ella felt she had fallen into a snake pit. Would Sully and the "bad people" come after her? For all they knew, she had died when *Merlin* exploded into flames and sank to the bottom of the sea. If they knew about Davis's buried treasure, they'd probably come after Sam first. And when they learned that he was dead they'd go after Nikki, who would be all too willing to point them in her direction. She needed to start thinking about her next move.

Her cell phone rang. She hesitated, then took the call.

"Falco?"

"You okay? Rich is in the hospital."

"Have you talked to him?"

"No," said Falco. "He's still unconscious but his vitals are strong."

"That's great news. You know he'll have amnesia when he wakes..."

"We need to meet."

"No."

"Where are you?"

"It's all gone." Ella knew better than to talk to Falco over a cell phone, but she didn't want to face him in person. "It was Carlos—along with Davis, Sam, and of course Nikki."

"Where are you?"

"Far away and still going. I'm through with smuggling."

"I need to talk to you."

"There's nothing more than what I just told you. Goodbye, Falco."

A few seconds after she hung up, Falco called back. She picked up; she didn't want to worry about Falco tracking her down.

"How'd the boat catch fire?"

"Carlos," she lied, then paused for a moment. "I have to go."

"The money?"

"Lost in the fire."

"Sam's dead," said Falco. "Nikki said it's your fault."

"No, she's lying. He was chasing me out of Davis's driveway." She regretted the words as soon as they left her mouth.

"Why were you at Davis's?"

"I wanted to see if he was there. He wasn't. Someone had trashed his house. Was it you?"

"Of course not," Falco said. "Ella, I'm glad you're okay. Get some rest. I'll call you later."

"No..." But Falco hung up before she could finish her sentence.

She fell back on the bed, watched the overhead fan spin round and round and wondered if she would ever need Falco again. Why would she? She slipped off the bed and walked out to the beach. The air had a stillness at sundown, when it was no longer day but not yet night. She stopped at the water's edge, wound back and pitched the phone as far out to sea as she possibly could.

CHAPTER 31

Ella feared Nikki or someone from Davis's gang would be coming for his money. She needed to keep out of sight, but she couldn't leave until she was sure Rich was okay and somehow let him know where to find the duffle. In preparation for leaving the Keys, she had put the bulk of Davis's money in a Marathon bank safe deposit box and, back in Fort Lauderdale, secured the duffle on *Caroline*. Rich always stowed his dinghy inverted on the cabin top when he was out of town, and Ella had stuffed the duffle under its seat, using a tarp she found in the lazarette to cover it and lashing it down so that even hurricane winds couldn't blow it off. While she waited for him to recover, she moved her boat to a private dock on Hendricks Isle, a secluded hideout for what she hoped would be only a few days. Finally, on the fifth day of calling the hospital from a pay phone, Rich answered.

"Yeah."

"How are you?" Ella noted the time, worried that the call might be monitored or traced: after all, Rich was the only survivor of a shipwreck and possibly the only witness to a crime.

"Fine. Don't worry."

"I do." Ella kept it short. "I'll keep in touch, but I'm going away."

"You should, it would do you good."

"Yeah." She looked at the time—fifteen seconds. "Umm, you know that Winslow Homer painting we were talking about, the one with the small tender on deck?"

"Yeah, yeah, I sure do."

"It's gone up in value."

"That's good to know. Take care."

"I will, thanks." She hung up the pay phone, wishing she could have said more.

*****

Ella wasted no time preparing the *Gina Marie* for the four-day sail to the Abacos. She settled her dock fees and, in case anyone came around inquiring, told the owner she was sailing back to Rhode Island. She waited a few days, and when there was a fair-weather window promising a smooth Gulf Stream crossing, she was ready to go. Sailing was in her blood, and it relaxed her when the sea wasn't trying to prove it was tougher than she. She spent the first night anchored off the westernmost settlement of Grand Bahama Island, then sailed along the Northwest Providence Channel, hugging the Little Bahama Bank. On the fourth day she reached Great Abaco, a place where she could safely catch her breath, collect herself and wait until people had forgotten about her.

To Ella, part of the beauty of the Abacos Islands lay in their seeming impermanence. Under a bright blue sky, the slivers of land stood just a few feet above sea level; and the rolling Atlantic, held back by a thin barrier reef, was perpetually poised to overtake them. But they had stood for ages against the tide, and offered Ella a haven where no one would expect to find her.

It was Rich who had first told Ella about these out islands of the Northern Bahamas, settled in the late seventeen hundreds by boat builders and Loyalists who moved there to escape trouble on the mainland—just as she hoped to do.

After two years of living onboard, she welcomed the expansive feeling of the open-walled home she'd rented—a sea-to-sea waterfront house nestled in the protected cove of Treasure Cay with a small dock to berth the *Gina Marie*. It was a quiet retreat where she could take time to weigh the dizzying options that a million dollars afforded a woman who had grown up poor.

The seaside home offered a luxury she wasn't accustomed to: gracious rooms with tiled floors and French doors that opened onto a screened veranda, a marble bath by a picture window overlooking the dunes. But best of all was the modern kitchen that rivaled the culinary academy's, with expansive marble counters and new appliances.

When the empty rooms and her wide-open future overwhelmed her, she retreated to curl up in the comforting quarters of her old bunk aboard the *Gina Marie*. But most nights she chose to sleep on the veranda where the soft ocean breeze lulled her to sleep.

*****

Ella awoke in a panic, threw off the tangle of sweaty covers and frantically checked her chest and back, feeling for a wound she was certain was there. Heart racing in her throat, she pulled a pillow to her chest and fell back onto the bed.

In yet another haunting dream, she had stood abandoned on the shore of a small island, watching her father sail away on the *Gina Marie*. A hundred yards out, Davis struggled to swim ashore, gasping for air, stretching his head above the water as waves washed over his face. He was drowning, and she scrambled around for something to throw to him. A piece of driftwood stuck up from the sand and she tugged it free—but when she did, the island on which she stood began to rapidly sink. The water quickly rose above her ankles, then her knees; she was in the middle of the ocean, with no other land in sight. The waves muffled Davis's angry shouts. She knew he wanted the driftwood that could keep him afloat. Closer to her now, he waved a gun above the water, aimed at her and fired point-blank. She swung the driftwood like a bat, hitting him squarely on the side of his head. He sank below the surface, revealing his terrified son floating behind him, alone in the open sea.

Ella lay with her eyes closed and listened to the soothing voices of children drifting up from the beach as her fear subsided. The soft whoosh of the bamboo ceiling fan beat out a steady breeze, accompanying the rhythm of the waves rolling in to shore. Assuring herself it was just a dream, she pushed aside the mosquito netting, stepped from the posted bed and opened the mahogany louvered doors to the outside.

Coconut and date palms framed a view of the sea in a medley of blues, and a light rain was falling. It was the last vestige of a storm that had brushed over the Abacos before heading down the chain of islands, leaving a damp chill in the November air. She pulled on a sweater and walked barefoot across the patio, wondering if the nightmares would ever go away. Would they follow her for the rest of her life, slowly driving her mad? Or would she find the strength to push them aside and focus on the good?

It was still too early for the island fishermen and party boats. The harbor was quiet and all was peaceful, yet her heart was in turmoil. Killing Carlos had been horrifying, and the memory of Burke's gruesome death was wrenching, as was Sam's senseless accident that he had caused by his own greed. But Davis had pushed his way into her heart, gaining a deep trust that hadn't come easily to her, then shattered that trust the night he attacked *Merlin*. His betrayal still felt devastating in spite of all her efforts to shed him. She had no idea whether he was alive or dead, whether she had killed one man or two, and it haunted her. Nevertheless, she had emerged with a strong resolve to set her own fate and she vowed to put an end to this. She thought of the letter from Siani, the woman in the photograph, with the return address of a Matanzas convent. She'd write to Siani, as a friend of Davis, to find out if he had died.

*****

After six weeks of waiting, Siani's response finally came: a letter from Cuba routed through her Fort Lauderdale address, then on to Treasure Cay Post Office, general delivery. Ella waited until she was in the privacy of her home to open it. She walked out into the garden, uncertain she wanted to know its contents, then slipped her thumb under the envelope's flap and tore it open. The letter confirmed that Davis had died from the bullet she'd fired that night on *Merlin*. She dropped to the garden wall, blindly facing the sea. So there it is, she thought. Davis really is dead.

Anger rose in her like a great heat. "I am not a murderer!" she screamed. She grabbed a wooden chair and smashed it hard against the rock face of the garden wall, shattering it into pieces. "I am not!" Grabbing a chair leg with both hands, she beat it again and again against the wall until it cracked.

How could one bullet take down a man she had always thought to be invincible? She paced the patio, picking up pieces of the broken chair and flinging them overhand toward the beach. Facing the sea, she caught her breath. She thought of Davis's money and how she had come to have it. It was nothing but blood money, she decided, unless she could do some good with it.

The nightmare had stayed with her; even now, weeks later, it felt as vivid as real life. She looked to the open ocean and saw Davis's son alone and terrified. His fear washed over her as if it were her own. Suddenly, she realized what the dream was telling her: the key to her redemption was saving the boy.

There are worse things than betrayal, she thought—like nurturing the seed of hatred in your heart. That's not going to happen to me, she vowed. She looked at the letter, thinking of the boy, and sat down to re-read what Siani had written.

The letter had a menacing tone, even though Ella had written that she had something of Davis's to return. Ella had been intentionally vague, knowing that the word "money" would trigger scrutiny from the Cuban censors. Siani had given her a date and time, three weeks from today, to meet her on the steps of Saint Christopher's Cathedral in Havana. Siani's last line stuck out to her: "It would be best for you to return his property before our men find you." A chill ran through her, and she rubbed her arms, remembering the tall, wild-haired man Davis had called out to that night: Paco.

Let them try, she thought. They'll never find me. If they were counting on Carlos to help stateside, then they hadn't heard the news that he was dead.

*****

Ella pushed off in her Avon inflatable to explore the islets closest to where she lived, and found a private sandy spit on Green Turtle Cay. She ran her dinghy up onto its sugary-white sands, stepped out of her shorts, slipped off her top and waded into the shimmering, brilliantly clear water. At seventy-five degrees, it was the same temperature as the winter air. Floating face down in the shallow waters, she reached for bits of shell, flipping over on her back to study them, keeping a few and letting the others drop.

She drifted along, thinking of Davis's son, an orphan like herself, and began putting together a plan that would secure the boy's future so he would stand a chance of a decent life.

CHAPTER 32

Ella pulled the bill of her baseball cap lower over her face, tucked the Swarovski binoculars inside her windbreaker and zipped it closed. Affecting a male stride, she made her way down a narrow cobblestone street of Old Havana, trying to blend in. The day's commerce was in full swing, and vendors pushed brightly painted carts, wobbly and dented with ages of use, through a lively crowd. Salsa music floated down from an apartment above, and people sat on crates in doorways chatting and laughing, their chickens milling about, while shouting children played stickball in the street. Through all the cacophony of the warm December morning, Ella heard the twelve haunting chimes from the bell tower of Saint Christopher's Cathedral—one hour before she was to meet Siani on its steps.

She hurried, anxious to get to the plaza ahead of Siani and whomever she'd have hiding in the shadows. Shooting a look behind her, she moved quickly along the crumbling wall that lined the street, searching the crowd and peering down alleyways for the tall, thin Paco. He was sure to be here with Siani, and she feared it was possible, even though she was disguised as a man, that he could recognize her from that dark night off Cay Sal Bank.

She felt for the bulky envelope, tucked in her waistband, that she had decided to hand-deliver in order to avoid the meddling eyes of the postal authorities. The envelope contained twelve thousand Euros along with paperwork for the trust she had drawn up for Davis's son: five hundred thousand Euros deposited in a growth fund at Bank of the Bahamas, Nassau. Her letter, translated into Spanish, outlined the monies Siani would receive for taking care of Nicholás; the cash was her first payment. At the bottom of the envelope was the stone necklace.

The Nicholás Davis Trust stipulated that Siani would receive twelve thousand Euros yearly to care for the boy—more than twice the average Cuban's income. Once Nicholás had completed secondary school and earned a diploma, he would receive the entire trust and the remaining balance of the million dollars. Those were the terms; Ella offered no plan B. Nicholás had to attend school and graduate. If he failed to do so by his nineteenth birthday, the account would revert to her.

Ella had no idea if Siani knew how much money Davis had stowed away, nor what she was expecting, but the deal was surely going to be a disappointment to her—especially since most of the money was tied up in a trust for Nicholás. There would be no way that she, or Davis's cohorts, could get their hands on it. The Lady of Charity convent in Matanzas had agreed to monitor the fund after Ella offered a sizeable yearly donation; the mother superior had responded quickly, grateful that someone was providing for the boy's future. Had Ella been looking for thanks, it would probably be all she would get, but she wasn't here for gratitude: this was about absolution, quieting the nightmares and turning toward her future.

She had realized too late that her plan was flawed: she should never have agreed to meet Siani face-to-face, on her turf, in this foreign land. She slowed her pace, trying to think of what to do. She was in a country whose language she only modestly understood, where she didn't know whom to trust or where to go for help if things went against her.

What she needed now was a safer plan. She trudged toward the Cathedral Square, trying to come up with one as she headed to a café she had chosen from her *Moon Cuba* guide. Located at the plaza on the second story, it had a clear view of the cathedral's steps so she could watch the arrival of Siani and whoever accompanied her.

The streets narrowed in the older section of the city and she kept to the side in deep shade, hands shoved into her pockets, lifting her head only to check behind her. Ahead, a woman leaned out of a second-story window to hoist a basket filled with vegetables from the street vendor below: a father with his son. Ella stopped and watched from across the street. The boy looked to be about ten and seemed eager to help his father. He turned and, seeing Ella, approached her.

"Cigarros de mejor calidad, sir," the son offered, promoting his own side business.

"Buenas tardes," Ella nodded. An idea had just come to her. "Do you speak English?"

"Buenas tardes. Sorry miss, I mistake you," he said, looking confused. "Yes, I speak very good English."

Ella smiled; he was just what she was looking for. "Can I ask for your help?"

The boy glanced over at his father. "What do you need, miss?"

"How would you like to earn two hundred pesos in one hour? All you have to do is come with me to La Bodeguita del Medio cafe by the cathedral."

"I know La Bodeguita. Two hundred pesos is big money. Why?"

"I need an envelope delivered to someone who will be coming to the cathedral steps." Ella could see the boy hesitate. "I'll buy you lunch while we wait, enough to bring some back to your father."

"Is it dangerous?"

"No." Not to you, Ella thought.

"One hour? All I have to do is deliver envelope?"

"Exactly, yes."

"How come you dress like a man?"

Ella smiled; the kid was smart. "What's your name?"

"Cruz."

Ella shook the boy's hand. "For two hundred pesos, Cruz, you don't get to ask questions." She turned, scanning the streets before coming back to the boy. "What do you say? Yes or no?"

The boy nodded. "I tell my father I be back in one hour."

"Part of the deal: you are *not* to tell him I'm a woman, not until tomorrow."

"Why?"

"Deal or no deal?"

"Deal."

Ella caught sight of the cathedral bell tower through a tangle of draping electrical wires and the day's laundry hanging on clotheslines from windows of apartments lining the street. In the distance a band started to play and the sound of trumpets and conga drums wafted from the direction of Cathedral Square. People came out from their apartments, children ran and bicyclists pedaled to the beat of the drums, all headed toward the music. Ella and Cruz pushed their way through the crowd, heading for the square. She checked the time: it was twelve-thirty. Siani expected her at one, and would likely arrive early if she planned an ambush. Turning a final corner, they stepped into the open square.

It was a Saturday, the sun was out, and so were crowds of tourists mingling with the locals. Ella scanned the plaza, looking for Siani. The National Revolutionary Police stood watch over the crowd from the foot of the statue of St. Christopher and guards with machine guns were scattered around the perimeter. It was possible that Davis's clan was under surveillance. Siani's letter had been mailed through the parish convent in Matanza, but that likely hadn't kept the authorities from steaming open the envelope and, Ella assumed, reading it before sending it along.

At the café, Ella asked for an upstairs table next to the balcony railing with a view of the cathedral steps. The hostess smiled as she seated them, dropping menus onto the table as Ella took her seat and Cruz plopped down across from her.

"Order whatever you want—knock yourself out," said Ella.

"Knock yourself out?"

"American slang," she smiled. "It means don't hold back, have as much as you want."

"Okay, I'm going to knock myself out."

"Sounds a little different when you say it, but you got it."

"I got it."

Cruz ordered heartily and the dishes kept coming, lobster and shrimp, fried bananas, rice and beans, until the table was crowded with side dishes. Then he ordered for his father. While he ate, Ella nervously searched the plaza and its incoming roadways.

"Don't get so full you won't be any good to me," she said as the boy happily wolfed down another shrimp.

A tall man, at least a head above others, with wild frizzed hair, entered the edge of the plaza. Ella sat up, lifting her binoculars. It was Paco, with a shorter man in dreadlocks, walking in the shadow of the far building, heading to the cathedral. She watched as they split up, disappearing to either side of the church steps. Siani had something planned for her. She checked her watch: it was a quarter to one.

"They here, miss?" asked Cruz.

"Not all of them, not yet." She waved for the waitress to bring the bill.

"When do I get paid?"

"You get one hundred now." Ella pulled out a hundred pesos and handed it to Cruz. "After you make the delivery, when you come back for your father's lunch, you get the rest."

She lifted her binoculars again to see Siani and a boy, maybe a little younger than Cruz, walking toward the cathedral. What have they got planned? she wondered. Drag me off this plaza in front of all these people? Wait and follow me back to my hotel? Except I'm not going back to my hotel, she smiled.

Siani and the boy sat down on the cathedral steps, side by side, inches apart. Ella focused the binoculars on Nicholás, a wide-eyed child who strongly resembled his father. His black, wavy hair reached down to his shoulders, unlike the city boys of Havana who wore their hair cut short. Sitting with his arms crossed over his jiggling knees, he watched the crowd in the plaza with a distrustful gaze. She scanned to Siani, sitting straight-backed and strong with a silken braid of black hair draped across her chest. She had the full lips and high cheekbones of a Taino Indian; all the expression in her face came from her fierce, dark eyes.

The bells of the Cathedral de San Cristobal tolled once. Ella handed the boy the binoculars, helping him to adjust the focus.

"See the woman with the boy sitting on the steps? You are to deliver the envelope to her. Tell me what she is wearing."

Cruz described Siani and the boy. Assured that he recognized them, Ella took the binoculars and handed him the envelope.

"This has information for their family, especially the little boy. You are doing an important job. Understand?"

Cruz nodded vigorously.

"Okay, I want you to walk along the side of the plaza, not down the middle. Slowly. Don't just run and hand this to the woman. Her name is Siani. Can you remember that?"

"Siani." Cruz nodded.

"When you hand Siani the envelope, don't—*do not*—wait around, do not answer any questions, just leave. You can run, but not back here. Go around the block and circle back." Ella pointed out the route for him. "The waitress who brought your food will have the rest of your money. Maybe it would be a good idea for you and your father to take the rest of the afternoon off."

"You said it wasn't dangerous."

"Shouldn't be. But I'll be watching you. Do you have any pets, any animals?"

"A chicken," said Cruz.

"A chicken?"

"Peso."

"Okay. When you want to pick up Peso, you have to walk slowly up to her, right?"

"Si."

"That is how you will walk up to Siani—slowly, so she doesn't notice you coming. Understand?"

"Yes, miss. I know how to play it cool."

Ella smiled at his American slang and gave him a high five.

Cruz took off with the envelope, following Ella's instructions, skirting the edge of the plaza to arrive slyly in front of Siani. Ella watched through the binoculars as Siani nodded and took the envelope, then gasped with dread as Cruz turned to Ella, shooting her a thumbs-up.

"Ah, Cruz, no!" Ella said under her breath.

Siani followed his line of sight to the balcony where Ella sat, then grabbed for Cruz's arm but missed and he got away. She looked down at the envelope and tore it open, pausing for a moment, assessing what she saw. She glanced quickly over her shoulder to where Paco hid, then turned her back on him and the boy before pulling out the money and stuffing it into her bag.

"Siani, you are clever." Ella shifted her gaze to Nicholás. Had he seen the money? But the boy had turned, watching Cruz run away. She wondered if there was more she could have done to protect Nicholás. She sharpened the focus on him, trying to capture him in a single moment that would have to last her a lifetime.

Paco ran into the frame. Siani pointed in the direction that Cruz had signaled, then in the direction he had run. Ella studied their faces, burning them into her memory. She looked down at Nicholás, who stood behind them looking frightened, tugging at Siani's hand, trying to pull her away, wanting to leave—but Siani shook loose his grip.

"Help is coming, Nicholás, help is coming," Ella whispered.

She checked the perimeter of the cathedral. Paco's sidekick was slow to leave his cover and nearly knocked into Cruz running for the back entrance of the plaza. She double-tipped the waitress in return for holding on to Cruz's final payment, then looked out over the plaza for Paco. He was pushing his way through the crowd, scanning the balcony and the outside patio as he hurried toward the restaurant.

She pulled down her cap and tucked the binoculars inside her jacket, grabbed a soiled newspaper from the busboy's station and calmly took the steps down to the patio. The patio seating was full except for an empty seat at a family's table. Ella dropped into the chair and hunched over the newspaper just as Paco banged past the patrons and rushed up the stairs, pulling a gun from the back of his pants. She looked for the other man, but he must have gone after Cruz.

Musicians gathered in the plaza, lighting people up with rumbas, and pedestrians shifted into dance as they passed, adding an element of chaos that could aid her escape. Ella smiled at the tourists across the table, then calmly stood up and walked into the crowd and across the plaza to the nearest side street. She stole a last look in the direction of the cathedral. Siani and Nicholás remained on the steps, Nicholás tugging at Siani's arm. She watched Siani pull the letter from the envelope and look at the papers inside. Ella guessed their next move would be to visit the convent and learn the meaning of the agreement.

She hurried down the side street, stealing nervous glances over her shoulder and worrying about Cruz, then spotted him tucked into an alley. She paused near him, pretending to put out a cigarette with the toe of her shoe.

"They're still at the cathedral steps. Wait until they've gone, then go get your money from the waitress. Her name is Karmina."

"Sorry," said Cruz. "I should not give you thumbs up."

"That's okay, kid, you did great." She started to walk away, then turned back to Cruz. "Muchas gracias, my friend."

Ella stole along the narrow cobblestone street, eyeing those around her to see if she were being followed, jumping at the blast of a car horn behind her. A vintage Pontiac with taxi plates and the name 'Victor' painted in gold script on its door sat empty at the curb. It sounded to Ella like victory, and she hopped in.

"You free?"

"Free?" The driver turned around to see her sunken low into the back seat. He looked more Apache than Cuban, with a turquoise scarf wound around his forehead, holding his long black hair in place.

"Available?" said Ella. "English?"

"Sí. Where you want to go?" The driver adjusted the rearview mirror to study her.

The rear door sagged on its worn hinges and screeched with resistance as she tried to pull it closed. On her second attempt, Victor hopped out of the driver's seat and body-slammed the door. He grinned broadly, showing off his gold tooth, as he leaned in the window to reassure her. "Don't worry, Miss, it is very good car."

"Okay, but please, just start driving." Ella twisted around and waved back at Cruz. She lifted her gaze and saw Paco pounding down the street toward the boy as the taxi began to pull away. "Cruz," she gasped. "Oh God, what have I done?"

"Wait. Stop!" She stuck her head out the window and screamed, "Run, Cruz, run!"

The boy didn't hear and was waving back at her when Paco came at him from behind and spun him around.

"Popi!" Cruz screamed. "Popi, ayudar, popi!"

Paco had hold of the boy's shoulders, fiercely shaking him and shouting demands whose meaning Ella could only guess. The taxi came to a stop and she watched through the rear window as a man in the street rushed Paco, yelling and swinging a baseball bat.

Paco kept his grip on Cruz and shouted what sounded like curses. The man brandished the bat, but Paco only barked back. Other men gathered, but he held his grip on Cruz. Finally, the man slammed the bat into Paco's legs, knocking him to the ground. Cruz broke free and ran toward his father, who raced to meet him. One of the men grabbed Paco's gun out of the back of his pants and held it on him while others shouted and kicked at Paco as he struggled to his feet, trying to break free of the growing crowd. He stumbled a few paces and then turned, a head taller than the others, and scanned the street looking for Ella.

She slid down, peeking over the seat, watching. Paco hold out his hand, no doubt demanding his gun, but instead the men closed in, one holding his gun aimed at him and another forcibly prodding him with the bat. Paco limped away at a quickened pace, holding his injured leg, and the men followed, yelling and shoving him further down the street. She watched until they turned the corner.

Ella could see Cruz wrapped in the protective arms of his father. He turned to look back at her, giving her a secretive thumbs up. She smiled and waved from the rear window.

"Where to, miss?" The driver followed her gaze to the street behind them, then pulled away from the curb.

"Away from the cathedral, away from Old Havana. I need to go to Jose Marti airport, but take your time. I've got three hours." Ella kept her eyes on Cruz until he was out of sight. "What were they shouting?"

"Someone has taken one of our little boys." The driver looked at her in the rearview mirror when he spoke. "That man was not one of us. They think it could be him."

"I'm happy this boy is safe," said Ella.

"We watch out for each other."

"What will they do to the man?" Ella asked.

"Depends. If they think he is guilty..." the driver shrugged.

Ella caught his eye in the mirror, then turned to watch out the back window, her nose still inches above the seat. The cab bounced along on broken springs, its sputtering engine coughing like an old smoker, and wallowed around a curve as its body shifted loosely on its frame.

It was finally over. There was nothing left for her to do, and nothing was expected of her. She pulled off her baseball cap, shook out her hair and rubbed the tension from her face before settling back against the lumpy seat. She stared out the window as they drove from Old Havana to the city's modern central district and then crossed through slums that redevelopment funds hadn't reached, beyond the tourist hot spots of Old Havana. Crowded tenements and shells of Colonial buildings stood in various stages of crumbling. It was a sadder glimpse of Havana, one that reminded her of a remark Davis had once made about the paralyzing effect poverty had on his country. Who could hate a thief who came from here? she asked herself.

Ella knew she had been lucky to survive a serious error in judgment, saying yes to a risky shortcut to big money, naively unaware that our experiences make us who we are. She was a different person now, indelibly affected by all that she'd seen and done. Her future was up to her, and she would learn to make her own luck.

The taxi stopped at a light alongside a low garden wall. "Creemos en Sueños" was splashed across it in graffiti-styled block letters of bright orange and emerald green. At the top edge of the final letter a lofty, sapphire-blue owl was depicted facing outward, taking flight. Its eyes seemed to focus on Ella, and its dream-like quality was riveting.

"What does it mean?" she asked the driver.

"We believe in dreams."

"Is that true?" She looked out at the disintegrating roadway patched in shades of time, its broken curb leaving only the slightest distinction. But beyond, men stood on tall scaffolds restoring the face of an old building and painting it the color of the sea.

"Sí, señorita. When you reach for something, you grow. That is what is important."

Had this sordid adventure taken her dream with it, she wondered? She had all the money she would ever need, but she couldn't have the restaurant. Owning a restaurant was a public life. Falco would find her, or possibly Siani or Paco, and there was always Nikki. But what no one could take, she thought, was her love of cooking.

She thought about Cruz and the shrimp and lobster he had ordered at the café, and wished for one bite of anything. She was starved—she hadn't eaten all day.

She leaned into the front seat. "Do you know where I could get an authentic Cuban meal?"

"I know a very good paladar, just up ahead."

"What's a paladar?"

"It's where you find our real food. Family-run private restaurants, not state-run—they have terrible food. Paladars can be in someone's home or in a little back alley place."

"They serve food to the public in their own homes?

"Sí."

"Where do the people eat?"

"Outside in the yard, inside in the living room or in a hallway. I have once eaten in someone's bedroom."

"Really?"

"Who cares where you eat, if the food is good. Do you like Cuban-Creole?"

"I don't know. I've never had it."

"I'll take you to a place that makes very good camarones a la criollo, sweet shrimp creole. It's on the way to the airport."

"Is it in someone's home?"

"Sí."

"An adventure," she smiled. "Would you have lunch with me? My treat and I'll pay for the time." Ella wasn't just hungry, she longed for the company of a normal person to help pass her remaining time in Cuba.

The driver lifted his bright eyes to the rearview mirror, "Sí."

"Muy bueno," said Ella.

She sat back in a long breath, letting the idea take hold. With a smile she whispered, "Paladar. Table d'hôte. The Host's Table." What a great idea. And as Rich said, there is always more than one solution—one that would've made her father proud.

The End

ABOUT THE AUTHOR

Toni Bird Jones

Toni Bird Jones spent years diving in the Northwest's Georgia Straits before moving to South Florida to pursue a life on the water. Over ten years in the sailing community of the Caribbean and South Florida, she refinished and delivered boats to the Lesser Antilles, Bahamas and the Eastern Seaboard. She received her U.S. Coast Guard OPUV Captain's License in Puerto Rico while based in Saint Thomas, Virgin Islands. Today, she and her husband sail the San Francisco Bay on their Erickson 29 *Hai Lien*.

A novelist and short story writer in adventure-thriller and literary genres, Jones studied Creative Writing at the University of California, Berkeley and the University of Arizona, Tucson. Her stories address moral questions of the human dilemma and are often set in the Caribbean. *The Measure of Ella* is her first novel.

Toni Bird Jones

www.tonibjones.com

If You Enjoyed This Book
Visit

PENMORE PRESS
www.penmorepress.com

All Penmore Press books are available directly through our website.

VITAL SPARK

BY

LEAH DEVLIN

After eking out a living as an adjunct professor in Washington DC, fisheries ecologist Alex Allaway lands a job running a small marine station back in her hometown. Arriving in River Glen to surprise her grandfather with her the good news, Alex is horrified to discover him dead, a bloody dagger in his heart. His clenched fist grasps a piece of pirate gold and a cryptic map with her name on it.

While the police investigate the murder, Alex begins her own search for answers. Aboard the tugboat Vital Spark she sails the Chesapeake in pursuit of treasure that belonged to a distant relative, the pirate Giles Blood-hand. But descendants of a rival pirate family are also looking for the bounty that's been hidden for over three centuries, and they'll think nothing of dispatching Alex once they discover she's in the way.

The first book in the Chesapeake Tugboat Murders series, Vital Spark draws us into a world where ancient feuds lurk beneath hidden waterways.

Leah Devlin is rapidly establishing herself as a writer of modern day mystery-thrillers. This story is as tight as a piano wire. Life at a seaside town in New England is full of treacherous undercurrents and peril, as residents are threatened by a menace from a thousand years ago. Murder, romance and deceit are a potent mix in this gripping novel, which I didn't want to put down.—James Boschert, author of the Talon Series and *Force 12 in German Bight*

PENMORE PRESS
www.penmorepress.com

Force 12 in
German Bight
by
James Boschert

Considering that oil and gas have been flowing from under the North Sea for the best part of half a century, it is perhaps surprising that more writers have not taken the uncompromising conditions that are experienced in this area – which extends from the north of Scotland to the coasts of Norway and Germany – for the setting of a novel. James Boschert's latest redresses the balance.

The book takes its title from the name of an area regularly referred to in the legendary BBC Shipping Forecast, one which experiences some of the worst weather conditions around the British Isles. It is a fast-paced story which smacks of authenticity in every line. A world of hard men, hard liquor, hard drugs and cold-blooded murder. The reality of the setting and the characters, ex-military men from both sides of the Atlantic, crooked wheeler-dealers, and Danish detectives, male and female, are all in on the action.

This is not story telling akin to a latter day Bulldog Drummond, nor a James Bond, but simply a snortingly good yarn which will jangle the nerve ends, fill your nose with the smell of salt and diesel oil, your ears with the deafening sound of machinery aboard a monster pipe-dredging ship and, above all, make you remember never to underestimate the power of the sea.

–Roger Paine, former Commander, Royal Navy .

PENMORE PRESS
www.penmorepress.com

Penmore Press

Challenging, Intriguing, Adventurous, Historical and Imaginative

www.penmorepress.com

CPSIA information can be obtained
at www.ICGtesting.com
Printed in the USA
LVHW032210090919
630429LV00002B/201/P